Praise for Julie Kagawa and the Blood of Eden trilogy

"Kagawa wraps excellent writing and skillful plotting around a well-developed concept and engaging characters, resulting in a fresh and imaginative thrill-ride that deserves a wide audience."
—*Publishers Weekly* on *The Immortal Rules*, starred review

"Allie's a smart, strong and compelling heroine, and readers will gladly join her for this adrenaline-rich ride."
—*Kirkus Reviews* on *The Immortal Rules*

"Infused with the moral dilemmas of a society on the brink of destruction, and stocked with continually developing characters whose reactions to these questions are complex and distinct. This series stands out."
—*Booklist* on *The Eternity Cure*

"Kagawa's vivid prose and unexpected plot developments will keep fans entranced."
—*Publishers Weekly* on *The Eternity Cure*

"A bloody good way to end a trilogy."
—*Kirkus Reviews* on *The Forever Song*

"Kagawa winds up her dystopian vampire Blood of Eden series with a cinematically gory and action-packed finale that never forgets the moral quandaries that have shaped the previous installments."
—*Booklist* on *The Forever Song*

**Books by Julie Kagawa
available from Inkyard Press
(Each series listed in reading order.)**

Blood of Eden

The Immortal Rules
The Eternity Cure
The Forever Song (paperback edition includes
"Dawn of Eden"** prequel novella)

The Iron Fey

The Iron King (special edition includes "Winter's Passage"* novella)
The Iron Daughter (special edition includes the "Guide to the Iron Fey"*)
The Iron Queen (special edition includes "Summer's Crossing"* novella)
The Iron Knight (special edition includes "Iron's Prophecy"* novella)
The Lost Prince
The Iron Traitor
The Iron Warrior

The Iron Fey: Evenfall

The Iron Raven

Shadow of the Fox

Shadow of the Fox
Soul of the Sword
Night of the Dragon

The Talon Saga

Talon
Rogue
Soldier
Legion
Inferno

*Also available as an ebook and in print in *The Iron Legends* anthology
**Also available in the *'Til the World Ends* anthology by Julie Kagawa,
Ann Aguirre and Karen Duvall

THE
FOREVER
SONG

BLOOD OF EDEN

JULIE KAGAWA

ISBN-13: 978-1-335-20999-3

The Forever Song
First published in 2014. This edition published in 2021.
Copyright © 2014 by Julie Kagawa

Dawn of Eden
First published in 2013. This edition published in 2021.
Copyright © 2013 by Julie Kagawa

This edition published by arrangement with Harlequin Books S.A.

For questions and comments about the quality of this book, please contact us at CustomerService@Harlequin.com.

Inkyard Press
22 Adelaide St. West, 40th Floor
Toronto, Ontario M5H 4E3, Canada
www.InkyardPress.com

Printed in U.S.A.

CONTENTS

To Nick. Your ideas are invaluable.

And to my readers. Your tears feed my muse.

THE
F⊕REVER
S⊕NG

"I don't expect you to understand, little bird. I expect you only to sing. Sing for me, sing for Kanin, and make it a glorious song."

—Sarren

Part I

DEMON

CHAPTER 1

The outpost gate creaked in the wind, swinging back on its hinges. It knocked lightly against the wall, a rhythmic tapping sound that echoed in the looming silence. A cold breeze swirled through the gap, and the scent of blood lay on the air like a heavy blanket.

"He's been here," Kanin murmured at my side. The Master vampire was a dark statue against the falling snow, motionless and calm, but his eyes were grave. I regarded the fence impassively, the wind tugging at my coat and straight black hair.

"Is there any point in going in?"

"Sarren knows we're following him" was the low reply. "He meant for us to see this. He wants us to know that he knows. There will likely be something waiting for us when we step through the gate."

Footsteps crunched over the snow as Jackal stalked around us, black duster rippling behind him. His eyes glowed a vicious yellow as he peered up at the gate. "Well then," he said, the tips of his fangs showing through his grin, "if he went through all the trouble of setting this up, we shouldn't keep the psycho waiting, should we?"

He started forward, his step confident as he strode through

the broken gate toward the tiny settlement beyond. After a moment's hesitation, Kanin and I followed.

The smell of blood grew stronger once we were past the wall, though nothing moved on the narrow path that snaked between houses. The flimsy wood and tin shanties were silent, dark, as we ventured deeper, passing snow-covered porches and empty chairs. Everything looked intact, undisturbed. There were no bodies. No corpses mutilated in their beds, no blood spattered over the walls of the few homes we ducked into. There weren't even any dead animals in the tiny trampled pasture past the main strip. Just snow and emptiness.

And yet, the smell of blood soaked this place, hanging thick in the air, making my stomach ache and the Hunger roar to life. I bit it down, gritting my teeth to keep from snarling in frustration. It had been too long. I needed food. The scent of blood was driving me crazy, and the fact that there were no humans here made me furious. Where were they? It wasn't possible that an entire outpost of mortals had up and disappeared without a trace.

And then, as we followed the path around the pasture and up to the huge barn at the top of the rise, we found the townspeople.

A massive barren tree stood beside the barn, twisted branches clawing at the sky. They swayed beneath the weight of dozens of bodies hanging upside down from ropes tied to the limbs. Men, women, even a few kids swinging in the breeze, dangling arms stiff and white. Their throats had been cut, and the base of the tree was stained black, the blood spilled and wasted in the snow. But the smell nearly knocked me over regardless, and I clenched my fists, the Hunger raking my insides with fiery talons.

"Well," Jackal muttered, crossing his arms and gazing at the tree, "isn't that festive?" His voice was tight as if he, too, was on the edge of losing it. "I'm guessing this is the reason we haven't found a single bloodbag from here all the way back to New Covington." He growled, shaking his head, lips curling back from his fangs. "This guy is really starting to piss me off."

I swallowed the Hunger, trying to focus through the gnawing ache. "Why, James, don't tell me you feel sorry for the walking meatsacks," I taunted, because sometimes, goading Jackal was the only thing that kept my mind off everything else. He rolled his eyes.

"No, sister, I'm annoyed because they don't have the decency to be alive so I can eat them," he returned with a flash of fangs and a rare show of temper. He glared at the bodies hungrily. "Fucking Sarren," he said. "If I didn't want the psychopath dead so badly, I would say the hell with it. If this keeps up, we're going to have to break off the trail to find a meatsack whose throat hasn't been slit, which is probably what the bastard wants." He sighed, giving me an exasperated look. "This would be so much easier if you hadn't killed the Jeep."

"For the last time," I growled at him, "I just pointed out the street that wasn't blocked off. I didn't leave those nails in the road for you to drive over."

"Allison."

Kanin's quiet voice broke through our argument, and we turned. Our sire stood at one corner of the barn, his face grim as he beckoned us forward. With a last glance at the tree and its grisly contents, I walked over to him, feeling the sharp stab of Hunger once more. The barn reeked of blood, even more than the branches of the tree. Probably because one whole wall of the building was streaked with it, dried and black, painted in vertical lines up and down the wood.

"Let's keep moving," Kanin said when Jackal and I joined him. His voice was calm, though I knew he was just as Hungry as the rest of us. Maybe more so, since he was still recovering from his near-death experience in New Covington. "There are no survivors here," Kanin went on, with a solemn look back at the tree, "and we are running out of time. Sarren is expecting us."

"How do you figure, old man?" Jackal asked, following me to the side of the barn. "Yeah, this is the psycho's handiwork, but he could've done this just for the jollies. You sure he knows we're coming?"

Kanin didn't answer, just gestured to the blood-streaked wall beside us. I looked over, as did Jackal, but couldn't see anything unusual. Beyond a wall completely covered in blood, anyway.

But Jackal gave a low, humorless chuckle. "Oh, you bastard." He smiled, shaking his head and staring up at the barn. "That's cute. Let's see if you're as funny when I'm beating you to death with your own arm."

"What?" I asked, obviously missing something. I stared at the barn again, wondering what the other vampires saw that I didn't. "What's so funny? I don't see anything."

Jackal sighed, stepped behind me, and hooked the back of my collar, pulling me away from the wall. "Hey!" I snarled, fighting him. "Let go! What the hell are you doing?"

He ignored me, continuing to walk backward, dragging me with him. We were about a dozen paces away from the wall before he stopped, and I yanked myself from his grip. "What is your problem?" I demanded, baring my fangs. Jackal silently pointed back to the barn.

I glanced at the wall again and stiffened. Now that I was farther away, I could see what Kanin and Jackal were talking about.

Sarren, I thought, the cold, familiar hate spreading through my insides. *You sick bastard. This won't stop me, and it won't save you. When I find you, you'll regret ever hearing my name.*

Painted across the side of the barn, written in bloody letters about ten feet tall, was a question. One that proved, beyond a shadow of a doubt, that Sarren knew we were coming. And that we were probably walking right into a trap.

HUNGRY YET?

It had been two weeks since we'd left New Covington.

Two weeks travel, of walking down endless, snow-covered roads. Two weeks of cold and wilderness and dead, silent towns. Of empty houses wrapped in vines, deserted streets, ancient hulks of cars rusting in the gutters. No movement, except for the skitter of wildlife, both large and small, overtaking the streets humans had once ruled. The Jeep, as Jackal had so eloquently pointed out, was dead, leaving the three of us to wander the empty roads on foot, following a madman who knew we were coming. Who was always one step ahead of us.

Time was running out, Kanin had said. In a way, I supposed that was true. What Sarren had, what he carried, could spell the end for a lot of people. Maybe the whole world. Sarren possessed a mutated version of the Red Lung virus that had destroyed the world six decades ago, only this one came with a nasty little side effect: it killed vampires, too. The three of us—me, Jackal, and Kanin—had been exposed to Sarren's virus when we were in New Covington and had seen the true horror of the plague. Humans had turned into insane wretches who screamed and laughed and clawed at their faces until their skin was all but gone, and attacked anything they came across. For vampires, the effects were even more horrific; the virus ate their dead flesh, and they rotted away from the inside. In the final confrontation with Sarren, we'd learned that the insane vampire was using New Covington only as a test site, that his real intentions were far more sinister.

He planned to kill everything. All humans, and all vampires. Wipe the slate clean, he'd told me, and let the world finally heal itself. His virus, when he released it again, would be unstoppable.

There was just one small kink in his plans.

We had a cure. Or at least, we'd *had* one. It was in Eden now, that small bit of hope for the rest of the world. That was what Sarren wanted; the cure, either to destroy or to turn against us. He thought we were tracking him to Eden to stop him, to prevent him from destroying the cure or releasing his virus. He thought we were trying to save the world.

He didn't know. I didn't care about Eden. I didn't care about his virus, or the cure, or the rest of the world. It made no difference to me if the humans found a cure for Rabidism, or if they could stop Sarren's new plague. Humans meant nothing to me, not anymore. They were food, and I was a vampire. I was done pretending that I was anything less than a monster.

But I *would* kill Sarren.

He would die for what he'd done, what he'd destroyed. I would tear him apart, and I would make him suffer. There had been four of us that night in New Covington, when we had faced the mad vampire for the last time. When I had cut the arm from his body and he'd fled into the dark, only to return later for his most horrible deed yet. Four of us: me, Jackal, Kanin...and one other. But I couldn't think of him now. He was gone. And I was still a monster.

"Hey."

Abruptly, Jackal slowed and dropped back to where I trailed several paces behind Kanin's dark, steady figure, following the road that stretched on through the frozen plains. We'd left the outpost and its slaughtered residents a few miles back, and the scent of blood had finally faded into the wind. That didn't stop the Hunger, though; I could feel it even now, a constant throbbing ache, poised to flare into an inferno of raw, vicious need at the slightest provocation. It even raged at Jackal, annoyed that he wasn't human, that I couldn't spin around and sink my fangs into his throat. Jackal seemed happily oblivious.

I ignored him and kept my gaze straight ahead, not really in the mood for a fight or listening to his barbed, obnoxious comments. That, of course, never stopped my blood brother.

"So, sister," Jackal went on, "I've been wondering. When we finally do catch up to Sarren, how do you think we should kill the old bastard? I'm thinking maiming and torture for as long as we can stand it." He snapped his fingers. "Hey, maybe we can tie him half in and half out of the sun, that's always interesting. Did that to some undead bastard who pissed me off several years back. The light began at his feet and crawled up toward his face, and it took a very long time for him to finally kick it. By the end, he was screaming at me to cut off his head." He snickered. "I'd love to watch Sarren die like that. If that doesn't offend your delicate sensibilities, that is."

He smirked then, his gold eyes burning the side of my head. "Just wanted to give you a heads-up, little sister, in case you decide to go bleeding heart on me. Of course, if you have a suggestion for how we should do the old psycho in, I'd love to hear it."

"I don't care," I said flatly. "Do whatever you want. As long as I get to land the final blow, I couldn't care less."

Jackal huffed. "Well, that's not very fun."

I didn't answer, walking faster to get away from him, and he quickened his pace to keep up.

"Come on, sister, where's that obnoxious morality you kept throwing in my face every two seconds? You're making it very difficult to take any sort of pleasure in mocking it relentlessly."

"Why are you talking to me?" I asked, still not looking at him. Jackal let out an exasperated sigh.

"Because I'm *bored*. And the old man doesn't give me the

time of day." He jerked his head at Kanin, still several yards ahead. I suspected Kanin could hear us, but he didn't turn around or give any indication that he was listening. And Jackal probably didn't care if he was. "And because I want to know your thoughts on our brilliantly disturbed serial killer." Jackal waved an impatient hand at the plains surrounding us. "It's still a long way to Eden, and I get the feeling we're not going to find any bloodbags—living ones anyway—from here to Meatsack Island. I don't particularly like the idea of facing the nut job with you and Kanin on the edge of losing it."

I flicked a glance at him and frowned. "What about you?"

"Oh, don't worry about me, sister." Jackal grinned. "I always come out on top, no matter what. I just want to point out that this annoying 'Scorched Earth' policy Sarren has picked up is going to make it very difficult for you. A couple more days of this, and the next human we see is going to be ripped to shreds—and you'll be the one doing it."

I shrugged. Jackal's revelation wasn't surprising, and I found that I really didn't care. Wherever Sarren went, whatever forgotten corner of the country he fled to, I wouldn't be far behind. No matter what he did, no matter how far or fast he ran, I would catch up to him, and then he would pay for what he had done. "So what?" I asked, returning my gaze to the road. "I'm a vampire. What does it matter?"

"Oh, please." I could hear the pity in his voice, and the disgust. "Enough with this 'I don't care anymore' shit. You know you're going to have to deal with it sometime."

A cold fist grabbed my insides. Jackal wasn't talking about feeding, and we both knew it. Memories rose up—memories of *him*—but then the monster emerged, swallowing them before I could feel anything. "I have dealt with it," I said calmly.

"No, you haven't." My brother's voice was suddenly hard. "You've just buried it. And if you don't get a handle on it soon, it's going to come out at the worst possible time. Probably when we're facing Sarren. Because that's how the psychopath's mind works—he knows just what to say, and when, to throw us off and give him the full advantage. And then he's either going to kill you while you're down and I'll be annoyed, or I'm going to have to do it myself."

"Better be careful, Jackal." My voice came out cold. Empty, because I couldn't feel anything, even now. "It almost sounds like you care."

"Oh, well, perish the thought, sister." Jackal gave me a sneer and moved away. "I'll stop talking, then. But if we reach Sarren, and he says something to make you fall apart, don't expect me to pick up the pieces."

You won't have to worry about that, I thought as Jackal walked on, shaking his head. A memory flickered, jagged and indistinct, and my inner demon pushed it back. *There's nothing left to break. Nothing Sarren says can touch me now.*

We walked a few more miles, through empty flatlands frozen under a layer of snow and ice, until the stars faded and a pink hue threatened the eastern sky. I was just starting to get uncomfortable when Kanin turned off the road and headed toward a gray, dilapidated barn sagging at the end of an overgrown field, a rusting silo beside it. The inside of the ancient building was musty and filled with broken beams and stacks of moldy straw. But it was also dark, secluded, and didn't have many holes in the roof where the sun could creep through. Ignoring Jackal's complaints about sleeping in a filthy, rat-infested barn, I pushed open a rotting stall door, found a shadowy corner behind a stack of rancid hay, and sank against the wall to sleep.

For just a moment, memory stirred again, like fragments of someone else's life, rising up from the dark. I remembered another barn like this one, warm and musty, filled with the soft bleats of livestock and the murmur of the humans around me. Hay and lanterns and contentment. A spotted baby goat, sitting in my lap, two human kids pressed close on either side, watching me feed it.

The monster roused. I'd been Hungry then, too, and had watched as the two humans fell asleep, baring their unsuspecting little necks to the vampire they'd unwittingly curled up against. I remembered bending forward, toward the throat of the child on my lap, as my fangs lengthened and slid out of my gums...before I'd caught myself in horror. I'd fled the barn before I could lose control and slaughter two innocent kids in their sleep.

The monster sneered at the memory. That seemed like a long, long time ago. A lifetime ago. Now, with the Hunger clawing at my gut and burning the edges of my mind, I thought longingly of the sleeping humans, so vulnerable beside me, imagined myself leaning down the rest of the way and finishing what I'd started.

The next night was more of the same. More empty plains and wilderness. More trackless snow, crunching beneath our boots, and an endless road snaking its way northeast. More of the Hunger gnawing my insides, making me irritable and savage. I concentrated on putting one foot in front of the other, trying to ignore the ache that refused to go away. I could feel the monster within, perilously close to the surface, a cold, dark thing that growled and stirred restlessly, always searching. It could hear the shuffle of tiny feet in the darkness, raccoons or possums or other nocturnal creatures, moving through the brush. It could sense the swoop of bats overhead and smell the deep, slow breaths of deer, huddled together in the undergrowth. It wanted to attack, to pounce on some living creature and rip it open, spilling hot blood into the snow and down our throats. But it knew, as I did, that wasting energy slaughtering animals was useless. That would not satisfy the Hunger. Only one type of prey would ease the hollow emptiness inside, and that prey was nowhere to be found.

So, we walked, Kanin leading, Jackal and I trailing behind. Three vampires who didn't need to rest, who never got cold or tired or winded, traveling through a wasted world that would kill most humans. That, in all honesty, already had.

And Sarren was well on his way to finishing the job.

Kanin turned suddenly in the middle of the road, his expression alert as he gazed back at us. I paused, too, surprised and a little wary. We hadn't spoken much after leaving New Covington. The Master vampire had walked steadily onward, silent and cold, without looking back at his two offspring. That was fine with me. I didn't have much to say to him, either. There was a wall between us now. I could sense his disappointment, the look in his eyes whenever Jackal made some snide, evil comment about humans and bloodbags…and I said nothing. Not even Kanin's silent disapproval would change the fact that I was a monster.

"Someone is coming," Kanin said, looking at the road behind us. I turned as well, straining my senses, but there was no need. The growl of an engine cut through the darkness, getting steadily closer.

The Hunger surged to life, and, close to the surface, the monster shifted eagerly. Vehicles meant humans, which meant food. I imagined sinking my teeth into their necks, imagined the hot blood rushing into my mouth, and felt my fangs lengthen, an eager growl escaping my throat.

"Get back," Kanin said, walking past me. I curled my lips at him, defiant, but his back was to me now, and he didn't notice. "Get off the road, both of you," he went on, as the engine noise grew louder and headlights glimmered through the trees. "Stopping for three strangers on a lonely road at night is a risk many would avoid. Better that they see a lone, unarmed traveler than a group." His voice grew harder. "Get off the road, Allison."

Jackal had already moved back, melting into the darkness. Kanin wasn't even looking at me, his gaze on the approaching headlights. With a growl, I stepped off the pavement and slipped behind a large twisted tree at the side of the road. And I waited, the Hunger clawing at my insides and the demon watching with barely restrained violence.

The lights grew brighter, and around a bend came a once-white van, now more rust than metal. Kanin stepped forward, raising his arms in a flagging motion as the vehicle sped forward, bathing him in the headlights.

It didn't slow. It angled toward Kanin, sped up, and a rough-looking human poked his head out the passenger window. He grinned and raised a dull black pistol, aiming it at the stranger in the road.

Kanin jumped back as several shots rang out, flaring white in the darkness. The van squealed past with hoots and harsh laughter, and the monster surged up with a roar.

I leaped out as the van came toward me, drawing my katana as I did. As it careened by, I lashed out with a snarl, aiming for the front tire, cutting through rubber and metal with a metallic scream and a flare of sparks. The van swerved wildly, screeched over the pavement, and crashed headlong into a tree.

I leaped after it, bright Hunger burning through my veins, the monster shrieking viciously in my mind. The driver and passenger lay against the shattered windshield, bloody and still, but the side door rasped open, and two men emerged, both clutching guns, and large ones at that. The first raised his weapon drunkenly as I raced up. My sword flashed, and he screamed as the gun hit the pavement along with both his arms. The second barked a terrified curse and tried to run. He got as far as the edge of the trees before I pounced on him from behind and drove my fangs into his neck.

Blood filled my mouth, hot and addictive. I growled in pleasure and sank into the feeling, the human going lax in my grip. Why had I ever shied away from this? I couldn't remember now.

"Well, that's just fabulous. Four humans to start with. Now two are dead and one's bleeding out like a ruptured fuel hose." The cold, exasperated voice cut through the ecstasy. I raised my head, warm blood running down my chin, to see Kanin and Jackal standing at the mangled remains of the van. Kanin was observing the armless, nearly delirious human writhe over the ground, moaning and sobbing, but Jackal was staring at me, a half amused, half disgusted look on his face.

"Oh, don't worry about me," he remarked. "You go ahead and enjoy that bloodbag. I'm not that Hungry anyway."

I swallowed, retracting my fangs, feeling faintly guilty. Kanin and Jackal were Hungry, too, and I was hoarding the only healthy source of food. Vampires didn't feed from the dead, even the newly dead. Drinking from a corpse had the same result as drinking from an animal; it did nothing for the Hunger. Not to mention, most vampires found it repulsive. Our prey had to be human, and it had to be alive; that was one of the ancient, unfathomable rules we lived by. One of the rules you just didn't question.

Turning, I dragged my prey a few steps into the road, back to where Jackal watched with amused exasperation. "Here," I said, and shoved the human at him. It collapsed bonelessly to the pavement. "That one is still breathing, mostly. I'm done with it."

Jackal curled a lip. "I don't want your leftovers, sister," he said contemptuously. I smiled back at him.

"Good. I can finish it, then?"

He gave me a murderous look, stalked across the pavement, and hauled the human upright. The man's head fell back limply, his neck a mess of blood, and Jackal plunged his fangs into the other side of his throat.

I glanced toward the van to see Kanin gently lower the armless human to the ground, where he slumped, lifeless, to the pavement. The stumps of his forearms no longer oozed, and his skin was white. I wondered how much blood Kanin had been able to get out of him before he died. Not much, I guessed, but even a little was better than nothing. I should have just cut off the one arm. Or a foot, perhaps. Then he wouldn't have been able to run.

Somewhere deep inside, a part of me recoiled, horrified with myself and my current thoughts. The old part, the Allison that was still a little human, screamed that this was wrong, that I didn't have to be like this. But her voice was tiny, indistinct. I shivered, and the monster buried the voice under cold indifference. It was too late, I thought, feeling blessed numbness spread through my core again. I knew what I was. Sympathy, mercy, regret—those had no place in the life of a vampire. The old Allison was stubborn; it would take a while for her to die for good, but I heard her voice less and less now. Eventually, it would disappear altogether.

Vampire indifference firmly in place, I glanced at my sire. Kanin had stepped away from the dead human and was now peering into the darkened interior of the van. A brief, pained look crossed his face before it smoothed out again. Curious, I walked up beside him and gazed into the vehicle.

There was another body in the van. A young woman, only a year or two older than me, dressed in a filthy white shift. Her hands were tied in front of her, and she lay crumpled against the wall of the van, her neck at an unnatural angle.

Curly yellow hair spread over her face, and glassy blue eyes stared at nothing out the open door.

Oh, no. She was a captive, an innocent. I caused this. For a moment, I felt sick. The dead girl's eyes seemed to bore into me, accusing. I'd killed her. Maybe I hadn't torn out her throat or cut off her head, but she was dead all the same, because of me.

I could feel Kanin's dark gaze on my back, and I heard Jackal's footsteps crunch over the thin layer of snow behind us as he came to peer over my shoulder. "Huh," he remarked, as if he was staring at a dead bird on the sidewalk. "Well, now we know why the bastards were in such a hurry. Shame she didn't make it—I'm still a bit peckish." He sniffed, and I felt his gaze shift to me, hard and reproachful. "That human you so generously left me barely took the edge off."

"I didn't know she was there," I muttered, not turning around. Not knowing if I'd said it to Kanin, Jackal, or myself. "I didn't know...."

But that wasn't much of an excuse. I knew it, and Kanin knew it. He said nothing, just turned and walked away, but as always, his silence spoke volumes.

"Oh, well," Jackal shrugged. "Nothing for it now. It just reminds you how very fragile these meatsacks are. Can't even look at them funny without breaking their bloody necks." He glanced down at me. "Aw, don't beat yourself up too hard, sister," he said, grinning. "It's not like the human had much to live for, not where she was headed. You did the bloodbag a favor, trust me."

I stared at the girl again and felt the monster creep forward, cold and practical, burying the guilt. *What does it matter?* it whispered. *So, you killed another human. It wasn't the first, and it won't be the last. They're prey, and you are a vampire. Killing is what we do.*

"Yeah." I sighed and turned away from the van, away from

the human and her flat, accusing eyes. Jackal was right; there was nothing I could do now. The girl meant nothing, one more death to be added to the endless, eternal list. Kanin was already walking down the road again, and we hurried to catch up. Leaving the vehicle, its slaughtered passengers, and another small piece of my humanity behind.

CHAPTER 2

✦

Three nights later, there was a body in the road.

Or, rather, scattered all over the road. Not much was left except the stripped, broken bones of some unfortunate creature, lying in a dark smear in the snow. From the looks of it, the body had literally been torn to pieces and left to rot in the center of the pavement. We had stumbled upon yet another dead town, the road cutting through rows of rotting buildings, overgrown and falling apart, roofs caved in and windows smashed. An ancient playground stood on the corner, swings piled high with snow, a rusty slide lying twisted and bent on the ground. Empty, like everything else around us.

"Sarren?" I asked, regarding the broken skeleton with a mix of annoyance and apathy. It wasn't human, so there was nothing wasted, nothing to regret. But the Hunger within still raged at the amount of blood spilled, demanding to be fed. Even the aftereffects of violence sent it into a frenzy now. I wished it would shut up.

Kanin shook his head.

"No," he murmured. "Sarren wouldn't bother with an animal. Not if he wanted to send a message. Besides, it's too fresh. This was done tonight."

"Rabids," I guessed instead, and he nodded grimly. "Can we avoid them?"

"We can try," he said, earning a snort from Jackal. "But we cannot deviate from this path. We must reach Eden soon, if not to beat Sarren there, then to stop him from using that virus." His gaze lifted to the horizon. "I fear we may already be too late."

I felt a tiny prick of worry. I knew people in Eden. People I'd risked everything for, just to see them to their vampire-free sanctuary. Caleb, Bethany, Silas and Theresa. What if Sarren got there before me and unleashed his terrible virus? What if, when I finally got to Eden, everyone I'd known was dead? Or worse, infected, bleeding, and tearing themselves apart? I thought of cheerful Caleb, shy little Bethany, and kind, patient Theresa. They didn't suspect anything. They thought they were safe in Eden, and now, a madman and a horrifying virus were heading right for them.

I shivered, and the darkness within rose up to shield me. If Sarren reached Eden before us, then those humans were dead. I couldn't do anything for them, and it wasn't my concern to protect them anymore. They didn't matter. I just wanted to find my enemy and bury him in pieces.

I felt the weight of Kanin's gaze on me, grim and searching. As if he knew what I was thinking, because he always knew. I met that stare, unflinching, the monster staring back without remorse. Not long ago, that look would've made me cringe, bristle, try harder. Now, I didn't have the will to care what even Kanin thought of me.

He didn't say anything, however. Just turned away, his step heavy, toward the northeast. And we continued on.

It began snowing again, large flakes drifting from a black sky, settling on my head and shoulders. The road continued past crumbling buildings, gutted-out stores and gas stations, and rusty hulks of old cars. Skeletal trees pushed their way through pavement and rooftops, their limbs frozen and bare, their roots splitting stone, wood and concrete as nature slowly engulfed the town. Maybe in another sixty years, it would vanish entirely. Maybe in another sixty years, no trace of mankind would be left anywhere.

We wove through a maze of ancient, snow-covered vehicles, several of them smashed against each other in the intersection, and came to a crossroads.

Kanin stopped in the middle of the road and abruptly drew his dagger. The thin, deadly blade flashed in the darkness as it appeared in his hand, and the vampire went perfectly still. Jackal and I froze as our sire stood there, unmoving.

"They're coming," he said softly.

We didn't hesitate, pulling our weapons and moving up beside him. The former raider king reached into his duster and withdrew a steel fire ax, the head stained dark with old blood, and gave it an easy twirl. Unsheathing my katana, I raised the curved, razor-sharp blade in front of me and listened.

Feet. Feet shuffling through the snow, and lots of them. From all sides of the intersection. I caught flashes of movement through the sea of cars, glimpses of pale, emaciated forms darting between vehicles. Wails and raspy hisses rose into the air, the screech of claws on metal echoed through the night, and the dead, awful scent came to me over the breeze.

"About time," Jackal growled as he swung his ax up, fangs flashing in a defiant grin. His voice echoed weirdly in the night, and the wailing around us grew louder. "Come on, you little bastards. I'm *so* ready to tear something's head off."

As if in answer, a creature leaped to the roof of the car beside him. It was vaguely human-shaped, with matted hair and white skin stretched over an emaciated body, and it reeked of death. Mad white eyes, with no irises or pupils, blazed down at us as the rabid bared jagged fangs and flung itself at us with a howl.

It met the edge of Jackal's ax as the vampire whirled and smashed the rabid headfirst into a car door, shattering glass and making a hollow *boom* against the metal. Dark blood spattered across the side of the vehicle, and the rabid dropped to the snow with its skull caved in. Jackal raised his head and roared, vicious and defiant, as a swarm of the pale, shrieking things scrambled over car roofs and hoods and descended on us. My own monster within howled an eager challenge in return, and I let it go.

A rabid leaped at me, claws slashing. As it fell, I whipped up my katana and sliced clean through the spindly middle, cutting it in two with a spray of black blood. Another lunged over the hood of a van, and I whirled toward it, bringing my sword down to cut the head from its body. A savage glee filled me as the skull bounced and rolled at my feet, and I leaped onto the roof of the van with a snarl, welcoming the swarm as they wailed and sprang at me. Rabids lunged over cars and clawed at my feet, trying to scramble up the vehicle or pull me into the mob. I spun and danced over the metal, leaping from roof to roof and slicing the monsters that followed, cutting off limbs that reached for me.

Below, Jackal and Kanin fought side by side, a deadly pairing despite their differences. Jackal's fire ax spun through the air and connected with bone-crushing force, cracking skulls, smashing opponents into cars and pavement. Kanin's thin, bright dagger was a blur as he moved gracefully around the flailing monsters, slitting throats and severing heads with surgical precision. They didn't need my help; both were doing just fine.

In the split second that my attention strayed to Kanin and Jackal, a rabid landed on the car roof beside me and lashed out with its claws. I jerked back, sweeping my blade up to cut it open, but a stinging pain erupted over my face as its talons scored my cheek.

The world went red. Screaming, I leaped down into the middle of the swarm and began laying waste with my katana. Limbs and heads parted for me as I carved my way through the horde. My demon reveled in the chaos and destruction, howling in delight with every body that fell, painting the snow and the cars around me with dark blood.

A shadow fell over me, and the ground shook with a roar. I spun to see a huge rabid, well over six feet, fill my vision one second before a large, claw-tipped hand struck the side of my head with an explosion of pain. I was knocked into a car, glass shattering around me as the giant roared, towering over the others, and came at me again.

I dove aside as the rabid struck the car, talons screeching off the metal and leaving long furrows behind. Despite its monstrous size, it was more skeleton than flesh. Below the ribs jutting sharply against pale skin, its stomach was a yawning, concave valley that seemed to press into its spine. But its shoulders were massive, and heavy, deformed arms hung past its knees, the hands tipped with sicklelike claws. It screamed at me and pounced, and I rolled away, cutting at its middle as I came to my feet. The katana struck a few ribs, severing them, and the creature whirled with a howl.

Blood ran into my eyes, making it hard to see. I blinked and shook my head, trying to focus. The rabid roared and lashed out with those long arms, and I met the blow with my sword, hammering it into the thing's forearm. The blade struck the thick limb and cut deep, but the force still knocked me aside, sending me sprawling to the snow. It was strong, and I was going to have to hit something vital if I wanted to kill it for good.

Still clutching my weapon, I pushed myself to my hands and knees. But before I could stand, something grabbed the back of my neck, lifted me up a few feet, and then slammed me to the pavement with crushing force. I felt my nose break and my jawbone snap, and pain exploded behind my eyes. The thing bashed me to the ground three more times, bones popping and crunching with every blow, before it turned and flung me into the hood of a car. More glass shattered, biting into my flesh, and fresh stabs of pain joined the agony already pounding through my head. The rabid bellowed in triumph, lumbering forward, and my delirium shifted to a sudden, all-consuming rage.

Ignoring the pain, I snatched my katana from where it lay on the hood and roared a challenge to the giant bearing down on me. As it loomed overhead, smashing down with a huge fist, I dodged aside, and its arm crunched into metal, leaving a deep hole behind. Snarling, I leaped toward my enemy, launched myself off its elbow, and brought my sword down as hard as I could. The blade sliced through the rabid's collarbone and carved through its pale body, splitting it open from neck to stomach.

The huge creature staggered, the two halves peeling off in different directions, before it slid slowly to the pavement, twitched once, and was still. Fangs bared, I gazed around for my next attacker, raising my sword, but nothing else moved in the night. The horde was gone, scattered in pieces behind and around me, filling the air with the foul stench of their blood. I was alone.

And I hurt. I hurt everywhere, inside and out. I needed food, blood. I needed to hunt, but there was no prey here. The pain within was fading; I knew I was healing, but I was Hungry now. *So very Hungry…*

"Well, little sister, I'm not too proud to say it. That was almost impressive."

A voice, snide and challenging, echoed behind me. The Hunger roared, and I spun, baring my fangs in a snarl. Another vampire stood several paces away, smelling of blood and power, yellow eyes widening in shock. Older than me, possibly stronger than me, but that had never given me pause before. My lips curled, and I stepped toward him, raising my sword.

"Sister." The vampire's voice was a warning, and he raised his hands, one of which held a bloody fire ax. "Don't be stupid. Get a hold of yourself. Don't make me smear your brains all over the pavement."

His voice rang oddly in my head, almost familiar. Did I know him? I hesitated, confused, but the fiery ache inside rose up, consuming me. I faced the vampire across from me and hissed, an invitation and a challenge. To my surprise, he didn't take it.

"Allison."

Another figure appeared from the maze of cars, striding to face me across the pavement. I cringed back, feeling the immense power radiating from that dark form. The first vampire was of no consequence now. This vampire was far older, and far, far stronger than us both.

"One of the bastards got her good," I heard the other vampire say, not making any sense. "She's close to frenzy. Doesn't recognize either of us."

The ancient one gazed at me, dark eyes boring into mine, and fear shot through me. I couldn't fight him; he would tear me apart. I snarled and stepped back, tensing to flee into the shadows, away from that terrifying presence.

"Allison, stop." The Master's voice, soft and compelling, lanced into me, holding me still. "Look at me," he continued, and I had no choice but to obey. "Calm your mind," he murmured, the words soothing the swirl of chaos and darkness within. "You know me. You know who you are." His voice flowed through me, becoming more familiar, and the rage began to subside. "Remember," the Master vampire continued, staring me down. "Remember what we are trying to accomplish." His voice hardened, becoming unyielding and stern. "You cannot lose yourself to frenzy. I will not allow it. Who am I?"

Memory flooded in at last. Closing my eyes, I slumped to the hood of a car, bowing my head. "Kanin," I whispered as everything came back. I could feel my fangs pressing against my lip, the blood on my cheek left by rabid claws, the damage done to me inside. The Hunger flared, painful and demanding, but I shoved it into the darkness once more.

His footsteps crunched through the snow until he stood over me, gazing at the top of my head. Shame burned, hot and intense. I'd lost control. The very thing I had promised would never happen again, nearly had. I'd been one step away from Blood Frenzy, from losing control of the Hunger and attacking anything that moved.

No, Allison. Don't lie to yourself. The truth emerged, making me feel cold. *You didn't lose control to the demon—you welcomed it this time. You gave in, willingly. And Kanin knows it.*

"How injured are you?" My sire's voice was grave, disapproving. I clenched my fists against the metal, pushing back the shame and the last of the Hunger, and rose to face him.

"I'll live." I flicked blood from my katana, then sheathed it calmly, keeping my own voice neutral. I refused to feel guilty, refused to let Kanin shame me for what I'd almost done. I'd been badly hurt, and Blood Frenzy was a fact of life for vampires. Sooner or later, we all lost control.

"I was careless," I muttered, turning away from my sire and seeing Jackal at the edge of the road. It was easier to face Jackal than Kanin; my blood brother stood with his arms crossed, smirking at me, but that was more bearable than the disappointed stare of a Master vampire. "It won't happen again."

"It will," Kanin said and walked past me, heading down the road, but in a different direction than before. I blinked after him.

"Where are you going?"

"We're breaking trail," Kanin said matter-of-factly. "Sarren will have to wait. We must go hunting before one of us falls to Blood Frenzy." That pretty much meant me, I guessed.

"No," I growled, and stalked after my sire, making him turn. "Kanin, I'm fine. We don't have to do this."

"Allison." Kanin's eyes narrowed. "Of the three of us, you are closest to the edge. You are making no effort to control yourself, and the monster is very close to the surface. Having you so close to frenzy is dangerous for us all. As it is, I am not certain you can restrain yourself in the presence of humans. I am less certain that you will even try."

It wasn't the muted disapproval in his voice that got to me; it was the sorrow, the regret. As if he had failed. As if he had been proud of me, once, but now had second thoughts about bringing me into this world, making me a vampire.

And suddenly, I was angry. I was angry that he could make me feel shame for what I knew was my base nature. I was angry that no matter what I told myself otherwise, how hard I tried to deny it, I wanted to make him proud. I was angry that he expected more from me, that he held me up to some ridiculous standard that I could never reach.

I raised my head and stared him down. "Maybe I won't," I said carelessly. "Why should that bother you?"

Anguish flickered across his impassive face before it became calmly aloof once more. "This is not what I taught you, Allison," he said in a voice meant only for me. "You are stronger than this."

I shrugged. "Maybe I realized it's futile, and I don't want to fight my nature for the rest of eternity. Maybe I realized Jackal was right all along."

"No." Kanin's voice was suddenly hard, terrifying. "You are simply using your demon to hide from what you really feel. Because you are afraid of what that means, that it might be painful. It is far easier to be a monster than to confront the truth."

I snarled back, baring my fangs. "So what?" I demanded, wanting Kanin to react, to show some kind of emotion, but he didn't even blink. "I tried, Kanin. I really did. But you know what I discovered?" I curled my lip into a sneer. "We *are* monsters. No matter how long I fight it, I'm always going to want to hunt and kill and destroy. *You* taught me that, remember? What happened with—" my mind recoiled from his name "—with that human—that was stupid and wrong and eventually, I would've killed him. It was…better…that he died." I nearly choked on the words, but forced myself to continue, to believe it. "He would've only been used against me. Now there's nothing holding me back."

"Very well." Kanin's voice sounded hollow. "Then the next time you are teetering on the edge, I will not pull you back from it. But be warned, Allison." His gaze sharpened, cutting into me. "There is a difference between killing while in the throes of Hunger or Blood Frenzy, and giving in to the monster. Once you fall, once you willingly cross that line, it changes you. Forever."

We glared at each other, two monsters facing off in the tangle of cars and dead rabids, the snow falling softly around us. Kanin's gaze was icy, but I sensed no anger from him, only weary acceptance, regret and the faintest hint of sorrow. He understood, I realized. He knew, better than most, the lure of the monster, how hard it was to deny our base nature. He was disappointed that he had lost another to the demon, but he understood. I wondered if Kanin, in his long, long existence, had ever fallen to his own darkness, if it was even possible to hold out forever.

I decided that I didn't care. Let Kanin do and think what he wished; *I* was still a monster, and that would never change.

"So, anyway." Jackal's impatient voice broke through our cold standoff. "Not to interrupt this riveting family drama, but are we going to go hunting anytime soon, or are you two going to glare at each other until the sun comes up?"

We took the road due north, a direction that pointed away from Eden and Sarren. I didn't want to postpone the chase, to let our quarry pull farther ahead. But Kanin insisted, and when Kanin insisted, there was nothing else to do. For the rest of the night, we walked, passing forests and plains and the broken remnants of civilization, well hidden in the snow and overgrown forest.

Kanin ignored me, walking silently ahead without looking back. Not that his behavior was any different than on most nights, but now it had this icy, untouchable feel to it. He had washed his hands of me, it seemed. I told myself I didn't care. Kanin's values were no longer my own. And he was wrong about me. I wasn't burying the pain left over from that night in New Covington, or using the monster to shield myself from hurt. I'd simply accepted what I was. What I should have accepted from the beginning.

"So, sister," Jackal said at length, dropping beside me with his ever-present grin. "Looks like we're in the same boat now. How does it feel, being one of Kanin's many disappointments?"

"Shut up, Jackal," I said, mostly out of habit. Knowing he wouldn't.

"Oh, it's not so bad," Jackal went on, with a nod in Kanin's direction. "Now you don't have to hear him go on and on about his stupid bloodbags and 'controlling the monster.' It gets so tedious after a few months." He gave me a wicked smile. "Isn't it easier down here, sister? Now that you've fallen from his ridiculously high expectations? You can finally start living the way a vampire should."

"Is there a point to any of this?"

"Actually, there is." His smirk faded, and, for a moment, he looked almost serious. "I want to know what you're going to do after we catch up to Sarren and beat the ever-loving shit out of him," he said. "I don't expect the old man will want either of us around much longer, now that you've finally accepted the fact that you actually like the taste of blood, and he tends to frown on such things. Where will you go once this is all over? Assuming you survive, of course. And that our dear sire doesn't decide to off us both for 'the greater good.'"

"I don't know," I said, ignoring that last part. I didn't think Kanin would try to kill me, but...he had tried to end Jackal's life once, long ago. Had I fallen so far that Kanin thought Jackal and I were one and the same? Mistakes that he should never have brought into the world?

"I don't know where I'll go after this," I said again, gazing off into the trees. I couldn't see myself staying in any one place, not among the humans who hated and feared me, and who I would systematically kill, one by one, to feed myself. Maybe I'd wander from place to place, forever. "I guess it doesn't matter."

"Well, I have a suggestion," Jackal said, the echo of a grin in his voice. "Come back with me to Old Chicago."

I glanced at him in surprise. He seemed completely serious

about the offer. "Why?" I asked warily. "You never struck me as the sharing type."

"You do have a very selective memory, you know that, right?" Jackal shook his head. "What have I been saying all this time, sister? I've made this offer before, several times in fact, but you were too hung up on your precious bloodbags to even consider it. No, I don't tolerate other bloodsuckers in my city, but you're not just a random, wandering mongrel vampire. You're kin." He smiled widely, showing the tips of his fangs. "And we could do great things, the two of us. Think about it."

Still wary, I asked, "And what are these 'great things' we would end up doing?"

Jackal chuckled. "For starters," he said, "once we get that cure from Eden, we could start working on that whole vampire-army thing I've been talking about. We could have our own vampire city, and the other Princes would bow to us. We could rule everything, you and me. Wha'd'ya say?"

"And you'd just share all that?" I gave him a skeptical look. "What's to stop you from stabbing me in the back the second we have a disagreement?"

"Sister, I'm hurt." Jackal gave me a mock wounded look. "You make me sound completely unreasonable. Isn't it enough that I want to get to know my dear little sister, my only surviving kin besides Kanin?"

"No," I said, now even more wary. I glared at him, and he gave me a smile that was way too innocent. "Don't try to feed me any crap about family and blood and kin. You'd throw us to the rabids if you thought you could get something out of it, you said so yourself." Jackal snorted, but he didn't deny it, and I narrowed my eyes. "What's the real reason you want me around?"

"Because, my thick-headed little sister…" Jackal sighed. "I trust you."

I nearly tripped over my own feet in shock. I stared at him, not really believing what I'd just heard, and he glared back. Like this was vastly annoying, and he needed to get it over with quickly. "Because I know that you, at least, won't turn on me if something better comes along," he elaborated. "Because you have that disgusting sense of loyalty that keeps getting you into trouble. And because you aren't half bad in a fight, either." His expression moved between arrogance and pity. "I figure I can be the smart, practical, logical one and you can be the pretty, hotheaded, overemotional one, and between us, we'll be ready for anything."

"So you want me around because I can fight, and I won't turn on you." My voice echoed flatly in my head, tinged with bitterness. "That's a pretty nice deal on your side. I seem to notice *you* aren't making those same promises."

Jackal shrugged. "Look at it this way, sister," he said, his golden eyes seeing way too much as they gazed down at me. "At least you won't be alone."

His words sent a shiver through my insides. *Alone.* I would be alone again. After this was all over, even if we beat Sarren, I'd be right back where I started the night Kanin and I had fled New Covington and been separated. I hadn't been able to return to the city, but I'd had no clue what to do next. With no sire, no friends and no direction, I'd wandered aimlessly through an empty, unforgiving world, not knowing what to do or where I was headed. Not knowing how lonely I was, until I stumbled upon a small group of pilgrims searching for a mythical paradise. They'd given me a goal, a purpose. I'd given everything to get them to Eden…but they were gone now. And once Sarren was killed, it would be like that again.

Kanin would leave and I'd be alone once more, wandering the world by myself. Unless, I accepted Jackal's offer.

"I don't know," I said once more, making him sigh again. "I'll…think about it."

"Think fast," Jackal said, but at that moment, Kanin stopped in the middle of the pavement, gazing at something at his feet. Curious, we strode over, hopping the trunk of a tree that had fallen into the road. We'd been following a narrow, broken trail through a stretch of forest that was doing its best to smother everything we passed, and the few houses I'd glimpsed through the thick trunks were barely more than rotted beams wrapped in vegetation. Nothing moved out here; even the wildlife seemed to be asleep or in hibernation, and the snow covered everything in a silent blanket, muffling all sound. I hoped Kanin knew what he was doing, leading us so far afield.

Kanin still hadn't moved when we came up, but his gaze followed something off into the woods. Gazing down at the road, I saw what had stopped him.

A pair of straight, narrow tracks cut through the snow, went across the road, and continued up the bank into the forest on the other side. I blinked. A vehicle of some sort? It would have to be a really small one, to be able to travel through dense woods. And there were animal prints of some kind between the lines. At least, they certainly weren't human.

"A horse and cart went through here," Kanin explained, perhaps seeing my confused expression. "Not long ago. A few hours, perhaps." He gazed into the trees, and his voice was suddenly grave. "Whoever left these tracks isn't far."

"About time," Jackal growled at my side, and an evil grin crossed his face as his gaze followed Kanin's into the forest. His eyes glowed dangerously, and his fangs glinted as he smiled. "Let's just hope there's more than one. I don't particularly feel like sharing."

There are humans nearby. The Hunger surged up with the realization, twisting and painful. I felt my own fangs slide out, poking my bottom lip, and suddenly resented the two vampires nearby—competition for my food.

"Come, then," Kanin said, sounding weary. He stepped off the road, heading into the forest without looking back. "Let's get this over with."

CHAPTER 3

The trail didn't take us far.

We'd followed the tracks about two hundred yards into the forest when the trees thinned and a small field stretched out before us, penned in with crudely cut logs. The ground past the barrier had been trampled to mud, and when I took a breath, I caught the familiar scent of manure and livestock hanging in the frozen air. The pasture, of course, was empty. No one left domestic animals outside at night, for the same reason no human ever ventured out at night: they'd be ripped to shreds by rabids in short order.

Eagerly, I stared past the field, searching for any signs of where these humans might live. When I had traveled with Jebbadiah's band, we'd stumbled across the Archer farm one night, an isolated homestead surrounded by a protective fence that kept rabids at bay. The barn and enormous farmhouse both sat within the wall, and the Archer clan had been able to move freely about even at night, so long as they stayed within its boundaries.

But, to my shock, there was no wall out here, not even a small one. Sitting at the edge of the field, smoke curling lazily from a brick chimney, was a house. It was dark, two stories high, and completely unprotected, sitting brazenly in the open with no fires, gates, or anything to shield it from the walking horrors outside.

"Well, that's interesting," Jackal murmured, leaning against the fence with his elbows on the railing. "No wall. And there are definitely bloodbags inside, unless the rabids have suddenly discovered they're not afraid of fire." He frowned, regarding the house like it was some new curiosity he'd never seen before. "So, I'm guessing these meatsacks are either the luckiest sons of bitches to ever walk the earth, or that house is going to have a few nasty surprises waiting for us." With a snort, he pushed himself off the railing, shaking his head. "Course, it's not going to matter either way. I'm still going to eat them. How much is going to depend on how seriously they piss me off by the time I get in there."

I growled at him, the monster rearing up in protest. "You'd better not kill them all," I said coldly, making him raise an eyebrow. "At least not until I'm done. Find your own human to feed on. I'm not sharing this time."

"Oh, sister," Jackal mocked, pretending to wipe away a tear. "Listen to you, sounding just like a real vampire. I'm so proud."

"We are not," Kanin said in a calm, terrifying voice, "going to kill anyone. Executing men who are shooting at us is one thing. There is no need to massacre a sleeping household. When we part ways, you both can do as you like. Until then, as I am the oldest and technically the head of this coven, we will do things my way. If you cannot abide this, you are always free to go. I am not stopping you."

He'd once said those words to Jackal, who'd taken him up on that offer and betrayed us to Sarren, only to switch sides once more at the last minute. But now, Kanin's dark gaze fixed solely on me, hard and cold. It sent a sudden, sharp pang through my stomach. My sire didn't trust me; he really had lumped me into the same boat as Jackal, the vampire whom I'd once despised for treating humans as food. Jackal's own words came back to taunt me. *"That's what I like about you, sister. You and me, we're exactly the same."*

He was right. My ruthless, murdering blood brother had been right all along.

I met Kanin's piercing gaze and shrugged. "Fine," I said, matching my coldness to his. "You've made your point. I'll try not to kill any of the bloodbags."

A flicker of what might've been pain crossed Kanin's impassive face on that last sentence. That last word, one I'd never used before. *Bloodbags.*

Jackal snickered then, shooting Kanin a dangerous leer. "Aw, what's the matter, old man?" he asked. "Didn't expect your little spawn to fall so far from grace? Did you really expect her to retain your ridiculous, unfeasible morals?" He gave me a sideways glance. "Open your eyes, Kanin. Your favorite hellspawn is a demon, just like the rest of us. Only now, she's finally realized it."

Kanin stared at us, his features coolly remote once more, then turned away. "We do this quickly and quietly," he said, following the cart tracks around the field toward the house up top. "Go in, take what you need, and leave. There might be guards nearby, so let's be careful."

As we approached the monstrous house sitting at the edge of the pasture, the reason it wasn't surrounded by a wall became quite clear. It didn't need to be.

Up close, the building was a fortress. The walls were brick, reinforced in places with steel bars and plates. A wide trench surrounded the whole house, with sharpened iron poles bristling from the bottom and stabbing up on the other side. Windows had metal bars running across them, and the heavy double doors, armored and plated with steel, seemed able to withstand the most vicious rabid attack.

But it didn't account for vampires.

"Creative bastards, aren't they?" Jackal mused as we silently circled the house, looking for points of entry, potential weak spots we could exploit. There weren't many; every window was barred, the back door was armored, and spikes bristled around the perimeter and even from the roof. "If I wasn't planning to eat the little bloodbags, I might be reluctantly impressed. As it is, this is just obnoxious. Hey, Kanin," he called in a louder whisper, gazing at the other vampire a few paces away, "you still sold on this 'enter quietly and leave' bullshit? Right now I'm thinking a good 'kick in the door' approach would work better."

Kanin stopped at the edge of the pit and calmly assessed his surroundings. My demon was intrigued by Jackal's suggested approach, anything to get us into the house sooner, but the Master vampire suddenly leaped the twenty-foot trench like it was a crack on the sidewalk, landing gracefully on the other side without impaling himself on the spikes. Grasping the thick iron bars in front of the window, he pulled them apart with as much effort as bending a wire and slid through the opening. Jackal snorted.

"Or you could do that, I suppose."

We followed Kanin into the house, jumping over the trench, somehow avoiding the bristling spikes waiting on the other side, and sliding through the window. The interior was sparse and clean, with wooden floors and old, simple furniture, a bed of hot embers glowing in the hearth. We had come into what looked like a living room, with a kitchen off to the side, a dark hallway next to that, and a staircase to the second floor in the center of the room. I took a deep breath and caught the mingling scents of smoke and cut wood, livestock and dirt, and the distinct smell of warm-blooded creatures. The Hunger awoke with a vengeance, and I stifled an eager growl, feeling my fangs burst through my gums.

Kanin, a dark figure against the wall, gestured at us to be silent, his eyes hard. I bit my lip, trying to calm down, though the Hunger refused to be ignored, now that prey was so close. The Master vampire pointed two fingers down the hallway, then again up the stairs. Four humans: two on the first floor and another two upstairs. All asleep. All thinking this fortified house would keep them safe.

From rabids, perhaps. But not from me.

Jackal shot me a hard yellow glare that very obviously meant *don't follow me* and stalked away down the hall, making no noise on the wooden floor. I watched him go, relieved that he was staying out of my way, and headed toward the staircase in the center of the room. I felt Kanin watching me as I started up the stairs, but between the Hunger and the anticipation of the end of the hunt, I barely noticed him.

I glided up the staircase, silent as a ghost, and the Hunger grew stronger with every step I took. Until it was a dark, raging fire within, consuming me. My fangs pressed against my bottom lip, eager to rip and tear, to find a human and release the hot flood of power that pulsed through its veins. So many times, I'd pushed down the Hunger, denying my nature and the monster within. The old Allison, desperately fighting to stay human.

No longer. I was a vampire, and I knew the outcome of this hunt. It was so easy to release my human conscience and emotions, to let the monster guide the way. I didn't know why I'd been so stubborn. Trying to remain human had brought nothing but pain. I would not open myself up to that kind of hurt again.

At the top of the stairs, another narrow hall stretched before me, with two identical wooden doors sitting across from each other. One was halfway open, revealing a bathroom. The other was firmly closed, but even through the wood, I heard the faint sounds of snoring.

I smiled. Walking up to the door, I turned the handle and gave it a soft push. It swung back with a creak, revealing a small bedroom cloaked in shadow. A dresser, a mirror and a closet stood against one wall, two grimy, barred windows on the other. Pale moonlight filtered through ragged curtains and touched the foot of a large bed in the corner. I could see a lump beneath the covers, a head resting on the pillow, dark hair spilling over the edge. The Hunger surged up with a roar.

Stepping into the room, I closed the door behind me with a faint click. It was all I could do to control myself, to not fly across the room with a snarl and sink my fangs into that exposed neck, ripping it open, spilling hot blood onto the white sheets. But Kanin would disapprove of a violent, bloody massacre, and besides, I would not let the Hunger overtake my will this time. I might be a monster, but I was not an animal.

With deliberate steps, I walked across the room until I stood at the edge of the mattress, gazing down. A woman lay there, long hair unbound, breathing peacefully. Her face, though young, was lined and haggard, her forehead creased in a faint, consistent frown. I stood there, my shadow falling over the bed, watching my prey sleep, feeling the Hunger blaze like fire through my veins. I felt it beating the edges of my mind, howling at me to feed, to rip my prey apart and paint the sheets in blood. And still, I waited.

The moment I knew I could turn and walk away, leave the room and its occupant unharmed, I struck.

Gently pushing the long hair aside, being careful not to wake my prey, I parted my lips, dropped down, and sank my fangs into the side of her neck.

She stiffened for the briefest of moments, a tiny gasp escaping, before slumping deeper into the pillow and the near delirium of a vampire's bite. Hot, glorious blood filled my mouth, and I growled in ecstasy, sinking my fangs in deeper. The Hunger raged as I drank in my prey, wanting more, always more. Never satisfied. I reached the point where I'd be sated for another two weeks, where the Hunger would be demanding and constant, but not overpowering. Where, if I drew back and left now, my prey would be weakened and tired from blood loss, but still alive.

I closed my eyes…and kept going. Continued feeding, never wanting to stop. Warmth and power filled me, intoxicating and overwhelming, and I didn't resist. The demon and the Hunger approved, howling in glee, stifling any feelings of guilt or remorse I might've felt. Kanin would be displeased that I'd killed this mortal, drained it to an empty husk, but I'd already disappointed him beyond repair. The one person I'd wanted to keep my humanity for was gone. I might as well succumb to my base instincts once and for all and accept that, no matter what I did, I would always be a monster.

The human grew pale beneath me, the skin taking on a deathly pallor. She made a tiny, breathy sound, a name breathed through pallid lips, as if she was lost in a nightmare. And, for just a moment, a tiny flicker of shame, of uncertainty, cut through the icy darkness within. I ignored it, sank my fangs in deeper, and continued to feed. This would be over soon. There'd be no more nightmares after this.

"Mommy?"

The muffled voice that came through the doorway was barely more than a whisper, but it gave me just enough of a warning. Retracting my fangs, I swiftly sealed the puncture wounds by pressing my tongue to my victim's throat, just as the handle behind me clicked and turned. As the door began to creak open, I rose, swept across the room with vampire speed and grace, and ducked into the closet.

Later, as I reflected on my actions, I didn't know *why* I'd chosen to run, to hide. Maybe it was guilt after all, not wanting anyone to see me prey on a human. The shame of what I had to do to live. Or maybe it was just habit now. But I pulled the door shut behind me, leaving only a narrow strip to see through, and hovered there in the darkness. A literal monster in the closet, watching and waiting.

Through the crack in the closet door, I saw a small figure in a ragged blue nightgown walk silently across the room to stand beside the bed. She was young, probably no more than eight, with stringy dark hair hanging down her shoulders and thin, birdlike arms. Those arms were wrapped around some kind of stuffed creature, holding it tightly to her chest, as she padded up to the mattress, her eyes large and frightened. Strangely, though I'd never seen this girl before, I felt a prick of recognition, making me frown. This scene was... familiar, somehow.

"Mommy?" The little girl hovered at the edge of the covers, clutching her stuffed thing. "I had a nightmare. Wake up. Mommy?"

Her whispers grew louder and more frightened as the figure in the bed refused to stir. Finally, the little girl reached out and shook the woman's arm.

"Mommy!"

"Mmm?" The figure under the covers finally moved, dark head raising off the pillow to gaze at the child. She was very pale, her skin having taken on an unhealthy grayness. But, seeing the girl, she rose higher from the mattress, reaching out to stroke the child's hair. "Abigail? What's wrong, baby?"

There was a sudden tightness in my chest. Something squeezing at my heart, making my throat ache with longing.

Memories of another time, another life, much like this one. A tiny bedroom, ratty curtains fluttering in the icy breeze, a woman and a child in a single bed…

Terrified, I clamped down on those emotions, shoving them back, trying to bury them in the darkness once more. I didn't *want* to remember. I knew, with a grim certainty, that if I did remember, something inside me would unravel, and I didn't want to face the fallout of whatever came to light.

The little girl sniffled. "I had a nightmare," she murmured. "I dreamed there were rabids climbing in the window. I was scared and came to find you, but you didn't wake up."

"Come here, sweetheart," the woman said, struggling to sit up. Her arms trembled as she pushed herself into a sitting position, leaning back against the headboard. But she didn't seem to notice or care about her sudden weakness as she patted the sheets beside her. "Come up with me. Do you want me to tell you a story?"

My stomach churned, that cold fist crushing my dead heart.

Do you want me to read you a story, Allison?

I took one staggering step back from the door. The woman and child vanished from sight, but that didn't stop the realization. I recognized them now. I knew why this felt so familiar.

It was me. This scene, the child in the room with the bed and ratty curtains…was me. Not the same place, obviously, and not the same circumstances, but I could still see myself in the girl: a skinny waif of only ten, climbing into bed with my mother. Listening to her soft voice as she read me a story I'd heard dozens of times before.

The ache of longing spread, growing more painful, and I bit my lip to keep the sudden jealousy in check. Clenching a fist, I listened as the girl clambered onto the bed beside her mom and curled up with her beneath the covers. I remembered doing that, once. Feeling peaceful and content and not scared anymore, because my mom was right there, holding me. Outside our hovel, vampires stalked the night, and humans preyed on each other when they could, but when I was with her, I knew I was safe.

Even though it was all a lie. When you lived in a vampire city, you were never safe. Even though my mother had followed the rules and was Registered, even though she had faithfully given blood every time it was required, they still came for her when she was too weak to get out of bed. They'd taken her blood, not caring that she was sick, not caring that a terrified ten-year-old watched from the corner, silently judging. Hating. Not caring that, after they left, the girl would see her mother waste away to nothing, that she would be out on the streets alone. And that hatred, planted inside her when the vampires' Pets forced their way into her home, would grow into a searing, burning determination that would keep her alive when most others would've died. She would never submit to the vampires. She would never give them her blood. And she would hate them for the rest of her life. Because she had watched the most important thing in her life wither away and die…to feed *them*.

Just like this girl.

Oh, God. I staggered farther away from the door, brushing aside the handful of coats and dresses in the closet with me, and collapsed against the wall. Shock and horror rose up, breaking through the numbing cold, shattering the emptiness at last. *I'm… I'm doing the exact same thing. That kid in there could be me. And I…*

I had become that monster. The thing that I hated most in the world. The demon that preyed on humans and cared nothing for what it left behind—a broken family, a distraught parent…or a little girl who had only grief and hate to sustain her.

Sickened, I slid down the wall until I was sitting in the

corner, while the murmuring voices of the woman and girl came to me through the closet door. *What's happened to me?* I thought in numb despair. *What the hell am I doing?*

The monster snarled, angry and dismayed, reminding me that I was a vampire. It was my nature to hunt and kill and destroy. Human emotions meant nothing to me. Mortals were food, prey, nothing else. I felt its cold apathy to the scene outside, the welcome, icy indifference, and for just a moment, I teetered on the brink of falling into it again. Letting the monster shield me from pain, grief and the horrible, crushing guilt just beginning to emerge from the darkness. It was safer in the dark, the demon whispered, soothing and enticing. I wouldn't feel anything, remember anything. I wouldn't have to face the reason I'd sacrificed my humanity. Why I had let the monster win.

Why...

My hand rose to my neck, finding the thin silver chain that rested there, tracing the image of the tiny metal cross beneath my shirt. And just like that, all memories of *him* came rushing back.

Oh, Zeke.

My eyes stung, turning my vision red and blurry. The knot in my chest unraveled, the barrier holding those emotions back fraying to shadows, releasing everything in a flood. And in that tiny closet, with the humans I'd nearly slaughtered murmuring just outside the door, I put my head to my knees and shook with silent sobs. For the horror of what I was, what I had almost let myself become. For the shame of my lost humanity, even if it was for just a moment.

And for Zeke. I cried for the boy I had lost, the human who'd believed I was more than a monster, even if I couldn't believe it myself. I'd never said a proper goodbye to him, had never let myself grieve his death before tonight. Vengeance had been the only thing on my mind, my utter hate for Sarren driving me forward. It hurt now, to realize Ezekiel Crosse was truly gone, and I would never see him again. In this world, or the next. Because Zeke's soul had surely gone to its final resting place, far from the misery of this godforsaken hell, a place where demons and monsters and soulless creatures of the night could never follow. He was safe now, truly safe. He was with his father and all the people he had lost on the way to Eden, and they would never have to fear anything, ever again.

Gradually, the bloody tears slowed and finally stopped, leaving me empty and drained in that tiny corner. My face felt sticky, my throat ached, and my chest felt painfully tight. But, for the first time since I'd left New Covington, I could face the horror of what had happened in that lab without falling apart. I could finally remember. Sarren torturing Zeke for information about Eden and the cure, Zeke's anguished screams and cries, that shining, terrible moment when he'd whispered... that he loved me. Right before Sarren had killed him.

I wondered if he could see me now, if he was horrified and disappointed at the thing I'd become. Or had he forgotten me? Maybe he didn't even remember his mortal life. Maybe all the pain, grief and darkness he'd endured was nothing but a fading dream where he was now. I hoped so. I wanted him to forget. It was better that way, that he forget this world with its demons and monsters and darkness that smothered any tiny bit of hope or warmth. I would still have to endure, for eternity.

Bitterness joined the swirl of sorrow and regret. Kanin and Jackal had been right; I'd been hiding from this, letting the monster shield me from the pain, because I didn't want to face the truth. Zeke was dead. I had to let him go.

Wiping my eyes, I rose to my feet, grief, shame and a hundred other emotions weighing me down. I welcomed them this time. Even if it was painful. Even if remembering made me feel like I'd never smile again. It meant that some tiny part of me was still human. I'd been so close to the edge tonight, on that brink of no return, as Kanin had warned. What would've happened if the monster had truly won?

Pulling out the chain, I closed my fingers around Zeke's cross, closing my eyes. The edges pressed into my palm as I remembered, forcing myself to recall what he'd told me once. *"You're not evil,"* he had whispered, those bright, solemn blue eyes staring into me, peeling away every defense. *"No one who fights so hard to do the right thing is evil."*

I had to believe that. I had to believe that *something* in me was still human, that I wasn't a complete monster.

Keep me human, Zeke, I thought, feeling a sharp flare of determination through the suffocating regret and guilt. My eyes burned once more, but I bit my lip and forced the tears back. *I swear, I'll keep fighting. I won't forget again.*

When I peeked through the closet door, the woman and little girl had fallen asleep, the mother curled protectively around her child. Easing into the room, I watched them silently, feeling that sharp ache of longing as I remembered my mother doing the same. The little girl sniffed and burrowed closer, her young face blissfully calm, free of worry or fear, and I smiled sadly.

Then I turned and glided silently from the room, into the hall, and down the steps to the first floor.

That dark figure waited for me in front of the window, silhouetted against the glass. As usual, Kanin gave no hints as to what he was feeling, what he thought I'd been doing, whether he was annoyed that I'd taken so long. His eyes were blank as I approached, and I couldn't meet his gaze, staring at the floor when we stood but a few feet apart.

"Is it done?" His voice was barely a murmur in the looming silence. I couldn't be sure, but I thought I heard the barest hint of hope, a last stubborn plea, beneath the quiet surface. Praying that he was wrong. "Did you kill her?"

I shook my head. "No," I whispered, and finally looked up at him. "I didn't. I…" A face swam through my head, blue eyes shining as he smiled at me, and I swallowed hard. "I couldn't."

Kanin didn't respond, but I could feel the tension leave him as I said this. But he only nodded. "Then let's go," he murmured, turning to the windowsill. "Jackal is waiting for us at the fence line. By now, Sarren has pulled even farther away. We need to find his trail again and head for Eden."

Numbly, I followed my sire out the window to the edge of the house, where the Master vampire pulled bars into place once more. After leaping the trench, I looked around and noticed that a new, very large pile of wood had been stacked next to the chopping stump, and I smiled to myself. Kanin's "payment" for tonight, *for the harm his actions would bring,* in his own words. I thought of the woman I'd fed from, pale and weak because of me, and swallowed hard. Maybe I should do something, too, leave something behind that would help.

"I've already taken care of it, Allison," Kanin said behind me, as if reading my thoughts. "Though firewood and a day's supply of meat is hardly compensation for the loss of a family member. I am glad it did not come to that."

"Yeah," I whispered, feeling a burning shame spread through me again. I felt his eyes on me and wondered, briefly, if I would ever earn Kanin's trust again, if he would ever see me the way he did before.

"I'm sorry, Kanin," I said quietly, not looking at him. I didn't have to say more; he knew what I meant. *For everything. For being a monster. For letting myself become a monster. For disappointing you and letting you think you failed. I know you, of all people, never wanted to see me like this. Like Jackal.*

Kanin watched me in silence. Just long enough for me to

wonder if it was too late, if he had given up both his offspring for lost. Then I felt his presence behind me, his strong hands coming to rest on my shoulders.

"We all have regrets, Allison," he said, his voice unbearably gentle. "We all have succumbed to the darkness and the monster. There is not one vampire in the world who has not. Even James has points in his past he would change, if he could. The important thing is that you do not let these points define you. James gave up fighting it long ago. For you and I, it is a constant uphill battle not to give in, not to become that demon, and it will be that way for eternity. I will not lie and tell you it gets any easier.

"But," he continued in that same quiet voice, "you have achieved something few vampires ever could—you have chosen to master your demon, to remember your life before you became immortal. Even though it is hard. Even though the Hunger will always tell you that it is easier to give in, to not remember anything human. It is the reason I told you, from the very beginning, that you would always be a monster." His voice, already low, went even softer. "I'd hoped that, when I Turned you, you would choose a more noble path than James, that you were tenacious enough to retain some semblance of humanity. I hoped that, if I taught you well enough, your will to live would help you in the fight to contain the beast." A ghost of a smile entered his voice then, and he dropped his arms. "As it turns out, I greatly underestimated that stubbornness."

"Yeah, well…" The barest hint of a smile tugged at one corner of my lips, even through the crushing guilt. "I had a pretty good teacher."

Kanin's voice returned to normal. "Regardless of the circumstances, you walked to the very edge tonight, looked into the darkness, and turned away. You did not take that final step to become a true monster. That's not to say that it won't happen again, sometime in the future. It will. You will always be fighting it, because we are never far from that edge, and it is a very thin line between human and demon. One day you might eventually go over, but until then, be very certain. Is this truly the path you want?"

"Yes," I said immediately. "It is."

This time, there was no doubt. No hesitation. Even if it hurt. Even though remembering Zeke ripped my heart into a million tiny pieces, I would not let this thing win. And if that meant fighting the monster until the end of time, that's what I was going to do.

I felt a brief, light touch on my shoulder before Kanin stepped away. "I expected nothing less," he said, nearly inaudible. "And, knowing you, perhaps you will be the very first to pull it off.

"Come," he continued, walking away from the house and its residents, all still alive and unaware of how narrowly they'd avoided death this evening. "It will take us the rest of the night to return to our original trail. And Sarren has extended his lead even farther now. If we are going to have any hope of stopping him, we need to pick up the pace."

I nodded and hurried after him, and together we walked across the snowy yard, toward the field and the tangled woods beyond. Back toward the road, and the trail that would take us to Eden.

CHAPTER 4

✦

"I can't believe you've gone all bleeding heart on me again."

"Shut up, Jackal."

We were back on the road again, and the forest had finally thinned out. Though it still wrapped its barren claws around everything it could touch, we were seeing more houses and buildings huddled in the snow through the trees, stubbornly clinging to existence. Rusty hulks of cars were sprinkled about the road, though usually on the other side, heading away from us. In my experience, that meant we were nearing a city, but all the nights had sort of blended together, and I had no idea how close to Eden we were. If we were close at all.

"So, all those fun plans we made—finding the cure, undead army, our own vampire city—all that's gone right out the window, hasn't it?"

"Yes. I told you before, I don't want any of those things."

"Typical." He snorted. "Silly me, thinking you actually had potential. I thought, *Finally, she's realized she's a* vampire. *Now we're getting somewhere.* But now you're just a big fluffy bunny with sharp teeth."

"Shut *up,* Jackal!"

"If you two do not stop," Kanin said without turning

around, "I am going to find another road to Eden without you. James, it has been two days. Let it go."

"Whatever you say, old man," Jackal said, holding his hands up. "Though I don't know why you're complaining. You got your little spawn back. You must be so proud."

"What's the matter, James?" I couldn't keep the grin from my face as he turned on me. "Don't tell me you're jealous."

He snorted. "Of *you?* Don't make me laugh, sister. If I feel anything right now, it's pity. I...wait a second." He stopped in the middle of the road, gazing around, making Kanin and me stop, too. His gold eyes swept over an ancient road sign, most of it eaten by rust, the words unreadable. "I recognize this town," he muttered, as Kanin and I watched cautiously. "I know where we are. These are the outskirts of Old Chicago."

I stared at him. "Are you sure?"

"Yeah, sister. I think I know my own territory." Jackal grinned, eyes shining eagerly as he gazed down the road. "No question. Follow this road for another two days, and you'll hit Chicago, right in the heart of Raidertown."

"How nice for you," I said, though the thought of being close to another vampire's territory, especially *this* vampire's territory, made me nervous. "You can finally go home. I'm sure your murderous raider friends will be thrilled to see you again."

"Oh, I'm sure they couldn't care less," Jackal returned, waving an airy hand. At my surprised look, he chuckled. "Please, sister. I might be an egotistical bastard, but I'm not blind. The minions follow me because I promise them power, freedom and all the carnage they can stomach. And because I'll tear the head off anyone who challenges me. If I never come back, it's no loss to them. They'll do what they've always done. So, yeah..." He shrugged. "I don't have any illusions of them showering me with flowers and puppies when

I return. However, it's a good place to grab a snack, a place to sleep that's not completely disgusting, and maybe a couple bikes for the road. We can shave a lot of time off getting to Eden if we're not on foot."

He had a point. Chasing Sarren would be easier if we had a working vehicle. And, I wouldn't lie, the thought of riding a motorcycle again was tempting. I'd "borrowed" one from the raiders the last time I was in Old Chicago, and had discovered the thrill of flying down an empty highway at top speed. Nothing compared, really.

Kanin narrowed his eyes, looking troubled. "And what if Sarren has gotten there before us?" he asked.

Jackal snorted. "Then he's either crazier than I thought or completely suicidal. Even Sarren can't take out a whole city of armed, bloodthirsty minions." He curled a lip in disgust. "And if he *can,* then you'll have to excuse me, because at that point I'm going to say the hell with you both, you can chase after Sarren without me. Though I don't think that's going to be a problem. The minions are stupid and savage, but they have one thing that makes them semi-useful—there's a whole fucking lot of them." He smirked, crossing his arms. "If Sarren wants to take out my city, he's welcome to try. The minions aren't a bunch of cowering little meatsacks, and four hundred raiders with automatic weapons are a match for any bloodsucker, crazy or not. Trespassers always get the same reception—a bunch of lead through the brain."

"And what about me?" I asked, frowning at him. "I'm pretty sure your army hasn't forgotten what happened when I was in Old Chicago. The last time I went through, they were trying to kill me."

"Give them some credit, sister." Jackal gave me an exasperated eye roll. "You *had* just burned down my theater and killed a whole lot of them on your way out. Which, frankly, I'm still a little annoyed about. I happened to like that theater.

"But don't worry," he went on, confident and unconcerned. "You're with me, and the only way the minions will shoot at you is if I give the order. They're a stupid lot, but they know their place on the food chain."

"Just don't get any ideas," I growled at him. "Actually, I don't know if I like the idea of going into your city of blood-thirsty killers. You've stabbed us in the back before—what's to stop you from doing it again?"

"You're never going to let me live that down, are you?" Jackal gave me an annoyed look. "Even though it probably saved your soft little hide from being carved into a pentagram by Sarren. Everyone seems to forget that part. Would it kill you to have a little faith in your older brother?"

"It might."

"Well, you'll just have to take your chances now, won't you?"

I scowled and glanced at Kanin, who stood a few feet away, watching his offspring argue with a stoic expression. "Kanin? What do you think?"

The Master vampire sighed. "If we are already headed in that direction," he said, "I see no reason why we shouldn't go through Old Chicago. If we can procure a vehicle and reach Eden in a shorter amount of time, it will be worth the detour. But..." And his brow furrowed slightly as he looked at Jackal. "I fear what we might find when we reach the city," he mused, ignoring the other's disdainful look. "Let us hope Sarren has left your humans undisturbed."

We started off again, and now that I knew where we were, where we were headed, certain landmarks began taking on a familiar feel. I thought I recognized a bend in the road, a rusty car half buried in weeds and snow on the side of the pavement. I wondered if I hadn't passed them on my way to Old Chicago the first time I'd come through. Though it had been only a few months before, it felt like a lifetime ago.

We came to another town, empty and deserted like all the ones before it. But as we walked down cracked, snow-covered roads, passing ancient structures falling apart and smothered by weeds, something felt strange. The sense of déjà vu was growing stronger, to the point where I finally stopped in the middle of the road, gazing around and racking my brain for the reason this seemed so familiar.

"Allison." Kanin turned, dark eyes searching as I stood there, frowning. "What are you doing?"

I know this place. The feeling was stronger than ever, beckoning me down a certain street, and my curiosity was too insistent to ignore. I had to know. Without answering, I headed off the main road and began walking deeper into town. The other two vampires hesitated a moment, then followed.

"Uh, sister? In case you didn't know, Chicago is *that* way."

Still ignoring them, I continued down the sidewalk, past crumbling buildings and the hulks of dead cars. Everything looked different now, because of the snow, but I felt like I'd been here before.

Then I walked around the collapsed wall of an old gas station…and froze.

I had definitely been here before.

Across the street, a building sat on an empty corner, desolate and still in the falling snow. It had been burned, and charred, blackened beams stood out harshly against the snowy backdrop. The roof was gone, but I remembered the wooden cross that once stood atop it, and the flames that had engulfed it on that last night. The night Jackal's men had attacked Jebbadiah Crosse and his followers, kidnapping everyone but Zeke to bring them to Old Chicago.

Silently, I crossed the road, stepped over the curb, and walked onto the tiny strip of land beside the church. Crosses and headstones poked out of the snow as I gazed around, my eyes falling on the very place I'd seen Zeke and Jeb Crosse together for the last time.

I heard Jackal and Kanin cross the road as well, but both vampires halted at the edge of the sidewalk, disdaining to step onto the cemetery grounds. "A church," Jackal said in obvious distaste. "Of course it would be a church. Why am I even surprised? You *really* don't get this whole demon thing, do you, sister?"

I gave him a strange look. In New Covington, all churches had been razed and burned by the vampire lords long before I was born. There were stories and speculation as to why, of course, but some of the more colorful rumors said that vampires couldn't cross the threshold of a church, couldn't set foot on holy ground, and burned up if they tried.

Obviously, they were wrong. I was standing right here, in the shadow of a church, and I was fine. But Kanin and Jackal still looked reluctant to approach, and I grinned at my brother over the strip of earth separating us.

"What's the matter, Jackal? Afraid you're going to burst into flames if you set foot on the grounds?"

His sneer had an edge to it. "Isn't that cute? A brand-new demon spawn, all puffed up and smug, thinking she's invincible. Let me make one thing clear, sister," he went on, still keeping well back from the edge of the lot. "I'm not afraid of the Big Guy, never have been, never will be. But, unlike some newbie vamps that won't be named, I have never been confused as to what I am. Even if God is dead, even if He's not here anymore—hell, even if He's nothing but a boogeyman made up by pathetic humans desperate for some sort of hope—I, at least, am still a demon. I've never pretended anything different. And God, if He is real, still hates us."

Jackal crossed his arms, smirking at me. "So, go ahead, my dear little sister. Stomp on His territory a while longer. Maybe He's dead after all. But if a lightning bolt strikes you dead in the next thirty seconds, I'll save us some time and say 'see you in hell' right now."

My stomach twisted. I remembered something Jebbadiah Crosse had asked me, long ago, when I hadn't been a vampire for long and had first stumbled upon his group.

"Do you believe in God, Allison?"

"No," I said immediately. "Is this the part where you tell me I'm going to hell now?"

"This is hell," Jebbadiah said. "This is our punishment, our Tribulation. God has abandoned this world. The faithful have already gone on to their reward, and He has left the rest of us here, at the mercy of the demons and the devils. The sins of our fathers have passed on to their children, and their children's children, and it will continue to be so until this world is completely destroyed. So it doesn't matter if you believe in God or not, because He is not here."

I'd been skeptical before. I didn't know what I believed now.

"Allison." Kanin's soft, cool voice came to me over the silent graveyard. I looked up, expecting him to call me back, to tell me we were wasting time, that we had to keep moving. His eyes were dark and hooded, his expression blank, as he gazed at me from the edge of the lot. "Do you know this place?"

I nodded. "I've been here before," I told him, stepping around a headstone, brushing the cold rock with my fingers. The same tombstone Zeke had braced himself against when Jeb had whipped him for a crime I couldn't remember now. "We—Zeke's group—passed through this town on their way to Eden," I continued, looking at the burned, blackened church. "They stopped here to rest, but they were attacked the next night." I turned my head and shot a glare at Jackal, angry again. "By Jackal's thugs."

"Huh." Jackal gazed around with interest now, unconcerned with the icy glare I was giving him. "So this is the spot where they nabbed everyone, is it? Small world."

"They killed a woman, you know," I spat at him. "Shot her in cold blood, and she couldn't even defend herself. Oh, forget it." Shaking my head, I curled my lip into a sneer. "Why am I telling you any of this—you certainly don't care."

"At last," Jackal returned, smiling. "It starts to sink in. I was afraid I'd have to listen to another sermon."

I wanted to snap at him, but it was useless. Instead, I turned and brushed snow off the cold tombstone as memories rose up to swirl around me. I recalled what had happened in this cemetery—seeing Zeke and Jeb from the cover of darkness. Watching as Jeb used a car antenna to whip his adopted son for an earlier sin. Watching Zeke with his head bowed, saying nothing. And what had happened after—the sudden attack, finding Zeke and traveling with him to Old Chicago to rescue the others—it all came back, reminding me yet again of what I had lost. That frozen piece of time in utter darkness, when Zeke had finally leaned in and kissed me, was forever etched into my memory and would never fade. I could see him now, standing beside me, as clearly as that memory would allow, his bright blue eyes shining with hope and determination. And I knew why I'd wanted to come here, to this spot, one more time.

Reaching back, I unhooked the chain from around my neck, drawing it and the tiny silver cross over my head. Refastening the clasp, I set it and the cross gently down on the gravestone, my fingers lingering on the metal winking against the rock.

Goodbye, Zeke.

Then I turned and crossed the grounds to where the two vampires waited on the sidewalk. Jackal shook his head as I joined them, but Kanin's dark eyes remained on me, sympathetic and appraising.

"Are you finished?" he asked gently, and I nodded.

"Yeah," I whispered, with one last glance at the church and the phantom memories that still lingered. The glint of silver, tiny and bright, caught my eye in the darkness, and I turned away. "Let's go. I'm done here."

We headed back toward the main road. No one, not even Jackal, said anything, leaving me to my thoughts and the persistent, swirling memories that refused to leave me alone. Several times, I almost turned around and went back; that cross was my last connection to Zeke, the only part of him I still had. But in the end, I left it on the grave in the middle of a lonely cemetery. I couldn't dwell in the past. Zeke was gone. I had to move forward.

As we stepped between two dead vehicles and the road stretched away once more, the sudden growl of an engine cut through the silence. I jerked up, caught a glimpse of flying snow and red taillights as two motorcycles flashed between cars and vanished. The tracks from the tires shot away through the snow and followed the motorcycles into the dark, down the highway, and out of sight. The whine of their bike engines echoed over the buildings, ebbing away into the night.

I whirled on Jackal. "Those were raiders!" I exclaimed, almost an accusation. He raised a patronizing eyebrow, and I narrowed my gaze. "Why are they here? What do they want?"

The raider king gave me a serene smirk. "What makes you think they were mine, sister?"

"Uh, because we're a couple days from Old Chicago? Because this is the same town where they attacked us last time?"

He continued to smirk at me, and I scowled. "Don't play innocent—those were your bikers. What did they want?"

"Haven't a clue," Jackal said breezily. "They didn't exactly stick around for tea and gossip, did they?"

I bared my fangs at his obnoxiousness. "Aren't you their king? Wouldn't they at least try to talk to you if they knew you were here?"

Jackal snorted. "Sister, please. The minions aren't stupid. If you were a bloodbag and you saw three vampires walking up the road toward your house, what would you do? Stay and have a nice little chat? Or run like hell?" He shook his head. "The minions, if they *were* mine, did exactly what they always do—saved their own worthless hides. As well they should. I don't want them getting comfortable with vampires. I worked very hard to make sure they're all scared shitless of me, and I'll thank you not to screw that up. My raiders, especially, know better than to hang around, waiting to be eaten. I'm their king, not their pal. So, yes, we saw two bikers, and they peed themselves and ran away. What's the problem here?"

"Just that… I mean…" I trailed off, frustrated that I knew something was wrong, and I couldn't put it into words. Kanin, however, spoke up from behind me.

"And is it usual that two of your humans would stake out a town for the sole purpose of watching for vampires?" he asked. "And that they chose *this* town, which they knew we would have to pass on the way to Old Chicago?"

Jackal shrugged. "Maybe. Who gives a damn, anyway? Don't glare at me, old man," he added, facing Kanin down. "I'm not a mind reader. I can't tell what the minions are thinking every second of every day. It's just a couple bloodbags. What do you think they're going to do?"

"I don't know," Kanin admitted, his dark gaze moving to the road ahead. "But I think we should proceed with caution."

★ ★ ★

Nothing unusual happened that night. We met no more raiders on the road, heard no motorcycles tearing away from us at top speed, encountered no human life at all. The path to Old Chicago was as it had always been: silent, cold and dark, twisting through woods and deserted towns, past the skeletons of houses and the ancient remains of cars buried in the snow. Near dawn, we split up to bury ourselves in the frozen earth, as Kanin was suddenly wary of being aboveground and exposed. I slept in my dark grave, silent, dreamless and undisturbed, and rose the next night to a still, icy world. It had stopped snowing, but sometime during the day the snow had turned to sleet, and everything was outlined in a thin layer of ice. I shook snow from my hair and clothes and paused a moment to concentrate on Kanin and Jackal, searching for them through our blood tie.

They weren't far. I backtracked through the trees until I found the road again and saw Jackal leaning against a dead tree at the edge of the pavement. He raised an eyebrow as I came up, but didn't move.

"Where's Kanin?" I asked, gazing around for the Master vampire. Our blood tie allowed me to sense my sire's general direction, and even that he wasn't very far, but it didn't let me know what he was doing. Jackal shrugged.

"You know as much as I do, sister. The old bastard is off that way—" he nodded over a rise on the other side of the road "—but of course he hasn't told me what he's doing. For all I know, he could be chasing squirrels to make a necklace from their little squirrel balls." He looked content not to move from his position as I glared at him. "If you're so curious, why don't you go ask him?"

"Yeah. I'll do that."

Following our blood tie, I trekked over the rise and through the snow, weaving through trees and around a rotting cabin, until I found him. He stood with his back to me at the edge of the road where it curved around a bend, his tall, imposing form a featureless silhouette against the snow.

"Kanin." I walked to his side, not expecting him to acknowledge me but knowing he knew I was there. As predicted, he didn't turn, but continued to gaze down the road, his face unreadable. I peered into the darkness, saw nothing unusual, and glanced back. "What are you looking for?"

"I don't know." Kanin sounded suspicious, and I caught the barest note of frustration beneath his cool tone, a hint I would have never caught a month ago. The Master vampire stared down the winding pavement, and his eyes narrowed. "I feel we are being watched."

I frowned. The road and the forest surrounding it were empty. Nothing moved or made a sound in the shadows; no tracks lay in the snow except our own. "Rabids?" I asked.

"No." Kanin shook his head. "Rabids would not simply watch from the woods. They would have attacked us by now."

"Raiders, then?"

"Perhaps. Though I am uncertain as to why they would be stalking us. And I cannot sense, or smell, any humans nearby."

I gave him a faint smile. "Is it possible you're just being paranoid after last night?"

He finally looked at me, a hint of amusement crossing his face. "One does not live to be several centuries old without a little paranoia," he said, the corner of his mouth curving just slightly. "But perhaps you are right. In any case, there is little we can do about it now. Let's keep moving. Once we reach Old Chicago, I am sure we will find answers."

Several hours later, the road widened and became a highway, and the buildings around us grew larger and more numerous as we approached the outskirts of the city. According to Jackal, we were still a day out from Old Chicago, though we'd left the wilderness behind and had entered the surrounding suburban districts. The tangle of trees and undergrowth now wrapped themselves around houses, stores and road signs, and the once-empty highway slowly grew choked with cars. One side of it, anyway. The other side, the side leading toward Old Chicago, was completely barren. I'd seen this before: the endless stream of dead, crumpled vehicles, thousands of people trying to flee the cities all at once. I stared at the cars we passed, repressing a shiver. It must've been chaos, back then. Vehicles lay smashed against each other, sometimes flipped to the side or all the way onto the roof. A skeleton lay half in, half out of a broken windshield, splayed across the hood in the snow. The blackened hulk of a van lay overturned in a ditch, one small bony arm reaching through the shattered window, as if trying to claw itself free.

Kanin and Jackal continued on, barely glancing at the silent vehicles and their grisly contents. I guessed that Kanin had been alive for so long, nothing surprised or disturbed him anymore. And Jackal certainly wouldn't care about a bunch of dead meatsacks, as he would so elegantly put it. I wondered if that would ever happen to me, if I would eventually live so long, the sight of mass death and destruction wouldn't faze me at all.

Ahead of us, the mouth of a tunnel loomed over the river of cars, a yawning black hole set into a rise. The tunnel was pitch-black, and though my vampire sight allowed me to see in utter darkness, I couldn't glimpse the end of it.

However, something was coming out of that dark hole that made me stop in my tracks. Silent and unseen, but unmistakable. It roused my demon and caused the Hunger to stir restlessly, spreading a low ache across my insides.

The scent of blood. A lot of it. Freshly spilled, coming from somewhere within that looming blackness.

I hurried forward, joining Kanin and Jackal at the entrance. Both vampires were gazing into the mouth of the tunnel warily, though the smell was probably making them just as Hungry as I was.

"Huh," Jackal remarked, arms crossed as he stared into the darkness. "That's interesting. Last I checked, there wasn't anyone living on this stretch of road. The minions killed off anyone in a twenty-mile radius of Chicago."

I gazed into the tunnel, trying to ignore the familiar ache spreading through my insides. "Do you think someone is in there?"

"If they are, their guts are all over the pavement, judging from the smell." Jackal sniffed, curling a lip in distaste. "Nothing is going to be alive in there, sister. I wouldn't get your hopes up."

A scream rang out, somewhere in the darkness, and I snarled in return. "Someone's in trouble," I hissed at the other vampires, and drew my katana. "Screw it! I'm going in."

Without waiting for a reply, I sprinted into the passageway.

The road through the tunnel was even more clogged with vehicles than the outside. Cars lay on both sides of the road, some knocked sideways or smashed into walls in their desire to escape. I wove through a maze of vehicles, sometimes having to scramble over hoods or roofs in order to navigate. Once, I had to duck beneath an enormous rectangular truck—a semi, I remembered they were called—sitting at an angle and blocking both lanes. I heard Jackal and Kanin behind me, and Jackal's comment that I was a pain in the ass reached me over the labyrinth of cars, but I concentrated on moving forward. In this dark, confined space, the scent of blood was overpowering, clinging to everything and making it impossible to sense anything else. The Hunger was raging inside, but I kept a tight hold on it, determined to stay in control. When I found the owner of that scream, I was *not* going to pounce and ravage them like a wild animal.

Though it wouldn't have mattered, anyway.

As I reached the spot where the blood scent was strongest, the maze of cars suddenly thinned. I stood in a small open space, several cars forming a circle around me, as if they had been deliberately moved or pushed aside. It was definitely the source of the smell. Fresh pools of blood stained the pavement, still wet and glimmering, in the middle of the circle. But there was no one here, no bodies or other signs of a scuffle, though I was sure this was the place I'd heard the scream.

That's weird, I thought, walking up to observe the pools of blood, keeping my Hunger firmly in check. I would not, I told it, lap up the puddles from the ground like some damn stray dog. *Fresh blood with no bodies. Where...*

Something warm dripped onto my face from above. Briefly, I closed my eyes, bracing myself, then looked up.

There were three of them. Two men and a woman, hanging from the ceiling of the tunnel with their hands tied behind them, the ropes around their necks creaking as they dangled in lazy circles. They had been split open, gutted from chin to groin, intestines spilling from their stomachs like pink snakes. Blood soaked the entire front of their bodies, wet and black, filling the air with the smell of death.

I backed away, nearly running into Jackal as he and Kanin emerged from the maze of cars, both gazing up at the bodies. "Oh, for fuck's sake," Jackal remarked, shaking his head at the corpses. "You'd think stringing bodies up would get old after a while. I think the old nutbag is losing his creative touch."

"This wasn't Sarren," Kanin muttered, as I looked to him for answers. "This was done recently. Tonight. Someone

wanted us to see this—they knew we would be here…." He
cast a grim look around the enclosed space. "We have to leave
now."

A clang, hollow and metallic, echoed through the tunnel
ahead. What immediately followed raised the hair on my neck.
Shrieks and wails rose into the air, the sound of claws scraping
over metal and pavement, and the stench of carrion, death and
wrongness filtered through the overpowering smell of blood.

"Rabids!" I snarled, surging back toward Kanin and Jackal.
A *lot* of them. I could see their pale, skeletal forms leaping over
cars, skittering over roofs or under tires, hissing and screaming. They were frenzied, crazy from the scent of blood, and
coming right at us.

"Fall back!" Kanin ordered, drawing away from the open
circle. "They'll stop when they reach the bodies, and we can
find a way around."

But a sudden screeching and wailing from the other direction made us freeze. More rabids, foaming and wild-eyed,
rushed toward us over the maze of cars. We were trapped in
the middle.

With a snarl, Jackal brandished his fire ax, and I swung
my katana as the horde came on, their screams reverberating
through the tunnel in a deafening cacophony. No going off
on my own this time; I stood back-to-back with Kanin and
Jackal, facing the monsters as they clambered over cars and
swarmed toward us. I lashed out at the first rabid, cutting clean
through its body, splitting it in two, then whipped my sword
down to behead the next that sprang forward. Then it was
just chaos: shrieking rabids, slashing claws and fangs, an endless wave of pale bodies flinging themselves at me. I moved
on instinct, spinning from one attack to the next, the blade
dancing in my hands.

A roar behind me made me turn. Jackal stood in the center

of a writhing heap of rabids, several spindly monsters clinging to his back, biting and clawing. He bashed the head of his ax into the ones leaping at him, knocking them away, but more piled on him, and sheer numbers were beginning to drag him down. His face was streaked with blood, and dark crimson stained his collar and the back of his neck.

Snarling, I rushed in from the side, plunged my blade into one of the rabids clawing at his shoulders, and ripped it away. While Jackal continued to fend off the rabids springing at him, I began cutting away the monsters that clung to his back, freeing him from the pile. I couldn't see Kanin, didn't know where he was, but the Master vampire was the strongest and most lethal fighter of us all. He could take care of himself.

As I cut down the last of the rabids clawing at Jackal, something hit me from behind, shrieking in my ear, sinking curved talons into my chest and shoulder. I yelled as the blow drove me to my knees, but a moment later the weight was gone, as Jackal grabbed the rabid by the back of the neck, spun, and smashed its head through a car window. Knocking aside another body that lunged at me, he glanced down with a savage grin and held out a hand.

"Come on, sister. On your feet. We're not done with these bastards yet."

I grabbed his wrist, and he yanked me upright. The rabids were still coming at us, insane with bloodlust, but the swarm was smaller now. From the corner of my eye I caught a glimpse of Kanin, surrounded by pale bodies, smoothly decapitating a rabid that lunged at him, and the monster's body collapsed like its strings had been cut while the head bounced once and rolled under a tire.

Side by side, Jackal and I cut our way through the last of the horde, crushing skulls and slicing necks until the final monster leaped at us and was struck down, meeting Jackal's ax across its face and my sword through its middle. As it dropped, twitching, to the pavement, the echo of its dying shriek faded away, and the tunnel fell silent once more.

"Well. That was entertaining." Jackal lowered his ax with a grimace, hunching his shoulders. The back of his duster was shredded, long gashes left by curved talons, though the scratches across his face were already healing. His eyes gleamed dangerously as he stared around at the carnage. "Anyone else get the feeling we've been set up?"

Kanin strode back to us, his bright, thin blade already vanished from his hand. "Let's keep moving," he ordered, his tone brisk. "We don't want to stay here. Hurry."

We rushed through the maze of cars until we came to the edge of the tunnel, back into the open. Another semi truck blocked most of the entrance, its doors flung back, showing an empty interior. The unmistakable stench of rabids wafted from the opening, and a pair of motorcycle tracks sped away down the road and vanished into the night.

"Well, well," Jackal mused, glancing from the truck to the empty road before us. "Isn't that amusing? Looks like we were set up, after all. Oh, someone is going to die. Very painfully, I think." He met Kanin's dark stare and narrowed his eyes. "Old man, if you say anything along the lines of 'I told you so,' you both can figure out how to get into Chicago without me."

Kanin didn't reply, but I stared at the tracks until they vanished around a bend, and frowned at Jackal. "Why are your people attacking us?" I growled, glaring at him. "I thought you had a handle on them." He scowled back.

"If I knew the reason, sister, I wouldn't be here." His eyes glinted. "But you can be sure I *will* get to the bottom of this. And when I do, the backstabbing little shits are going to wish they were never born." Glancing at me and Kanin, he curled a lip. "You two can go around, if you want. Keep chasing the psychopath. I'm going back to my city, and I'm going to bash in some heads until they remember who their king is."

"No," I shot back. "There's no time to go around." I looked at Kanin, silently watching us both, and hardened my voice. "We have to catch up to Sarren, and we can't do that if we keep taking detours. Old Chicago is the only place we have a chance of catching up. We'll grab a couple bikes while Jackal is bashing in heads and keep going to Eden. But we can't turn back now."

"I am not disagreeing with you, Allison," Kanin said. His gaze drifted to the road behind us, at the tracks fading in the snow, and his expression turned dark. "If the straightest way to Eden is through Old Chicago, we will continue in that direction. But I would advise extreme caution now, as it seems there are humans who wish us harm."

"Oh, don't worry, old man," Jackal growled, a dangerous promise in his voice. "There won't be for much longer."

CHAPTER 5

We reached the outskirts of the city later that night.

I'd forgotten how huge Chicago was; even the urban sprawl leading up to the main city seemed to go on forever. Miles and miles of empty, silent streets and decaying houses, vehicles rotting along the shoulder, streetlamps and signs lying in the road. The last time I'd come through here, I'd been riding a stolen motorcycle and hadn't paid much attention to my surroundings as they flew by. My focus had been on steering the bike and avoiding obstacles…and on the person sitting behind me, his arms around my waist.

I shot a glance at Jackal walking beside me, his expression dangerous. And for a brief, irrational moment, resentment flickered. He probably wasn't thinking of what had happened the night I'd come through his territory, and if he was, he didn't care. But I remembered. Darren's screams when Jackal had thrown him into a cage with a rabid and let it rip him apart, just to set an example. Fighting an army of raiders to rescue the rest of Zeke's group, and setting a building on fire to escape. And, of course, the fight atop Jackal's tower, where I'd faced my blood brother for the first time, and he'd nearly killed me.

Jackal caught me looking at him and raised an eyebrow. "What's that look for?" he challenged.

I faced the road again. "Nothing."

"Bullshit." Jackal's gaze lingered on me. "You're thinking about Old Chicago and the last time you came through. You're remembering all those fun little moments when I killed your humans, tortured them, threw them into the ring with rabids—all those good times." His gaze narrowed. "Don't try to deny it, sister. It's written all over your face."

I snarled at him, baring fangs, tempted to draw my sword and slash it through his smirking mouth. "Don't you ever shut up?" I spat. "Yes, I'm thinking about Old Chicago, and what a bastard you were when we first met. I'm wondering why the hell I'm even talking to you now and not trying to cut the stupid head from your body. We should've had that rematch a long time ago."

"Aw, sister, I'm hurt," Jackal mocked, putting a hand to his chest. "That's not how I remember it. I remember discovering I had a blood sibling. I remember offering to share everything with her. Because, why not? She was a decent fighter, and I was getting kind of bored talking to brainless minions. Could've been fun. But, no." His voice hardened. "I remember having the cure for Rabidism right at my fingertips, decades of searching, planning, about to pay off. And then, my own sister turned her back on the cure, on ending the virus, in order to save a few pathetic humans."

"You staked me and threw me out a window!"

"You had already made up your mind by then." Jackal glared back, completely serious. "I couldn't talk you out of it—you'd chosen your side, and it was with the bloodbags. So, yes, I tried to kill you. Because you had waltzed into something that had been cumulating for years, without even knowing what you were threatening, and you destroyed it." His eyes narrowed, mouth setting into a grim line. "I would've ended Rabidism, sister. If that old human had discovered the cure, I would've shared it. I want the rabids gone just as much as anyone. But then you came along, and you were so worried about saving a few humans, you couldn't see the bigger picture. If you'd let me finish what I'd started years ago, all of this could've been avoided. Sarren would've never gotten the virus, he wouldn't be on his way to destroy Eden right now, and your sappy little human might still be alive."

I roared and spun on Jackal, swinging my blade at his throat. It met the head of the fire ax as Jackal whipped it up to block, sending a ringing screech into the air as the two weapons collided. Snarling, Jackal swung the ax at my face, the broad, bloody edge barely missing me as I ducked. I slashed up with the katana, aiming for his chest, and he dropped the ax down to meet it. There was another clang as the weapons met, and we glared at each other over the crossed blades.

"Enough!"

And Kanin was there, grabbing me by the collar, pulling us apart. The Master vampire easily held Jackal back with one arm and kept a tight hold of my coat with the other. "That is enough," he ordered in his cold, steely voice. "Stop it, both of you. We don't have time for this."

Jackal shrugged off Kanin's arm and backed away, sneering at me. I growled and bared my fangs, daring him to say something, but he just walked away. I watched him go, fury making me see red. Murdering, insufferable bastard. I'd tear him in half and the world would be a better place for it.

"Allison, stop," Kanin said, putting a hand on my arm. I was shaking with rage, and gripped the sword hilt to force the anger down, back into the darkness that it came from. Kanin waited with me, keeping a light but firm hold on my elbow, until I was in control again.

When the rage had faded somewhat, I sheathed my katana, feeling the weight of Kanin's stare still on me. "I'm fine," I told him, angry with myself now. "Sorry. Jackal was being a bastard, again. I shouldn't have let him get to me."

Kanin released my arm but didn't move. "What did he say?" the Master vampire asked.

"That…it's my fault we're chasing Sarren now. If I hadn't come after the group in Old Chicago, none of this would've happened. Jeb might've discovered a cure. Sarren wouldn't have released the virus. And… Zeke would still be alive."

Kanin was silent a moment. It had begun snowing again, soft flakes drifting from the sky, swirling around us. "Do you believe that?" the vampire finally asked.

"I don't know what to believe anymore, Kanin." I raked hair out of my face, shoving it back, and faced the road again. "It seems like every decision, every choice I make, somehow backfires on me in the end. No matter what I do, things just get worse. Maybe…" I swallowed hard. "Maybe it *is* my fault… that Zeke died. Maybe the whole damn world will go extinct, because of me."

Kanin chuckled, nearly making me fall over in shock. "You are far too young to carry that burden, Allison," he said. "If we are going to be throwing around blame, let us go back even farther, before you were ever born. Let us go back to when the virus and the rabids were first created."

Embarrassed, I ducked my head. "I… I didn't mean it like that."

"I know." The Master vampire sighed. "But, if we are talking about choice and regret, what has happened cannot be undone. And dwelling on the past changes nothing. You will only drive yourself to insanity if you do." He sighed again, sounding like he carried the weight of the world on his shoulders. "Trust me on that."

A shot rang out in the darkness.

I jerked, tensing as the bark of gunfire echoed over the rooftops, sounding fairly close. It faded, but was quickly followed by a roar of fury that was instantly familiar. *Jackal.*

Kanin and I took off running toward the sound, as the scent of blood and smoke drifted to me over the breeze. I pushed my way through a weed-choked space between two buildings and caught sight of my brother in the road ahead. He was sitting against a dead car, his ax lying in the road beside him, one hand pressed to his chest. The pavement beneath him was spattered in red, and Jackal's fangs were out in a grimace of agony.

I darted across the road and dropped beside him, blinking in shock. The scent of blood was everywhere, but I couldn't see a wound until Jackal dropped his hand. A tiny hole had been torn through his duster right below the collarbone, no larger than a dime. It didn't look big enough to account for all the blood...until Jackal slumped forward and I saw the exit wound.

I winced as Kanin joined us, his dark gaze going to the massive hole in Jackal's back, nearly the size of my fist. It was healing, but I knew it had to hurt. Kanin's eyes narrowed, and he peered through the broken glass, scanning the street.

"Where are they?" he muttered as I cautiously poked my head around the hood. A booming retort rang out, and something struck the car a few inches from my face, sparking off the metal. I flinched and ducked behind the barrier again, and Jackal gave a strangled laugh.

"I wouldn't poke my head up if I were you, sister," he said through gritted teeth. "A rifle shot to the forehead might not kill you, but it'll give you one hell of a headache." He grimaced, pushing himself off the car, leaving a dark smear behind him. "I think the bastard is in that house," he told Kanin, nodding to a two-story ruin at the end of the street. "Shoot-

ing at us from the attic window." His eyes gleamed, and he
bared his fangs in an evil grin. "Cocky little shit, isn't he?"

I risked a quick peek through the broken glass of the car
window, and caught the glint of metal from the tiny darkened window at the very top of the house. "Okay," I mused,
ducking back down. "We know where he is. How do we get
past without getting shot full of holes?"

"Get *past* him?" Jackal glanced at me and snorted. "You
think we're going to sneak around our trigger-happy friend
and continue our merry way—that's cute, sister. Me, I'm a little
Hungry right now, and a lot pissed off. I'm planning to shove
that rifle so far down his throat, he'll feel it out the rectum."

"So, we're going to charge the crazy man's house while he
has an open street to fire on us. That sounds like a great plan."

"And what were you planning to do? Offer cookies and
ask the psycho murdering bandit to please stop shooting us?"

Kanin sighed and half rose, taking in the street, the cars
and the house in one practiced glance. "I'll draw his fire,"
the Master vampire said calmly. "You two stay low, and keep
moving. I'll meet you upstairs."

He stepped into the street, and instantly a shot rang out,
shattering the window of a truck behind us. I flinched, but
Kanin kept walking, a black silhouette against the snow and
cars. He moved like a shadow, fading in and out of the darkness, always visible but sometimes no more than a blur. Shots
echoed in the street and sparked off metal and pavement, but
nothing seemed to touch the vampire, who continued down
the street as if out for a stroll.

Jackal swatted my arm. "Quit gaping," he ordered, ignoring
my glare, and jerked his head up the road. "Come on, while
the old man has his attention."

We raced up the street in a half crouch, darting behind
cover when we could. The human, whoever he was, contin-

ued to fire, but not at us, though I had no idea where Kanin was after the first few minutes. Whatever he was doing, however, seemed to work. We reached the doorway of the rotted, half-crumbling building and ducked inside, the reports of the gun now echoing somewhere above us.

Jackal stalked forward with a growl, his eyes glowing a vicious yellow in the darkness, but I paused. Something about this felt wrong, though I couldn't put my finger on what. Cautiously, I followed Jackal through the house, tensing as we passed old rooms full of dust and rubble, overturned chairs and rotting furniture, remnants of the time before. I was wary of ambushes, but the rooms were abandoned, and Jackal moved swiftly up the floors without slowing down.

A peeling, broken staircase led the way to the third floor, and we had just started up it when a shout rang out overhead, followed by a flurry of cursing. A moment later, footsteps clattered across the floor, and a human appeared at the top of the steps, gazing down at us, wide-eyed. He was dressed in dusty leathers, and clutched the long barrel of a rifle in one hand.

At the sight of us, the man let out another curse and quickly turned to flee back up the stairs, but Jackal gave a roar and surged forward, grabbing him by the neck and lifting him off his feet.

"Ah ah ahhhh, where do you think you're going, minion?" Stalking into the attic, the raider king threw the human into a wall with enough force to put a hole in the plaster, and the man slumped to the floor, dazed. Jackal loomed over him, his eyes murderous. "I think you're going to sit right there and tell me what the hell is going on, before I start ripping off important body parts. If you tell me what I want to know, right now, I *might* start with your head, and not your arms."

I caught a glimpse of a dark silhouette in the corner by the window: Kanin, watching impassively from his place against the wall. Briefly, I wondered how the Master vampire had gotten in without being shot…but it was Kanin. There was a whole lot I still didn't know about him.

The man groaned, pawing weakly for the rifle. With a growl, Jackal reached down, grabbed him by the throat, and slammed him into the wall. I forced myself not to interfere. I knew Jackal had to be starving, on the brink of losing it, the blood from the gunshot wound still wet and glimmering against his back. But he smiled evilly at the raider, his voice ominous but under control when he spoke.

"I believe I asked you a question, minion," the raider king said in a conversational tone, though his fangs were bared and fully extended. "And I don't have a lot of patience to spare right now. So, if you don't want me to rip the arms from your sockets, I'd start talking. Why are you attacking us? Who's involved? Is this some offshoot of discontents I'm going to have to wipe out, or does the entire city have a death wish?"

The human gagged, clawing futilely at the hand around his throat. But, shockingly, he looked up at the raider king, his eyes bright with pain and fear, and gave a raspy chuckle. "You're…not in charge…anymore, Jackal," he gritted out, with the defiance of someone who knew he was dead. "You promised immortality…and you never delivered. Well…we have a new king now. One who agreed to Turn…whoever got rid of you."

My insides went cold.

"Is that so?" Jackal continued, his voice gone soft and deadly. "And does this new king have a name, or do I have to guess?"

"He said…you would know who he is," the raider choked out. "And…to come find him…in the flooded city." He coughed and held up his hands. One was empty, but the other held a tiny metal box, which he clicked open to reveal a small flame. Glancing at the raider king, he gave a last defiant sneer. "If you make it that far."

Against the wall, Kanin straightened. "James—" he began, but it was too late. The raider opened his fingers, and the item, whatever it was, dropped to the floor.

A few things happened all at once.

As soon as the flame dropped from the raider's hand, Jackal leaped back, flinging himself toward the wall. Abruptly released, the raider's body hit the ground at about the same time as the metal box. There was a short hiss—

—and a wave of fire erupted from the tiny flame, racing across the floor and up the walls, turning the room into an inferno. It engulfed the human on the floor, who screamed and thrashed, flailing about in agony as his clothes caught fire. I barely heard him. Terror rose up, blinding and all-consuming, and I looked wildly around for an escape route. The walls were a mass of rolling orange flames, snapping and tearing at me; I could feel the awful heat against my cold skin and cringed back with a hiss. I had to get out of here, but there was nowhere to go; wherever I looked, there was fire....

"Allison!"

Something grabbed my arm as I stood there, on the verge of panic. "Calm yourself," Kanin ordered, as I snarled and tried yanking back. "Listen to me. We cannot take the stairs; the lower rooms are completely engulfed, and it will take too long to reach the door. We must go through the window."

The window? I looked to the far wall, at the opening where the human had been shooting. I could barely see the window through the snapping flames, and cringed back. "You've got to be kidding me."

"No." Kanin's voice was ruthlessly calm. "It is the only way. Jackal has already gone through. We must follow him if we are to survive this."

The flames roared at me, filling my mind, until all I could see was orange and red. I couldn't think; I could almost feel the skin peeling from my bones, blackened and bubbling in the heat. If it wasn't for Kanin's grip on my arm, I would've fled, though I didn't know where I would go. All I could think of was getting away from the flames. And Kanin wanted me to leap *through* the fire? "I can't!" I told him, baring my fangs in fear. "I'll never make it."

"You must. I'll be right behind you."

"Kanin…"

"Allison." Kanin grabbed my other arm, forcing me to look at him. His voice compelled. I *felt* it reverberate through me, a quiet, undeniable thrum. "Trust me."

I bit my lip, and squeezed my eyes shut, blocking out the flames. "You can do this," Kanin went on, in that same soothing tone. I focused on his voice, ignoring the roar of the flames around us, the heat burning my face. "The fire won't touch you. It will be over in a few seconds, but you must be quick. Are you ready?"

Swallowing, I clenched my fists, pushed back my fear, and nodded.

"Then go." Kanin released me. I turned and sprinted for the wall of flames.

They loomed before me, horrifically bright, snapping and clawing in the wind. For a second, I almost balked, my vampire instincts screaming at me to stop, to run away from our deadliest enemy besides the sun. Kanin's voice echoed in my head, pushing me forward. I reached the roaring, living wall and dove through the flames, praying I wouldn't catch fire.

There was a moment of blinding pain, a scalding heat ripping across my face and hands. And then cold winter air hit my skin as I tumbled through the window, hit the edge of the roof, and fell into the bushes below.

Snarling, fangs bared, I struggled to my feet and lurched away from the house. Heat clawed at my back as I ripped through vines and branches and fled into the road. Only when I was on the other side of the street did I turn and look back.

My instincts cringed, urging me to move even farther away. The house was a raging inferno against the sky, tongues of fire snapping in every direction. I panicked for a moment, not seeing Kanin anywhere, afraid that he was still trapped upstairs. But then a shadow melted away from the house, and Kanin's dark form glided across the street toward me, making me slump in relief.

"Are you injured?" he asked, joining me on the sidewalk. I shook my head, still trying to calm down. My face and hands stung, and I caught a faint scent of burned hair that I tried to ignore, but I didn't seem to be badly hurt. Another few seconds, and it might've been a different story.

"Where's Jackal?" I asked, looking around. I vaguely remembered Kanin telling me that Jackal had gotten out, but everything from the past few minutes was sort of a blur.

"He leaped out the window the second he realized what was happening," Kanin replied, his voice taking on a slight edge. "I expect he's around here somewhere."

I shook myself. The fire had apparently made my brain stop working; the only thought on my mind had been to get away, but it was slowly starting to focus again. "I don't understand," I said. "What do you mean, when he realized what was happening?"

"This was a trap, Allison." Kanin looked back at the inferno. "Nothing catches fire that quickly unless it has been doused in something. Gasoline, or alcohol. I didn't notice when I first came in, and I expect you and Jackal didn't, either, but the walls and floor had been soaked in something flammable. Sometimes, not having to breathe is a blessing, but not this time." He shook his head, looking annoyed, with himself or with us, I couldn't tell. "I'm certain our raider friend did not intend to set the house on fire with himself still inside," Kanin continued grimly, "but when we surprised him, he figured he was already dead."

"Which is a shame, if you ask me," said a familiar voice, and Jackal sauntered out of the darkness. Ignoring me and Kanin, he shot an annoyed glare at the burning house. "I didn't even get to rip his heart out before he went up in smoke. Inconsiderate bastard."

I scowled at him. "You're one to talk. You left us in there! No warning, no hesitation, nothing. I bet you didn't even look back when you hit the ground."

"And what would you have had me do, exactly?" Jackal questioned, baring his fangs. I smelled the blood on him, soaking his shirt and duster, and realized he was probably starving after taking that shot to the chest. "Hold your hand while you jumped out the window? Go back inside with the whole house about to collapse on top of me?" He sneered. "We're still vampires, sister. We still look out for number one. If *I'd* been trapped up there, I wouldn't have expected you or the old man to come back."

"Guess you don't know me as well as you think," I said in a cold voice. "Because I *would*."

"Really?" Jackal mocked, crossing his arms. "I find that a little hard to believe. I bet you can't even look at the house now without wanting to figuratively piss yourself."

"I believe," Kanin said, sounding exasperated, "that you both are forgetting the more pressing bit of information we've learned tonight." He looked past the burning building, the firelight dancing in his dark eyes. "Namely, who has turned the raiders against us, and who is still waiting in Old Chicago."

Sarren. The thought made me tense, and hatred flared up

again, searing and deadly, pushing back everything else. I hadn't forgotten. Sarren would still pay for what he'd done. Just because I refused to become a demon didn't mean I wouldn't kill him. When I found him, I'd stop at nothing until his head was impaled on my sword, and his body was a pile of smoldering ash.

"Sarren," Jackal agreed, and there was something new in his voice, too. A dangerous edge that hadn't been there before, speaking of violence and retribution. "Okay, you psychopath. You want to play games? I'll play games." His eyes gleamed, and he looked back at the burning house, a completely humorless smile crossing his face. "Screw around with my city and my minions, will you? Think you're going to be the new king?" He chuckled, and the sound made me shiver with anticipation. "I'll slaughter every human and burn the entire city to the ground before I give it up to you."

"Let's not get ahead of ourselves," Kanin warned. "Vengeance can easily cloud the mind, and Sarren is hoping for that. We cannot become so caught up in revenge that we rush straight into a death trap, like we did tonight." His gaze flickered to the inferno, just as there was a roar from within and the roof collapsed in a burst of embers and sparks. I flinched, and Kanin's voice turned grave. "Sarren has us at a disadvantage," he murmured. "There is an entire army between us, and he knows we're coming for him. From here on, if we are to even reach him alive, we must be *very* careful. And ready for anything."

I met Jackal's eyes, and he gave a small smirk. For once, both of us were thinking the same thing. It didn't matter how many thugs Sarren had between us and him, it didn't matter what kind of nasty surprises he had waiting. We would fight our way through an army if we had to, carve them down one by one, until we found Sarren.

And destroyed him utterly for what he'd taken from us.

* * *

We took a winding, indirect route into the city that night. True, we had every intention of finding Sarren, even if we had to slice our way through the entire raider army to do it. But, as Jackal pointed out, there was more than one way to skin a vampire. The raiders were likely watching all the main roads into Old Chicago; there was no reason we shouldn't try to sneak up on Sarren and avoid having to fight the whole city. Instead, Jackal took us through a series of rubble-strewn alleys and old buildings, claiming that the raiders never used them because they couldn't get their bikes through.

Also, rabids still lurked in the empty corners of Old Chicago, a fact I discovered when we followed Jackal through an underground mall and several pale monsters leaped at us through the broken windows. After cutting our way through the mob, we continued to slip through narrow, deserted streets, always alert for guards and sentries, though the city remained eerily still. At one point, Kanin put out an arm and pointed silently to where a pair of raiders leaned against the railing over a levee, their backs to us. Jackal grinned, motioned us to stay put, and slipped into the shadows. A few minutes later, both men were yanked into the darkness with separate yelps, and Jackal returned reeking of blood, a satisfied grin on his face.

A few hours later, we stood on the banks of a sullen black lake so vast you couldn't see the other side. According to Kanin, in the time before, it was called Lake Michigan, and Chicago had stood proudly along its edge. Now, the lake and the rivers that cut through the downtown area had crept over their banks and merged together, flooding part of the city but also creating a natural barrier against rabids.

I gazed over the rough waters, narrowing my eyes. I remembered Jackal's city from the last time I'd come through; a tangle of narrow bridges, walkways and platforms that crisscrossed submerged buildings. From where I stood, it looked much the same. I could see the old barge that sat in the center of the river, and the ramshackle bridge that spanned the dark waters. Motorcycles and a few other vehicles were parked in haphazard rows along the surface of the barge, the final stop before you crossed into the lair of a raider king.

Or a deranged psychopathic vampire hell-bent on destroying the world.

"Home, sweet home." Jackal sighed. "Or it will be, once I slaughter all the bastards who turned on me, stick their heads on pikes, and decorate the city with them. Maybe shove a torch through their teeth and use them to light the walkways, wha'd'ya think, sister?"

"It would definitely be you." I gazed out over the water, seeing the distant lanterns and torchlight glimmering in the haze. Even from this distance, I could tell something was wrong. "There's no one on the bridges," I mused, remembering that the last time I'd come through, the walkways had been swarming with raiders. Now, the bridges and platforms stood empty, abandoned. "Everything looks deserted."

Which meant we were walking into a trap, of course.

"Where do you think Sarren will be?" Kanin asked quietly. The Master vampire gazed over the water, observing the city with dark, impassive eyes. Jackal shrugged.

"Only one place he would be." He pointed to where a tall, narrow skyscraper stood against the skyline. A light shone near the top, bright and familiar, making my skin prickle with recognition.

Jackal's tower. The place I'd met my blood brother for the first time. Where we'd fought, on the top floor of the building, and he'd nearly killed me.

The place where Jebbadiah Crosse had died.

"It's the only building in the city that still has power," Jackal continued, staring up at the tower and the flickering light at the top. "And you can see everything that's going on below. If I were Sarren, that's where I would be."

"Then that's where we're going." The light shimmered across the water, taunting me, and I felt my fangs slide out. Sarren was close. This time, I wouldn't just cut off his arm. This time, I was going for his head.

"I suggest we do so quietly," Kanin interjected, his low, calm voice breaking through my sudden hate. "Sarren knows we're coming, and the whole city will be on high alert. If we can, we should avoid alerting them to our presence. It would be wiser to deal with Sarren first, before confronting the rest of the army. If we remove their new king, they will have lost their reason to fight us."

Jackal snorted. "Sneak into my own city and skulk around like a sewer rat," he muttered darkly, shaking his head. "Oh, heads are going to roll for this. I'm going to set up a special lane and use their skulls for bowling balls."

Ignoring him, I glanced at Kanin. "How are we going to sneak in?"

My sire gave a tight smile. "I expect the roads will be well guarded, but slipping into a flooded city is not hard. As large as this army is, they cannot watch the whole river."

Great. Looked like we were going for a swim.

CHAPTER 6

We crossed the river easily, as silent as the shadows that clung to the waves. Thankfully, though there was a thin sheet of ice clinging to the edges of the bank, the rest of the river was clear. And navigating large bodies of water wasn't difficult if you didn't have to worry about things like breathing or hypothermia. We slipped below the hulk of the huge barge, vampire sight piercing the pitch-black waters, as we continued into the flooded streets of Jackal's territory. Fish glided past us in large schools, flitting through an eerie underwater world of drowned buildings and submerged roads, rusty cars lining the pavement. A massive dark shape, almost as long as me, swished by my head, making me grit my teeth. Kanin had assured me that fish could not become rabid—and Jackal had laughed at the question—but I had no issues with drawing my katana underwater and slashing the next thing that came out of the depths toward me.

Above us, the city was silent. Bridges and walkways sat empty, platforms were deserted and still. Nothing moved overhead, and the ominous silence began to eat at me. This was a trap; I knew it, and the others had to know it, but there was nothing we could do except press forward. I'd face whatever Sarren could throw at me if it meant I would find him waiting at the end, with nothing between us but my katana.

"Careful." Kanin grabbed my collar when we surfaced, drawing me back a pace. We'd come out beneath a bridge, a flimsy walkway of wood and metal that stretched from one roof to another. Puzzled, I frowned back at him, and he pointed to the underside of the planks.

A strange metal device had been taped to the bridge, wires poking out in every direction. I didn't know what it could be, but the blinking red light on one corner looked fairly ominous.

"That's why the city is deserted," Kanin mused as Jackal looked up at the strange device and swore. "He likely has the whole place booby-trapped. Step on the wrong bridge, and it won't be there anymore."

"Huh," Jackal remarked, gazing at the wired bridge with the hint of a smirk. "That must've taken him a while. Bastard sure went through a lot of trouble, just for us. I feel so special, don't you?"

I paused. Something about Jackal's comment didn't feel right. "Why is he doing all this?" I asked as we began moving again, keeping well back from the mine. "Isn't he trying to reach Eden? Why stop here?"

"I don't know," Kanin murmured, and he sounded troubled, too. "Perhaps he wants to stop us for good, so he can continue his plans undisturbed. But that does not seem like him." His brow furrowed, and he shook his head. "Sarren is as unpredictable as he is brilliant and cruel. If he is in the city, he has a reason for it."

"Does it matter?" asked Jackal behind us. "Who cares what he's up to? He can be planning to fill the world with puppies, and I'm still going to rip the shriveled black heart from his chest and shove it down his throat until he chokes on it."

A memory flickered to life then, making my stomach cold, and I whirled on Jackal. "Wait," I said, as realization dawned. "The lab! You had a lab set up at the top floor of your tower. That's why you kidnapped Jeb—you wanted him to develop a cure for Red Lung, and you had given him everything he needed to do it—"

"Well, shit." Jackal raked a hand through his hair. "I forgot about that. Now I'm kinda embarrassed."

"There's a lab here?" Kanin echoed, his eyes grim. I nodded. "Then we must hurry. If Sarren uses that virus now, it will be New Covington all over again."

"Great," Jackal said as we struck out again, moving a bit faster now. "More bat-shit crazy bleeders. Hey, sister, here's a riddle for you. What's worse than infected killer psychos tearing their faces off?"

I frowned, confused for a moment, until it hit me. "*Armed* infected psychos tearing their faces off?"

"Bingo," Jackal growled. "So if you do see any of my former minions, do me a favor and cut their heads off, hmm? It'll save me the trouble of burning this place to the ground after we kill Sarren."

We encountered no resistance as we made our way toward the looming expanse of Jackal's tower. Kanin did point out a few more mines and traps, stuck to bridges or placed innocuously along walkways. Sarren was definitely here, and had been expecting us for a while.

Put out all the traps you want, you psychopath, I thought as the shadow of the huge tower encompassed us, dark and threatening. *Block the way, sic your army on us, do whatever you want. I'm still coming for you. And when I find you, one of us is going to die.*

The last stretch to the tower was made completely underwater. Jackal took us down until we reached the cracked pavement of the flooded city, weaving through cars and rubble piles with the fish. The base of the tower rose from the riverbed, the front doors ajar at the top of the steps, but the raider king didn't use the front entrance. Instead, we swam around back, slipping through a shattered window into what appeared to be an office. The remains of a desk sat disintegrating on the floor, silvery schools of fish darting through it. We followed Jackal through the office door and into a long, pitch-black hallway. Chunks of wall filled the narrow corridor, and metal beams lay slantwise across the passage, forcing us to weave through or move them aside. I received a shock when I swam around a corner and nearly ran into a bloated, half-eaten corpse floating in the water. It was a good thing I didn't have to breathe, because I snarled and quickly jerked back, filling my nose and mouth with river water as the corpse drifted by. Jackal turned, and I didn't need to hear his voice to know he was laughing at me.

Finally, Jackal wrenched open a peeling metal door, the rusty screech reverberating through the water and making fish flee in terror. Through the gap, I saw a flooded stairwell ascending into darkness.

We trailed Jackal through the door and followed the stairway until it broke free of the water, continuing its spiraled path up the side of the wall. Jackal watched, grinning, as I emerged, dripping wet from the river, water streaming from my hair and coat to puddle on the landing.

"What?" I asked softly, my voice echoing weirdly in the flooded stairwell. Kanin emerged at my back, making no noise at all even in the water. Jackal's grin widened, and he shook his head.

"Oh, nothing. You've never drowned a cat before, have you, sister?"

"Where are we?" asked Kanin before I could reply. His

voice carried a faint undertone that warned us to stay on target. That we were in Sarren's territory now, and he was waiting for us. The raider king raked his hair back and looked up the stairs.

"Third floor, back stairwell," he muttered. "No one ever uses it because some of the higher floors collapsed and the stairs are blocked on this side. But there's a second stairwell we can reach from the ninth floor, and that one goes all the way to the top." Jackal crossed his arms, smirking. "I figure everyone will be expecting us to use the elevator, and the minions might surprise me and cut the cables when we're near the top. And trust me when I say that falling from the top floor of this tower is *not* a pleasant experience."

He looked at me when he said this, narrowing his eyes. I thought again of our fight on the top floor, him staking me through the gut, the intense pain that had followed. Dangling from a broken window high above Chicago, desperately clinging to the ledge as my strength slowly gave out. Looking up, seeing Jackal standing above me, ready to end it—and Jebbadiah Crosse slamming into him from behind, hurling them both into open space.

"I always wondered how you survived," I told him, and his smirk widened. "You're like a rat that's impossible to kill—no matter what you do, it always comes back."

"One of my best qualities, sister." Jackal lowered his arms. "You'll appreciate it one day, trust me. Now..." He gazed up the steps again, a dangerous glint coming into his eyes. "What do you say we find Sarren and beat the ever-loving shit out of him?"

That I could get behind. My enemy was close, and I had never wanted someone's death as badly as I wanted Sarren's.

"Let's go," I told Jackal.

We started up the stairs, Jackal in front, Kanin silently

bringing up the rear. Around us, the stairwell creaked and groaned, the sounds echoing through the tight corridor and making my skin crawl. I did not like small, enclosed spaces with no way out, especially when it seemed the ancient, crumbling stairs could collapse at any moment. I concentrated on taking one step at a time and focused my anger and rage into a burning determination. Because if I concentrated on my hate, I could almost forget the fact that Sarren still terrified me, he had an entire raider army under his control, and that facing him again would be the hardest fight of my life. That he was still stronger than me, and even with Kanin's and Jackal's help, we might not be able to beat him. Especially since he knew we were coming.

None of that mattered. I didn't know how he planned to spread his awful virus, but I did know he was fully capable of destroying everything without a second thought. And I wouldn't let that happen. No matter what it took, no matter what nasty surprises he had waiting, we had to kill Sarren, tonight.

The stairs wove around the walls of the building, spiraling ever higher, before they ended in a blockade of stone, metal beams and twisted pipes. Jackal stopped us on the final landing and nodded to a peeling metal door set into the concrete.

"The other stairwell is through here. We'll have to cross the floor to get to it, but once we do, it's a straight shot to the top floor and Sarren."

I nodded back, but then I caught something that made me freeze. Filtering through the door, slipping underneath the crack, was an unmistakable scent.

The other two vampires paused, as well. "Blood," Kanin mused, his gaze dark and grim. "A lot of it. Something is waiting for us beyond this door. It appears your humans are expecting us, after all."

"Yep." Jackal sighed. "The minions aren't completely stupid all the time. And they know that blood is an excellent way to mask your presence from a vampire. We won't be able to pinpoint exactly where they are. If the whole army is waiting for us, it could get messy." He glanced at me, fangs shining in the darkened corridor. "Ready for this, little sister? No turning back now."

I drew my katana, the soft rasp shivering through the stairwell, and smiled grimly. "Ready," I whispered. Jackal grinned and pulled open the door with a rusty screech.

A cold breeze ruffled my hair, hissing into the stairwell. The room beyond the frame was huge, with a low ceiling and shattered windows surrounding us. Low sections of wall created a labyrinth of cubicles and narrow aisles, perfect for hiding behind or staging an ambush. Rubble, fallen beams and rotting desks were scattered throughout the floor, silent and still, and the room seemed to hold its breath.

It was also completely saturated in gore. Blood streaked the walls and ceiling, splattered in arching ribbons across the cubicle walls. Some of it wasn't human; I could pick out the subtle hints of animal blood in the room—dogs and cats and rodents, musky and somehow tainted. But the rest of it was definitely human, and the Hunger roared up with a vengeance.

"Well," Jackal remarked, gazing around the carnage-strewn space, "that doesn't scream 'trap' at all. Is this the best Sarren could come up with? I'm rather disappointed." Raising his head, he bellowed into the room: "Hey, minions! Daddy's home, and he's *not* happy! But because I'm such a nice guy, I'm going to give you a choice. You can make it easy for yourself and blow your brains out right now, or I can slowly twist your head around until it pops right off your neck. Your move!"

For a moment, there was silence. Nothing stirred beyond

the door, though if I listened hard enough, I thought I could hear the acceleration of several heartbeats, the scent of fear rising up with the blood.

Then something small, green and oval came arching through the air toward us, thrown by an arm behind an overturned desk, and Jackal grinned.

"Wrong answer," he muttered.

Lunging past me, he grabbed the object before it could hit the ground and, blindingly fast, hurled it back into the room. There was a muffled, "Shit!" from behind the desk.

And then something exploded in a cloud of smoke and fire, flinging a pair of bodies into the open, mangled and torn. Jackal roared, the sound eager and animalistic, as a few dozen raiders leaped up from behind desks and half walls and sent a hail of gunfire into the room.

I lunged behind a desk as bullets sprayed the floor and put a line of holes in the walls behind me. Gripping my katana, I peeked around the corner, trying to pin down where the attacks were coming from. I didn't see Kanin, but Jackal charged a cubicle with a roar, fangs bared. Several bullets hit him, tearing through his coat and out his back, but the vampire didn't slow down. Leaping over the desk, he grabbed one raider by the collar, yanked him off his feet, and slammed his head against the surface. Blood exploded from the raider's nose and mouth, and Jackal hurled him away to go after another.

Raiders were screaming now, firing their weapons in wild arcs, shattering glass and tearing chunks out of plaster. I saw two humans emerge from behind a pillar, aiming their guns at Jackal's back. I growled and darted from my hiding place, then lunged toward them. They saw me coming at the last minute and turned, shooting wildly. I felt something tear into my shoulder, sending a hot flare of pain and rage through me. Snarling, I slashed my blade through one raider's middle and, as he collapsed, whipped it up through the second's neck. Headless, the man toppled forward, and I leaped past him toward a cluster of raiders in the corner.

The demon in me howled, and bloodlust sang through my veins as I hit the group of men hard, katana flashing. They turned on me, faces white, guns raised. And then everything dissolved into screaming, gunfire and blood. I was hit several times, sharp stabs of pain that barely registered as I gave in to my anger, hate and grief. Raiders fell before me, cut down by my blade, their hot blood filling my senses. The Hunger raged within, stirred into a near frenzy with every kill, every bullet that ripped through me. But through it all, I kept a tight hold of my demon, refusing to lose myself again, even if killing these men brought me one step closer to Sarren. I would avenge Zeke's death, but I would do so on my terms.

As I fought my way to the center of the room, slicing my way through a trio of raiders, a sudden beeping filled the air, shrill and rapid. On instinct, I leaped back just as the pillar in front of me exploded, sending rocks and shrapnel everywhere and catching two raiders in the back. I was hurled away, crashing through a half wall and into a desk on the other side. Dropping to the floor, I lay there a moment, stunned. My coat was in tatters, and I could feel warm wetness spreading out from my middle a second before the pain hit, making me clench my jaw to keep from screaming. My katana lay several feet from my hand, glinting in the bursts of gunfire around me.

Another shrill beeping went off, and a second explosion rocked the room, filling the air with screams and the stench of smoke. Wincing, I struggled to rise, shrugging off rocks and debris, pushing away the wooden beam that had fallen across my chest. A shadow fell over me, and a raider glared down, eyes wild and crazy, as he pointed the barrel of a shot-gun at my face.

I jerked to the side and threw up my arm, just managing to knock the barrel away as a shot rang out, booming in my ears and making my head ring. Fire flared from the tip of the weapon, searing the air close to my face, and my demon re-coiled with a shriek. Snarling, I yanked the raider down, tore the gun from his hands, and sank my fangs into his throat. Hot blood filled my mouth, easing the pain as my wounds healed, mangled flesh knitting back together. I continued feeding until the body shuddered and went limp in my grasp, and I let it slump lifelessly to the floor.

Wiping my mouth, I grabbed my katana and rose, looking around for my next enemy.

The chaos in the room had quieted down. Bodies lay every-where, cut open and torn apart, scattered in pieces through-out the room. I could see my own carnage-strewn trail that led to the ruined pillar, and the two dead raiders who had been caught in the blast. Smoke hung in the air, along with the acrid stench of explosives and burned flesh.

Jackal emerged from the slaughter, blood-drenched and dangerous-looking, crimson streaking his face and hands. Gaz-ing around, he nodded in satisfaction. Kanin also appeared, seemingly out of nowhere, stepping over bodies as he made his way to the center.

"All righty, then." Jackal kicked a body out of his path and sauntered forward, grinning. "I feel better already. Noth-ing like massacring a bunch of filthy traitors to get the blood flowing. Wonder where the rest of the bastards are hiding."

I blinked at him. "There's more?"

He sneered at me. "This wasn't even half the army, sis-ter. When I said there's a whole fucking lot of them, I wasn't exaggerating. I'm guessing this was just the welcome-home party, and the rest of them are somewhere between this floor and Sarren."

"Then perhaps we should keep moving," Kanin suggested. "Unless there is another way to the top."

"Not unless you want to climb the elevator shaft," Jackal said, and began walking across the floor, weaving between beams and rubble, stepping over dead bodies. We picked our way through the room, the scent of blood now mingling with the stench of lingering smoke and charred flesh, until we reached a metal door on the other side.

"Ladies first," Jackal grinned, and pushed open the door to the stairwell.

I stepped through, frowning, then paused. Directly across from me, on the far wall, someone had written a message. In blood. Below that, a wet, unrecognizable lump of...something...had been speared to the wall with a knife. Stepping closer, I looked up at the top line, and my blood went cold.

Little bird, it read, making my stomach turn in hate and revulsion. There was only one sicko who called me that. I could see his scarred face, hear his awful, raspy voice as he smiled at me, whispering his insane plans. *"Sing for me, little bird,"* he'd told me once, holding up his knife and smiling. *"Sing for me, and make it a glorious song."*

I shivered and forced myself to read the rest of the message. *This is yours,* the bloody note went on, the letters dripping into each other. *Or, at least, I believe Ezekiel wanted you to have it.*

I went numb with dread. Fearfully, unable to stop myself, I looked at the lump at the bottom of the message, recognizing it for what it really was. Immediately wishing I hadn't.

A human heart.

Behind me, Jackal swore, and Kanin called out to me, his voice urgent. I barely heard them. I didn't register the words. I couldn't see anything but that awful token Sarren had left behind. It was like he'd reached into my consciousness, found the one thing that scared me more than anything else, and dragged it, twisted and perverse, into the light. My eyes burned, hot tears welling in the corners, but they weren't tears of sadness or grief. They were tears of blinding, uncontrollable rage.

My vision went black and red. Baring my fangs, I gave a strangled cry that was part roar, part scream, my voice echoing up the stairwell. Gripping my katana, ignoring Kanin's cries for me to stop, I leaped up the stairs, my mind only on one thing. Finding Sarren, and ripping him to pieces bit by bit. Driving my fist into his chest and tearing the warped, evil heart from his body, making sure he watched me do it.

I heard Kanin and Jackal start after me. But as I raced up the stairs, a sharp, ominous beeping echoed behind me, making the hairs on my neck stand up. I turned just as an explosion boomed through the stairwell, making the whole structure shake. Rock, dust and rubble rained down on me, and I staggered away, shielding my face. When the smoke and debris cleared, the stairs behind me were collapsed, and a wall of concrete, rubble and steel beams blocked the way down.

"Kanin!" I scrambled to the edge and tugged on a massive iron girder, trying to yank it aside. I was strong, but the girder was huge and half buried under a few tons of rock; it groaned but didn't budge. "Kanin! Jackal! Where are you? Can you hear me?"

A familiar annoyed voice came from somewhere below, muffled through the stone and rock, but there.

"We're fine, Allison," Kanin called over Jackal's swearing, making me slump with relief. But a gunshot rang out, followed by distant shouting, and the sound of bullets sparking off the walls below. Jackal snarled.

"Well, shit. There are the rest of 'em. I was wondering where they were hiding."

"Allison!" Kanin called, as the shouts and gunshots grew louder. "Wait for us! We'll find another way up! Do not take on Sarren by yourself, do you understand?"

A yell echoed somewhere below, and bullets ricocheted off the walls. "We gotta move, old man," Jackal yelled, his voice booming through the stairwell. "Now!"

"Kanin!" I called, but there was no answer. Kanin and Jackal had already moved back into the room. I listened as the screams, shots and roars of furious vampires raged below for a few seconds, then faded away, growing distant as if the fight had left the room. Or as if Jackal and Kanin had fled, taking the army with them.

Alone in the stairwell, I straightened, backed away from the cave-in, and gazed up the stairs. *He* was up there, somewhere. Waiting for me. Everything he'd done so far—the trap, the horrible message… Zeke's heart—was to separate me from my group. He wasn't interested in Kanin and Jackal. He wanted me.

Okay, you bastard, I thought, gripping my blade. A cold resolve filled my heart, and I glanced up the stairwell. *You want me? Here I come.*

I met no one on my journey up the tower, probably because all the raiders were busy dealing with Jackal and Kanin. I desperately hoped they were all right, though it was pointless to worry; I couldn't help them now.

The long, twisting stairwell went on, dark and empty but never silent. The stairs creaked under my weight, and every so often a rusty groan would echo through the shaft, making my skin crawl. I tried not to imagine the whole thing collapsing beneath me, and concentrated on putting one foot in front of the other.

As I neared the top, the scent of old blood hit me, faint and indistinct, and I proceeded more cautiously. Reaching another landing, I stopped, stifling the tiny ripple of fear that crawled up my spine. Overhead, a light flickered, casting erratic, disjointed shadows over the wall, and the message written on it in blood.

Almost there, little bird.

I swallowed hard. *Almost there,* I agreed. *And you're going to pay for what you did to him. Watch me, Zeke. I'll send your killer to hell, and I'll smile while I'm doing it.*

Gripping my katana, I climbed the final few steps to the top landing, wrenched open the door, and stepped through.

A long hallway greeted me, lined with windows on one side, most of them blown out or shattered. Far below, Old Chicago huddled in the shadows and dark water, and beyond it, the moon glimmered off the surface of the enormous Lake Michigan, stretching over the horizon.

I began walking toward the door at the very end of the hall, feeling as if I'd been here before. As I passed another corridor, I glanced down and saw a darkened elevator shaft along the walls, and everything jolted into place. I *had* been here, on this very floor, when I'd tried to rescue Jeb. I'd come up through the elevator instead of the stairwell. And I knew where I had to go. Through the door at the end of the hall was the laboratory, where Jebbadiah Crosse had died. Where I'd met Jackal for the first time.

Where Sarren waited for me now.

The door loomed dead ahead, and I didn't stop. I didn't pause to reconsider my plan. Whether I was walking into a trap or straight to my death. Katana at my side, I strode up to the door and kicked it below the knob. It flew open with a crash, nearly ripped off its hinges, and I stepped into the room.

The lab was dark, silent, and I paused in the frame, listening. When I'd been here last, it had been brightly lit, with no shadows or dark corners to hide in. I stepped through the door, sword out, searching for my enemy.

"Sarren," I called, easing forward, wary of traps and explosions, or a sudden horde of raiders pouring out to shoot at me. But the room remained silent. Still wary, I stepped through the doorway, a sense of familiarity stealing over me as I gazed around. I remembered this place. There was the desk and the ancient computer in the corner, mostly undisturbed, though the screen was dark and shattered now. There was the counter, covered in broken beakers and chips of glass, where Jackal had held me down and rammed a stake through my gut. And beyond it, the wall of cracked and shattered windows, through which my brother had fallen to his supposed death, glinted in the darkness, the remaining shards of glass sharp and lethal.

I paused. A chair sat against the back wall, silhouetted against the glass of an unbroken window and the night sky. The floor around it was streaked with old blood, and the scent reached me a moment later, stirring the Hunger. Wondering if this was Sarren's latest handiwork, I eased forward a bit, then froze.

A body sat in the chair, slumped forward with its head bowed, arms tied behind the chair back. The body was still, far too still to be alive. A raider, perhaps? I edged closer, studying the corpse. Moonlight filtered through the glass and cast a dark shadow over the floor, outlining the lean, ragged body, glimmering off its pale hair.

Oh, God…

My katana dropped from nerveless fingers, striking the ground with a clink. I couldn't move. My mind had snapped; I was seeing things that weren't there. Because I knew this wasn't real, it couldn't be. He was dead; I'd listened to him die.

Dazed, I took one step forward, then stopped, clenching my fists. *No,* I told myself furiously. *Don't believe it, Allison. That's what Sarren wants.* This was a trick. A ploy to make me fall apart. Like the heart in the stairwell. Sarren was playing me, and if I went up to that body, it would explode, or trigger a trap, or leap up and try to kill me. It wasn't him. Or maybe it *was,* and I'd walk up only to see a half-rotted corpse with a gaping hole in his chest where his heart had been.

"It's not him." My voice was resolute. Squeezing my eyes shut, I bowed my head, cutting off my emotions. Willing myself to believe my own words. This would not work. I would not give Sarren the satisfaction of breaking me. Zeke was dead. It still killed me, ripped me to pieces inside, but I knew he was gone. "It's not him," I said again, a cold numbness settling around my heart. Reaching down, I picked up my sword, rose with icy resolve, and deliberately turned from the body. "Stop hiding," I told the darkness and shadows. "I am not falling for it. Come out and face me, you fucking psychopath. I'm done playing games."

"Allison?"

My stomach dropped, and for the second time that night, the world froze. Sarren might be able to disguise a body. He might even be able to alter a corpse, make it look like someone I knew, someone I longed to see again. He could not disguise a voice. Especially one so familiar, one that had been on my mind for weeks, in my thoughts every single day. A voice I'd thought I would never hear again.

Slowly, I turned. The body in the chair hadn't moved, still

slumped forward with its head bowed. But as I watched, it stirred, raising its head...and I felt the earth shatter as his familiar, piercing blue eyes met mine across the floor.

"Hey, vampire girl," Zeke whispered, his voice slightly choked. "I knew...you'd come for me."

This...can't be real.

I stared at the body across from me, unable to process what was happening, not daring to believe. This was wrong; it had to be a trap. Sarren was still playing his sick games, and in a moment this would all fall apart. I couldn't start believing, didn't dare to hope. My heart was just beginning to heal from being so brutally shattered; if I started to hope, only to have that hope crushed again, I didn't know if I would recover.

"Allie?" The human's voice drifted to me, weak with pain and exhaustion. A trickle of dried blood ran from one corner of his mouth, and dark circles crouched beneath his eyes. He looked beaten, bloody and in pain, but alive. He coughed, shoulders heaving, and gazed at me, imploring. "What's wrong?"

I shook my head, trying to ignore my heart, the way it seemed to leap in my chest, like it was alive again. Around us, the world had stopped; time had frozen into this brittle, dreamlike moment where nothing was real. "It's not you," I told the body in the chair, knowing I sounded insane. "You can't be here. I listened to you die."

"I know," he whispered, holding my gaze. I didn't move, wary and disbelieving, pleading for him to prove me wrong. The human sighed. "I know...how it looks," he went on. "But it's all right. This isn't a trap, or a trick. I don't...have a bomb strapped to me, I swear." He gave a faint, rueful smile, so familiar I felt my throat close up. "I'm still here. It's...really me, Allison."

My knees were suddenly shaky, and I couldn't take it anymore. In a trance, I crossed the room to kneel in front of the chair. The wood was hard, chips of glass poking me through my clothes, but I barely felt it. I needed to touch him, to make certain this was real, that it wasn't an illusion. My trembling hand rose to his face, brushing his cheek, as he gazed down at me, blue eyes never leaving mine. A shiver went through me the moment I touched his skin. He was pale and cold, dried blood covered his face, and his clothes were in tatters. But it was him.

It was Zeke.

"See?" he murmured, smiling at me. "Still here."

I choked back a sob, and the world pitched into motion again. "You're alive," I whispered, running my fingers down his cheek. He closed his eyes and turned his face into my touch, and my heart lurched, blood singing, as it did only when around him. "How?"

Zeke smiled, then bent forward with a shudder, shoulders heaving. "I'll tell you…everything later," he panted, looking up again. "Right now…let's just get out of here. Can you cut me free?"

Still in a daze, I stood, walked around the chair, and began slicing through the ropes tying him to the seat. In the back of my mind, I knew this was wrong. This was too easy, too good to be true. Sarren wouldn't just let me saunter up, free Zeke, and walk out again. But my arms continued to move, almost by themselves, and I could only stare at the boy I'd thought was dead. Dried blood covered his shoulders and the back of his shirt, but there didn't seem to be any wounds that I could see. Zeke waited patiently, head bowed, as I cut the bindings at his wrists, arms and waist. "Where are Kanin and Jackal?" he asked as the ropes began falling away.

"I don't know," I answered. "They said they would find

another way up." *I hope they're okay.* Tearing my gaze from Zeke, I looked around the room once more, a last-ditch effort to be cautious. "Where's Sarren?"

"Not here," Zeke muttered weakly. "Don't know…where he is now. Think he might've gone ahead to Eden.…"

The last ropes parted, and he slumped forward, nearly falling out of the chair. I caught him around the waist and pulled him upright, steadying us both.

Zeke gazed down at me, his face so familiar, his hair falling jaggedly over his forehead. Our eyes met, and he offered a faint, familiar smile, exhausted, pained, but full of hope. My throat closed, and with a little sob, I collapsed against him, burying my face in his shirt. He murmured my name, and I closed my eyes, feeling him, solid and real, against me. The last time I'd seen him, held him like this, was in New Covington. Where, in the safety of Prince Salazar's tower, I'd kissed Zeke and promised I would go back to Eden with him. Before Sarren had returned and stolen him away. Before I was forced to listen to the awful sounds of his torture. His screams and sobs and pleas for Sarren to kill him, before his wish was finally granted.

Or so I'd thought.

"I can't believe you're here," I whispered, feeling one arm slide around me, the other reach for something at the small of his back. "I thought Sarren killed you."

"He did."

His voice sounded strange now, cold and flat. Puzzled, I tried to pull back, but his arm tightened like a steel band, holding me close. He was strong, much stronger than I remembered. Putting both hands on his chest, I started to push him away, but stopped in horror as my nerves prickled a terrified warning.

Zeke...had no heartbeat.

Chilled, I looked up, into his face. I could see myself reflected in his eyes, as he gave me a familiar, too-bright stare—the gaze of a predator—and smiled.

"He told me to say hello," Zeke whispered, his fangs gleaming inches from my throat.

And he plunged a blade into my chest.

PART II

LOST

CHAPTER 7

I gave a soundless gasp and lurched back from Zeke, my hand going to my chest. He watched impassively, blue eyes cold, the hint of a smile still on his face. I found the hilt of something poking between my breasts and grasped it, sending a ripple of agony through me. Clenching my jaw, I gathered my will and pulled. The knife slid back through my chest, ripping and slicing, and I screamed as it came free.

Shaking, grasping the hilt with limp fingers, I looked up at the boy who had haunted me every day since before New Covington. The boy who had seen past the monster and the demon to the girl beneath, and hadn't been afraid to love her. The boy who'd once begged me never to Turn him, who had made me promise to let him go. To let him die…as a human.

"What's wrong, vampire girl?" Zeke whispered, stepping forward. He smiled, fangs glinting in the shadows, his voice cold and mocking as he approached. "Aren't you happy to see me?"

"Z-Zeke." I staggered away from him, fighting to stay on my feet. Pain blazed through my center, agony making it difficult to move, even as I felt myself healing. The knife dropped to the floor with a clatter, leaving a spray of crimson over the broken glass. "What…happened to you?"

"I died," Zeke said, in a way that made my skin crawl. Flat and blunt, like he was discussing the weather. "I died, and Sarren brought me back." His lips twisted in a cruel, mocking grin. "Why, Allie? What did you think happened?"

I was too horrified to answer. This…this was all wrong. This couldn't be Zeke. "No," I whispered, backing away from him. "Zeke, don't you recognize me?" He cocked his head with a patronizing look, as if I was being ridiculous. Desperate, I stammered on, frantic to fix this, to snap him out of it. "Do you remember…us? Me and Kanin and Jackal, fighting Sarren, trying to stop his new virus? Do you remember being human?"

"I remember pain," Zeke said softly. "I remember there was blood, and pain, and darkness. And then…nothing." He blinked, seeming to shake himself from a trance, smiling again as he turned to me. "But we all started out human, didn't we, vampire girl? I don't need to remember that life, because that human is dead now."

"No," I choked, shaking my head. "No, Zeke, you don't mean that."

Walking to a shelf beside the counter, Zeke reached up and pulled out a familiar blade, his machete, then regarded the weapon intently. A tiny furrow creased his brow, as if he was remembering. "I sang for Sarren," he whispered, and everything inside me went cold. "I sang and I sang, until I died. And Sarren gave me a new purpose, a new song. But the requiem isn't over yet."

Turning his head, he gave me a chilling stare, one that was instantly familiar. Terror lanced through me as I saw Sarren gazing at me through Zeke's eyes.

"This is your melody, vampire girl," Zeke said, his quiet,

lilting voice making my skin crawl. "Tonight is your final per-
formance." He smiled, and it turned my blood to ice. "Sing
for me, Allie," he crooned, in a voice that was all too familiar. "Sing for us, and make it a glorious song."

I staggered away from him as he stepped forward with a
demonic grin, eyes and fangs bright. My katana was still on
the floor beside the chair, and a part of me knew I should grab
it, but I was in so much pain, and nothing seemed real. My
mind was screaming denials, my body was trying desperately
to heal itself, and all I could do was back away as the thing
that looked like Zeke came closer.

"Zeke, please." I continued to back away. It still hurt to
move, but my wound was smaller now, and I could walk without feeling like I might collapse. That pain was nothing, however, compared to the anguish clawing at my insides as I faced
Zeke. The blank look in his eyes made me want to scream, but
I swallowed my despair and tried to speak calmly. "I don't...
want to fight you. Not after everything. Not after..."

Pain shot through me as I stumbled on a loose plank and
nearly fell. Gritting my teeth, I pressed a hand to my bleeding chest, keeping my gaze on the vampire slowly pressing
me back. An evil smile crossed his face. I was weaker than
him right now, in pain, and his vampire instincts were goading him to attack, to take advantage of a wounded opponent.
I remembered my Zeke: brave, determined, compassionate.
The boy who hadn't let the fact that I was a vampire scare
him away, who had offered his heart to a monster, because he
could see the human inside. The only living being I would
ever open myself up to, because I'd trusted him. Because I'd
known he would never hurt me.

To see him like this crushed something deep inside. I felt
broken, as if my soul had shattered like a mirror, and the pieces
were cutting me from within. I stared into the face of the boy

I'd once known, and for the first time, I wished he was dead. I wished he was dead, my memories of him intact and un-broken—so that I didn't have to remember him like this. As the monster he'd vowed never to become.

"Zeke, please, don't do this," I whispered, feeling something hot slide down my cheek. "What about Caleb, and Bethany, and Jeb? What about Eden?"

Zeke shook his head. "It's too late, Allison," he whispered, trapping me in a corner. Broken metal frames pressed against my back, and the cold night wind tossed my hair through the opening. Zeke regarded me without emotion. "All I remem-ber of that life is pain," he said, almost in a daze. "I sang, I died, and Sarren brought me back." He raised his machete, the blade and his fangs gleaming in the shadows. "And now, I'm going to destroy you, Allie, because he wanted it to be me. He wanted you to see me tear the heart from your chest and crush it in my fist. It will be poetically ironic, he said, what-ever that means. So, take a good look, vampire girl, before I kill you." Zeke paused, and Sarren's evil smile crossed his face again, his eyes going blank. "Or should I say…little bird?"

That jolted me out of my trance. I threw myself to the side as Zeke's blade came whipping down to sink into the wall be-hind me. I hit the ground, rolled to my feet to face him, and barely dodged the next blow as Zeke lunged in with a snarl, slashing viciously. The machete blade passed inches from my head; as I jerked back, it sliced a shallow cut across my cheek. He was much faster than I remembered, vampire speed and strength adding to his already lethal fighting skills. I had to stop him before he could use that blade. As his follow-up blow hammered down toward my neck, I threw up a hand, catching his wrist, and braced myself as he crashed into me.

"Zeke, stop—"

His free hand shot out and clamped around my throat. I

snarled and grabbed his arm, trying to pry him off. Fangs bared, he turned and rammed me into the wall with the full strength of a vampire behind him. My head struck the concrete with a dizzying crack, making me see stars, and I desperately fought to keep my focus.

Dragging me off the wall, Zeke spun and pushed me into the counter, bending me backward, the machete suddenly at my throat. Panicked, I grabbed the hilt, trying to keep the blade from sliding forward to cut off my head. He grinned and leaned his weight into me, pushing the edge closer to my neck.

"Look at me, Allison," Zeke whispered as the blade inched closer to my skin. And, despite myself, my gaze flicked up to meet those glassy blue eyes. Zeke smiled. "That's right, vampire girl. Look at me as I kill you. I want my face to be the last thing you see before I send you to hell."

The blade touched my neck and sank in, drawing blood. With a desperate hiss, I brought my knee straight up, striking between his legs as hard as I could. Zeke snarled and convulsed; I grabbed the first thing my fingers closed around—a jagged chunk of ceiling—and bashed it against the side of his head.

The blade at my throat vanished as Zeke staggered away, blood smeared across his temple, and dropped to a knee, one hand pressed to his face. Coughing, I staggered across the room to the chair, snatched my katana from where it lay beside it, and whirled to face him again.

Zeke staggered to his feet, still holding the side of his head. Blood trickled over his fingers as he stumbled across the floor and nearly fell, grabbing the shelf to keep himself upright. Glass vials and instruments clattered to the floor, shattering on the tile as Zeke groped for something at the back of the ledge, his machete lying on the floor beside him.

Gripping my sword, I stared at him in anguish, feeling

warm blood ooze from the cut in my throat. My center still throbbed, sending ripples of pain through me, though everything else felt numb. What did I do now? I didn't want to fight him, but if he came at me again, I'd have little choice. Zeke wasn't playing around. Another few inches, and my head would've been lying on the floor at his feet.

My eyes burned with desperate tears. This couldn't be happening. It didn't seem real, but the throbbing pain in my chest said otherwise. Vaguely, I realized that this was what Sarren must've planned all along; a cruel, cruel trick to bring Zeke back, only he wasn't the same.

Zeke was still leaning against the shelf with his back to me. His head was bowed, and blood covered one side of his face, though I could tell the wound had already healed. But he hadn't moved or picked up his weapon, and I felt the tiniest thread of hope rise from the despair.

"Zeke…"

"Get away from me, Allison." The hoarse sound made my stomach leap. It was his voice, *Zeke's* voice, choked and raspy-sounding, but it was him. "Get out of here, vampire girl," Zeke muttered, hunching his shoulders. "Go. Find Kanin and Jackal and just go. Leave me here."

"No." Relief shot through me. Lowering my blade, I stepped toward him. "No, Zeke, you're coming with us. I won't leave you." *I'm not losing you a second time.*

Zeke's shoulders trembled. I took another step toward his stooped form, intending to draw him away, to take him far from this twisted place so we could both forget. I heard short gasping breaths and thought he might be sobbing….before I realized it was laughter.

Smiling, he turned back and raised his arm, the deadly curve of a crossbow pointed right at my chest.

"You're so easy," he whispered.

There was a sharp, clear snap, and something slammed into my center, hot and blindingly painful. It punched a hole through my chest, a strip of white-hot fire that made my limbs seize up and froze the scream in my throat. I felt myself falling, and the world blacked out for a second.

When my vision came into focus again, I was lying on my back, unable to move. Vaguely, I was aware of what had happened to me, but it seemed unreal—though the throbbing pain radiating from my center was all too real.

I've...been shot. Even thought was a struggle now, and I tried desperately to stay conscious. *The stake...needs to come out. Have to pull it free.*

My limbs felt like stone, but I raised my arm and felt along my ribs to where the strip of fire was lodged in my chest. My fingers brushed a slender wooden dart, only a couple inches protruding from my skin. The rest was inside me, searing and agonizing. I clawed weakly at the quarrel, desperate to get it out, but my fingers felt wooden and numb, and my limbs were losing all feeling.

A shadow fell over me, and Zeke loomed overhead, peering down at my limp body. I couldn't see his features clearly; his face was blurred, and the rest of the room seemed to be shrinking, vanishing at the end of a long tunnel. I blinked hard to clear my vision, but the blackness returned, hovering around the edges of my sight.

"Don't go to sleep just yet, vampire girl," Zeke whispered, and I heard a metallic scrape as he picked up my katana and raised it in front of him. "We're just getting to the climax." He regarded the sword appraisingly, then gave it an expert twirl and held it out, the edge poised right above my throat. "Any last words, Allie?"

"Why?" I whispered, gritting my teeth against the pain, the woodenness of my body. Blinking away tears, I looked into his face, searching for any hint of the boy I knew, but his face remained cold. "Why…are you doing this, Zeke?"

Zeke's cruel smile didn't change. "I died, vampire girl," he repeated, as if it were obvious. "And Sarren helped me forget. I forgot the pain of being mortal. The human you knew before…he's dead. Dead and gone." He stepped forward, raising the katana above his head, eyes bright with glee and madness. I could barely see his features through the haze darkening my vision, but his voice rang out, cold and ruthless. "And now, you can join him."

"Boss!"

There was a sudden, deafening crash. Behind Zeke, the door flew open, and a raider staggered through, reeking of blood and smoke. Zeke lowered the blade and turned as the man lurched toward him, looking panicked.

"They're coming!" the human blurted, heaving in great gasps. "The bloodsuckers… Jackal and the other one…we couldn't stop them. They're on their way—"

Zeke grabbed the man by the throat and lifted him off his feet. "You were supposed to kill them," Zeke said calmly, as the raider choked and gagged. "That's all you were required to do. Are you telling me that three hundred armed humans cannot destroy two vampires? What are you all good for?"

"Tell me about it." A body came hurtling through the air, crashing into the wall in a spatter of blood before slumping, lifeless, to the floor. Zeke dropped the raider and spun, eyes narrowing as a tall figure stepped through the door wearing a vicious smile. "It's so hard to find good help these days, isn't it?"

My vision finally went dark. I tried to shake it off again, but teetered on the edge of succumbing to the pressing blackness. Sound was becoming muffled and dim. The stake throbbed inside me, searing and agonizing, and all I wanted to do was

escape the pain burning a hole in my chest. But I forced my
eyes to stay open, watching through the fog as Jackal crossed
the room, his eyes gleaming as they locked on Zeke. The
raider king was covered in blood, clothes tattered and burned,
and one eye was blackened and squeezed shut as if something
had exploded in his face. Close behind him, Kanin swept into
the room amid a flurry of shouts and gunfire.

"Well, look who it is," Jackal remarked, smiling dangerously
as he advanced on Zeke, who stepped away from me to face
him. His voice was tight, fangs bared in a painful grimace, and
his movements were stiff. "What a surprise. Our little bloodbag is back from the dead, and the new king of Chicago."

The tunnel across my vision shrank even more. I could
barely see Jackal and Zeke facing off in the middle of the
room. Zeke might've said something in return, but his back
was to me, and I couldn't make it out. The noise around us
now seemed to come from a great distance. Then I felt a presence next to me, and someone lifted me off the ground, holding me to his chest.

"Kanin," I whispered, but my voice must've been too soft
to hear because he didn't answer. Gunfire rang out, shattering glass and peppering the walls and floor, as raiders began
spilling into the room. Kanin flinched, holding me closer and
protecting me with his body. I felt him jerk as a few bullets
struck him, but he didn't run. Whirling, he ducked behind a
shelf and peered back into the room.

"James!"

I could just see Jackal, crouched behind a counter, bullets
sparking all around him. His gold eyes met ours, and he bared
his fangs. "Move, old man," the raider king snarled through
the cacophony, though everything sounded like it was taking place underwater. "Get her out of here! I'll hold 'em off
for a few seconds—"

A crossbow bolt came from nowhere, flying through the shelves, striking Jackal below the collarbone. He fell back with a muffled howl of pain, and Zeke lowered his arm and calmly walked forward, my katana in his other hand.

No! I wanted to scream, but the raiders unleashed another barrage of gunfire, pressing us back. I felt Kanin turn, cutting off my view of the room, Jackal, the raiders and Zeke.

Kanin, no! We can't leave them. But my voice was gone, and Kanin didn't slow down. Bullets zipped past us as he rushed forward, toward the wall of broken windows and empty space.

There was a crash, a feeling of weightlessness for a few seconds, and then we began to fall.

CHAPTER 8

When I opened my eyes, the world was silent. Voices had disappeared, gunshots and screams and cries of pain had vanished from existence. It was dark, and I lay on my back on the hard cement, staring up at a low, bare ceiling. There were no windows that I could see, and no light filtered in from outside.

I shifted on the floor and winced as my chest throbbed, a dull ache that went all the way through my body. Gritting my teeth, I struggled to sit upright, finally slumping back against the wall to ease some of the pain.

What...happened? I felt sluggish and heavy, my thoughts a hazy, tangled mess. Something hovered at the back of my mind, dark and terrible, and my thoughts kept shying away from it. Where was I? I didn't remember coming here.

"Allison."

Kanin's voice echoed somewhere close, soft with relief. A piece of shadow melted off the wall as the Master vampire rose from where he'd been sitting in the far corner. His head nearly brushed the ceiling as he approached and knelt beside me, the dark gaze searching and intense.

I blinked. Up close, his face was lined with worry, his expression grave. That ominous memory stirred again, brushing my consciousness, but it slipped away before I could grasp it.

"Kanin," I gritted out, my voice strangely hoarse and raspy. "Where are we? What happened? I—" My chest throbbed, and I winced. Kanin put a hand on my arm.

"Easy. Don't move around just yet. It will be a couple hours, now that you're awake, for your body to heal completely after the damage it sustained. Here, this will help. Try to drink it slowly." He handed me a cracked bowl, filled with something that smelled hot and thick, and the Hunger flared up with a roar. I downed the blood, not knowing where Kanin had gotten it and not caring, and warmth seeped through my veins. The ache eased somewhat, though not completely.

"What's wrong with me?" I asked, shifting against the wall. It sent a tiny jolt through my center, and I clenched my teeth, almost angry at the pain. "Why haven't I healed yet?"

"Allison." Kanin turned a dark, agonized gaze on me. "It's been two days. You went into hibernation for a little while." He paused, letting the gravity of that statement sink in before continuing. "I've been working to bring you out of it, but until now, I wasn't certain you would revive. It's extremely lucky that such a young vampire would wake up at all, after being staked right through the heart."

"Staked?" Gingerly, I prodded my chest at the point where the ache originated. It was sore, but there was no indication I'd had a long piece of wood shoved through me. "What happened?" I asked again. "I don't remember...."

"Jackal's tower," Kanin said softly. "We went there to find Sarren."

Jackal's tower. Fragments of that night came back to me. The silent walkways. The journey underwater to reach the building. Fighting raiders and being separated from Jackal and Kanin. The long flight of stairs, leading to the top floor of the tower and...

My hand went to my mouth as the darkest piece of the night emerged from my subconscious, horrific and terrifying. "Zeke," I whispered. "He's...he's a *vampire*. Sarren Turned him. And..."

And he tried to kill me. He nearly succeeded, too. God, what happened to him? Why would he turn on us? It was like he was a completely different person.

"I'm sorry, Allison." Kanin's voice was grim. "I underestimated Sarren. I didn't expect him to Turn Ezekiel like that." He sighed, briefly closing his eyes. "I should have predicted this."

I was numb with misery, from remembering that fight, where Zeke had come after me with pure, ruthless intent, his eyes hard. So Kanin's words took a moment to register. "What do you mean?" I choked out. "That Sarren would Turn Zeke?"

"Yes," Kanin said slowly, "but it is more than that. Sarren did not simply Turn Ezekiel, as I did you. No, he went further. He made him a childer."

"I don't know what that is, Kanin."

"It's when a vampire—and only a Master can do this—creates a spawn in his own image. He wipes his mind clean, destroys all memories of his life before, and shapes a new personality based on what he wants that childer to be. Sometimes he will force a mind compulsion on the childer—think of it as a stronger version of the blood bond we share—to make certain his offspring does what he wants. In ancient times, many old Masters created their covens this way, making sure their childer would not rise up or betray them. But it is such an invasive, barbaric practice, it is frowned upon by nearly all our kind and used only in rare, extreme cases."

"So, that...really wasn't Zeke?" I snatched at the only ray

of hope I could find in this horrible situation. "He didn't act like that because he wanted to?"

"Yes and no." Kanin sighed. "It depends on his state of mind, and how strong the compulsion is. It could be that Ezekiel's memories have been repressed, that he is fighting the compulsion. That somewhere deep inside, he still retains a sense of who he is. Or..." Kanin paused, then went on in a grim voice. "Or it could be that Sarren shattered his mind completely, drove him to madness, and remade him into the vampire you saw in the tower. If that is the case, then you won't be able to reach him, because there is nothing left of the boy you once knew."

I squeezed my eyes shut as stupid bloody tears stung the corners and leaked from under my lids. "But...there could be a chance, right?" I whispered, looking back up at Kanin, who regarded me with pity and not much hope. I didn't care. I refused to believe Zeke was gone. "I won't leave him like that, Kanin," I said stubbornly. "Now that I know he's alive..."

"What would you do, even if you could reach him?" the Master vampire asked gently. "Ezekiel never wanted to be a vampire. He would have rather died than Turn. Even if his mind is still intact and you somehow manage to break the compulsion, what then? Do you think he could live as one of us, feeding on humans, preying on those around him? It would destroy him, Allison. He wouldn't be able to live with himself." His voice softened even more, though I hated him for saying it, knowing he was right. "If you do face Ezekiel again, I think you know what you have to do."

I turned away from my sire and rose, unable to look at him anymore. Despair weighed me down, heavy and suffocating, and I pressed my forehead to the stone wall, trying to keep the awful rage and grief in check. Dammit! What did Kanin want from me? I'd followed his rules. I'd tried to find the balance between human and monster. I'd done everything I could think of to fight the demon, to not give in, to keep some semblance of humanity. Even though it was hard, it hurt like hell, and all I had to show for it was a broken heart.

I'd promised Zeke I would keep fighting the monster. And I would. But now, Kanin was asking me to destroy the one thing that kept me human, the only thing I had ever truly wanted for myself.

But, even through the anger and grief, and the stubborn voice inside me shouting protests, I knew he was right. Zeke had never wanted to be a vampire. And as shocking and confusing as my own Turning had been, I couldn't imagine what it must be like having Sarren for a sire. I remembered those first few days with Kanin, his careful, patient lessons as he taught me how to be a vampire, and that had still been terrifying even when I'd *chosen* to Turn. There was no telling what Sarren had done to Zeke, what he'd made him do. Maybe Sarren *had* twisted his mind beyond repair, and the Zeke I'd known was truly gone, replaced with that cold, ruthless killer I'd seen in the tower. A spawn in Sarren's own image.

If that was the case, if Zeke really was lost…then he'd be better off dead. I thought of everything I'd had to learn as a vampire: the feeding, the bloodlust, the constant struggle with the Hunger. It had been hard, and there had been many nights when I'd questioned my decision to become a monster, knowing I would struggle with my choice for eternity. I tried to imagine Zeke—gentle, compassionate, selfless Zeke—forcing himself to hunt and kill his once fellow humans…and couldn't. Kanin was, as always, right. The most merciful thing would be to destroy Zeke now. He would want it that way.

I just didn't know if I could do it.

Numb, I gazed around for my sword, feeling the empty

sheath against my back, light and disconcerting. When I didn't immediately find it, I panicked for a moment…before I remembered. It had been left behind when Kanin jumped out the window with me. My weapon was still on the top floor of the tower…with Zeke.

And then, I remembered something else.

"Where's Jackal?" I whispered, spinning toward Kanin as he rose, his shoulders slumped. The last thing I remembered from before I'd blacked out in Kanin's arms was Jackal, surrounded by raiders, struck down with a crossbow bolt, and Zeke advancing on him. Kanin gave me a look that was full of regret.

"He's not here, Allison. He didn't make it out of the city."

No. I clenched my fists, refusing to believe it. *No, not Jackal. He can't be dead; he always makes it out.*

On impulse, I reached out for Jackal's presence, searching for him through our blood tie. Suddenly terrified, I braced myself to feel nothing, solid proof that my infuriating, inscrutable blood brother was no longer in the world. That something had finally killed him.

There was a pulse, and I closed my eyes in relief. It was faint and erratic, like the dying heartbeats of a bird, but it was there. Desperately, I followed it, needing to see open sky, to get out of this suffocating tomb. The steps were blocked with decades of rubble and stone, but a hole in the floor led down into an ancient, rusty pipe, which eventually emptied into a storm drain. I crawled from the opening and found myself at the edge of the lake, cold water sloshing at my boots.

From where I stood, I couldn't see Jackal's old city, but I could feel him, that faint tug from somewhere over the turbulent waters, telling me he was still out there.

Headlights suddenly pierced the darkness, and I shrank back as three raiders cruised out of the shadows, one after the other, riding along the edge of the lake. They vanished down another street, the growl of their engines fading into the night, but I knew what they were searching for.

"They come by every few hours, searching along the water's edge," Kanin said, emerging from the pipe. "There are more in the ruins, going through buildings and empty houses, looking for us. Thankfully, they have not found this place yet, but they know we are still in the city."

"How?" I asked.

"Because not all of them make it back," Kanin replied gravely, and looked down at me. "You were badly hurt, Allison. You needed blood, and a lot of it, to have a chance of coming out of hibernation. The lake's edge was a good spot to take shelter; it allowed for easy disposal of the bodies. But they've noticed that their numbers have slowly dwindled, and they now patrol the city in groups of at least three." His mouth thinned in a humorless smile. "It appears Ezekiel is not about to let us go."

Zeke. I forced my thoughts away from him, trying to suppress the horror of the task before me. I would deal with that when I faced him again. I would not think of him now, because then I would fall apart.

"Jackal is still out there," I muttered. Kanin nodded grimly.

"Yes, he's still alive," my sire agreed. "I feel him, too. But he hasn't moved in two days, and I fear where he might've ended up. I believe he is somewhere deep within the flooded city, unable to move or feed himself." Kanin's eyes narrowed in the direction the bikes had gone. "It seems they have not found him yet, but he will not be able to hide forever. And there is still the matter of Sarren." His gaze grew distant and troubled. "This was likely his plan all along, to slow us down, give himself more distance and time. He is likely very close to Eden now, if he has not already arrived."

I bit my lip. "We…we're going back for him, right?" I asked, and Kanin glanced down at me, his expression blank. "We can't leave him behind, Kanin," I argued. "I know he's a bastard, and he'd probably leave us if he were in the same situation, but…" I trailed off with a helpless gesture, unable to explain. I felt empty and defeated, weighed down with despair, the knowledge of what I had to do: destroy the evil thing Zeke had become. I was so tired of it. I didn't want to lose anyone else, not even Jackal. He was ruthless, infuriating, selfish, and would sell us out without a second thought, but he was my brother, the only family I had left besides Kanin. "I'm going back for him," I whispered, trying to keep my voice steady under my sire's steady gaze. "You don't have to come. Keep going to Eden. Find Sarren, stop the plague. That's always been your objective. I understand." I swallowed hard as he continued to stare at me, unblinking. "But I'm going back for Jackal." *And Zeke.*

Kanin cocked his head at me, appraising. "Is it worth it?" he asked, making me frown. "Two lives for the rest of the world?" he continued. "Are you willing to sacrifice everything to save one and destroy another?"

"What do you—"

"Answer the question, Allison," Kanin continued in a quiet but ruthless voice. "I want you to understand exactly what you are deciding, right now. If we return to the city for Jackal and Ezekiel, Sarren could reach Eden, complete whatever he is planning, and unleash a virus that could destroy everything. And if that happens, everything we've done here will be for nothing. Do you understand that?"

I blinked at him. "We?"

Kanin sighed. "I cannot take Sarren alone," he said in a matter-of-fact voice. "If we are to have any hope of stopping him, we must face him together. But, regardless of that, I refuse to leave one of us behind, even one as volatile as him. I created him. I am responsible for his life. So, you will not be going into the city after James, Allison. I will."

I blinked in shock. He peered down, dark gaze boring into me. "I just want you to understand the potential consequences of tonight," he went on. "If we are killed, if we cannot get to Sarren in time, everything could die. It will be like it was sixty years ago. You aren't old enough to remember the days Before, but when Red Lung was at its peak, the entire world was madness and chaos. And when the rabids appeared, it be-came hell on earth." Kanin paused, brows drawing together as he gazed at the ruined city around us. "It is…a very heavy weight to carry, Allison, the damnation of a world. I want you to be very certain, before we go any further. Is it worth it? Is *he* worth it?"

His words chilled me, but I already knew my answer. It was selfish, it was unreasonable, and I knew it was the wrong choice. But I looked up at Kanin, into his impassive face, and whispered, "Yes."

"You are willing to let others die for this. To let Sarren win."

"He won't win," I said. "You and Jackal will get to him in time, I know you will. But… I have to do this, Kanin." Turn-ing, I gazed over the dark lake, feeling Jackal's faint glimmer of life, and the ugly yawning decision that awaited me with Zeke. "I won't leave Zeke like that. He's suffering, even if he doesn't realize it. If it were me, you'd do the same."

"And how do you expect to fight him?" Kanin asked softly. "Your weapon is gone."

"I don't know," I muttered, feeling a sharp pang of loss at the reminder. I missed my sword; without the familiar weight across my back I felt oddly naked and incomplete. "I'll find something, I guess. A pipe, a broken bottle. The end of a stick, it doesn't matter."

Kanin sighed. Without a word, he stepped close, took my wrist, and placed the sheath of his thin, razor-sharp dagger into my palm. I blinked as he wrapped my fingers around it, the blade light and lethal in my hand, and looked up at him.

"Kanin, I can't—"

"Take it, Allison." Kanin pulled his arm back, leaving the blade and sheath gripped loosely in my fingers. "You will need something to defend yourself with, as I am not coming with you. If you insist upon facing Ezekiel alone, I will not send you into battle empty-handed."

I swallowed the lump in my throat. "I'll return it, Kanin. I swear."

Kanin raised a hand. "Just listen a moment, Allison. Before we take another step, I want you to be very sure of what you're about to do." He gazed down at me, his eyes and face dark, his mouth pulled into a grim line. "We have done exactly what Sarren wanted, what he planned for us, every step of the way. It was never random chance that you found Ezekiel. He was put here to stop us—his orders were likely to kill us all, keep us from reaching Eden. But Sarren specifically left him behind for *you,* Allison. And Ezekiel will be his most dangerous creation, because he knows you so well." Kanin's gaze narrowed. "No matter what he says, no matter what you tell yourself, you must remember that your human is gone. And the thing Sarren left behind is just a twisted mockery of Ezekiel Crosse."

I bit my lip to stop the stinging in my eyes, struggled to keep my voice from cracking. "I know," I almost snarled. "I know he's gone. Why are you telling me this now?"

"Because I want your eyes to be fully open," my sire replied. "You must know what you are walking into. You cannot let your feelings for Ezekiel cloud your judgment. He will try to kill you, Allison. And he will succeed if you are not fully prepared to end his life." His gaze sharpened, cutting into me. "Are you absolutely certain you can do this?"

No, I thought in despair. *But I won't leave him...like that.*

"Yes," I told Kanin, and my voice was almost steady. The Master vampire regarded me a moment longer, then nodded.

"Then this is where we will part," he stated, turning toward the lake. A cold wind hissed across the water, tugging at our hair and clothes, as Kanin's dark gaze swept over the vastness before us. "I am unsure where Jackal is," he murmured. "I simply know that our blood tie will lead me to him. But I don't know what state he will be in when I find him, if he is in hibernation, severely wounded, or close to Blood Frenzy. It might take me a while to locate his body, and even longer to help him. We might be separated for a good length of time."

I didn't like the idea of splitting up, but there was no better choice. Jackal had to be found, and I had to face Zeke. Better that Kanin find the raider king and get them both out of Old Chicago. That way, if I died—if Zeke killed me—at least they would still have a chance of stopping Sarren. And even that seemed like a long shot now. Time was slipping away from us; Sarren might've already gotten to Eden and destroyed the only hope left for the rest of the world. We might already be too late.

"Where will you go from here?" Kanin asked, turning back to me. I shrugged.

"Back to the city, I guess. Unless you think Zeke is riding around with the patrols?"

"No." Kanin shook his head. "If I know Sarren's mind, Ezekiel will be waiting for you to come to him. Probably in a place that has significance to you both. I do not know where that will be, but..." His brow furrowed. "I'm certain you will find it, and him, fairly soon."

"All right, then." I sighed, taking a step back. Nothing left to do now but go, face the boy I had to kill. "I guess... I'll see you and Jackal when this is over." *One way or another.*

"Allison."

Kanin was still watching me as I turned back, his expression unreadable. "When you have dealt with Ezekiel," he said, "wait for us on the eastern road out of the city. If we're not there by tomorrow evening, go on to Eden without us." Something passed through his eyes, a flicker of emotion, before it was gone. "Be careful."

I nodded. "You too, Kanin."

He turned then, and walked into the black waters of the lake without looking back. I watched until his dark head vanished below the surface, then made my way up the bank, into the street, and back toward the flooded city. Back to Old Chicago and Zeke.

As I slipped through the silent, ruined city, canyons of cement and rusting steel towering overhead, I could feel the lingering pain in my chest start to fade—the physical ache, anyway. My body was finally healing; the blood Kanin had given me was repairing the last of the damage from the wooden spike that had been driven through my heart by the boy I had lost.

My stomach clenched, and not from Hunger this time. I... was really going to do this. Kill Zeke. Because some sick, demented vampire had Turned him into a monster. Wiped his mind clean, destroyed his memories, and twisted him into something I didn't recognize.

I'm going to destroy you, Allie, because he wanted it to be me.

He wanted you to see me tear the heart from your chest and crush it in my fist. It will be poetically ironic, he said, whatever that means.

"Damn you, Sarren," I growled, as the stupid angry tears pressed behind my eyes again. "If I survive this, nothing will stop me from finding you and tearing you in half. The world could be falling apart around us, and I'll still see you dead before it's over, I swear it."

But that didn't stop the ache at what I had to do now.

I shot a quick look at the tops of the ruined skyscrapers, crumbling and skeletal, against an ominous navy blue sky. Not much night left. Maybe a couple hours to sneak into the flooded city, find Zeke, and kill him. But I couldn't turn back. By this time tomorrow night, I would either be on the road to Eden, hopefully with Kanin and Jackal, or I would be a pile of ashes swept away by the wind.

At the edge of the river, I paused, gazing over the water into the flooded city. Apparently, the traps and mines Zeke had set when we'd first come through had been taken down, because the city was no longer empty. Torches and lanterns were lit again, glowing orange in the darkness, and humans milled about the platforms and crossed the walkways and bridges without fear, though not in the numbers I'd seen before. In fact, only a few people seemed to be out, in small groups or pairs, or just wandering the bridges alone. I wondered if the majority of the raider force was out patrolling the city, looking for three escaped vampires. Or maybe they were all with Zeke, and I was walking into another trap.

Slipping into the water, I retraced my steps from the night Jackal had led us through. I swam to the base of his tower but, instead of going through the flooded stairwell, entered the building through the front doors and surfaced in the lobby.

It was empty. No raiders or guards lurked in the shadows or paced the walkways overhead. It seemed odd that no one was expecting me, but I wasn't going to question it. Silently, I made my way to the far wall where, just like on the very first time I'd come through, the elevator sat, still coughing and spitting sparks, in the corner of the room. Not bothering with the lever or the questionable machinery, I climbed atop the rickety box, grabbed the cable, and shimmied up the shaft, going hand over hand, until I reached the very top floor.

It was still quiet, despite the evidence that a brutal fight had raged here not long ago. Streams of bullet holes dotted the floor and walls, punched through plaster and the remaining windows, shattering them. Dried blood was smeared everywhere, on the floor, laced across the walls; there was even a spatter of it on the ceiling, evidence that the two vampires who'd fought their way to get to me had left carnage in their wake. I swallowed hard, gripping Kanin's dagger beneath my coat. Both of them had sacrificed so much to get me out. The least I could do was destroy the evil that Sarren had left behind.

The door to the lab stood open, creaking on its hinges. No guards stood before it, no raiders, no Zeke smiling his awful smile. But sticking out of the wooden frame, glimmering in the dim light through the shattered windows, was a familiar sword.

My sword.

Warily, I edged forward, barely stopping myself from reaching out and snatching the blade from the wall. I couldn't smell any humans nearby, and there was nothing on the ground or the sword itself to indicate a trap. Nothing seemed unusual or out of place, except a small scrap of paper, folded over and shoved halfway down the blade itself.

Carefully, ready to leap back if needed, I reached up, grabbed the hilt of my weapon, and pulled it from the frame.

It slid out easily, and I stepped back, waiting. When nothing happened, I glanced down, tore the slip of paper from the blade, and flipped it open.

I'm at the Pit, the note read, making my insides go cold. *Face me.*

The paper fluttered from my hand and blew away down the hall as I closed my eyes, gripping the sword tightly with my other hand. *All right, Zeke,* I thought, swallowing the lump in my throat. Opening my eyes, I gazed out the broken windows to where a smaller, blackened building sat several blocks away on the corner. Of course, he would be there, just as Kanin had said. A place that was significant to us both. *You've made your point. Let's end this.*

I didn't swim below the city this time. I didn't bother to hide my presence. Zeke knew I was coming; he was expecting me. I walked down the ramp and across the bridges, striding in plain sight toward the Pit, my sword strapped to my back and my face set into a blank, *don't fuck with me* mask.

No one did. Humans took one look at me and quickly backed off, cringed away, or fled my presence entirely. Perhaps Zeke had told them I was coming. Perhaps the rest of the army was away, searching for Kanin and Jackal. No one stepped up to challenge me as I made my way over the rickety bridges and catwalks, ignoring the men and women who watched from the shadows, reeking of fear. That, and the scent of warm blood, stirred the Hunger, urging me to attack, to paint the platforms in red, to drench myself in it before I faced my enemy. I firmly shoved it down. I was here for one person, though if someone *did* try to interfere, they wouldn't live long enough to regret it.

The Pit loomed before me at the end of the walk, the old theater where Zeke and I had first seen Jackal, several months ago. Back then, it had been a crumbling but still majestic brick building, its neon-red CHI AGO sign blazing against the night. That was before we'd rescued our group and set the Pit on fire. Now, the old building was blackened and charred, the roof had partially collapsed, and steel beams poked into the sky like the skeleton of an ancient beast. The CHI AGO sign had gone dark, never to be lit again.

I strode up the walkway and ducked through the window above the submerged front door...and stepped into the Pit.

The place was a mess. What was once the foyer was now a tangle of charred, broken beams, rubble, dangling wires and blackened walls. The walkways circumventing the room had collapsed and were now poking out of the water at odd angles. I picked my way over downed pillars, piles of brick, and scattered shingles, searching for a way into the grand hall. The stairwells leading to the upper levels had been destroyed or completely blocked off, so I followed the wall until I found a section I could climb. Ducking under a fallen beam, I stepped through the door frame and looked around in grim amazement.

I barely recognized the place. Before, this had been an enormous circular room filled with folding seats and aisles where raiders had gathered. I stood on the second-floor balcony, though most of it had collapsed to the flooded ground level, and chairs lay twisted and molding beneath the surface of the water. At the front of the room, a floating stage had once sat beneath an enormous red curtain—the spot where I'd seen my blood brother for the first time. The place where Jackal had stood and promised his raiders he'd find a way to make them immortal.

Now, it looked ravaged. The stage and curtain were gone, burned to nothing, and the once-majestic ceiling was charred and black. From where I stood, I could see that the rows of folding seats were now reduced to black metal frames. Part of the roof had fallen in, creating a giant crater in the center of the room, and water lapped sluggishly over the uneven floor. Far overhead, past jagged beams and collapsed floors, I could see the sky. A faint blue glow filtered down through the hole, creating a hazy light in the center of the room and making me shiver. Dawn was close. Whatever I did, I had to do it fast.

Drawing my sword, I stepped onto the balcony, walked down the aisle of charred seats, and dropped to the first floor. Water sloshed against my boots, soaking the hem of my coat as I made my way into the room, and got deeper the farther I went. By the time I reached the middle of the floor and the circle of hazy light in the center, it was up past my knees.

I paused, gazing around the darkness, searching for him. It was quiet, the only sounds being the rhythmic lapping of water and the faint groans of the building above me. Nothing moved in the shadows. But I knew he was here. I could feel him, watching me.

"I'm here, Zeke," I said quietly, knowing he would hear my voice, that he was close. I hoped that he could not sense the anguish stabbing me through the heart. "Let's get this over with."

There was a faint rustle behind me, and I turned just as Zeke dropped from somewhere overhead, landing with a splash several feet away. His machete was already in hand as he rose, his expression a vacant mask, the hazy light falling around him and making him glow. Meeting my gaze, he smiled, and the light caught the gleam of his fangs as he stepped forward.

I backed away, raising my katana, and Zeke gave an empty chuckle that made my skin crawl.

"Too easy, vampire girl," he said. He shook his head and gave me a mock-sorrowful look. "You shouldn't have come back. You should've left the city, gone after Sarren, and left me here. But you couldn't do that, could you, Allie? Because you couldn't bear the thought of leaving me like this."

I swallowed hard, gripping the hilt of my sword, keeping the deadly blade between us. "I don't want to do this, Zeke."

He cocked his head, smirking. "You could always let me kill you," he suggested. "Make it easy for both of us."

"That's not going to happen, either."

"No? Why not?" The grin faded, and he turned serious. "I would think it's the least you could do, Allie. After all, I'm dead…because of you."

It felt like he had punched me. I staggered away from him, ice spreading through my veins, and my voice came out choked. "That's…that's not true," I protested weakly. "You don't mean that, Zeke."

"Don't I?" Zeke sneered at me, his face hard. "Think about it. *Everything* that's happened—from New Covington, to Eden, to here—is your fault, vampire girl. Jebbadiah is dead, because you couldn't save him. Kanin was tortured and nearly killed, because you *had* to see if Stick was all right, and he betrayed you both to the Prince. Everyone in Eden is going to die, because you let Sarren get away." His eyes glittered with hate. "And I… I'm dead, because you came into my life, and I was stupid enough to fall in love with a monster. *You* killed me, Allie. Not Sarren. I'm a vampire now, because of you."

Every word, every accusation, hit like a knife, slicing me open. But the last nearly dropped me to my knees. Tears blurred my vision, and I turned from Zeke, slumping against a section of roof that had fallen in. *My fault.* Jackal had been right. It was my fault that Zeke was dead, my fault for everything.

"You should have died," Zeke went on in that cold, ruthless voice, stepping forward. I looked up, blinking through tears, to face that accusing glare. "If you had only refused Kanin's offer, if you had just let yourself die as a human, instead of becoming a monster, none of this would have happened." He raised his machete, the light gleaming down the deadly blade, and pointed it at me, narrowing his eyes. "You owe me, vampire girl. Let me end it, tonight. No more pain, no more grief, no more senseless, bloody deaths. I promise, you won't feel a thing. And you can take your evil from the world for good."

I blinked, shaken from my paralyzing indecision, as Zeke's voice came back to me. Something he'd told me once, not very long ago, before he'd died and become this twisted monstrosity.

You're not evil. No one who fights so hard to do the right thing is evil.

I backed away. This wasn't Zeke, I reminded myself. Zeke, *my* Zeke, was dead. This was a vampire who'd been sired by my worst enemy, who knew exactly what to say to throw me off, make me question everything. He could get to me because he *knew* me, or he had when he was human. He knew my secret fears and worst nightmares. The difference was, the real Zeke would never use them against me.

"No," I said, bringing my weapon up in a gesture of defiance. "I admit, I made some mistakes in my life, but what's done is done, and I can't go back and change them. And even...even if what you say is true, that it is my fault that you died... I don't regret anything that happened between us. This is Sarren talking, not you. Not the Zeke I remember." He stared at me blankly, and I straightened, wiping away the last of the tears. "I promised someone I'd keep fighting, and I intend to do that, for however long it takes. No one gets to decide what kind of monster I am but me." I remembered my vow, made in that tiny closet when I'd nearly lost myself, and my resolve grew. "And I'm not going to kneel down and die. Not for you, not for anyone."

Zeke smiled. Not one of his old smiles; this one was cruel and bloodthirsty, his fangs sliding out of his gums as he bared them in an evil grin. "All right, vampire girl," he said, twirling his blade in a graceful arc. "You want to do it the hard way. That's fine. I was actually hoping you'd say that."

And he lunged.

CHAPTER 9

I dodged, bringing the katana up to meet his blow, and the two blades clashed with a metallic screech that rippled down my spine. The shock of it vibrated through my arms, even as I ducked Zeke's second swing, a vicious cut to the neck that would've severed the head from my body if I hadn't moved. Stumbling back, I blocked yet another strike to my face, seeing Zeke's eager, hungry gaze across the swords. His blows were savage, lethal; he wasn't holding back, and if I didn't get my act together, he was going to kill me.

I snarled my anger, my rage at the unfairness of it all, and lashed out, putting all my hatred and grief behind the blow. The katana met Zeke's sword, hammered through, and bit deep into his shoulder even as he twisted out of the way. He hissed in pain, stumbling back, and I went for him again, sweeping my blade down at his neck.

He dodged, swiping his machete at my face, leaping away to put distance between us. Retreating a few steps, he reached back and grabbed the twisted hulk of a theater chair, half buried in water and fallen rock. With a snarl, he wrenched the entire seat free, metal frame and all, and hurled it at my head.

I ducked, nearly flattening myself to the ground to do so,

and the chair crashed into the rubble pile behind me with an earsplitting screech. Bits of rock and stone showered me as I scrambled upright, barely raising the katana in time to deflect Zeke's sword as he attacked again. I caught his blade, but didn't see the rock clutched in his fist until it hammered into the side of my head, knocking me down.

Pain erupted through my skull as I hit the water and instantly rolled to my back, hearing the hiss of the machete strike the place where I'd just been. I could feel something hot running down my face as I kicked out desperately, striking Zeke's knee and causing him to fall, too. We both stood unsteadily, dripping with water and blood, raising our weapons to circle each other again.

Blinking blood from my eyes, I struggled to contain the Hunger and bloodlust, which had emerged with the sudden violence and was burning like fire through my veins. I couldn't lose control now. Zeke, facing me across the water with blade in hand, had lost that eager, bloodthirsty smile. His fangs were out, his eyes flat and cold as he circled, every inch a predator. My stomach twisted. Human Zeke, for all his determination, grit and stubborn resolve to fight, had never been a killer.

"Come on, vampire girl," he taunted in a low, snarling voice. "Don't tell me that's all you've got."

I hissed in return and lunged, cutting at his head, and he leaped back. As I slashed at him a second time, he darted forward, blocked with his weapon, and lashed out with his fist, striking me in the temple. I staggered, pirouetted with the motion, and brought my blade sweeping up, slicing a gash across his stomach and chest. He snarled, backing away as blood seeped through his shirt, and reached for something at the small of his back. I realized what he was going for and tried to get to him before he could pull it out, but wasn't fast enough. Zeke yanked a pistol from beneath his shirt and fired six shots into me, point-blank. My chest exploded with blood and agony, and I screamed, knocked back with the force of the eruptions.

Slumping to one knee in the water, I pressed a hand to my chest, feeling blood seep between my fingers as the wounds slowly healed, and the Hunger surged with a roar. Gritting my teeth, I raised my sword to meet Zeke's weapon slicing down at my neck. The katana met the knife edge and thrust it away, but the weapon was knocked from my hand. The machete instantly whipped back at my face, and I threw myself aside, feeling it miss my head by millimeters. Landing in the water, I rolled to my feet and instinctively raised my arm to block the vicious slash coming at my neck. I struck Zeke's elbow with jarring force, felt something snap with the blow, and Zeke howled. Lashing out with a kick, he struck me in the chest and sent me flying backward.

I hit the ground again with a splash, striking my head on a fallen beam lying in the water. Dazed, I looked up to see the blade in Zeke's other hand, slicing down at me, and jerked to the side. The machete struck the pillar behind me, sinking deep, leaving him exposed for a split second.

Lunging to my knees, I ducked beneath my enemy, grabbed Kanin's knife from beneath my coat, and stabbed up, plunging the thin, straight blade through his chest, into his heart, and out his back.

Zeke went rigid, his mouth gaping in shock and pain, and for just a moment, I was staring right into his eyes. Zeke stared back, eyes bright with agony, but I thought I saw a flicker of recognition, a hint of the boy I'd known before. Then his eyes glazed over, and the reality of what I'd done caught up to me. With a sob, I tore the blade free and stumbled back, and Zeke swayed a moment in place before falling to his knees in the water.

My hands shook, and I gazed down at the form kneeling in front of me, head bowed and the back of his neck exposed. This was it. It was time. One quick slash; that's all it would take to end this, put Zeke out of his misery for good.

My arms shook as I raised Kanin's dagger, aiming for the back of his skull, though the tears running down my face were making it difficult to see clearly. Zeke didn't move, kneeling motionless at my feet with wounded arm cradled to his chest, as if he knew what was coming. I took a deep breath, steeled my emotions, and brought the blade slicing down.

It never touched him. Halfway down, I jerked myself to a stop, shaking. The blade hovered in the air for a long moment, and try as I might, I couldn't make myself complete the motion. Dammit, what was wrong with me? This wasn't Zeke any longer. If I didn't end this now, he would only heal and come after me again. I couldn't let myself remember. I couldn't allow myself to see those memories of the past, of myself and Zeke...before. Our first meeting in the abandoned town, a vampire and a human boy with wary blue eyes, aiming a gun at her head. That first, secret kiss in absolute darkness, my entire being consumed with wanting him. Lying with Zeke in my old room, my fangs inches from his throat, just listening to his heart as I fell asleep. His smile, his touch, the way he looked at me, with complete and utter faith that I wasn't a monster.

Stop it, Allison. I choked back a sob, cursing my stupid traitorous thoughts. It didn't matter now. This had to be done. Zeke had to die, and there was no one around to do it but me.

I'm so sorry, Zeke.

I gripped the weapon tightly and raised it again, trying to focus through the tears. *One cut,* I told myself. *One quick slice, and it'll be over. He won't feel a thing, and then you won't feel anything, ever again.*

"Do it."

The voice was a strangled whisper, and I froze, staring at the hunched form in shock. Zeke hadn't moved, his head was still bowed, but I could see his shoulders trembling. I tensed, remembering the way he had tricked me in the tower, when I thought he had come back to himself. This was likely another ploy to get me to lower my guard. I'd be stupid to fall for it again.

And yet… I still hesitated, that crazy, stubborn hope insisting on rising up to torment me. What if he was still in there? What if Sarren hadn't destroyed him completely? I gripped Kanin's dagger, feeling like I was being torn in two. I knew the thought was foolish; I knew I should end it right now. This was what my sire had warned me about; I was letting my feelings get in the way of what had to be done. But if I killed Zeke now, I would question this moment for the rest of my life. For eternity.

"What are you waiting for?" Zeke gritted out, and his hands clenched on his knees. I knew he was healing, was probably almost healed, but he still didn't move. And even though his head was bowed, I heard the tears in his voice. "Do it, Allison. Kill me. Please, get it over with."

I made my decision. Foolish, emotional and irrational as it was. Lowering the blade, I stepped back, shaking my head. "No," I whispered, and he gave a strangled sob. "No, I won't kill you, Zeke. Not like this."

"Allie…" A violent shudder racked Zeke's body. Slowly, he pushed himself to his feet, dripping water and blood, wrapped his arms around himself, and didn't move. He stood with his back to me, shivering, the machete shining in the water at his feet. Cautiously, I stepped toward him, and his head rose and turned, just a little, in my direction.

"Wrong choice, vampire girl."

He whirled with frightening speed, clamped one hand around my throat, and slammed me back into a pillar. I instinctively brought my weapon up, but Zeke grabbed my wrist with his free hand, the one that had been fractured a few seconds ago, and turned the weapon back on me. I felt the razor edge of Kanin's dagger against my throat and looked up to meet Zeke's blank smile.

"You should've killed me," he whispered, and pressed the blade forward.

I tensed, fighting his arm, feeling the knife's edge bite into my neck. "Zeke," I gritted out, straining to keep him and the dagger at bay. "I know you can hear me. I know this isn't what you want. Please...stop...."

Zeke suddenly closed his eyes, and a shudder racked his body. "Allie," he whispered, his voice strained and desperate. "No. No, I won't do this. Enough." The knife halted, and the arms pinning me to the cement loosened, though Zeke's eyes stayed closed. "Allison," he whispered, like he didn't have much time. "Kill me now. I can't fight this much longer. Hurry!"

"I can't." My eyes burned, and I blinked hard to clear my vision, to keep my gaze on him. "I can't kill you. Please don't make me do this, Zeke."

He growled again and shoved the knife at me. I grabbed his arms, whirled around, and pushed him back into the pillar, wrenching the dagger from his grasp. His eyes snapped open, vicious and crazy once more, and he bared his fangs in my face.

"Make your decision, vampire girl," Zeke snarled, and at that moment, I didn't know which personality was in control. Or if both were speaking. "You're running out of time."

Tears streamed down my face, and I shook my head, frantically trying to think of something. Dammit, there had to be *something* to shock him out of it. What could stop a vampire in its tracks besides a stake to the heart? Was there nothing I could do? Only watch as Zeke slipped from me once more, and in the end, be forced to destroy him after all?

No, I couldn't. I would not lose him again. Not this time.

"Allie," Zeke groaned, and I sensed him slipping, changing into the thing Sarren had created. He tilted his head back, squeezing his eyes shut, and I made my choice. As Zeke opened his eyes, his expression savage once more, I dropped the dagger, stepped forward, and sank my fangs into his throat.

He gasped, going rigid against me. His hands came up to grip my arms, crushing them in a grip of steel, but I barely felt them. His blood seeped past my lips and spread over my tongue, a thick, sluggish river. Different. It was different than when he'd been human, sweet and earthy and very much Zeke. This was darker somehow. Hot and strong and powerful, and completely intoxicating. I could suddenly *feel* him, the real him. I could feel his thoughts and churning emotions. *Confusion. Despair. Fear.* And below that, a rippling undercurrent of something so powerful it was almost overwhelming.

Flashes of memory invaded my thoughts, carried through his blood. The horrible night with Sarren; his agony as the vampire slowly cut him open, demanding he betray everyone he loved, and his absolute despair when he gave in to the torture. Another scene: him standing in the shadows, watching me struggle with a flimsy tent on an open, windy plain, hoping the tent would fall just so he could go talk to me. A flash of pain as he endured one of Jebbadiah's many beatings, knowing he would never live up to the old man's expectations. A memory of New Covington, of slow dancing with me in a dark corner, piano music swirling around us, and realizing how much he would sacrifice, how far he would go, for us to be together.

That very first night in Old Chicago, when we went to

rescue our group from the raider king and, kneeling across from me in utter darkness, he realized that he was completely, irrevocably in love...with a vampire.

A little frightened at the depth of emotion sweeping through me, I tried drawing back, but Zeke shivered and slid his arms around me, pressing me to him. Urging me to go on. Closing my eyes, I sank my fangs in deeper, melting into him, and Zeke groaned softly.

I took only a little, knowing he was badly wounded and had little blood to spare. But it was hard, pulling away, forcing my fangs to retract. For a second, I'd seen the deepest, darkest parts of him, known every emotion and secret fear. I'd never felt so connected to anyone.

Looking up, I met Zeke's gaze and trembled. His eyes were no longer blank, but shone with an intensity I'd never seen before. His lips were partially open, and his fangs gleamed inches from my face.

I swallowed, knowing what he wanted...and tilted my head back, baring my throat to him.

He lunged, and for a split second, I felt a jolt of fear, remembering the horrible pain when Kanin had bitten me. I tensed, but then Zeke's fangs sank into my flesh. There was a tiny, initial stab of pain, and then warmth spread through me, turning my bones to liquid. It burned through my veins, soothing and wonderful, silencing even the constant ache of the Hunger, the raging of the demon. I closed my eyes, holding his head to my neck as he yanked me against him. Zeke growled, driving his fangs deep, and I gasped, arching into him, desperate to get closer.

He can see you. A tiny, panicked voice emerged from the layers of bliss, making me frown. *He can see you now, the real you. Who you really are, behind that wall you put up for everyone.*

What will he think now that he knows what you really are? A killer.
A monster.

I didn't care. *Let him see,* I thought, holding him more
tightly, urging him on. I thought of the moments we'd shared,
my reluctance to trust anyone, especially a human, and how he
had broken down every wall with his unshakable faith until I
had to let him in. I remembered the look in his eyes just before he'd kissed me, knowing I was a monster, not letting it
scare him away. I let him see the utter devastation his death
had brought, how the demon had nearly won, and how it was
my memory of *him* that finally drove it back.

This is me, I thought, wondering if he could hear my
thoughts, as well. *All of me. I'm here, Zeke. I won't let you go.*

Abruptly, Zeke stiffened. Pulling his fangs from my throat,
he shoved me backward, his eyes wide with horror, as if just
realizing what he'd done. I stumbled, caught myself, and faced
him again, ready to leap away if he attacked.

He stared at me, blood smearing his lips and trickling from
the corner of his mouth, his face contorted in anguish. With
a shaking hand, he touched a finger to his lips and pulled it
down to stare at the crimson spotting his skin. His eyes went
dark with shock and disbelief, and he took one staggering step
back, shaking his head.

"Zeke," I whispered, stepping forward. My legs shook,
possibly from blood loss, and I nearly fell. Zeke didn't notice,
staring at his bloody fingers. He looked horribly sick, like he
might actually throw up if he could. "Wait."

"Why didn't you kill me?"

I stopped. His voice was so harsh it was almost a growl, his
gaze desperate and accusing as he glanced up. "Why, Allie?"
he whispered. His fangs were still out, and he bared them
at me in an unconscious snarl. "Why didn't you end it? You
promised me you would."

I swallowed my own desperate reply, meeting his con-
demning stare. "I promised I wouldn't Turn you if you were
dying," I choked back, trying to steady myself. "I promised
I'd let you go. I never said I would help you destroy yourself."

"No," Zeke agreed, slumping. "No, you didn't. I can't
blame you for that." For a moment, he stood there, the hazy
blue light falling softly around him. Raising his head, Zeke
looked at the ruined ceiling, letting the light wash over his
face. Glancing at the hole, I felt a twinge of nervousness. The
stars had faded, and dawn was very close.

I looked back at Zeke, who had closed his eyes, hands
clenched at his sides. "It's up to me, then," he murmured, his
voice broken but determined. He took a step back. "I'll have
to do it myself."

"Zeke." Suddenly very afraid, I started forward, wooziness
forgotten. "Wait. What are you doing?"

He gave me one last, anguished glance. "Thank you," he
whispered. "For…bringing me out of it. For helping me remember. I… What you showed me… I don't deserve it. Not
now. But at least I'm free of Sarren." He glanced up at the ceiling, at the open sky overhead, his expression resigned. "Kill
him for me, vampire girl," he murmured. "Promise me you'll
kill him. Send him to hell, and then I'll finish the job myself."

Ice shot through my veins. "Zeke, no."

But he turned and fled, covering the room in several long
strides, ignoring my cries for him to stop, and vanished from
the chamber.

I chased him, following him out one of the doors and up a
crowded, rubble-filled staircase, scrambling to catch up. Zeke
ignored my calls, not looking back once, moving through the
ruined theater like he was possessed. When his path became
blocked by debris or walls or the fallen roof, he quickly chose

another direction, but continued to move steadily upward. I had to push myself to keep pace with him, sometimes even climbing the crumbling walls of the theater, toward the roof and the lightening sky.

Finally, I pulled myself up a final beam, onto the blackened, skeletal roof of the old theater. Wind tossed my hair as I straightened, gazing around frantically. The gaping hole of the building plunged straight down several feet away, crisscrossed with steel girders that hung precariously over the edge. The top of the CHI AGO sign hung crookedly from the far wall, and beyond it, a terrifying orange glow had crept over the horizon.

A lean figure in black stood across from me on the rooftop, facing that oncoming light. He perched at the very edge of a metal girder, suspended out over nothing, the wind tearing at his hair and clothes. My vampire instincts were screaming at me to get inside, away from the killing rays of the sun. There wasn't any time left. But I forced myself to walk carefully across the roof, easing around the gaping pit, to where the lean, pale figure stood, awaiting the dawn.

"Zeke." My voice shook. Terrified, of both the rising sun and the thought of watching Zeke slowly erupt into flame right in front of me, I stepped to the very edge of the building and stared at the figure at the end of the beam. So close and yet, a lifetime away. "Don't do this."

He barely inclined his head, continuing to face the rising sun. "Go back inside, Allison," he whispered, his voice calmer now. Resolute. "You don't want to see me burn. From what Sarren told me, it's quite painful."

His voice trembled on the last sentence. I swallowed my fear, the instinct to take his advice and flee inside as quickly as I could, and inched forward. "Not without you." He didn't reply, and my voice became desperate. "Zeke, please, listen. You can fight it. I can show you how."

"Do you want to know my first memory as a vampire?" The words were flat, emotionless. He didn't seem to have heard me. The wind tossed his hair and clothes as he stood unmoving, silhouetted against the horizon. "The first few nights," he went on, "I didn't know what was happening. It was all flashes, blips of emotion and memory, like a fever dream. I didn't know what Sarren was doing, or even how long it lasted—everything was hazy. Until one night."

He bowed his head, oblivious or uncaring of the faint pink glow spreading across his skin. I trembled, clamped down on my instinct to run, and stayed where I was.

"I woke up in a barn," Zeke went on, in that same dead voice. "And when I did, I couldn't remember anything. I didn't know where I was, or who I was. I just knew… I was starving."

Dread twisted my insides. I suddenly had a horrible suspicion of where this story was going, and wanted to rip Sarren apart for his cruelty. I remembered my first awakening as a newly Turned vamp; the confusion, fear, rage and Hunger that followed, and my mentor's patient care in explaining everything. That hadn't happened for Zeke.

"I wasn't alone, of course," Zeke continued softly. "Sarren had locked me in and barred the door from the outside along with about a half dozen other people. Just simple farmers, women and a couple kids. They weren't even armed." He paused, clenching his fists, as if the next memories were more than he could bear. "And I… I killed them, Allie. Every single one. I slaughtered them all."

He choked, one hand going to his face, as I fought back tears, as well. "Zeke," I managed, knowing I couldn't imagine what he was feeling now, the guilt and utter horror of what he'd done. "I know it sounds horrible, but…that wasn't you. When we're Turned, when we first wake up, we don't know what we're doing. The Hunger takes over and we attack the first thing we see. Sarren knew that. You can't blame it on yourself."

"No." He whirled on me, his gaze feverish. The desolation on his face made my stomach twist. "You don't understand. I remember killing those people. I remember tearing them apart and...and I *loved* it, Allie." His face screwed up with revulsion and self-loathing. "Don't you see?" he whispered. "I'm not like you. You've fought this thing since the day you were Turned. I've...already fallen." He blinked, and twin tracks of red slipped down his cheeks. "I'm a demon, and the sooner I take myself out of this world, the better."

It was very bright now, or it seemed that way to my light-sensitive eyes. I didn't know how much time we had left, but I couldn't leave him here to die alone. "You're not a demon," I pleaded, as my own tears spilled over to join his. "You're just as strong as I am, Zeke. You can fight this. It doesn't have to control you—"

"I'm a vampire now!" Zeke exploded, his face anguished. More crimson lines coursed down his skin as he gestured violently toward the rising sun. "I died, Allison. I'm dead! What kind of existence can I expect from now on? Feeding on humans, only coming out at night, constantly fighting to stay in control, to not rip people apart for fun. Living for eternity as a cursed thing?" He sobbed. I couldn't answer, because my own throat was filled with tears. Wiping his eyes, Zeke looked up at me, his expression desolate.

"My father is dead," he whispered with a hopeless gesture. "I can't go back to Eden. My family won't have anything to do with me now that I'm a vampire, and I can't ever go near them, because I don't want to put them in danger. Everyone I love will hate and fear me, and they have every right to."

He gave another sob, closing his eyes and turning from me. "I should have died," he choked out. "Back in that lab with Sarren. I wanted to die. What's keeping me here, Allison? Why should I stay?"

"Because *I* love you, you idiot!"

He blinked, looking stunned. I slumped, feeling the tears still trickle from my eyes as I looked up at him, beseeching.

"That night in the lab," I began in a soft, resigned voice, "when you...died... I lost myself for a little while. I almost became the monster you always hated." Shame and guilt rose up once more, mingling with the fear and desperation. Memories of the night I had nearly crossed the line. "I thought it would be easier to let go of everything that made me human, to feel nothing. But I didn't let it win, Zeke. Because of *you*."

Zeke didn't move or look away from me. I met his gaze head-on, uncaring of the red lines down my cheeks or the sudden, instinctive fear of those three words that left me wide open. "You told me once I wasn't evil," I said firmly. "That I wasn't a demon, and I believed you. I still believe you." I took a careful step forward, so that I was right at the edge of the girder, just a few feet away if I reached for him. "And I swear to you, Zeke, I'll help you fight it. Every step of the way. I won't let you become a monster. But you have to trust me now. *Please*."

The top of the sun broke over the horizon. Faint orange light spilled across the rooftops, and a blinding pain speared me right in the eyes. I hissed, half turning away, feeling the skin on my cheeks, forehead, hands, everywhere that wasn't covered, erupt with pain.

"Go back," Zeke choked out, his voice tight with agony. I peeked up and saw him silhouetted against the light, tendrils of smoke beginning to curl from his bare arms. His eyes were anguished as they met mine. "Allie, get inside. Leave me."

"No." Straightening, I turned to face the sun, feeling the light sizzle across my face. Putting one foot on the beam, I held out a hand, my fingers already red and raw. My tears felt like acid, searing down my cheeks. "I'm not leaving without you," I said hoarsely. "So, you either come with me, or we both burn."

Zeke closed his eyes. For another moment, he stood there, head bowed, fighting with himself. Finally, he let out a sob, a heartbroken, defeated sob...and stepped forward, placing his hand in mine. I pulled him from the edge, hurried to the gaping hole in the roof, and dropped into darkness, as the sun climbed fully over the rooftops and painted everything behind us in orange light.

CHAPTER 10

I woke the next night starving and momentarily confused. I didn't recognize the room I was in, and there was a body curled next to mine, still as death. Carefully, I levered myself to an elbow and looked around, taking in the small, windowless room. Moldy chairs sat on top of each other along the wall, and boxes of rags covered in dust and cobwebs were stacked in the corners. A huge, once-white dresser stood at the front of the room, the large, square mirror above it now fractured into a dozen pieces.

Then my gaze flickered down to see Zeke's pale, unconscious form beside me, and everything from the night before came flooding back.

He's really here. For a moment, I just watched him, letting relief spread through me like a slow flame, driving away the dark. Last night, I'd thought I would have to kill him. Last night, I'd experienced the worst moment of my life when he'd stood atop that roof, waiting for the sun to end his existence.

But it hadn't. He was here, miraculously back from the dead, technicalities aside. It still didn't seem real, like this was some sort of dream, though vampires didn't dream. Zeke was back. Against all odds, against torture and mind compulsions and death and everything that Sarren had done to him, he was still here. Still alive.

The tricky part would be keeping him that way.

I won't let you become a demon, I swore, gazing down at him. He lay motionless beside me, no slow breaths, no heartbeat, no warmth radiating from his skin. Thankfully, we had both healed from our deadly brush with the sun; no traces of burned flesh remained. Though I remembered looking down at my hand just before I fell asleep, and seeing that the tips of my fingers were black and charred. The memory made me shiver. I'd almost died last night, almost let the sun cook me alive, turn me into a smoldering pile of ashes.

I'll do it again, if it means saving you.

Zeke slept on. I put a hand against his cheek, feeling the smooth, cold skin beneath my fingers. He was a corpse—a living corpse, like me, but we would deal with this together. *I promise, Zeke. You won't become a monster. I'll fight for both of us if I have to, I swear it.*

A darkness invaded my thoughts then, the reality of my decision rising up to overshadow everything; I'd gone to face Zeke instead of continuing on toward Eden and the insane vampire hell-bent on destroying the world. Of two impossible decisions, I'd chosen to turn my back on my survival instincts…and follow my heart. A year ago, Allie the Fringer would've done anything to keep living. She would've mocked the attachments to the small group I now considered family, encouraged me to sever all ties to protect myself. But I couldn't do that anymore.

I wonder if Kanin ever found Jackal?

Suddenly anxious and feeling a little guilty, I shifted to one knee, closed my eyes, and reached out for my kin.

The instant pulse through our blood tie nearly made me collapse in relief. They were there. Both of them. I felt Kanin's presence, strong and steady, and another, fainter tug that had to be Jackal. I didn't know where they were. I didn't know if they were waiting for me outside Old Chicago, or had gone ahead to Eden. I just knew they were alive. That was enough. If anything, the two of them could stop Sarren if I failed.

They're all right. I relaxed, slumping back against the wall. *They're alive. Even Jackal is alive. We're all okay for now.* I glanced at Zeke, still dead to the world, knowing he could wake at any moment. *Now, we just have to get out of Old Chicago without being pumped full of lead.*

The floorboards creaked beside me as Zeke stirred, coming out of sleep, and I tensed. I didn't know what state of mind he'd be in when he woke up. If he was teetering on the edge of Blood Frenzy, I'd have to stop him from losing it. With his wounds, he had to be just as Hungry as me, and he had less practice in controlling himself.

I desperately hoped that he hadn't woken with a new resolve to meet the sun or to have someone drive a stake through his chest, but the possibility hovered at the edge of my mind, dark and terrifying.

Zeke rose slowly, pushing himself to one elbow, then to his knees. I shifted behind him, not touching, just letting him know I was there, that I was close. But he didn't make any attempt to get up. He wasn't shaking, or crying, or hunched forward in misery. He just knelt there with his hands on his knees, staring at the floor, at nothing.

"It wasn't a nightmare, then."

I swallowed. His voice was low, flat. The tone used when you're so numb you can't feel anything anymore. When you've been so cut open from the inside, you've completely bled out, and there's nothing left. Fear twisted my stomach. This was going to be hard. For Zeke, it might be impossible.

"No," I told him simply. "It wasn't."

I waited, dreading his next words, that he might ask me to take my sword and end his life. Or that I leave so he could do it himself.

"Where are Jackal and Kanin?" he finally asked, surprising me. "Did you come here alone?"

I nodded. "Yes, but they're okay. At least, I think they are." Briefly, I searched for them again, feeling two separate pulls, coming from the same direction. "I can feel both of them, through our blood tie. Jackal was pretty badly hurt when… when we fled the tower the first time, and we got separated. Kanin went back to look for him."

"So I didn't manage to kill him after all," Zeke muttered, and I couldn't tell if he was relieved or disappointed. I suspected the latter. I also suspected this stoic front Zeke was putting up was a horrible lie, that underneath he was a writhing mess of emotions, and it worried me.

"Are you all right?" I asked. My gaze flicked to the back of his shirt, and the tiny hole in it, right over his heart. Where I had shoved Kanin's knife through his body. "How are you feeling?"

"Hungry." Stated so bluntly that I shivered. This wasn't right. I hadn't expected Zeke to be perfectly fine when he woke up, far from it, but this utter lack of emotion wasn't him. I hoped it was just the shock, and he would eventually start acting more like himself again. Though now that he was a vampire, I didn't know what "normal" was for him anymore.

I had the sudden, disconcerting thought that, maybe, this *was* the real Zeke now that he was a vampire. I certainly had changed from the time I'd become undead; maybe the old Zeke, the human Zeke, really was gone forever.

"Starving, actually," Zeke went on, oblivious to my dark thoughts. "And that's a problem, now that I don't control the army anymore. Sarren put me in charge when he left, but I'm not their boss any longer. Once they find out I can't give them what they want, they'll try to kill me, too."

"They don't know that," I said. "No one has been here, no one knows what happened last night. As far as anyone can tell, I entered the Pit and never came out again. They probably think you killed me."

Zeke flinched. It was small, barely noticeable since he was turned away from me, but I saw it.

Sliding forward, I reached out and put a hand on his back. "I'm still here," I said softly. "We beat Sarren's sick little game, and he has no hold on you anymore."

I hope. I desperately hoped the compulsion was broken and Zeke was truly free. But if not, if Zeke fell under Sarren's control again, then I would snap him out of it one more time. And again, and again. As often as I had to, until Sarren was dead.

"Allie." Zeke bowed his head, and his shoulders trembled. I felt him take a deep breath, as if to compose himself, a reflex left over from his time as a human. "I know we have to stop Sarren," he continued, his voice a little stronger. "I know that's the most important thing now, that putting an end to his plans takes precedence over everything else, even my own feelings. I know that, and I'm with you. Don't worry about that part." He shivered again, though his voice remained calm. "I'll go with you to Eden, and I don't intend to stop fighting until I know Sarren is dead. But after that, after I'm sure everyone is safe and Sarren is gone…" Zeke paused, now uncertain. "I… I don't know if I can do this. If I even want to try." He hesitated again, then in a near whisper, added, "You might have to…"

"Stop it," I growled at him. "You've asked me this before, and it nearly killed me to say yes. I won't let you become a monster. I'll fight it with you every step of the way. But I will not help you destroy yourself."

"I never wanted this," Zeke said harshly, clenching his fists. "I would've rather died, and Sarren knew that. His evil is still inside me. What if it turns on you? What if I can't help being more like Sarren than like you and Kanin?"

Having Sarren for a sire was something I couldn't even imagine, and it made me feel cold inside. "It doesn't work like that, Zeke," I told him, praying I was right. "And even if that was the case, you still have the choice to fight it. To not be like him."

"And if I'm not strong enough?"

"I don't believe that for a second."

He shook his head. "You have more faith in me than I do, vampire girl," he murmured, almost to himself. "I hope you don't come to regret it."

"Boss!"

The shout came from below, rough and guttural. It was followed by another voice, both sounding rather desperate. Zeke raised his head at the sound, and his eyes gleamed. Hunger rippled across his features, and he shook himself before breaking away and rising to his feet.

"Raiders," he muttered. "They probably saw you come in last night and are wondering which one of us is dead."

As he said this, there was a burst of gunfire outside, making both of us jerk up. Almost instinctively, I reached out with my blood tie and felt two pulses, very close, coming from the same direction as the shots.

"Kanin," I whispered. "Jackal. What are they doing here? They were supposed to wait for us outside the city."

"Looks like they came back for you," Zeke said. Reaching to his back holster, he took out his pistol and checked the clip with a frown. "Three bullets left," he muttered. "And I don't have my blade. Do you?"

I shook my head. My katana was on the first floor where

I'd dropped it, frantic to stop Zeke from killing himself. I still had Kanin's dagger, but I really wanted my sword. Zeke nodded grimly, and holstered the gun again.

"Nothing for it, then. Let's go."

"Zeke, wait."

He ignored me and swept across the room. I followed him out the door into an open corridor where the entire wall had fallen away, showing the yawning crater several floors down. I hurried forward just as Zeke dropped from the edge of the balcony into the pit below. Frantic voices drifted up from the bottom, and I walked silently to the edge, gazing down.

"Boss!" Almost directly below, two large, brutish men suddenly turned, guns in hand, and rushed toward Zeke. I followed them, unseen, from above. "Hey, we got a situation," one said, not seeming to notice the way Zeke was advancing on him, eyes hard. "You need to get out there, right now." There was another burst of gunfire, closer this time, followed by a desperate yell. The raiders flinched and glanced back toward the walls.

"The vamps are here, boss," the second human gasped. "The little bitch's friends are coming. Our old king. We tried holding them off, but they got into the city somehow and are on their way right now—"

He didn't get any further. Zeke pounced on him with a snarl, driving him into the floor with a splash and a terrified shriek. The other yelled and raised his gun, but I dropped from the balcony and hit him from behind, burying my fangs in his throat. Hot blood filled my mouth, soothing and wonderful. There was no guilt this time. I kept drinking until there was nothing left, until the body was a limp sack of meat and bones, drained and lifeless.

Letting the corpse slump to the water, I looked around for Zeke.

He rose slowly, fangs out, watching his own raider's body sink below the water's surface and disappear. I kept a close eye on his face, waiting for the disgust and loathing to hit, for the horror of what he'd done to sink in, but there was nothing. His expression remained blank, his eyes flat, and my stomach twisted.

Shots boomed close by. I jerked, then searched frantically for my weapon, trying to spot the shine of steel beneath the water. I found my katana right where I'd left it, dropped when Zeke had kicked me in the chest. The fabric around the hilt was soaked through, but it seemed perfectly fine otherwise. I flicked water off the blade before sheathing it again. Zeke's machete lay a few yards away, glimmering in the spot where he'd knelt and waited for me to end his life. He sloshed over to pick up the weapon before turning to me, his expression still blank and cold.

"Let's go."

We started across the pit but had taken only a few steps when gunfire boomed along the balcony seats above us, flaring white, and a second later, a familiar roar shook the darkness. Pistol fire barked, fast and frantic. A scream, and then the scent of blood filled the air a moment before a body dropped from the balcony and hit the water with a splash. I tried not to notice that its head was missing as a tall, bloody figure stepped out of the shadows to the edge of the balcony and smirked down at us.

"Oh, good," Jackal remarked, his dangerous gold gaze fixed not on me, but on Zeke. "You're still alive."

He leaped from the balcony, making a splash when he landed, and grinned demonically as he rose, fangs gleaming. "I was hoping you'd be here," he said, glaring at Zeke. "No one takes what's mine and gets away with it, not even you, bloodbag. When I'm done, you're gonna wish you stayed dead the first time."

A pair of raiders appeared where Jackal had been moments before. Seeing their former king, they leveled automatic machine guns into the pit and fired, spraying the water with lead. Jackal snarled, sounding more irritated than anything, and we ducked behind rubble piles as bullets hissed around us and sparked off the stones.

Abruptly, the gunfire ceased. I peeked out to see another body drop into the crater as Kanin snapped the neck of the other from behind. More shouts echoed behind him, and the Master vampire melted back into the darkness.

Kanin is here, too? I thought as a growl echoed behind me. I whirled just in time to see Jackal lunge behind our section of wall, shoving me aside as he did. I hit the ground and rolled upright as my brother grabbed Zeke by the throat, turned, and slammed him into the broken stones. His face was vicious as he leaned in, smiling.

"You know, I didn't always hate you," Jackal said, as Zeke grabbed his wrists, trying to pry him off. "But I think I'd like you better if you were a little shorter. Maybe a head shorter, wha'd'ya say, bloodbag?"

I drew my sword, intending to leap in and force Jackal to back the hell off. But at that moment, Zeke bared his fangs with a savagely inhuman snarl and drove a fist into Jackal's ribs. I heard the distinct snap of bones, and Jackal jerked, grunting in pain. Before I could respond, Zeke spun and rammed the other vampire into the concrete, slamming his head into the rock with another sickening crack, before shoving him away. Jackal slumped into the water, holding his side, and I grabbed Zeke's arm.

He turned on me, and his eyes were cold. Merciless. The monster, staring back at me. It sent an icy lance through my insides, and I dropped his arm, resisting the urge to back up. Zeke's gaze shifted away as if he'd forgotten me, and I shivered with the sudden realization. For a split second, for the very first time, I had been afraid of him.

On the ground, Jackal started to laugh.

"Oh, yeah," he wheezed, rolling into a sitting position, one hand still around his ribs. His eyes still glowed as he stared at Zeke, appraising. "I forgot. The little bloodbag joined the undead club a few weeks ago. Now he can throw a proper punch. My mistake." He rose, shedding water, and gave himself a shake, glaring at Zeke with his fangs out. "I won't forget again."

"Jackal, stop it." Shaking myself out of my daze, I stepped in front of Zeke, my katana between him and my blood brother. Zeke didn't move; I could sense him watching us, patient and calculating, the monster barely restrained. I had the sudden, disturbing thought that this Zeke could be worse than the one Sarren had created, and violently shoved it back. "This is stupid. You can see he's not under the compulsion anymore."

"I see that," Jackal agreed, his smile no less ominous. "It's not going to stop me from tearing him in half. Like I mentioned before, I'm kind of a sore loser."

He stepped forward, and I did, too, raising my weapon. Shots still echoed around us, getting closer all the time, but I trusted that Kanin was still out there, taking care of the raiders. I couldn't worry about them now, not until I was sure Zeke and my blood brother wouldn't try to kill each other. Again.

"Take your city, if you want it," Zeke said. "It's yours, I'll gladly turn it over."

"Oh, will you, bloodbag?" Jackal sneered. "That's awfully generous of you. But you're missing the point." He gestured back at the balcony. "I don't give a shit about this place, or the minions. I can get more if I really need to. They were always just a means to an end." He narrowed his eyes. "But I'll be damned if I let any spawn of Sarren's share space with me. That kind of crazy sneaks up on you when you least expect it, and everyone around you suddenly has their throats cut."

"That's not going to happen," I argued, and Jackal shot me a disgusted look. "He's fine, Jackal. He's not a threat anymore." *And even if he is, I'm not going to let you kill him now.*

"If you believe that, then you're more gullible than I thought." Jackal shook his head. "Stop trying to fool yourself, sister. You know what's happening here. You're not that stupid." He jerked his head in Zeke's direction. "Look at him. Take a good, long look at your precious Ezekiel and tell me he's exactly the same. But I bet you can't stare lovingly into his eyes for two seconds without seeing Sarren looking right back at you."

I shuddered, and Jackal nodded slowly. "You know I'm right, sister. His mind is broken. It's only a matter of time before it falls apart. I'm not killing him because he screwed up my city, took my minions, and, frankly, pissed me off. I'm putting him out of his misery." He gave an evil, indulgent smile. "Consider this a mercy. Like shooting a three-legged deer."

"No," I growled and moved with Jackal as he came forward again, my katana raised. My mind was made up. "You want him, you'll have to go through me."

Jackal's face twisted like he'd swallowed something foul. "I'm surrounded by bleeding heart idiots," he muttered. "Sister, you realize you're protecting *Sarren's* progeny. The Grand Lunatic himself? For all we know, this is exactly what the psychopath wants."

"I don't believe that," I retorted, as gunfire nearly drowned out my words, making me wince. The army was almost here. I didn't have a lot of time to convince them—both of them,

Zeke *and* Jackal—that Zeke wasn't like his sire. Even if I was horribly unsure myself.

"Allison." Zeke finally spoke up from behind me, and his voice was resigned. I knew exactly what he was thinking, and snarled at him without taking my eyes from my brother.

"Zeke, don't you dare start with that!"

"What if he's right?"

"I don't care!" I roared, baring my fangs at them both. "I will not watch you die again. I promised I'd help you fight it, and I swear I'm going to kill Sarren. But you're going to have to trust me, Zeke! And you," I said to Jackal, jabbing at him with my sword. "You're one to talk. You want to Turn your whole army into vampires. If they're anything like you, you'll have to watch your back every second of every day. I may not know much about sires and offspring, but I know there's *always* a choice. You don't have to be like your sire. I mean, look at you." I narrowed my eyes at Jackal, curling my lip in a sneer. "Kanin Turned you, and you still became a bastard."

"Boss!"

Gunfire rang out once more. I tensed as a horde of raiders swarmed the room from above, pointing their weapons down into the pit. It seemed the rest of the army had finally caught up. Gripping my sword, I quickly gauged the distance between myself and the balcony, and winced. I was going to get pumped full of lead before this was over.

"Minions, stand the fuck down!"

I jumped as Jackal's voice boomed throughout the chamber, bouncing off rafters and making the water vibrate. It rang through my head, compelling and powerful, and amazingly, whether it was from force of habit or the intensity in Jackal's voice, the humans froze.

"That's better." The raider king gave us all a supremely exasperated look and crossed his arms. "I could hardly think anymore, with all the gunfire and screaming. Party's over, boys," he stated, his clear voice carrying through the stunned silence. "Your new king and I have had a little talk. We've decided you worthless meatsacks aren't worth dying over, and it's better for everyone if we come to an understanding." He turned and gave Zeke a pointed look, raising his eyebrows. "Fifty-fifty split sound about right to you, *partner?*"

He curled a lip on the last word, as if the thought of sharing was deplorable. But Zeke gazed at him and the raiders without interest and shrugged. "I don't care. Do what you want. Sarren is gone, and I'm through with this place."

I swallowed hard. The emptiness in Zeke's voice was even worse than the sadistic taunting, and for a moment, Jackal's warning cast a dark shadow over my thoughts.

"Which means you minions," Jackal added, sauntering up to Zeke and draping an elbow over his shoulder, a gesture which was ignored, "are in a flying shitload of trouble. Too bad you didn't think of that before deciding to stage this little coup. Not that it's terribly surprising, but I'm a little pissed off at the lot of you right now." He smiled, all fangs, as the humans shifted apprehensively. "But, hey, I'm a reasonable guy. I'll offer you bloodbags the same deal as before—follow me, and have a shot at becoming immortal. Refuse, and the three of us—" he gestured to me and Zeke "—will systematically rip the heads from your bodies and send you to a worse hell than this one. Your choice." He chuckled, vicious and eager, and glanced at something over their heads. "But if you meatsacks think you have a shot at taking out three very annoyed vampires *and* one stuck-up Master, then by all means, let's get this massacre started."

The humans turned, craning their necks up and looking behind to where Kanin's tall, imposing figure stood perfectly still on an overhead beam, gazing down at them.

"So, wha'd'ya say, minions?" It wasn't really a question. Jackal's voice was hard, the edge beneath the surface hinting at barely restrained violence. He grinned at them, the smile of a killer, all fangs and glowing eyes, and several raiders shuffled uneasily. "Do we have an understanding? Grovel for my forgiveness now, and I might kill only half of you later."

The raiders hesitated. Several of them looked to Zeke, standing motionless at the edge of the pit. "What about the other vamp's promise?" one called. "He said he'd Turn whoever killed Jackal and brought you his head. Does that offer still stand?"

Jackal laughed, his voice booming through the chamber. "You really think that psycho would've Turned any of you?" he mocked. "Really? Because the messed-up face and obnoxious riddles would've tipped me off." The raider king shook his head, his voice cutting. "He's not coming back, minions," he called. "And if any of you believed for one second that Sarren would keep his promise and not rip your hearts out through your jugulars, then do me a favor and shoot yourself in the face right now, because you're too stupid to keep living."

"Sarren is gone," added a deep, confident voice from overhead. Kanin, watching dispassionately from his perch. "And as Jackal said before, he is not coming back. We are the vampires you must deal with now." The raiders stirred, muttering among themselves, as the Master vampire continued. "You have two clear choices tonight—leave in peace, or stay and fight us all. You might win. Your numbers might overwhelm us. But we *will* decimate this city, and its inhabitants, before we are finished. And neither Sarren nor Ezekiel will protect you."

I stood quietly, sword in hand, waiting to see what the humans would do. I felt like I should say something, but Zeke and Jackal seemed to be handling it well on their own; they were the vamps who had been in charge of this city, not me.

And Kanin, by definition, was a Master and someone you'd best pay attention to. I just had to stand here and look dangerous—well, as dangerous as a thin, seventeen-year-old girl with a katana could look, I supposed. Hopefully the fact that I was a vampire made up for my height.

There were a few heartbeats of tense silence, before one raider snorted and stepped back from the edge.

"Fuck this," he growled, lowering his weapon. His voice echoed through the chamber, and the room seemed to let out its breath. "I ain't fightin' a goddamned pack of bloodsuckers. They want the city, they can have it. I ain't dyin' for this."

That seemed to be the tipping point. As the one raider walked away into the darkness, everyone else lowered their weapons and stepped back from the ledge. Jackal waited a moment longer, until it seemed the danger was truly past, then nodded.

"There, see? I knew we could be civil." Though his voice was amused, his eyes glittered, hinting at future retribution. "Murder and thieving aside, we're not barbarians. Now, get out of here, the lot of you. Your stupid faces are grating on my nerves.

"Oh, and minions?" he added as the room began to empty. Most of the humans looked back, and Jackal gave them a very dangerous smile. "Don't think for a second you've gotten off easy," he warned in a low voice. "I won't forget this. In fact, I think it's high time we brought back the public dismemberments, to remind everyone why it's a bad idea to piss off a vampire king." He grinned up at them, fangs gleaming brightly, and cocked two fingers. "Any volunteers?"

The raiders scattered. Guns clattering, they swiftly drew back from the ledge and fled the room, vanishing through doorways and even through holes in the walls in their haste. For a few seconds, chaos ensued as the army scrambled to get out of Jackal's immediate sight. Then the footsteps disappeared, the voices faded away, and soon the dripping of water and the faint moans of the building around us were all that could be heard.

Jackal smiled into the silence, then turned to the rest of us, smug satisfaction breaking over his face. "And *that*," he stated, looking mostly at Zeke, "is how you rule a raider city."

Zeke didn't answer, but I stepped forward, placing myself between him and Jackal, keeping my sword raised. Jackal eyed me and snorted.

"Relax, sister." The raider king waved an airy hand. "Put up the damn sword before I shove it down your throat. The minions have come to their senses, and as soon as I hang a few heads from the center of town, all will be as it should. We won this round, so untwist your panties and calm down."

I didn't relax. "What about Zeke?"

"What about him?" Jackal shrugged. "You won't let me put him out of his misery, he's your problem now. Besides…" He glanced at Zeke, watching us a few feet away, and smirked. "I'd never thought I'd say this, but the little meatsack has potential. If he doesn't have a meltdown and decide he needs a tan, he might actually be a decent bloodsucker. And by decent, I mean a proper, murdering, 'I eat babies for breakfast' vampire. It's always the nice ones you have to worry about." Jackal smiled at me, cruel and challenging. "Ironic, isn't it, sister? Your innocent, puppy-eyed human could become a worse monster than you. Or me. Or even Sarren. Wouldn't *that* be a hoot?"

I scowled, but at that moment Kanin dropped from the ledge, landing with a barely audible splash a few yards away. I blinked as he rose and glided toward us, his face impassive.

"I thought you and Jackal were going to wait outside the

city," I said, gazing up at him. "Wasn't that the plan? Not that I'm complaining, but why'd you come back?"

One corner of Kanin's mouth twitched, very slightly. "It wasn't entirely my decision to return, Allison," he said.

For a moment, I was confused. Then my eyes widened in shock, and I turned to Jackal, who was standing in the same place with his arms crossed, looking annoyed. "Jackal?" I sputtered, and he raised an eyebrow. "*You* decided to come back? Why?"

"Don't read too much into it, sister." My blood brother sneered at me, golden eyes mocking. "I didn't come back to save you from the big bad minion army, trust me. I just wasn't about to let lover boy get away with stealing my city. And I figured you wouldn't have the balls to off him yourself, once it really came down to it. Looks like I was right." He snorted and rolled his eyes. "I came to cut off a head and take back what's mine, nothing else. So, don't get all mushy on me."

"Regardless," Kanin said, interrupting us, much to Jackal's relief, I thought, "we are wasting time. Eden is still in danger. Ezekiel," he said solemnly, turning to Zeke, "I will ask you this only once. You know the stakes, how important it is that we reach Eden. You know we will have to face Sarren at the end of this journey. Can you do this?"

"I don't know," Zeke answered simply, unapologetically. "But I promised Allison that I would help you stop Sarren. That finding him comes before everything else. So, at least until we get to Eden, I'm with you. I can't promise anything beyond that."

"And if Sarren uses you again to stop us?"

"Then kill me," Zeke replied. Stated so bluntly, so matter-of-factly, that my stomach turned. "If something happens where it's either Sarren or me, don't hesitate. Stop him, even if you have to kill me, too." He avoided my gaze as he said this, his voice dropping to a whisper. "It would be a mercy."

"Oh, don't say that, bloodbag," Jackal said, ever-present grin back in place. "I was just starting to like you."

CHAPTER 11

We left Old Chicago that night, heading east toward Eden once more. Only this time, things were vastly different. One, Zeke was with us. Still shaken, dispassionate, and numb with what had happened to him, but alive. I was determined to keep him that way. And two, we had a working vehicle again.

"Not the prettiest hunk of metal on the road," Jackal remarked as we walked across the floating barge, passing rows of motorcycles to where a rusty old van was parked at the end of the line. "I would suggest bikes, but fuel's running a bit low, and it's a bitch to find more. Better to have to fill one tank instead of four."

Kanin regarded the van impassively. There were slats across the windows, and metal spikes welded to the hood and bumpers, making it bristle with ill intent, but he didn't say anything. Zeke also observed the van without emotion, which worried me. A van like this had been used to kidnap his people and take them to Old Chicago, but if he was remembering that night, it didn't show.

Wrenching open the side door, I peered inside. The interior was empty, seats torn out, rotting plywood laid across the floor. An old, flat tire sat in the corner, and a skull-sized hole, the edges lined with rust, was punched through the opposite wall. Water and snow had obviously seeped in, for the whole thing reeked of mold.

"Really?" I looked back at my blood brother. "We're going to Eden in this hunk of metal? It's two steps away from falling apart."

"Sorry, sister. I didn't realize you were such a car expert." Jackal sneered at me. "Does the chariot not meet her majesty's approval? Were you expecting white horses and gold wheels? You could always walk to Eden, you know."

"You're the king of Old Chicago. Can't you demand a better vehicle?"

"This *is* the better vehicle."

The growl of the engine interrupted us. Kanin had slipped into the driver's seat and turned the ignition, making the van cough and sputter to life. It stood there, shaking and wheezing like some ancient beast, and the Master vampire drummed his fingers on the wheel, staring out the front window. Clearly, he was done waiting for us to make a decision. Zeke stepped into the van without hesitation, sitting cross-legged against the far wall, and Jackal opened the passenger door with a smirk.

"Shotgun."

"What?" I said. But he had already slammed the door behind him, leaving me standing there by myself. Glowering, I stepped into the flimsy, rotting interior, pulled the door closed, and settled against the wall with Zeke. The van coughed once more and began to move, rolling across the barge, over a shaky, rattling bridge, and into the streets.

Back on the highway, Kanin turned the van east once more, weaving through cars and dead vehicles clogging the road, until we reached the outskirts of the city and the lanes opened up. As we picked up speed, the broken skyline of Old Chicago faded into the darkness, until it vanished from sight, and only the road was left, stretching on to Eden.

That first part of the night, the ride was hushed. Kanin drove, and Jackal rode beside him with the seat back and his hands behind his head. I sat with Zeke on the floor of the van, watching his still form and wishing I could reach out to him, somehow. He seemed to have retreated deep within himself, and my few attempts to talk to him were met with polite but vague one-word answers. He didn't want to talk, or he wasn't ready to talk, and the more I prodded, the further he withdrew. Eventually, I gave up and sat next to him in silence, just letting him know I was there. When he was ready, he would come around. Until then, I would let him sort everything out in peace.

The van lumbered on, the only sounds being the sickly whine and cough of the engine, and the occasional thump of tires rolling over debris. Sometimes, the road was clear. Other times, Kanin had to slow the van to a near crawl, weaving through clusters of abandoned, overturned vehicles or trees that had fallen into the road. Once, when he drove carefully around a rock slide that covered most of the pavement, the engine sputtered and died, and it took several tries to get it started again. I was relieved when it finally coughed and turned over, albeit very reluctantly. Ancient and unreliable as the van was, we were still covering ground much faster than had we been on foot.

"Oh, my, it's awfully quiet back there," Jackal remarked after several miles had passed and nothing had happened. Of course, my blood brother took personal offense to peace and quiet, and I could practically hear the grin in his voice. "Are you two making out?"

"Shut up, Jackal."

He snickered. Kanin drove on in silence, determined, I suspected, to ignore us all and the annoyances that were looming. I shifted closer to Zeke, just so that my arm brushed his, and waited for Jackal's next comment.

"So, little bloodsucker," the raider king went on, confirming my suspicions. "How's life as a vampire these nights? Not that I care, mind you, but we are chasing *your* crazy-as-shit sire. If he has something nasty waiting for us in Eden, I'd kinda like to know about it. Any hints as to what your psycho daddy is up to?"

"No," Zeke answered simply. "I haven't seen him since he left Old Chicago, a few days before you showed up."

"Well, that's unfortunate." Jackal crossed his arms, his voice contemplative. "Haven't seen the psychopath at all, huh?" He gazed up at the roof. "If only there was some sort of link that would let you know exactly where he is."

I jerked up. The blood tie. Of course, how could I forget? Zeke was Sarren's offspring, disturbing as that was, so he should be able to sense where the crazy vamp was through their shared bloodline. I wondered if we could somehow track Sarren down without alerting him to Zeke's presence. I also wondered how I could tactfully suggest that to Zeke without completely freaking him out.

But Kanin shook his head.

"No," the Master vampire stated, the first thing he'd said since leaving Chicago. "It's too soon. The blood tie takes time to develop, depending how strong the new vampire is. Sometimes it takes months. If neither sire nor offspring is a Master, it can take even longer. Often, it is triggered by intense emotion or pain; when one member subconsciously calls for help, it is felt by the whole bloodline. But I fear it is too soon for Ezekiel to have developed the link to his maker, at least not one that he can feel. The tie usually emerges after the off-spring has been a vampire for a while."

"Huh." Jackal didn't seem pleased with this, but I was relieved. Zeke certainly didn't need that kind of burden, having to feel Sarren's presence, like an evil taint, lingering in his consciousness. A constant reminder that he was still out there, waiting. The thought made me shudder.

Jackal shifted against the seat, making it groan loudly. "Guess you got lucky there, bloodbag," he muttered, and I wondered if even Jackal found the thought of being tied to Sarren disturbing. "Any hints as to what he's doing, then? Plans? Ideas? Creepy riddles?" He turned and peered back at us, raising a pointed eyebrow. "A message scrawled on a bathroom door in the blood of the innocent?"

"He didn't tell me anything," Zeke said, with a dangerous undertone that warned not to keep pushing him down this path. Jackal, of course, didn't get the hint or, most likely, didn't care.

"Well, you're just all kinds of useless, aren't you?" He shifted back, settling against the seat with his arms behind his head again. But he wasn't done, yet. "Come on, Ezekiel, you're the progeny of the Insane One himself. Sure you can't scrape something out of that screwed-up head to give us the jump on Sarren? I'm sure if you dig hard enough, you'll find his special brand of crazy right where you need it."

I slid forward and kicked the back of his seat, making him turn to glare at me. "Will you shut up? Leave him alone. How is this helping anything?"

"Hey, pardon me for wanting to be prepared," Jackal drawled. "We can't all be like you, sister, charging in blind and hoping your sword hits something as you flail about. You got lucky this time. That's not going to work with Sarren."

"Why don't *you* tell us what he's up to?" I challenged. "You worked with him back in New Covington. I'm sure the pair of you had plenty of chances to bond."

"You'd think so, but not really." Jackal didn't miss a beat. "Turns out, crazy psychotic vampires are really difficult to pal around with. They tend to be irrationally paranoid, and his poetry was about to drive me up a wall. So I'm afraid I didn't get any useful information out of Sarren because I was busy...oh, what was it again? I forgot why I was there." Jackal mock frowned, then snapped his fingers. "Oh, yeah! I was saving your skin."

"Funny, I was going to say setting us up."

"You're never going to let that go, are you?"

"If the two of you would like to walk to Eden," Kanin said at last, not taking his eyes from the road, "I can stop anytime." I fell silent, and Jackal gave a disgusted snort and turned to face the windshield again. Kanin sighed. "James, we will come up with a plan for dealing with Sarren when we have more information," he said, glancing at Jackal. "But antagonizing Ezekiel will not help, so I suggest you cease before your sister runs a sword through the back of your chair." I smirked triumphantly, though it didn't last. "Allison, your brother is right. You cannot go charging into Sarren's lair blind this time around. He will be expecting you." Kanin's voice turned grave. "And he will be ready for us all."

The van died an hour later.

Kanin had slowed again, driving carefully beneath an overpass that had partially collapsed, leaving huge chunks of concrete leaning against each other at treacherous angles. As we cleared the bridge's ominous shadow, the van shuddered, gave one final wheeze, and stopped moving. Kanin tried coaxing it to life, but no amount of prodding could revive it this time. It was well and truly dead.

"Great." I glared at Jackal as we piled out onto a lonely highway that stretched for miles in either direction. The trek to Eden had just become that much longer, and we didn't have time to spare. "I know it's irrational," I told him, "but I blame you for this."

"Whatever floats your boat, sister." Jackal ignored my glare and walked to the front of the van, then lifted up the hood with a creak. Gazing over the complicated jumble of metal and wires, he shook his head. "Could be the fuel hose, could be the alternator. Or the engine might be shot to hell. I won't know unless I fiddle with it." He eyed Kanin, who stood calmly at the front of the vehicle. "Unless that screws with your time schedule, oh, impatient one. This might take a couple hours, and I don't know if I'll be able to get it started again. But by all means—" he waved a hand down the empty, moonlit highway "—feel free to take the runts and start walking, and I'll meet you down the road. If you hear me coming, just stick out a thumb." Jackal grinned, his eyes glowing yellow in the shadow of the hood. "I'll slow down. Probably."

Kanin gave him a level stare. "No," the Master vampire said, as if that was the end of it. "We go to Eden together, or not at all. Unless someone truly wants to leave for good, we face Sarren as a unit. There is too much at stake to take chances." Jackal shrugged and stuck his head beneath the hood again as Kanin went on. "We can make up for a few hours if we have a working vehicle. What do you need to repair it?"

"Besides a bloody miracle?" There was a grunt, and Jackal swore. "Parts. Tools. And a new engine would be fucking fantastic. But since we're sort of screwed on any of those, peace and quiet, without a certain obnoxious sibling bitching at me every two minutes."

"Funny, I think that exact same thing every day."

"There were a few vehicles a couple miles back," Zeke said,

startling me. His voice hadn't changed; it still was empty as ever, as if none of this interested him. "They looked abandoned. Want me to go see if any of them start? Since this is going to take a while."

"The puppy speaks," Jackal mocked, peering up from the hood. "And he actually said something useful. Yeah, why don't you do that, bloodbag? And while you're at it, see if any of them have fuel. Fixing this thing won't matter for shit if we don't have gas."

"I'll go, too," I said, quickly pushing myself off the van.

Jackal snickered and muttered, *"Big surprise,"* as he ducked back under the hood, but I ignored him. No way was I letting Zeke out of my sight now. I didn't *think* he would head off down the road alone to meet the rising sun, but I honestly wasn't sure. This cold, emotionally detached Zeke worried me more than if he'd acted angry and bitter.

I wanted to talk to him without Jackal's snide comments or Kanin's silent but unmistakable presence. If I could just get him alone, talking freely, maybe I could break through the icy shell he'd built around himself. Or at least get him to tell me what was going on.

"Allison." Kanin's voice reached me over the van. I glanced at my sire, saw sympathy and understanding in his dark eyes. "Be careful," he warned. "You will likely not meet with rabids or humans, but still, remain on your guard. Return immediately if there is trouble."

"We will," I promised, and glanced at the vampire beside me. "Ready, Zeke?"

Zeke returned my gaze and nodded, but his eyes remained distant. Reaching into the van, he emerged with a faded red container and turned down the long stretch of highway behind us. "Let's go."

We followed the road for several minutes in silence. Zeke

walked next to me, gaze fixed on the distant horizon. Around us, nothing moved. The highway stretched on, empty and still, the only sounds the crunch of our boots on the snowy pavement. I was trying to think of a way to talk to Zeke, to breach the silence, when his voice echoed quietly into the stillness.

"Go ahead and ask."

Startled, I glanced at him, seeing his empty face, the cold, remote eyes, and swallowed painfully. "Zeke..." I hesitated, not really knowing how to put it, what to ask. *I can't reach you. You've pulled so far back, I don't even recognize you anymore. Is this a choice, or is this what you are now? Is there anything left of the old Zeke? The one I...fell in love with?*

"This isn't like you," I finally said, wishing I knew how to express my true thoughts. He didn't reply, neither agreeing nor disagreeing with me, and my concern spiked. "Talk to me, Zeke," I urged. "I know you have to have questions, about everything. I can help. I'm not as good a teacher as Kanin, but I'll do my best."

"I don't want to know," Zeke said. At my confused frown, he finally looked at me, a flicker of pain finally cracking his icy mask. "I don't need to understand vampire politics, or rituals, or if they have special holidays," he said. "I only have to understand one thing—I'm a demon. I may not have wanted it, but it's what I am now." His jaw tightened, brow furrowing as if he was in pain. "This rage, and bloodlust, and Hunger... I can *feel* it inside me. And if I let it go, for one second, I'll lose everything."

"You can control it—"

"I'm *trying,* Allison." He bared his fangs, then his face smoothed out, returning to that blank front of indifference. "I'm trying. If I don't think about...what I lost, if nothing matters, I don't feel it as strongly. If I give in to anger or hate or regret, it's that much closer to coming out."

"So, your answer is to feel nothing at all."

"Yes." Zeke's voice was hollow again, his eyes distant. "Better to feel nothing, to be numb, than to lose control. It's the only way I know to deal with it."

And...what about us? I wanted to ask. *Where do we stand, Zeke?*

I knew it wasn't the right time to ask. Being Turned against his will, the twisted mind games Sarren had played with him, the horror of everything he'd done while under the compulsion; he had so much to work out, to come to terms with, before he was anywhere near normal. He wasn't ready to face anything between us.

And to be honest, I wasn't either. I was afraid to ask, to hear what the answer could be. Afraid that my worst, secret fear would be confirmed: that Ezekiel Crosse truly had died on that table with Sarren, and the vampire walking beside me was a completely different person. One who couldn't love me anymore.

I didn't say anything else, lost to my own dark thoughts, and Zeke retreated behind his icy, blank wall. We continued the rest of the journey in silence.

"That took longer than I expected," Jackal remarked when Zeke and I returned. Poking his head from under the hood, he smirked at us. "Did you two get lost, or did you decide to jump each other's bones in the ditch?"

I wasn't familiar with that terminology, though I could guess what Jackal was hinting at, and figured it was best to play ignorant. "Shut up, and here," I said, setting the red plastic container on the ground beside him. "None of the cars would start, but there's about a half gallon of fuel in there. Did you get the van working?"

In answer, Jackal rose, pointed an imaginary shotgun beneath the hood, and "fired" point-blank at the engine. I grimaced. "I take it we're walking, then."

"Unless you can pull a working alternator from your tight little ass." Jackal wiped his hands on his jeans and slammed the hood so hard the van bounced. "Otherwise, I think it's safe to say we are S.O.L."

"What does that mean?"

"It means," Kanin broke in before Jackal could explain, "that we need to hurry. Without a working vehicle, Eden is still several days on foot." The Master vampire gazed down the road, to where the pavement met the night sky, and his eyes narrowed. As if he could sense what lay beyond that point, what waited for us at the end of the road. "Let's go," he murmured, starting forward. "I fear we are nearly out of time."

So we walked.

For three nights, we walked. Through snowy woods and deserted towns, Kanin leading, Zeke and I trailing behind, Jackal prowling his own path between us. With the exception of a certain loud-mouthed raider king, we didn't speak much. Kanin walked on, silent and steady, and Zeke continued to hide deep within himself, rarely talking, never showing any hint of emotion. He didn't act angry or bitter or lost—that I could have dealt with. He never complained, or expressed any kind of sorrow or regret for being a monster. He was just... lifeless. Empty. Like nothing mattered to him anymore, not even his own life. Eventually, I started asking him questions about Eden, about Caleb and Bethany and the others who had made it, just to get him talking. To see if he remembered.

He did. And that was even worse. He remembered everything, everyone, but would answer my questions with the same numb detachment that he showed everything else. It made me sick with worry and despair. Zeke was with us, but he had either retreated so deep within himself that I couldn't reach him, or Sarren had destroyed the human, and this cold, dispassionate vampire was all that was left.

One night, I climbed out of the hard, frozen earth beside the road to see Kanin leaning against the median with his arms and legs crossed, waiting for the rest of us. As far as I could see, Jackal wasn't around, and Zeke, being the youngest of us, hadn't woken yet. Shaking dirt from my clothes and hair, I stepped onto the pavement and walked over to where my sire waited, silent and motionless against the dark.

He acknowledged me with a faint nod, but otherwise didn't move. I leaned against the railing with him, crossing my arms as well, and together we stared into the shadows, each lost to our own thoughts. Briefly, I wondered what was on Kanin's mind; he'd been so quiet the past couple nights, not cold and shut down like Zeke, just…preoccupied. I doubted the Master vampire worried about the things I did, but then again, I rarely knew what my sire was thinking.

"Where's Jackal?" I finally asked, not because I really wanted to know—or couldn't find out for myself using the blood tie—but for something to say. My voice echoed weirdly in the stillness, almost out of place. The branches above us rustled, as if offended by human speech where there should be only ruins and wilderness.

Kanin stirred, nodding down the highway. "He went on ahead," the Master vampire replied softly. "Said he spotted a couple cars in the road and wanted to see if he could hotwire any of them. I doubt he has much hope, but I also sense he is getting rather bored with the lot of us."

I snorted. *You mean, he's not having any fun taunting Zeke,* I thought, frowning. Jackal's comments had been nonstop ever since we'd left Old Chicago, barbed, challenging remarks aimed at our newest vampire, but Zeke either ignored them or replied in the same flat, expressionless manner as he had everything else. Last night, Jackal had sneered that Zeke was about as fun as a dead cat and stalked off, shaking his head. I couldn't tell if he was disgusted by Zeke's passiveness or the fact that his comments had no effect on him.

Nothing did anymore, it seemed.

"How much farther to Eden?" I asked, looking up at Kanin. The Master vampire sighed.

"I'm not entirely sure. A couple days, I should think. I have never been there, so I could not tell you for certain." Kanin flicked a glance at me, dark eyes searching. "You and Ezekiel are the ones who have been to its gates," he reminded me. "Does any of this look familiar?"

"I…don't know." I gazed around helplessly, at the highway, at the choking woods on either side, and shrugged. "Maybe? We were in a car the entire way from Old Chicago, so everything pretty much looks the same."

Kanin didn't admonish me for not remembering. He only raised his head and went back to staring at the horizon. The stillness fell once more, darkness and falling snow seeming to engulf everything, swallowing all sound. An owl hooted somewhere in the trees, and then the world was silent again

"I'm worried about him, Kanin," I admitted, almost a whisper. Kanin didn't reply, and didn't ask who I was talking about; there was no need. "What will happen when he gets to Eden? They're going to know that he's not the same."

"Yes," Kanin agreed quietly. "I imagine they will."

"Can't you help him?" I gazed at my sire, imploring. "Teach him how to be a vampire? Like you did with me? I'm not getting through to him." Hurt and a little anger flickered, though I tried to push it down. Didn't Zeke realize he wasn't alone, that I'd been through all this, too? "Will you talk to him?" I asked Kanin. "He'll listen to you."

"No, he won't." I blinked, and Kanin's gaze shifted to me,

stern and sympathetic. "He's not ready to listen, Allison. He won't hear me, or you, or anyone. I was able to teach you because you had already chosen to Turn. Ezekiel was not afforded that choice. And until he comes to terms with what he is, no one will be able to help him." He raised his head, staring at the spot of disturbed earth and clay where I had slept. Where Zeke was still buried, a few feet away. "You can reach for him," Kanin murmured, "but it's up to Ezekiel to look up and see it. He has to take the first steps out of the darkness himself."

I clenched my fists against the railing, fighting despair. "What am I supposed to do, then?"

"Just be there, Allison." Kanin didn't look at me, though his voice was understanding. "When it's time, if Ezekiel does manage to accept what he is, he will not look to me or Jackal or anyone else for help. He will come to you."

We fell silent again. Jackal didn't return, and Zeke slept on in his shallow grave. I crossed my arms, waiting for him to wake up, hoping against hope that he would be himself again. He'd given us all the information he could about Eden: where it was located, how the town was set up, where Sarren would likely go when he arrived. All delivered in the same flat, emotionless voice he'd used since Old Chicago. I wondered if Zeke was steeling himself for what he might find when we got to the city. If he was preparing himself for the loss of everything he had loved. We'd been so focused on catching up with Sarren, intercepting him before he reached the island. But Sarren was probably already there, and if Sarren was in Eden…

"Kanin?" I ventured.

"Yes?"

I licked my lips. "Everyone in Eden…is probably dead, aren't they?"

My sire turned, looking down at me. His voice was calm. "What makes you think that?"

"Because...we couldn't catch up with Sarren? Because he's probably already there, doing whatever awful thing he's been planning?" I kicked at a rock in frustration. "We failed, didn't we? We did exactly what he wanted us to do in Old Chicago, and now there's no chance of catching up. Sarren knew I would go after Zeke. He knew exactly what he was doing when he left him there. I played right into his hand, and now he's in Eden laughing at us all."

Kanin still didn't answer, and I sighed. "I want to think they're all right," I said, feeling a lump in my throat as I thought of Caleb, Bethany, our old group. Probably all dead, because of me. "I want to believe that everyone in Eden is okay, but... I'm just fooling myself, aren't I?"

"No." Kanin's soft voice surprised me. The vampire raised his head, gazing off into the darkness, the hint of a smile on his face. "If there is one thing I have discovered over the centuries of watching humans," he murmured, "it is their stubborn and indomitable will to keep living. As a species, it is almost impossible to kill them completely. They survived Red Lung. They survived the rabid plague. True, many of them now live in vampire cities, enslaved and ignorant of the times Before, but there are still small settlements that exist outside the Princes' territories. Humans living free.

"Sarren is one vampire," Kanin went on, as I stared at him in amazement. "No matter how deadly, how terrible his plans, even he cannot wipe an entire city from the face of the earth in a few days. Humans are ever resilient, and their will to live surpasses everything else. Do not lose hope, Allison." He bowed his head, his next words so soft I barely caught them. "Your hope is the reason we have a chance to stop this."

A shifting of earth halted our conversation, the sound of

dirt being pushed back as a body rose from the frozen ground. Zeke, kneeling in his shallow grave, shook clay from his hair, brushed off his jacket, and rose, his face as blank and detached as ever.

"Sorry I kept you." His glassy blue eyes stared right through me, his voice low and indifferent. "Are we ready to leave?"

I resisted the urge to leap up and shake him, just to see some sort of emotion cross that empty face. Anger, surprise, disgust, *anything* was better than the apathy he showed now. "Almost," I told him instead. "We're just waiting on Jackal."

"Aw, isn't that sweet." And Jackal sauntered into view, smirk firmly in place. "But don't wait around on my account. It's not like I can't wait for yet another riveting night of listening to you people whine at each other. *Oh, woe is me, I'm a vampire. I'm a horrible monster who eats babies and murders bunnies, boo hoo hoo.*" He snorted and glared at Zeke. "I know that's what you're thinking, puppy. This robotic song and dance isn't fooling anyone, and it's starting to get really annoying." He bared his fangs, a brief, threatening grin. "So, why don't you stop playing the fucking whipped dog and start acting like a vampire? Or are you afraid you might actually like it?"

No response from Zeke. It was like Jackal hadn't said anything at all. The raider king shook his head in disgust, and I glared at him. "I don't suppose you found anything useful," I challenged, "like a working car."

Jackal rolled his eyes. "If I had, I would be driving to Eden right now," he said. "Being around the lot of you is like slowly pushing nails into my brain."

"Stick around," I told him. "Maybe I'll find a way to make it literal, as well."

Abruptly, Kanin shoved himself off the railing, brushed past us, and began walking down the highway without a word.

Left behind, Jackal, Zeke and I blinked at each other a moment, before Jackal gave a mocking snicker.

"I think the old man is getting a little tired of us," he remarked as we hurried to catch up. His eyes gleamed as he smirked back at me. "Maybe you shouldn't be such a wretched shrew, sister."

"Me?" I bared my fangs, and would've kicked him if he was closer. "You're the one he wants to kill. Come to think of it, you're the one *everyone* wants to kill."

"Hey, old man," Jackal called in a mocking voice, "you forgot to say '*if you kids don't stop I'm going to turn this car right around and then no one will go to Eden.*'"

Kanin didn't deign to answer, and together we continued our journey, four vampires on a long, lonely highway heading east.

Hoping our time had not run out.

CHAPTER 12

Two hours before dawn, we found Sarren's last message waiting for us.

We smelled it first, of course, the familiar, unmistakable scent of blood drifting over the empty highway like invisible threads. The highway had entered civilization again, taking us through empty towns and subdivisions, crumbling houses on either side and cars scattered about the road. Wary, we continued on, each thinking the same thing—that there was some kind of trap, ambush, or atrocity waiting for us down the road. We weren't entirely wrong.

The stench of rot, decay and wrongness soon joined the smell of blood, so it wasn't surprising when we approached an overpass choked with weeds and vines and saw a mass of spindly pale things swarming under the bridge.

"Rabids," Zeke muttered, as the four of us paused on a corner across the street, watching the monsters hiss and scramble over the hulk of an ancient, rusting semitruck that blocked the path we needed to take. The swarm wasn't huge, but there were enough to be dangerous. "Should we find a way around?"

"What if someone's in the truck?" I asked, watching him carefully. And though my voice was calm, I was almost terrified of his answer. If he shrugged or gave no indication of wanting to help survivors, then I would know my Zeke was truly gone. "Someone might be hurt," I went on, as Zeke gazed at me blankly. "If we leave them now, they're dead."

"If this is Sarren's work, they're probably already dead," Zeke answered, making my heart crash in despair. "But," he added, and pulled out his machete, his eyes going hard, "I suppose we have to make certain."

Relief flooded me. I glanced at my sire, hoping he thought the same. "Kanin?"

The Master vampire nodded once. "I'm right behind you, Allison."

Jackal groaned. "Oh, yeah, stroll merrily up to the van reeking of blood, placed very conveniently in our direct path. That doesn't sound like a trap at all." But his dinged, bloody fire ax emerged from beneath his duster, and he gave it an easy twirl. "Rescuing bloodbags and saving puppies." He sighed. "That sounds about right for this group. You bleeding hearts are going to be the death of me, I just know it." Gazing down at me, he smirked and gestured to the distant pack. "Well, this is your party, sister. Why don't you get it started?"

Drawing my sword, I stepped off the curb into the road, bared my fangs, and roared a challenge into the night. My voice carried over the wind, echoing off the rooftops, and the rabids jerked up, pale heads snapping toward me. With piercing shrieks and wails, the mob leaped off the truck and came skittering at us, claws and talons scraping the cement, jaws gaping to reveal jagged fangs. My monster surged up with the explosion of violence, eager and bloodthirsty, and I ran forward to meet them.

Zeke was suddenly beside me, cold and silent as the horde

bore down on us, his face the same killer's mask I'd seen in Jackal's tower. The first rabid sprang at him with a howl; Zeke's blade flashed, and the monster's head left its shoulders, bouncing into a car. Snarling a challenge, I slashed my katana at the next pair of spindly bodies, cutting through one and into the other. Their black, foul-smelling blood spattered the snow, and then the rest of the swarm flooded in, surrounding us, and everything dissolved into madness. I heard the savage crunch of bones as Jackal's fire ax connected, crushing skulls and knocking rabids away, and caught glimpses of Kanin's dark, graceful form from the corner of my eye as his knife parted heads with lethal precision. Rabids pressed forward, screaming, and I met them with my blade, feeling the shiver of metal as it passed through undead flesh, the monster inside howling with glee.

A different roar, icy and furious, made me whirl around. Zeke stood with his back against an overturned car, two rabids hounding him on either side. One had its fangs sunk into his sword arm, even as the blade itself stuck out of its collarbone. The other hissed and pressed forward, jaws snapping eagerly.

I lunged forward to help, but with a rabid still gnawing on his wrist, Zeke reached back with his other hand, pulled the gun from his back holster and shoved it between the rabid's eyes. There was a boom, blood and bits of skull exploding everywhere, and the rabid fell away with the back of its skull missing. At the same time, Zeke yanked his machete from the dead rabid's body, turned and sliced it through the second one's neck.

"Zeke!"

He spun on me as I came up, eyes bright and glassy, lips curled back to show fangs. Blood streaked his face and the front of his shirt as I stared at him, a cold-eyed, snarling vampire, and he raised his gun.

"Duck, Allie."

My instincts responded even as I was tempted to stand there gaping. Instead, I threw myself aside just as the pistol barked, and a rabid shrieked behind me and slammed into a car.

I darted to Zeke's side, and we faced the last of the horde together, back-to-back. Rabids leaped at us, wailing, and fell before our blades as we moved around each other, guarding the other's flank. I stuck my katana through a rabid's chest, ripped it out and turned to slash another lunging at Zeke's blind spot. Zeke decapitated a rabid, spun, and fired his pistol into the face of another behind my shoulder. The roar of the gun made my head ring, but the rabid was flung back, its face a bloody mess, and didn't rise again.

And then, it was over. Zeke and I stood in the center of a gore-strewn circle, limbs and bodies scattered at our feet. Lowering my blade, I stared at the field of carnage, looking around for Jackal and Kanin. They stood a few paces away, the Master vampire calmly wiping his blade on his sleeve while Jackal pried his ax from a rabid's severed head and tossed away the skull in disgust.

I looked up, met Zeke's gaze, and my insides fluttered. He was gazing at me with a faint, familiar expression, one I hadn't seen on him since he'd Turned. The icy mask had cracked a bit, admiration, respect and a little awe filtering through the terrible blankness in his eyes. The corner of his mouth curled, very slightly, and he shook his head.

"Still incredible, vampire girl," he whispered, sounding almost like himself again. "Dangerous, beautiful and unstoppable. You haven't changed."

"Oh, isn't that sweet," came Jackal's loud, mocking voice before I could reply. "Let's make goo-goo eyes at each other in the middle of a stinking corpse field, how very romantic." Ignoring my glare, he kicked an arm out of his way and sauntered forward, the ax vanishing beneath his duster once more. "But before you two start making out, maybe we should check the thing we fought all the rabids to get to?" He glanced at the back of the semi and rolled his eyes. "Don't want Sarren's trap to go to waste, after all."

We approached the doors cautiously. Now that the fight was over, the scent of blood returned, stronger and more powerful than ever. The truck practically threw off waves of the smell. I didn't know what we would find when we opened that truck, but knowing Sarren, it was probably going to be worse than I could imagine.

A beam was set across the thick double doors of the back. Keeping rabids from getting in, I wondered, or preventing something from getting out? No sounds came from inside the container; everything was eerily silent again, muffled and still in the falling snow. Jackal leaped onto the back of the truck, grabbed the beam, and yanked it out with a raspy screech that made me wince. After tossing it behind him, he paused and observed the truck critically.

"You know this is not going to be pleasant, right?" he stated to the rest of us. "Whatever the sicko has in here, he obviously wants us to see it. Which means it's probably going to fuck with at least one of us, really badly." He snickered, shaking his head. "Course, that's the trap now, isn't it? We could walk away, right now, but not knowing what's inside is going to drive us bat-shit crazy."

I frowned. He was right. I couldn't walk away now, even if I knew there was something awful waiting for me inside. Bracing myself, I took a steady breath. "Open it."

Jackal shrugged. Dropping to the ground, he gripped the bars running vertically up the truck doors, tensed briefly, and threw them open with a squeal.

A wave of cold billowed out of the container, and with it

the smell of blood, death, offal and human insides hit me like a slap in the face, making my stomach clench. Peering into the long, shadowy interior, I realized I had been right; what Sarren had left for us was far worse than I had imagined.

I clenched my fists, fighting the urge to turn away. Even with all the atrocities I'd seen, the horrible things Sarren had done, this one took the prize. The wall's original color was impossible to tell, because it was streaked floor to ceiling in blood, thick and dried and black. The floor of the container was caked with it, a congealed, slimy carpet nearly an inch thick, glistening dully in the moonlight. Humans hung on the walls, staked or nailed in place, their skin peeled back in grotesque star patterns around them. A few didn't even have skin, raw muscles and bones bared to the light, their faces twisted into masks of horror.

For a brief moment, I was relieved I was a vampire. Because if I'd been human, I would have fallen to my knees on the ground and puked up my last meal. Even now, though the Hunger raged at the amount of spilled blood and the monster looked on with indifference, I felt sick. Sick, and filled with a sudden, blinding hatred. No one with even a sliver of humanity would do this. I was a monster, and I traveled in the company of monsters, but even Jackal had lines he wouldn't cross. This...depravity was just further proof that Sarren had no humanity left; he was a true demon in human skin who had killed, maimed and tortured all these people, just to prove a point. And a terrible one, at that.

On the far wall, a message glittered, stark and black. Written in blood, of course. Only, I had been wrong; this one hadn't been left for me, or Jackal, or even Kanin. No, it was far more horrible, and filled me with a cold, lingering dread.

Welcome to your future, it read. *Ezekiel.*

"No."

Zeke's voice was a strangled whisper. He stumbled back from the container, eyes wide, face contorted in agony and horror. Hitting a rusty car, he turned from the semi and its grisly contents, putting a hand against the door as if to brace himself.

"No," he choked out, closing his eyes. "Oh, God, I can't do this. I can't do it anymore." Bowing his head, he pressed his face into the metal, his voice dropping to a moan. "Let me die," he whispered, making my insides clench. "Before I become… that. Just kill me already."

"Zeke." I stepped toward him, and he flinched, shoulders hunched in anguish. "Look at me." He didn't raise his head, and I took another step, my voice urgent. "Dammit, listen to me. Don't let Sarren get to you. This is just another one of his twisted mind games, and if you start listening, you're giving him exactly what he wants."

"Because, it's true, Allie." Zeke finally looked up at me, his eyes a little wild. I blinked as that searing, glassy blue gaze met mine. "You don't know me anymore," Zeke whispered. "You don't know what I've done. Those people in the barn, they weren't the only humans I killed. I helped Sarren murder an entire village, kill every soul there." His eyes closed, and he dropped his head into his hands. "And then, when we were done, we strung their bodies from a tree and painted a wall with their blood."

My stomach turned. I remembered the slaughtered outpost, the tree of corpses and the barn streaked with blood. Zeke had done that, been a part of it. I realized how blind I'd been. If I had done that, even if it was under a compulsion, I wasn't certain I could live with myself, either.

"It haunts me, every night," Zeke whispered, clutching at his hair. "I can't get their screams out of my head. But no matter how much that disgusts me, no matter how much I hate myself for it…there's a part of me that wants to do it again. And it will never go away, will it?" He looked up, and his eyes stabbed at me, almost accusing. "I'm always going to feel like this, like I'm going to explode if I can't hunt down a human and tear it apart."

I bit my lip as he paused, waiting for my answer. I didn't want to say it, to confirm what he already knew, but I wouldn't lie to him. "No," I whispered. "No, the Hunger will never go away." He turned away, and I stepped forward, desperate to talk him down, to give him some kind of hope. "But you can control it, Zeke. We all have to learn to fight it. That's part of what being a vampire is."

"But I'm going to slip up one day." Zeke's voice was low, defeated. "One day, I won't be able to resist. And it will be the barn all over again." And I couldn't answer, couldn't deny it, because I knew that was true. That, one day, he *would* slip up. There was no question in my mind. Kanin's own words came back to me, that warning he'd given, not so very long ago, when I first became a vampire.

Sometime in your life, Allison Sekemoto, you will kill a human being. Accidentally or as a conscious, deliberate act. It is unavoidable. The question is not if it will happen, but when.

That held true for Zeke now, as well. And we both knew it.

"What if I get to Eden," Zeke went on, "and I can't control myself? The people there, my family, they won't suspect anything. What if Caleb or Bethany come running up to me, and I…" He closed his eyes, unable to continue, his face twisted with loathing. "I can't do it," Zeke whispered, his voice choked but resolved. "I can't go to Eden, not like this. Go on without me."

"I am *not* leaving you behind, Zeke." Anger and panic flared, and I bared my fangs at him. I would not lose him now, either to Sarren's twisted games or his own guilt. Atrocities aside, I had to make him see that he wasn't alone.

"Do you think you're the only one who's gone through this?" I demanded. "Do you remember all those times I said we couldn't be together, because you were a human and I was a vampire? When I told you I couldn't go to Eden, because I was afraid I would kill someone? Remember what you told me, then? You said I'm not a monster, and I'm not evil. Why is it different for you?"

"Because I *am* a monster!" Zeke snarled back. His fangs flashed as he whirled around, glaring at me. "This is what I am, Allison! I'm a demon—you know it as well as me."

"Oh, for fuck's sake!"

Jackal abruptly shoved himself off the truck and came stalking forward, eyes glowing yellow, his lips curled into a grimace of disgust. "Puppy, I am getting *so* tired of listening to you whine about this," he snarled at Zeke. "This isn't rocket science. If you don't want to be a monster, don't be a bloody monster! Be an uptight stick in the mud like Kanin. Be a self-righteous bleeding heart like Allison. Or you can stop agonizing about it and be a fucking monster, it's actually a lot of fun." He narrowed his eyes as Zeke and I stared at him, stunned. "But for the love of piss, make some sort of decision. If you don't want to eat babies and nail bloodbags to walls, that's your choice. What Sarren did or made you do in the past has nothing to do with it now. You're a *vampire*. Do whatever the hell you want."

Zeke blinked, still in a state of shock, but I bristled and stepped forward, baring my fangs at my brother. "That isn't fair, Jackal," I growled. "He never wanted to Turn. Sarren forced this on him—"

"And you," Jackal interrupted, turning on me, "are part of

the problem. Bitching and crying because he's not acting like a human anymore. Here's a news flash, sister. He's *not* human anymore. He doesn't need you holding his hand every time a kitten dies. Maybe when he was a mewling, pathetic meatsack, he needed some kind of protection, but he's one of us now. Or he would be, if you didn't act like it was the end of the world because he likes the taste of blood. Stop treating him like a mortal and let him be a bloody vampire."

Taken aback, I fell silent, and for a moment, we all stared at each other. The wind picked up, blowing the scent of death and mutilated corpses into the road, and the rabids lay scattered around us like fallen limbs, bloody and broken. It caught Jackal's duster, causing it to billow out behind him as he glared at us, his expression twisted with mockery and disgust. Behind him, Zeke's face had gone blank again, glassy blue eyes staring out at nothing.

Then Kanin stepped into the circle, his voice weary but calm. "Dawn is nearly upon us," he said, giving no hints to his thoughts, his feelings about the sudden outburst between his two offspring. "I suggest we get out of the open. This conversation will have to wait until tomorrow night."

That ended it. With a final, disgusted snort, Jackal turned and stalked off down the road, shaking his head. He didn't look back, and within moments, the raider king had slipped between the sea of scattered cars and disappeared from sight.

"Allison." Kanin looked at me, his dark eyes impassive. "Take Ezekiel and find a place to sleep. Try to stay close. I'll find you both this evening."

"Right," I murmured, and Kanin too, disappeared, melting into the darkness surrounding us, leaving me and Zeke alone.

I glanced at Zeke, who hadn't moved from his spot next to the car, and jerked my head toward a peeling, two-story house on the corner of the street. "Come on," I said quietly. "Let's get out of the open."

He didn't say anything, just followed me across the road, over a sagging picket fence, and through a weed-choked yard to the steps of the house. Inside, rubble covered the floor, and the walls were cracked and peeling, showing rotting boards beneath, but it was in better shape than most empty houses I'd seen. A fireplace sat crumbling against the back wall, bricks scattered over the floor, and a gutted armchair lay overturned in front of it, covered in moss.

I spotted a staircase against a wall and motioned Zeke toward it, knowing the bedrooms would probably be on the second floor. The creaking, groaning stairs took us to an equally noisy hallway, with a trio of doors that led to individual rooms. The largest had a rusty brass bed and a mattress big enough for two people, but it also had several windows that faced east and nothing to cover them with. The room across the hall was smaller, but its one window was already boarded up, so in that regard, it was an easy choice. Of course, there were other factors to take into account.

A single bed sat in the corner, dusty but fairly clean, and I hesitated, not knowing if Zeke wanted to share the mattress with me. Or, honestly, if *I* wanted to be in the same room with him. Jackal's words still clawed at my mind, the accusation that I was making this worse, that I couldn't let Human Zeke go. I didn't want to admit it, but as infuriating and shameful and humbling as it was, my blood brother was right. I'd wanted Zeke to be like he was before, and that just wasn't possible. Not with what he had gone through.

It also confirmed something I'd known for a while now, but refused to believe: Zeke Crosse, the boy I knew before, the human I'd fallen in love with, *was* dead. I had to accept that. Just like Allie the Fringer had died that night in the rain with the rabids, Ezekiel Crosse was no longer human. He wasn't the same; he couldn't be. He was a vampire now, with all the bloodlust, Hunger, savagery and ruthlessness that came with it. He would never be the same sweet, innocent, selfless human I had known and loved. There would always be an edge to him, the knowledge that he was something dangerous, something lethal. That a demon lurked within and could come out at anytime. Was that something I could come to terms with? And, even more important, could he?

Or would I wake up this evening to find him gone, having finally chosen to meet the sun rather than put those in Eden at risk?

Angry, frustrated tears stung my eyes. I growled softly and clenched my fists, trying to drive them back. I was losing him. Zeke was slipping further and further away, and nothing I said or did could reach him. I'd told him how I felt; I'd laid everything bare, promised I would help him fight the monster, that he wouldn't be alone, and it didn't seem to be enough. I didn't know what more I could do, what else I could offer.

"Hey."

His voice was a breath, a flutter across my cold skin. I froze, then turned to find him watching me, blue eyes solemn in the shadows of the room. I swallowed, meeting his gaze, not caring about the single track of red crawling down my cheek. Zeke's expression tightened, a flicker of guilt and regret crossing his face. He looked like he wanted to say something, but couldn't find the right words. I didn't speak, just continued to watch him, and there was a moment of tense, awkward silence.

Then Zeke sighed, and the shadow of a wry, painful smile crossed his lips. "You know it's the end of the world when Jackal starts making sense," he whispered.

The wall between us shattered. I let out a choked, relieved laugh and fell into him. His arms enveloped me, pressing me close, and I clung to his waist, feeling his cool cheek against my neck.

"I'm sorry, Allie," he murmured. Raising his head, he pressed his forehead to mine, his voice low but steady. "I'm so sorry. I've been so consumed with this whole vampire thing, I didn't see you standing right there. And if I'd just listened, you were telling me exactly what I needed to hear." His brow creased in what might've been regret, or disgust. "It's…pretty bad when the egotistical murdering vampire has to set you straight. I guess I had that kick in the head coming for a while. At least Jackal is good for something." A painful chuckle escaped him, and he shook his head. "I was blind, but I see things a little more clearly now. I won't be a burden anymore."

"You were never a burden," I told him. "You were just… lost for a little while. We all were, at one point."

He squeezed his eyes shut for a moment, and his shoulders trembled. "I'm scared," he whispered. "I'm terrified that I won't be able to fight this, that I'll turn into a demon and lose my soul forever, if it's not already gone. The *only* reason I'm here, the one thing that's keeping me from going out to meet the sun and ending it for good…is you."

"Zeke…"

He took my arms, his gaze intense as he stared down at me. "I never wanted this," he said. "All my life, I was taught that vampires are evil and soulless, and that's what I believed, until I met you. You showed me that I was wrong, that vampires didn't have to be monsters, and you even made me believe that they could still have a soul. I know that you still have yours. After everything we've been through, you're still hanging on to it with both hands."

I bit my lip as tears threatened again, hot and stinging. There it was, that faith that I was more than a monster, even when he couldn't believe it about himself. Zeke raised a hand to my cheek, brushing it softly with his thumb, still gazing into my eyes.

"I'm not the same person, Allie," he said quietly. "I'm... not even a *person* anymore. I tried to kill you. I've murdered dozens of people, and I'm the offspring of an insane vampire who wants to destroy the world. The only thing that hasn't changed, the one thing I'm sure of, are my feelings for you. But... I'm different now." He drew back slightly, as if to let me see him better. "I died, Allison," he said in a soft, firm voice. "Part of me was killed on that table with Sarren. I'll still fight for my humanity, as hard as I can, but I know someday I'm going to slip up and give in to the monster. And when that day comes, I'm going to hate myself for a very long time." He clenched his jaw, his eyes going dark before he composed himself once more. "So, I have to know, vampire girl. Can you still be with me, even after all that? Even though I'm a monster, that I'll never be the same?"

I didn't hesitate. I already knew my answer. Zeke was a vampire. He would struggle with Hunger, rage and blood-lust in a way human Zeke could never fathom. But even as a human, he'd chosen to love a monster, and now it was my turn to trust him. To look past the demon and the monster, and find the human inside.

Reaching up, I slipped my arms around his neck, pulled him to me, and pressed my lips to his.

He sighed, and it seemed like it was a release, a letting go of fear, and doubt, and disbelief. A total surrender. His arms slid around me, gentle yet strong, and his lips moved with mine, kissing me back. Not fevered or passionate, trying to devour each other while desperately trying get close; this was tender and thoughtful and solemn, a promise without words.

I kept my eyes closed as we parted, my hands on either side

of his face. "I thought I lost you," I whispered, feeling the wet tracks on his own skin. "I thought we had more time, even though I knew better. Life is so fragile, and someone can be taken from you at any time. I've always known that." I slid my hand down his chest, to the spot where, not long ago, his heart had beat steady and sure against my palm. The stillness there now made me a little sad. "I guess I was trying to protect myself."

"Allie..."

"I love you, Zeke," I whispered, and he froze. This time, the words didn't scare me at all. "Vampire or human, it doesn't matter to me. Sarren could've forced you to kill a hundred humans, and it wouldn't change a thing. I would've come back for you regardless. And you're wrong. You're stronger then you think. You were the one who taught me that humanity is worth hanging on to, that it's worth fighting for at all costs. You always told me that I was more than a monster. Well, now you're going to have to prove it to yourself. But I'll be here. I won't let you fall."

I finally looked up at him, met those clear blue eyes, saw the raw emotion staring back at me. The doubt and fear still lingered, but for the first time since his death, he looked like Zeke again. I saw the shift from bleak, horror-filled despair to something that, while not completely optimistic, was at least hopeful. I put a hand on his cheek.

"There, preacher boy," I murmured, and forced a tiny half smirk as he closed his eyes. "I said I love you. Twice. Now, can we please move past this and get on with saving the world?"

He let out a breath that was half laugh, half sob, and yanked me to him, crushing me in his arms. I slid mine around his waist and held him tight, feeling him tremble.

"Don't let me slip," he whispered into my neck. "Please. When I get to Eden, don't let me give in to the monster."

"I won't," I told him, a promise to Zeke, to myself, to everyone. "You're going to be fine, Zeke. And after we beat Sarren, we'll have forever to figure this out."

Moving to the bed, we sank down together, still holding each other tightly. Eden, a mysterious virus, and Zeke's terrifying sire waited for us at the end of the road, but right now, all that seemed a little less urgent. I had Zeke back. He was different; he was a vampire, but we'd both taken that first step toward acceptance. It was enough for now. As the sun crept over the buildings outside, tinting the sky red and the roofs orange, I drifted off to sleep with the boy who had died held safely in my arms.

I would never let him go again.

As usual, I woke first, opening my eyes to darkness and taking a moment to remember where I was. The room was small, sparse and empty, a boarded-up window and ancient dresser on the far wall, and a body lying next to me in the tiny bed.

Propping myself on an elbow, I watched him. Zeke lay on his back on the edge of the mattress, unmoving and unbreathing, the sleep of the dead. I put a hand over his heart, missing the warmth, the pulse beneath my fingers, the slight rise and fall of his chest. He didn't stir, and I resisted the urge to shake him, to prod him awake. Both to see him move, and to see if he was the same Zeke I'd fallen asleep with this morning. Would he remember the convictions of a few short hours ago? I knew there was no reason for him to forget, to relapse, but he had been an emotionless zombie for so long, our last conversation almost felt like a dream. Even though vampires didn't dream.

I didn't rouse him. Instead, I reached out with my blood tie and found both Kanin and Jackal nearby, probably waiting for us. Kanin would be impatient to get on the road; I wondered if having to wait for younger, less experienced vampires who couldn't force themselves awake whenever they wanted annoyed him sometimes. I also wondered how far from Eden we were. We had to be close; it hadn't taken Zeke and I half as long the first time we'd traveled this road. Of course, we'd had a working car the entire way from Chicago.

Preoccupied, I didn't see Zeke move until cool fingers curled around mine. I blinked and looked down to see his eyes open, gazing up at me in the darkness. He wasn't smiling, but his gaze was steady and his expression was calm, not the cold, blank mask he'd worn ever since Old Chicago.

"Hey," I murmured. Zeke didn't answer, and I searched his face, hoping his conviction still held, that he wouldn't start doubting himself now. "You okay?"

His eyes closed. "No," he whispered, and squeezed my hand before I could worry. "But... I'm getting there. One day at a time, right? I can't turn back now, not when we're this close." Gazing at me again, he forced a faint smile. "We're almost there," he mused, and his hand traveled up to my face, brushing my hair back, skimming my cheek. "You'll be able to see Eden with me after all."

I ran my fingers down his chest, remembering what Kanin had said the night before. Sarren had likely beaten us to Eden. Who knew the state of the island now? Maybe everyone was dead, after all. But I wouldn't think about that. We couldn't give up. I would choose hope, to believe that they were still all right. It was all I could do now. "I'm just glad I won't have to explain to Caleb and Bethany where you are," I said, smiling down at Zeke. "I don't think they'd ever forgive me for coming back without you."

A shadow crossed his face, his brow creasing with worry and a little fear. I knew what he was thinking—whether he'd be able to control himself around those kids, both of whom adored him. "What am I going to tell them?" he whispered, his voice catching a little. "How am I going to explain what happened to me? When we were searching for Eden, before you joined us, everyone knew vampires were evil monsters that ate little kids. I told them that myself." His face tightened, his expression full of regret and pain. "What will they think of me now?"

"You have to tell them the truth," I said, and he flinched. "And they'll either accept it or they won't. But you're not the first vampire they've seen, Zeke. And I know Caleb, at least, isn't as terrified of vampires as he should be."

"Not anymore," Zeke said in a wry voice. "Not after he met you."

I smiled, remembering Caleb, a thin, dark-haired kid and the toughest six-year-old I'd ever met. He'd been through so much, seen so much, on his journey to Eden: rabids, wild animals, evil bikers and sadistic raider kings. He'd lost an older sister to rabids and had nearly died himself a few times, but had come out of that whole nightmare ordeal a true survivor. Perhaps a little more hardened than he should have been, but one thing that had disappeared completely was his fear of vampires. Or, at least, of one vampire.

"So, I think they'll understand," I finished. "They love you, Zeke. It won't matter if you're not human anymore." I put a hand over his wrist and squeezed gently. "And don't worry about the monster—I'll be right there. If you feel yourself slipping, just keep your eyes on me."

"Allie…" His eyes were suddenly sapphire pools of emotion and longing, peering up at me in the darkness. It sent a ripple of heat through my insides, a stirring of Hunger that was familiar and strange at the same time. Lowering my head, I kissed him, and his arms wrapped around me, pressing me close.

I slid my hands down his stomach, my fingers slipping beneath his shirt, and Zeke's grip tightened, his kisses turning hungry, too. My lips left his mouth and trailed a path down his jaw to his neck, and he moaned, arching his head back. Offering his throat. I paused, my mouth hovering over his skin, fangs throbbing against my gums. I wanted to feel him again, like I had in Old Chicago when the compulsion was finally broken. Not just his blood, but his emotions and thoughts and secrets and fears. I wanted to see him when nothing separated us, when everything was laid bare.

But if I started down that road, I wouldn't be able to stop. And we were so close to Eden now, with Jackal and Kanin just a few streets away. The last thing I wanted was for my sire to get impatient and come looking for us. Or worse, Jackal.

Raising my head, I kissed his lips, lingering and soft, taking us back into safe territory. Zeke didn't fight me, didn't press forward, letting us both cool down before I pulled back. Though his eyes still smoldered when I looked down at him, the tips of his fangs visible in the darkness.

"We should go," I said reluctantly. "Kanin and Jackal..."

"Yeah." Zeke sighed, sounding as grudging as I felt, and released me. We climbed off the mattress, checked and rebuckled our weapons in place, and left the room together.

Following my blood tie, we found Kanin and Jackal in a small garage a few streets down. Jackal was kneeling on the pavement, holding up the front of a car with one shoulder, his jaw clenched in concentration while he fiddled with the tire. At his back, Kanin watched impassively and turned as we came up.

"Good. You're here." The Master vampire nodded to us, his dark gaze lingering on Zeke. "We're almost ready to leave. As soon as James finishes, we can get on the road again."

"You know," Jackal grunted, gritting his teeth as he screwed the last nut into the hubcap, "this would've been a lot easier if

I didn't have to hold up the freaking car *and* change the tire at the same time. I suppose once you hit Master vamp status, you're excluded from such ignoble work. Wouldn't want those special fingers to get greasy, right?" He gave the screw a final twist, then let the vehicle drop and bounce to the pavement. "Then again, I doubt any of you would know the throttle from the gas cap."

Dusting off his hands, he rose and shot a quizzical stare at Zeke. "Well, look who's feeling better," he mocked, raising an eyebrow. "Did you two work through your feelings over a nice slaughtered baby or something?" His grin grew wider, turned into a leer. "Or...did something *else* happen to take your mind off things?"

"Wouldn't you like to know," Zeke answered coolly, before I could kick Jackal in the shin. Jackal blinked, taken aback for just a moment, before barking a harsh laugh.

"Aw, look at that. The puppy is finally showing some teeth." He snickered, then leaned an elbow against the car, regarding Zeke appraisingly. "Think you can manage to show those fangs when we face your big bad sire, puppy? Or are you going to slink off with your tail between your legs?"

Zeke smiled back, but it was a dangerous, lethal smile, fangs glinting in the shadows as he faced Jackal down. "I haven't forgotten," he said in a soft, ominous voice, as the temperature in the garage dropped a few degrees, and Jackal frowned in confusion. "What you did to my family, I haven't forgotten it. I still intend to keep my promise. One night, you'll look up, and I'll be there. So, don't get too comfortable. I'm still going to kill you when this is all over."

Jackal stared at him. Silence fell, and I resisted the urge to draw my sword. On the other side of the car, Kanin didn't move, but I could feel the tension in the room, four vampires waiting to see what the others would do.

Then Jackal chuckled and pushed himself off the door, shaking his head. "Well, you're welcome to try, puppy," he said, as the tension diffused somewhat. "It's going to be a shame to kill you—you have the potential to be a decent bloodsucker. But I'd wait until we find Sarren before you start making your little death threats. That lovely message we found? That means he knows the compulsion is broken. And I'll bet he's not too thrilled with his special minion having free will again. He'll be looking for any chance to turn you inside out." Jackal smiled evilly and leaned closer to Zeke, fangs gleaming. "So I'm not the one you need to worry about," he sneered. "Try me again when we have the psycho's head on the end of a long spike. I'll be more than happy to stick yours next to it."

"Enough." Kanin's deep, stern voice broke through the standoff. "Now is not the time to fight among ourselves," he lectured, narrowing his eyes at the three of us. "Sarren is very close. And he will use every opportunity to slow us down, turn us against one another." His gaze went to Zeke, who lowered his eyes. "If we are to stop him, we must put aside vengeance, put aside hatred and doubt and uncertainty, and trust each other. If only for a moment. Can you do that, Ezekiel?"

"Yeah." Zeke sighed, bowing his head. "I got it."

"Then let us go. We're nearly there."

"Oh, sure," Jackal remarked, opening the passenger door. "No, 'Hey, thanks, Jackal, for fixing the car. We'd all be hoofing it to Eden if you weren't here.'" He slid into the chair and slammed the door behind him. "Next time we get a flat, you're on your own. In fact, I think *some* lazy little fucks who won't be named need to learn the basics of changing a tire."

"Shouldn't be hard," I replied, sliding into the back with Zeke. "We'll just fill it using the hot air shooting out of your mouth."

"Allison." Kanin sighed. "Please." And we fell silent as he started the engine, turned the vehicle around, and cruised off down the road, back toward the highway and the last stretch of our journey.

CHAPTER 13

We drove on as if nothing had happened since the van had died near Old Chicago, with Kanin and Jackal up front pretending to ignore each other, and me and Zeke in the back. There were subtle differences, though. Zeke was quiet, but it wasn't the empty, hopeless silence of the nights before. I could sense him thinking, the worry plain on his face. His thoughts were probably with his family: with Caleb and Bethany, Matthew and Jake, old Silas and Theresa, the people he'd left behind. Eden was supposed to be their haven; that's what was promised, a city free of monsters and vampires. A place where humans were safe. But now, Sarren threatened even that.

Shifting closer, I put a hand on his knee, making him blink and glance over. His face was somber, eyes shadowed with worry, but it was far better than seeing absolutely nothing when I looked at him. "They'll be all right," I murmured, and the hint of a smile crossed his lips.

"I hope so."

"There you go again." Jackal sighed from the front. "Getting the puppy's hopes up. More likely, every bloodbag on Eden is screaming and tearing their faces off, but, oh, no, no one wants to hear that." He waved a hand. "So, go ahead, tell him that everything is going to be fine. All the meatsacks are perfectly content on their happy little island, Sarren has given up world destruction to raise kittens, and the magic wish fairy will wave her wand and turn shit into gold."

Zeke tensed under my fingers, and I glanced over at Kanin. "Can I stab him, please?"

"Hey, I'm just being a realist, here." Jackal laced his hands behind his head, leaning back with a snort. "Someone in this fucked-up family has to be."

Nobody said anything to that. Zeke settled back in the seat, eyes dark, but after a moment, he shifted close and pulled me against him, wrapping me in his arms. His gaze remained worried and preoccupied, his chin resting on my shoulder, but he never relented his grip. Like I was an anchor keeping him from plummeting into the dark. I relaxed into him and tried to keep my thoughts on Eden, Sarren and the task before us. Not the smooth skin of his throat, inches from my lips.

Maybe an hour into the drive, the dark, endless expanse of Lake Erie began appearing through the trees and crumbling buildings, keeping us company as we rode through the night. Still settled against Zeke, I watched the forest zip by through the windows, the black waters of the lake glimmering through the trees, and had the vague sense that this was all very familiar somehow.

A car flashed by in the headlights, a rotting hunk of metal on the side of the road, jarring my memory. The road before us was empty and lifeless, but I remembered: a night in the rain, a deserted stretch of pavement, a thousand rabids clawing themselves out of the dirt to come at us.

"Kanin," I murmured, gently freeing myself from Zeke's arms, "I think we're close."

More cars appeared, lying in ditches or abandoned on the side of the road, their doors gaping open. Zeke stirred beside me, peering out the front window, scanning the tops of the trees.

"The spotlight is gone," he said darkly. "They always keep it lit, to guide people to the checkpoint, let them know they're close." His eyes narrowed, and my uneasiness grew. "We have to hurry."

Kanin didn't answer, but his grip on the wheel tightened, and the vehicle picked up speed. The cars and trees thinned, vanishing altogether, until there was nothing but open pavement. A long, lonely strip of blacktop, leading to a pair of huge iron gates at the end of the road.

Kanin brought the car to a rolling halt, switching off the headlights. I clenched my fist against Jackal's seat, excitement warring with apprehension. There it was. Finally. Eden, or the last barrier before getting to Eden. Beyond those gates was a military compound where the ones who made it this far got a final checkup before being allowed into the fabled city. I remembered driving through those gates with Zeke and the others, the dazed relief from the humans because we were finally safe. We'd finally made it.

And I remembered walking out again, through those same gates, leaving it all behind. Because I was a vampire, and Eden, as I'd always known, was not for someone like me.

But the gates wouldn't be the only barrier keeping us from Eden tonight. A huge pale swarm milled around the wall, shrieking and clawing. Dozens of rabids, maybe hundreds, surrounding the gates that led into the checkpoint.

"Oh, no." Zeke stiffened beside me. "Something is definitely wrong. The rabids usually stay away from the gates— the soldiers use them for target practice if they get too close."

"Well, something's sure got them all riled up," Jackal said, his boots still propped on the dash, one arm dangling out the open window. "And they're not going to let us walk up and knock on the door, that's for damn sure. Any thoughts on how to get in? I guess finding a meatsack and using it for bait is out…." He sighed as both Zeke and I glared at him. "Hey, I'm just throwing out suggestions. And don't scowl at me, puppy. You certainly didn't have any qualms dicing a few minions to get us where you wanted in Old Chicago."

Zeke's lip curled, showing fangs, and I put a hand on his arm. Now was not a good time for a fight to break out; the rabids would notice and be on top of us in a heartbeat. "Kanin?" I asked instead, watching my sire. "Any ideas?"

Kanin stayed silent, observing the swarm claw and leap at the barrier. Without answering, he reached up and flipped on the headlights, then almost instantly switched them off again. He did this several more times, flashing the lights in a strange pattern I didn't recognize. Three short flashes, followed by three longer ones, then three short ones again. Several of the rabids noticed and broke away from the wall, edging toward the vehicle.

Jackal cocked his head, watching the approaching monsters. "Well, if you were trying to get their attention, old man, congratulations. Here they come. Not sure they get the whole Morse code thing, but who knows?"

Beyond the swarm, at the top of the wall, a light suddenly clicked on, the quick gleam of a flashlight. It flashed three times, and Zeke straightened quickly.

"Someone is up there," he said, his voice threaded with relief.

Kanin nodded. "Let us hope it is a human and not Sarren," he murmured, and glanced over at Jackal, still slouched back in his seat. "I'd roll up the window, were I you," he added.

Jackal frowned. "Roll up the window? Why…oh." Jackal quickly swung his boots off the dashboard. "Shit. Guess we're gonna go knock on the door after all."

His words were almost lost as Kanin slammed his palm into the center of the steering wheel, sending a piercing wail into the air. The rest of the swarm jerked up, spinning around at the noise, and hundreds of blank, dead eyes fastened on us.

"Well, here we go." Jackal sighed as the entire mob gave earsplitting cries and sprinted toward us over the pavement. Kanin put the car in Reverse and sped backward down the road, inciting the horde into a frenzy. When he was a few hundred yards from the gate, and about fifty yards from the rabids swiftly closing in, he slammed on the brakes and wrenched the car into drive again.

"Allison, Ezekiel?"

"Yeah?"

"Hang on to something."

The car leaped forward with a squeal, gaining speed, as we hurtled straight for the approaching swarm. Kanin didn't slow down but flipped on the headlights just as we crashed full speed into the first wave, knocking them aside with wet thumps. Rabids flung themselves at the vehicle, smashed into the windshield, and were hurled away. They leaped onto the hood, clinging desperately as they screamed and clawed at the glass, soulless white eyes peering madly through the barrier. One rabid's skull hit the windshield as it leaped at us, and a spiderweb of cracks instantly spread across the glass.

The wall loomed in front of us, the space in front of it clear, though the massive iron gates were still closed. With a few rabids still clinging to the van, we sped unerringly toward the metal barrier, Kanin not slowing down. Zeke muttered something inaudible and grabbed the back of Jackal's seat in a death grip. I followed his example with Kanin's.

"Hang on," Kanin muttered, and spun the wheel sharply to the left. The car gave an earsplitting squeal as it spun sideways, left the road, and smashed into the wall, crushing a few rabids between layers of metal. The impact threw me sideways, too, nearly wrenching my arms from their sockets as I clung desperately to the seat. There was a moment of chaos, of grinding metal, screaming rabids, and breaking glass, and the vehicle rocked to an abrupt halt.

"Let's go." Kanin jumped out and pulled open the side door, letting Zeke and I scramble free. The car lay in a crumpled, smoking ruin, the broken bodies of rabids lying beneath it or smashed into the wall. In front of us, farther down the road, the horde was coming back, screaming and bounding over the pavement.

"Get to the gates!" Kanin barked, and we ran for the entrance, which was still firmly closed. We crowded in front of the steel doors, drawing our weapons, as the frantic shrieks and wails drew closer. Zeke called up to the watchtower, banging his machete hilt against the metal, but there was no answer.

"This asshole had better open the door," Jackal growled, spinning his fire ax in a graceful arc as the horde came on. "I didn't come all the way to Eden to be eaten at the damn gates. Some might call it ironic, but that just pisses me off."

The first rabid lunged at me, howling, fangs and claws going for my face. I brought my katana up and sliced through the spindly middle, cutting it in half in a spray of dark blood. Another bounded in, and Zeke's machete sliced down, hammering into it and tearing the head from its neck.

With a deafening groan, the gate shuddered and finally cracked open, just wide enough for a single person to pass through. I turned just as a soldier poked his head out and beckoned frantically to us all.

"Get inside! Hurry!"

"Go!" Kanin snapped, and we didn't need encouragement. Zeke ducked through first, with Jackal right behind him. As the horde descended upon us, screaming and wailing, I cut down one last monster and backed swiftly away with Kanin until we reached the door. We slipped through the opening, and Kanin joined Zeke and the soldier in pushing the heavy gate shut. A rabid hit the gate and started to squeeze through, hissing, but my katana flashed, and it fell as its head bounced to the road. For a moment, peering through the crack, I was staring at a sea of rabids rushing toward me. Then the gate shut with a hollow, clanging boom, a heavy bar dropping into place as wailing, scratches and frantic thumps sounded on the other side.

I slumped in relief, then turned…to face a squadron of suspicious, hard-eyed soldiers, their assault rifles already trained on us all.

Okay, this wasn't starting off well.

The monster in me growled, urging me to attack, to take out the threat before it was too late and they shot us full of holes. I pushed down the bloodlust and lowered my sword, trying to appear nonthreatening. I hoped these weren't the same soldiers I'd encountered the first time I'd come through the checkpoint—the ones who would recognize me as a vampire. They had to believe we were just a group of normal humans looking for Eden. But something was definitely wrong. The checkpoint was on high alert, and the soldiers seemed twitchy; it hadn't been this way the first time we came through.

Sarren's doing? I wondered. *Or something else?*

Jackal snorted.

"Nice reception," he drawled, gazing at the squad of armed humans with a mix of amusement and disgust. "I feel so welcome here. Do all visitors get the red carpet treatment, or are we just special?" He shot a glance at Zeke, his smile dangerous. "Hey, puppy, I think your welcoming committee needs a few things explained."

Zeke quickly stepped forward, facing the squad. "It's all right," he said, as the soldiers turned, their eyes wary and hard. I watched him, hoping he was calm, that he had his monster under control, as well. Thankfully, he seemed composed as he continued, speaking to the soldier out front, the one who looked like he was in charge. "My name is Zeke Crosse. I'm a resident of Eden." Some of the men straightened, definitely recognizing the name, as Zeke continued. "Dr. Richardson knows who I am. If you tell him I've come back, he'll sort everything out."

The soldiers murmured and relaxed a bit, and the lead soldier lowered his gun. "Zeke Crosse," he repeated, his brow furrowed in thought. "You're that kid who was working with the scientists. The one they let off the island a few months back." Zeke nodded, and his gaze flicked to the rest of us. "What about them?"

"They're friends," Zeke replied without hesitation. And Jackal, much to his credit, managed not to roll his eyes or snort. "They're here to help."

The man relaxed, and the rest of the soldiers lowered their weapons. "All right," he said, and I breathed a small sigh of relief. "I've heard your name before, Mr. Crosse, though you picked a hell of a time to come back. Sorry for the welcome, but we can't be too careful anymore."

"What's going on?" Zeke asked.

"Come with us." The soldier jerked his head back down the road. "We'll explain as we go."

"Wait." Another soldier pushed to the front. The commander frowned at him, but the human's dark eyes were narrowed on me. "The girl," he growled, his voice hard, and my heart sank. "I know you," he stated. "I recognize you. You were with that group when they first came here, about five months ago. You're the one Keller let walk away." His jaw tightened, and he raised his gun as the other soldiers tensed. "She's a fucking vampire!"

All guns were leveled in my direction, and I bit down a snarl. Raising my hands, I forced my voice to be calm, steady. Oh, we did not need this now. Not with Sarren out there, possibly close. Something was definitely up, and I'd bet the deranged vampire was right in the middle of it. The humans might not even know the danger they were in. We had to find him, but getting shot full of lead or inciting a panic was not going to help any of us.

The soldiers glared at me, fear and anger plain on their faces, their fingers tensing around their weapons. The monster within growled, eager for bloodshed. "I didn't hurt anyone last time I was here, and I'm not going to now," I told the men, meeting their hostile, accusing stares. "We don't have to do this."

Zeke stepped forward and swept me behind him in one smooth motion, facing the soldiers and their guns. "She's with me," he said, keeping himself between me and the dozen assault rifles pointed at my chest. "I brought her here. At Dr. Richardson's request. She's not a threat to Eden or the people here, I swear it on my life." I caught the tremble in his voice, the bridled rage, and swallowed hard. The monster had emerged with the threat of violence, and he was barely holding himself back. I shot a quick glance at Jackal and Kanin. My sire watched calmly, patient and calculating, waiting to see what would happen, if he needed to intervene. Jackal stood a few feet away, observing the humans with his arms crossed and a rather dangerous smirk on his face, making me groan inwardly. If this got out of hand, these men were as good as dead.

The soldiers stared at Zeke, stunned and outraged. "Fetch Dr. Richardson," Zeke went on. "Tell him I'm here, and that

I have what they sent me for. He'll know what I'm talking about."

The lead soldier finally lowered his gun, though his expression wasn't friendly. "Well, that might be difficult," he stated in a flat voice. "Richardson is dead."

Zeke straightened. "He's dead?" he whispered. "When? How?"

"Eden has been compromised," the man said grimly, as the soldiers continued to hold their weapons on me. "The island is lost. We cannot give you any more details, but your vampire is going to have to come with us."

CHAPTER 14

I could sense the snarl rising in Zeke's throat as several of the men stepped forward, their guns trained on me. I heard the beginnings of a growl rumble through him, and quickly grabbed his arm. If he attacked, if he gave himself away as a vampire, the soldiers would turn on him, on all of us. They might start firing, and then everything would end in disaster. We couldn't afford that. Not now. Not with Sarren out there, probably within Eden itself.

"Zeke, wait!" He turned, his gaze angry and intense, the hint of fangs peeking through his lips. Dammit, I had to calm him down as well, before he lost it and savaged the humans. "I'll go with them," I whispered, then glanced at the soldiers. "I'll go with you!" I called, louder this time, and they relaxed, though not by much.

Turning back to Zeke, who still looked defiant, I leaned close and lowered my voice. "This is the best way," I told him. "Stay with Kanin and Jackal. Try to figure out what's going on."

"I'm not letting them take you."

"I'll be fine." I squeezed his arm, desperate to convince him. "What are they going to do, burn me at the stake?" *God,*

I hope not. "But you have to look for Sarren, Zeke. If they think I'm the only vampire here, they won't be watching the three of you. We have to find out what's happened to Eden, and where Sarren could be. That's more important now."

Zeke closed his eyes. "I'm sorry," he murmured, giving me an anguished look. "I didn't want it to be this way. I thought Dr. Richardson would be here to explain everything."

"You couldn't have foreseen what would happen." The soldiers were giving me impatient looks; I didn't have a lot of time. "This is the best option, Zeke. We don't want to start a fight. Better that it's just me then all four of us." I leaned in even closer, dropping my voice to a whisper. "You can't let them discover you're a vampire, not until you figure out what's happened to Eden."

Zeke sighed, looking angry and frustrated, but nodded. "I'll find you," he promised, briefly pressing a hand to my cheek. "I promise. I know the people here, they're not unreasonable. We'll talk to them and sort this out. Just hang on until then."

"I will," I said, though I didn't tell him my true thoughts. That humans in general were not very reasonable when it came to vampires. That the fear of monsters and predators usually took over any rational thoughts when it came to their own survival. That I didn't expect much sympathy or un- derstanding, and I was really just buying him and the others time to find Sarren.

And lurking in the darkest part of my mind was the fear that I kept even from myself. The whole reason Zeke had been allowed to leave Eden in the first place was to bring back a vampire. And now, here I was. A vampire, in a city full of frightened, desperate mortals.

Part of me said I was being incredibly stupid, putting faith in these humans, trusting they wouldn't strap me to a table and dissect me like a rat. Part of me was insisting that I fight my way clear. I was a *vampire;* who were these mortals to treat me like a prisoner and an animal? We could rip them apart, scatter their limbs in the road, and find Sarren without their help.

I pushed that voice aside. I was not that kind of monster, I told myself. We had come all this way; I wasn't about to slaughter the people I'd come to help. And Zeke still had family here; if I gave in to the monster, he could fall as well, and it would be even more devastating for him once he came out of it. No, if it meant keeping Zeke grounded and in control, if it meant the others would remain free to look for our real enemy, I would put myself in the humans' custody and not tear them in half. Even though I had zero faith that they would treat me as anything but a monster.

"Leave that weapon behind," the lead soldier told me, jabbing his gun at my katana as I walked up. "Bad enough we let a bloodsucker walk through the streets—it's sure as hell not going to be armed. Take it off."

I bristled, but calmed my anger, stripped off my weapon, and handed it to Kanin. Our eyes met as his fingers closed around the sheath. *Look after him, Kanin,* I thought, holding his gaze, hoping he could read my expression. *Don't let him succumb to the monster.*

He gave a tiny, almost inscrutable nod, and I relaxed. Kanin knew what was happening, what had to be done. He would take care of both Jackal and Zeke, and they could figure out what was happening in Eden, as well.

Turning back to the soldiers, I raised my hands to show they were empty and stepped forward. They surrounded me, keeping their guns trained at my center. The lead soldier eyed my companions over my shoulder, his mouth pulled into a grim line.

"You three wait right here," he told Zeke and the others. "Don't move until we return." Turning to me, he motioned us forward with his gun. "Let's go."

They escorted me down the road, where it became clear that something was terribly wrong in Eden.

Rows of makeshift tents and buildings lined the street, filled with humans reeking of pain, blood and fear. Lean-tos made of corrugated metal, wood or tarp had been hastily constructed into crude shelters, and people crowded together for warmth and body heat. Sometimes, a family or group didn't even have shelter; they huddled in blankets around a lamp or fire pit, their lips blue with cold. When I'd first come here with Zeke, this had been a sparsely populated outpost, with a few long cement buildings that held military units and the checkpoint clinic, where they tested you for infection before you were allowed into Eden. That was as far as I'd gotten; a well-meaning doctor had tried treating my injuries, only to discover I didn't have a heartbeat. I'd left immediately after, not thinking I'd ever see this place again.

"What happened here?" I asked the lead soldier. "Are all these people from Eden? What's going on?"

"Not at liberty to say, bloodsucker." The soldier's voice was clipped; he was obviously on edge. People stared at us as we walked by, eyeing me with suspicion. This was probably not the best time for a vampire to arrive at Eden's gates; nerves were shot, and tempers were already frayed thin with the chaos.

The soldiers ushered me to one of the long cement buildings, down a flight of steps, and into a small underground room. Two cells stood opposite each other in the dim light, small and cramped, and already occupied. A pair of scruffy-looking men looked up from the bench in one cell, their eyes going wide when they fixed on me. The lead soldier marched to a cell, unlocked it, and yanked open the door.

"Out," he snapped, glaring at the men in distaste. "Go on, then. Back to your zones, and stay out of trouble this time.

No one is happy, but we're working on the problem as fast as we can. I swear, if I have to break up any more fights, I'll start tossing people over the wall, you got that?"

"What, you mean you're not going to let the girl stay with us?" one of the rougher-looking men drawled, peering through the bars at me. "She must be pretty special, to get a whole cell block to herself." He leered at me, showing broken yellow teeth. "You can throw her in here with us, Sarge, we'll be good, I promise."

The monster perked at this, and I swallowed the sudden excitement...and fear. That would be a very, very bad idea. Me, in a tiny cell with a pair of humans, locked in, nowhere to go. Even if these men didn't try anything, I wasn't sure I could control my instincts. The soldiers might come back to a massacre.

"Funny." The soldier's voice was cold; apparently he was thinking the same thing. Stepping back from the cell, he jerked his thumb at the stairs, glaring fiercely. "Out," he barked again. "Both of you, get out. Now."

The men complied. Filing out of the cells, they shuffled toward the stairs, shooting me looks that ranged from curious to hungry. One of the soldiers jabbed a gun in my direction and backed me against the wall, away from the humans passing us. They kept their guns trained on me until the men clumped up the steps, and then the lead soldier pulled back the cell door with a groan, motioning me inside.

"Move, bloodsucker." A gun poked me in the ribs, and I went. Passing the sergeant, who watched me carefully, as if I might turn on him at the last moment, I stepped into the cell, and the door clanged shut behind me.

I took in the space in one quick glance: cement walls, heavy iron bars, no windows. That was something, at least. I wouldn't have to worry about the sun slinking across the floor, with me huddled in the corner, desperate to get away from it. I didn't think I'd be able to break out of here even if I got the chance; the door and bars seemed pretty heavy-duty. Kanin could probably bend them, no problem, but I wasn't a Master vampire and didn't have his strength. I might be stuck in here for a while.

I gazed back at the sergeant. "How long will I have to stay here?"

"Not my call, vampire." The men seemed a little more at ease, now that iron bars separated us. "We'll alert the proper authorities, but it's up to them to decide what to do. I suggest you get comfortable, and don't get any ideas. You poke one fang out of this room without authorization, I'll have every soldier in this place shoot you full of holes. You got that?"

"Yeah." I sighed, walking to the bench on the far wall. "I got it."

"Good. Make sure you don't forget." He strode away, barking orders to his men. "Lewis, Jackson, watch this room. No one comes down here without my say-so, and if the bloodsucker so much as sneezes, I want to know about it."

"Yes, sir."

"And check out the other three—the kid and the two strangers. I want to know who they are, where they came from, everything."

"Yes, sir."

Their footsteps clomped up the stairs, their voices fading away, and I was alone in the room.

Great. I'd been afraid it would come to this, locked in a cell while I waited for the humans to decide what to do with the vampire. I hoped that, when I woke next, I wouldn't be strapped to a bed while scientists in white coats milled around, poking me with needles and taking my blood. Like they'd done to Sarren, and all those other vampires sixty years ago. The ones they'd turned into the rabids.

Shivering, I hugged my arms to my chest and sat on the hard metal bench, trying not to think about that. This had been a bad idea; I should've known not to trust the humans. I hoped Zeke, Kanin and Jackal were all right, that they'd be smart enough not to wait for the soldiers to return. I worried most for Zeke. Would he be able to control himself in the presence of so many humans, many of them weak and vulnerable? I trusted Kanin would be able to keep him sane, but I also had my doubts that my sadistic blood brother wouldn't say or do something that would send him over the edge. And if that happened, we could all end up in here, waiting for the scientists to strap us to tables and poke tubes through our veins.

An hour, maybe two, passed in silence. No one came to check on me, and I alternated between sitting on the bench and pacing my cell. I tested the bars and door a couple times, wondering if I could break free if I had to, but the metal was thick and the door firmly locked. I wondered what Zeke and the others were doing, if they had found a way to Eden without me. Or had their secret been discovered and they were in hiding now, trying to avoid capture, or death? Zeke had promised that the Eden scientists wouldn't use me as a lab rat, but those scientists were no longer around. Growling, I clenched the bars of my cell, feeling my fangs slide free. If it did come to that, I wouldn't go quietly. A vampire could only be pushed so far. Keeping me locked up was one thing. If they came anywhere near me with a needle or a scalpel, I hoped they were ready for a hell of a fight.

I had just paced back to the bench to settle in the corner again when a noise on the steps made me look up.

A human stood at the foot of the stairs, watching me from behind his glasses with sharp black eyes. He was tall and slender, with a narrow face, thinning hair, and a pristine gray suit that looked slightly too small for him, showing off bony ankles and wrists. I narrowed my eyes. He reminded me of a Pet, of a boy I once knew, who'd betrayed me to become the aide to the vampire Prince of New Covington. It seemed Eden had their version of Pets, as well.

The man gazed at me, lips pressed into a serious line, then stepped briskly into the room. I tensed as he approached the cell and stopped several feet from the bars, well out of my reach should I decide to lunge at him. I eyed him wearily. I didn't know what he wanted, but if he was anything like that Pet I used to know, then I didn't want to talk to him. He was probably here to threaten, or ask questions, or maybe to inform me that I was bound for some kind of secret lab on the island. I wondered if I could get any information out of him regarding Zeke and the others.

"Miss Allison."

I blinked, frowning. I was surprised that he'd used my name; most humans just called me *vampire* or *bloodsucker*. But his tone wasn't condescending, or smug. It almost bordered on…civil. That was different. "Yes?"

He continued to stay well away from the bars, but his voice was serious as he folded his hands before him. "Please, forgive the accommodations," he said, as if he was soothing an annoyed yet important guest. "Rest assured we are doing everything we can to clear up this misunderstanding. Your friends are speaking with the mayor right now about the situation in Eden. We expect that you will be able to join them soon, if you can be patient just a little longer."

I stared at him, unable to believe what I was hearing. It had been so long since any human had spoken to me like I was a person, once they knew what I really was. "You…you do realize what I am, right?" I asked. Maybe he *didn't* know what he was talking to; maybe his boss hadn't told him the girl in the cell was really a monster. He blinked, then gave a somber nod.

"Yes. You are a vampire. That has already been established. But your friends have vouched for you, that you mean no ill to the people of Eden, and we will hold them to that. If you harm or kill anyone while you are here, it will be on their heads." The man's voice didn't change; it was still polite and matter-of-fact, but the warning in it was clear. If I hurt anyone, Zeke and the others would pay for it, too.

"However," the human went on, "Zeke Crosse has done much for Eden, and we have spoken to the doctors and soldiers who saw you the last time you were here. On their testimony, and the insistence of Mr. Crosse, we have decided to trust you. As soon as the mayor gives the order, you are free to go."

"He's letting me go. A vampire." Suddenly leery that this could be a trap, I narrowed my eyes, searching his face for the truth. "I find that a little hard to believe. What does he really want from me?"

"Only your cooperation, Miss Allison." The man's voice didn't change. "And the promise that you will not harm anyone here. The citizens of Eden do not know about you, nor should they, but the mayor realizes that a vampire could be of great use to us, especially now."

"If that means he's going to turn me over to the scientists, I'm afraid we don't quite see eye to eye," I said, showing the very tips of my fangs. But the man shook his head.

"No, Miss Allison. Never without your consent." If he saw my incredulous look, he didn't mention it. "The scientists you speak of did need vampire blood to continue their research, this is true, but we fear they are all dead now. They never got off the island when the catastrophe hit."

"What catastrophe?"

"I'm afraid you'll need to hear it from the mayor," the human said gravely. "He just sent me here to inform you that the situation is being resolved, and ask you to please not attack the citizens of Eden when you leave this place."

I continued to stare at him. That wasn't what I'd been expecting. Humans welcoming a vampire into their city? Treating her like she wasn't a monster, or a thing that could be turned into an experiment? The human outside the cell was being cautious, yes, but he'd spoken to me with respect, like I was a real person. Maybe… I'd been wrong. Maybe Zeke's version of Eden had been the right one, after all.

"Allie."

Footsteps echoed on the steps, and Zeke came into the room, followed by several soldiers. The lead soldier, the sergeant I had seen before, gave me a businesslike nod as they entered, then jerked his head at another human, who approached the cell door with a key.

Zeke stood back as the soldier unlocked the door and pulled it open with a rusty screech, but quickly stepped forward as I left the cell. His gaze was worried, hesitant, as if afraid that I blamed him for being stuck behind bars for three hours. "I'm sorry, Allie," he murmured, regret and concern etched into his face, along with a little anger and guilt. "This shouldn't have happened. I promised you wouldn't be treated this way—"

"It's fine," I assured him, lightly touching his arm. "They had to protect themselves. I get it. Where are Kanin and Jackal?"

"They're with the mayor right now." He paused as the sergeant approached, holding my katana out to me. Surprised again, I took it and slipped it onto my back, and the soldier motioned us up the stairs. "He wants to talk to you. Are you ready?"

I nodded, then glanced at the man I had thought was a Pet, still watching us from where he stood before the cell. He met my gaze, solemn and unsmiling, but his expression wasn't fearful or filled with hate. Perhaps I'd judged him a bit harshly, too.

"Thanks," I said softly, and he nodded.

We followed the soldiers up the stairs, out of the building, and into a large jeep humming at the edge of the road. No one spoke. Zeke and I sat pressed between two soldiers, guns held across their chests, gazing straight ahead. Outside the windows, I viewed the tent-and-rubble city, sprawled in messy rows past the pavement and reaching all the way to the distant wall. Ragged, shivering humans wandered the streets or huddled around metal drums, looking scared and miserable. Whatever was happening in Eden, it had to be horrible, to have driven the entire population here.

That did sound like Sarren.

"Do you know what's going on?" I whispered to Zeke. He nodded grimly.

"Mayor Hendricks will tell you everything," he murmured back. "Better that you hear it all at once. But it's awful, Allie. I didn't think it would be like this when I came back." His voice turned steely. "Sarren has to die. I don't care what happens to me, but we have to find Sarren and end this, once and for all."

The vehicle pulled to a stop at another long cement building, one I recognized from my last stay. It was here that I'd watched the rest of the group being shuffled off to different parts of the building, never to see them again. It was here that I'd whispered my goodbyes to a sleeping, post-surgery Zeke, turned, and walked out of his life without looking back.

"The hospital?"

"Yes," Zeke answered as we piled out of the car. "The

mayor was badly injured in the flight from Eden and has been recuperating here ever since."

The hospital was filled to capacity, rooms bulging with wounded humans, and the scent of blood and chemicals nearly knocked me down when I stepped through the doors. People in stained white coats shuffled through the aisles of cots, checking patients, administering aid, trying to make them comfortable because that was all they could do anymore. Groans and soft cries of pain followed us as we walked through the rooms, and, surrounded by the wounded and vulnerable, my demon stirred restlessly. Injured people were everywhere. They had even spilled into the halls, huddled in blankets or curled up in corners, looking miserable. The monster, of course, watched them intently, urging me to take advantage of the sick and weak, easy prey. I pushed it down, but the scent of blood and fear made it hard to think of anything else. Halfway through the walk, Zeke reached down and took my hand, squeezing tightly as we ventured deeper into the hospital. He did not look at the beds or the rows of moaning, thrashing humans, keeping his gaze rigidly in front of us. But his eyes were glazed, and his jaw was clenched to keep his fangs from sliding out. I kept a firm grip on his hand as we continued down the halls.

Finally, the soldiers led us to a door at the end of the hall. The two men guarding it eyed us warily as we approached but didn't say anything as the lead soldier pushed open the door and motioned us in. Beyond the frame was a room that had probably been an office once. But the desk was gone, replaced with a single bed, and a man in a white coat hovered over it with his back to us. A pair of soldiers in combat fatigues stood by the door, giving us the evil eye as we came in. Glancing around the room, I spotted Kanin in a corner, nearly blending into the wall, and Jackal slouched against the back window with his arms crossed. He met my gaze across the room and grinned.

"Oh, hey, there's the little stool pigeon herself. Make any new friends while in the slammer, sister?"

"Shut up, *James*."

The doctor turned at that, eyes widening behind his glasses when he saw me. He was a small, thin man with a balding head and long, elegant fingers. "You," he blurted, blinking rapidly in the florescent lights. "It *is* you. The vampire girl. I recognize you."

I recognized him, as well. He was the doctor who'd taken care of Zeke's injuries when we'd arrived several months ago. He was also the person who had discovered I was a vampire, when he'd tried to listen for a heartbeat I didn't have.

"Dr. Thomas," rasped the person in the bed, and a man struggled to sit up. The doctor turned as if to help him but was waved away by a thick, bandaged arm. "Doctor, please. I'm fine. Let me see the bloodsucker for myself."

The doctor stepped aside, and I stared in astonishment. The man in the bed was huge. Not tall or muscular, just…big. His stomach bulged against his hospital gown, his cheeks were pale but round, and his neck was thicker than anyone's I'd ever seen. I'd heard the term *fat* before, but had never encountered such a thing before this. Hunger and starvation were so common in my world; I couldn't imagine having so much food that your body would store it away for later.

His large torso was wrapped in bandages, his skin white and pasty beneath the cloth. His dark hair was short and damp with sweat, and the hand lying on his ample stomach was bandaged tightly, thick fingers twice the size of a normal person's.

But his eyes, tiny and black, regarded me with a sharp, piercing gaze, one pencil-thin brow raised in surprise. "This is the vampire?" he asked no one in particular. His voice was surprising, too. High and clear. "A girl? I wasn't expecting her to be so...small."

We can't all be walrus men, was the retort that sprang to mind, though I didn't voice it out loud. Dealing with volatile vampire Princes had taught me the value of diplomacy, especially when talking to the people in charge. Jackal, of course, snorted a laugh, and I glared at him.

"She's stronger than she looks," Zeke said in a quiet voice, making the mayor blink at him. "Trust me on that."

"Yes, but..." The mayor peered at me intently. "When they told me a vampire was being kept in the barracks, I was picturing something...older. Not a girl. She looks young enough to be my niece."

I held my tongue again. *You wouldn't know a vampire if it walked up and bit you,* I thought ungraciously. *You have four vamps standing in this room right now, one of whom is a Master, and you're making comments about my age? How did you get to be mayor of Eden, anyway?*

"It doesn't matter." Kanin's deep, calm voice echoed from the corner. "She is still a vampire, and you cannot afford to be choosy at this time, Mayor Hendricks. You need her."

I frowned, glancing from my sire to the mayor, feeling confused and left out. "What's going on?" I asked.

"Ah, of course." Mayor Hendricks sighed and sat up straighter in the bed. "My apologies. Let me explain." He winced, shifting his large bulk under the covers, trying to get comfortable. "As you've probably guessed by now... I'm sorry, what was your name again, vampire?"

"Allison," I supplied.

"Allison. That seems so normal." The mayor shook himself. "Well, as you've probably guessed, Allison, Eden is experiencing a bit of a...situation. With everyone driven from their homes, trapped between the lake and the rabids, tension is running a bit high. We didn't mean to be rude, but I'm sure you understand we had to protect ourselves. Especially now."

"I got that," I said cautiously, and he grimaced, more in pain then from anything else. "What exactly is going on?" This was crazy. How had Sarren managed to drive *everyone* out of Eden? Even if he was insane, unhinged and unpredictable, he was still just one vampire. He couldn't drive off an entire city by himself. "What happened on the island?"

"Well." Mayor Hendricks, pressed his lips together. "Turns out, that person you've been chasing is a sick, sick bastard. Early one evening…"

He grunted, clenching his jaw in pain, and the doctor stepped forward anxiously. Hendricks waved him off. "Doctor, please. I'm fine. I need to talk to the vampire before you knock me out again. Give me two minutes, and then you can stick me with whatever you want."

The doctor backed off, his face pinched with worry. Hendricks sighed and turned to me. "One evening," he continued, "a barge floated up to the island. On the western side, near the town square. People thought it was abandoned. There was no one aboard that we could see, nor did it answer any of our communications. A crowd of people watched it crash into the docks, and gathered on the shore to see if they could help." Hendricks shook his head. "Poor bastards," he murmured, running a chubby hand down his face, before looking up at me. "Take a wild guess as to what was on that barge, Allison."

My insides felt cold, and I briefly closed my eyes. I didn't have to guess. "Rabids," I whispered.

"Hundreds of them," the mayor confirmed. "They came pouring out like ants, screaming and killing, attacking everything they saw. Instant pandemonium." He snapped his fingers. "Eden was lost in minutes. Hundreds of people died fleeing the rabids or trying to get off the island. The military units were overwhelmed—there were just too many, and they caught everyone by surprise. Most of the army died that night, trying to protect the civilians and get them to safety. There just weren't enough boats for everyone to leave at once." Hendricks's mouth thinned. "My own guards sacrificed themselves so that I could get out of there, and even then, I almost didn't make it. But I know I'm luckier than a lot of people."

"I'm sorry," I said, because there was nothing else to say. Only Sarren would think of something that horrible. What had it been like, I wondered, being trapped on an island with a huge army of rabids? The one place that was supposed to be safe for humans, suddenly turning into a nightmare. I couldn't imagine it.

"Everyone out there has lost something," Hendricks continued, gesturing vaguely at the door. "A child, a parent, a friend and, at the very least, their home. We are stuck here. Every day, the soldiers go back to the island to look for those still stranded. Every day, they dig up and kill as many rabids as they can before the sun goes down again. But it's not enough, and we're running out of time. Supplies are almost gone, and the doctors can't keep up with the sick and injured. Something drastic has to be done, or Eden will be lost forever.

"And then," Hendricks went on, eyeing me again, "I get word that four strangers fought their way through the horde outside the gate to get here, and that one of them was Zeke Crosse. The same kid who left Eden to bring back a *vampire* for the scientists, because apparently they need vampire blood to finish their research." The mayor glanced at Zeke. "We all thought he was dead, or at the very least, crazy. But here he is. With a vampire, no less."

I caught Jackal's knowing smirk from the corner of my eye and deliberately did not look directly at him or Kanin. "So, what do you want me to do?" I asked, feeling Zeke tense beside me. "Clear out your island? Even I can't take on hundreds of rabids by myself."

"From what I understand," the mayor continued, glancing at Kanin, "we have a far bigger problem to worry about."

I glanced at my sire as well, and Kanin slid out of the corner to stand before us.

"Yes," he said, mostly to Mayor Hendricks. "The rabids, as I explained before, are only a distraction. A very clever, dangerous distraction, but they are not the source of your problems. You have a vampire on that island. It was he that set the rabids on you, and it is he that is using Eden for his personal testing grounds."

The mayor's gaze grew dark. For the first time, he looked dangerous, like he wasn't someone you really wanted to cross. I suddenly understood how he was in charge. "Why?" he asked softly. "What does he want?"

"He's after the cure," Zeke said. "He wants the Rabidism cure, either to destroy it or to turn it into something horrible. He already destroyed New Covington with that virus—think of what he'll do to Eden if we don't stop him. Allie is the only one who stands a chance."

"So, we'll send a vampire to fight a vampire," the mayor mused quietly, and gave a grim smile. "What a strange way to answer our prayers, but I'll take what I can get."

Glancing up at Kanin, his tone became businesslike. "What do you need?" he asked briskly. "Weapons? Ammo? I would send some of my men with you, but I honestly don't have many to spare. Or supplies, for that matter. But we'll give you what we can."

"That won't be necessary," Kanin said. "Transport to the island is all that we require."

"I can get you a boat," Hendricks said immediately. "And a pilot, if you need one. The ice hasn't completely frozen the lake yet. It'll be a bumpy trip, but you should be able to get there. When are you planning to leave?"

"Tomorrow." My sire spared a glance at me. "As soon as the sun goes down."

Hendricks started to reply, but gasped and started to cough, causing the doctor to scurry forward with a syringe. "I'm sorry, but he really needs to rest," he told us, over the mayor's breathless protests, pushing the needle into his arm. "You're welcome to stay in the infirmary, provided you can find an empty bed. And that the…er…young woman isn't a danger to the patients." His bespectacled gaze went to me, which I found ironic, given the circumstances. Especially with Jackal leaning against the corner, watching us all. I felt the smugness radiating from him even without turning around.

"I won't stay here," I told the doctor. "So, you don't have to worry about that."

"It's fine, doctor," said Hendricks, having recovered from his coughing fit. "Look at her. She's not going to go on a killing spree." He glanced in my direction. "Will you, Allison?"

"No," I said simply. *I'm not the vampire you have to worry about.*

"Oh, and Mr. Crosse." Hendricks looked at Zeke. "I had someone track down the names you gave me," he said in a solemn voice. "Would you like to know what happened to them now? I warn you, you might not like what you hear."

Zeke closed his eyes for a moment. I could see him bracing himself, preparing for the worst. Opening his eyes, he gave a stiff nod, his voice grim. "Tell me."

"Very well." The mayor nodded. "Silas and Theresa Adams died of natural causes not long after you left the island," he began, making my stomach clench. "They were both found in their bed one morning, no signs of struggle, no apparent wounds or sickness. It seemed they both just went in their sleep." He gave Zeke a sympathetic smile. "They're buried in the town cemetery on Eden, if you wanted to look for them."

Zeke took the news stoically, though a muscle worked in his jaw. "And the others?" he asked in a voice that wavered only slightly.

Hendricks sighed. "Jake Bryant and his wife, Anna, managed to escape the chaos when it first broke out," he continued. "Unfortunately, Mr. Bryant was struck with a stray bullet and badly hurt. He remains in the clinic with his wife, in critical condition, but they don't think he's going to make it. The others…" The mayor paused, and by the expression on his face, it was clear that he was reluctant to go on. "Mrs. Brooks made it off the island, but her husband was killed in the first attack, as was her adopted son, Matthew. Her other two children, Caleb and Bethany Brooks, remain missing. Alive or dead, we're not certain. All we know is that they are not here."

Zeke's voice was choked. "No one has gone to look for them?"

"We send out search parties every day," Hendricks replied, his voice gentle. "The men leave as soon as the sun rises, and remain on the island until an hour before it sets. Any longer, and it becomes far too dangerous for them to continue. They can't be everywhere at once, and lately, they're finding fewer and fewer survivors each time they venture in. This last time, they didn't find anyone. I'm sorry." He shook his head, genuine regret spreading over his face, then added, "I think you need to accept that they might be gone."

Zeke clenched his fists. Without a word, he turned and left the room, moving past me with his head down. I watched the door swing shut and hesitated, torn between rushing after him and giving him space. If he was upset, he might want to be alone to grieve for his family in peace. But he was also a vampire now. And I knew how quickly sorrow could turn into a blinding, bloodthirsty rage, as the monster lashed out at everything around it.

I looked at Kanin, and he nodded. "Go," he murmured, and I went, slipping through the door into the hall, searching for Zeke.

CHAPTER 15

I found him on a narrow pier over the lake, well away from the building and the wounded people inside. The icy wind tugged at his hair and shirt, tiny flurries dancing around him and settling on his bare skin, but he didn't move as I approached.

"Zeke."

He didn't answer. Stepping up beside him, I peeked at his face. It was dry, no red tracks slicing down his cheeks, but his expression was blank once more. Alarmed, I put my hand on his arm, trying to get him to look at me. "Hey."

"I'm fine, Allie." His voice was low, tight. He didn't sound fine. He sounded like he was barely hanging on to a swirling mess of emotion inside. I stared at him, worried. "I'll be all right," Zeke insisted. "I'm just…"

Bowing his head, he shuddered, and the first red tear slipped from his eye, dropping into the water. It made my throat tighten with sympathy, but it also sent a shiver of relief through me. Horrible as it was, he was still letting himself feel something.

"They're gone," he whispered, making a lump rise to my

throat. And I forgot about the monster's indifference, wishing I knew what to say. "My family is dead. I'm the only one left."

"We don't know that," I said gently. Near his feet, the waters of Lake Erie lapped against the pier, a quiet, somehow ominous rhythm. "They could still be out there."

"They're kids," Zeke murmured. "And it's been days. How could they survive, alone, with the rabids? And Sarren?"

I swallowed. I didn't know how they could still be alive, either. It wasn't fair that those two little kids had to die, killed by rabids and a deranged vampire, after they'd come so far. That they'd survived the entire journey to Eden, only to die in the very place that was supposed to be safe.

But the world didn't care about that; it was ruthless and brutal and merciless, just like Sarren, and not even people like Caleb and Bethany were immune to its darkness.

Zeke suddenly raised his head and roared, baring his fangs and making my heart jump to my throat. I tensed, but immediately after, he dropped his head, clenching his fists so hard his knuckles turned white. "My fault," he whispered. "This is my fault. I gave Sarren the information. *I* told him where Eden was. He wouldn't have come here if it wasn't for me—"

Stepping forward, I slipped my arms around him, pinning his arms to his sides as I pressed close. He stiffened, but didn't fight me, and we stood there on the banks of the lake, the wind tugging and snapping at our clothes.

"Enough," I whispered against his back. "Enough with the blame, Ezekiel. We all have things we regret, things we wish we could change, but we can't dwell on them. That's part of being a vampire now—learning to move on.

"You did everything you could for them," I continued, as his hands came up to grip my arms, squeezing tightly. "You brought them to Eden, you gave them a real home. It is not your fault that a psychopathic lunatic wants to wipe out everything."

"I should have been there with them," Zeke whispered. "If I'd never left the island—"

"I would be dead," I told him softly. "And Kanin would be dead. And Sarren would still be trying to destroy the world, with no one to stop him." I paused, then added, very gently, "I'm not discounting their deaths. And maybe they're still alive somehow. We don't know for certain that they're gone. But...you once told me everything happens for a reason. Maybe this is why."

Zeke gave a short, humorless laugh. "Why I became a vampire?" he asked. I'd never heard him sound so bitter. "Why an entire city is lost, and everyone I love is probably dead?" He shivered, gazing out over the lake. "My family is gone," he said in a flat, empty voice. "I've lost everything. Seems an awfully high price to pay."

My voice was almost a whisper. "*I'm* here, Zeke."

A tremor went through him. He didn't say anything more, and I didn't feel any tears drip onto my hands. I didn't know what he was thinking, but we stayed like that, silent and motionless, the waves lapping at the pier and the wind blowing flurries around us. I didn't move, feeling his skin grow cold under my cheek, until I felt another presence at my back, a dark set of eyes gazing down on us.

I turned. Kanin stood at the end of the dock, impassive and imposing against the night, his arms folded before him. Zeke hadn't turned, didn't see the Master vampire, but those depthless black eyes were on me, waiting. He didn't move, didn't beckon me forward, but I turned back to Zeke, lowering my voice.

"I have to go," I told him, and his head bobbed very slightly. "Will you be all right?"

"Yes." His voice was soft, but almost normal. I reluctantly let him go, and he hesitated before adding, "Allie…thank you."

I wanted to say more, but I felt the weight of Kanin's gaze on us both. So I lightly touched Zeke's shoulder and went, leaving him alone at the edge of the water, worry and sorrow still heavy on my mind.

The Master vampire waited for me at the end of the dock, watching as I approached. As usual, he gave no hints to his thoughts or feelings, though I was surprised he'd sought me out. Usually, my sire was the silent, neutral observer, leaving me and Jackal to our own devices—until our bickering got too annoying, anyway. I wondered why he'd chosen tonight to come after me.

"Come," he said simply, when I finally joined him at the edge of the wooden planks. "There is work to be done. Follow me."

"Work?" I frowned and hurried after my sire, jogging to keep up with his long strides. "What work? What are you talking about?"

"The people here have lost a great deal," Kanin said without looking at me, heading toward the main street and the huge tent city clustered beyond. "There are too many in need and very few with the resources to help. There are things that we can do to alleviate that."

"Why me?" We passed the hospital, where a pair of soldiers nodded to Kanin but eyed me with wary suspicion. Kanin smiled humorlessly.

"I would not ask James," he replied, making me snort. "And Ezekiel needs some time alone. There is only so much you can do for him, Allison. He must come to terms with this loss himself." His voice turned slightly grave. "Also, I fear with four vampires here, Eden might not come away completely unscathed. We might have to feed soon, so let this be part of that compensation. I only hope it does not come down to that."

Kanin and I worked through the night. The most pressing concern was the wall that kept out the rabids; there were places that had weakened with the relentless attacks and were in danger of crumbling entirely. The humans watched us come and go without suspicion, unaware of the monsters in their midst. After a few hours of fortifying the defenses, Kanin volunteered me for guard duty, watching the road for stragglers and making sure the rabids couldn't claw their way in. As I sat atop one of the towers, gazing down at the hissing, writhing mass outside the gates, I wondered if the real reason Kanin was doing this was to keep me away from Zeke. Maybe not with the intention to separate us, but to keep me occupied and to give Zeke a chance to deal with this loss alone. Maybe that *was* the best thing for him now.

Or maybe not. Maybe Kanin's reasons were as he said— payment for the harm four vampires might bring to the community. Or perhaps it was something else. I didn't know. My sire had always been inscrutable, and I'd given up trying to figure him out.

About an hour before dawn, I was relieved of sentry duty, and I returned to the hospital. In the quiet stillness before sunrise, most of the tent city was asleep, huddled between blankets and family members, their misery forgotten for a while.

As I headed toward the front door, a hint of fresh blood came to me over the breeze. Frowning, I followed it around a corner, where Jackal leaned casually against the outside wall, cloaked in shadow, his yellow eyes glowing in the darkness. He smelled of blood, but clean and untainted with chemicals, unlike the bandaged, wounded patrons in the hospital. I desperately hoped he hadn't eaten one of them. My Hunger perked up with a growl, and I shoved it back.

"Oh, hey, sister." Jackal grinned at me, then took something out of his duster: a plastic bag full of dark liquid. "Did they finally release you from manual labor? A vampire working for the sheep—how positively nauseating. If I were you, I would've told the old man to go sit on a campfire. But, hey, better you than me." He gave me a mocking salute, then bit into the plastic. I frowned.

"Where did you get that? No one here knows you're a vampire."

He pulled his fangs from the bag and smirked at me with bloody lips. "It's amazing what you can find if you go poking around back rooms when no one's looking," he answered. "Found this hanging in a fridge, and I got Hungry. Want one, sister?" He lifted the bag, and a few red drops fell to the ground, making my stomach churn with Hunger. "There's still a couple left, last I checked." He peered at me again, then arched a brow. "What's that look for?"

"Nothing," I said, smiling. "Just never thought I'd see you choose a bloodbag over a human to feed from. Are we finally rubbing off on the big, bad raider king?"

He rolled his eyes. "I'm a vampire, sister. I'm not stupid. If one of these meatsacks up and vanishes without a trace, who are they going to blame first? We don't need the heavily armed, vampire-hating soldiers poking around and asking questions, and it's so tedious to dispose of a large pile of corpses. But not to worry." He settled against the wall, crossing his long legs, and bared his fangs in a smile. "After we stop Sarren, I fully intend to indulge in a nice killing spree to get this taste out of my mouth, so don't think you've defanged me quite yet."

I grinned. "If you say so, James."

He glared at me. "Shouldn't you be saving orphans with the

puppy right now? Or pretending to be interested in Kanin's stories? Go bother someone else for a while."

Triumphant, I turned away, preparing to leave. "Where are Kanin and Zeke?"

"Hell if I know. Last I saw the old man, he was talking to the mayor, making plans to leave tomorrow and all that shit. They didn't look like they needed me, and besides, I was bored." Jackal took a long swig from the bag. "So I thought I'd do my own exploring. Oh, and by the way, they cleared out a room for you so you don't have to share the common area with the sickies. Guess having a vampire in the hospital made them a bit nervous after all." He waved the bag at me, arching his brows. "Sure you don't want one, sister? You could split it with the puppy over candlelight."

I walked into the hospital, leaving Jackal outside with his stolen blood. The rooms were quiet now, most of the humans sleeping, only a couple nurses milling around the beds, checking on patients. They ignored me as I made my way through the halls, not really knowing where I was going. I wondered if I should go look for Zeke, but figured I'd leave him alone tonight. Maybe he was weary of my constant hovering. Dawn was less than an hour away, and I was tired. Zeke knew I was here; if he wanted to talk, he would come to me.

I finally stopped a nurse in the corridor and asked where my room was. She pointed me in the right direction, then fled, hurrying around a corner as quickly as she could. So, apparently, some of the humans here knew of the vampire wandering the grounds. Hopefully, they'd keep that knowledge from the rest of the patients. I could only imagine what a mob of scared, panicked humans might do if they realized a vampire was sleeping in the room next door.

I walked into my room, which happened to be a large storage closet with a bed in the corner, and froze when I saw a figure leaning against a shelf, waiting for me.

"Zeke?" I blinked as the door swung shut behind me. "What are you doing here—"

Zeke took three steps forward, took me gently in his arms, and pressed his lips to mine. Shocked, I stiffened, but only for a moment. Then my arms snaked around his waist, and I leaned into him as he pulled me close. His mouth worked against mine, gentle but insistent, almost desperate. I could feel the hard cords of muscles in his back, in his arms, like steel bands dragging me closer. His hands rose to tangle in my hair, and I sighed against his lips, feeling a different hunger rise up, burning through my veins. I wanted to tip my head back, baring my throat, but Zeke held me so tight, it was all I could do to kiss him.

When he pulled back, I was a little dazed. His arms were still around me, pressing me close, and didn't feel like they would loosen anytime soon. I looked up at him, meeting that intense stare, and gave him a puzzled smile. "What was that about?" I whispered.

Zeke touched his forehead to mine, closing his eyes. "That was me...finally realizing what's important." He sighed, his voice full of regret. "It shouldn't have taken me this long, but it seems I've always had trouble seeing what was right in front of me. I guess..." His brow furrowed, and he shivered. "I guess everything had to be taken away for me to get it."

"Zeke..."

He pulled back, his eyes tormented as the stared into mine. "Eden is gone," he said, making my stomach clench. "My home has been destroyed, and my family...is probably dead. And I'm a vampire. I've lost almost everything." His grip tightened painfully, his gaze almost desperate. "I can't lose you, too."

"You're not going to lose me," I said, feeling my eyes prickle. "I've told you that before, Zeke. I'm here. I've been right here the whole time."

"I know," he choked out. "God knows I don't deserve it. I don't deserve a second chance, but… I can't imagine my life without you, Allie." His hand rose, pressing against my cheek, his eyes bright with emotion. "You're the only person that makes me feel human again. When I'm with you, I can actually see a future. One that isn't full of blood and death, one that I can live with." He paused, his voice soft but determined. "I can't change what I've done, but I *can* try to make things better. I want to live, and I want to spend forever with you. If… if you want it. If you want me around that long."

I swallowed hard to clear my throat. "You've always had me, Ezekiel," I managed, meeting his bright blue stare. "Time never mattered. Vampire or human, if we had forever or just a few years, I'd always choose to spend it with you."

He blinked, and his palm traced a searing path down my cheek, his gaze intense. "I love you, Allison," he whispered, making my stomach twist into a knot. "With everything in me—heart, mind and soul. Even Sarren couldn't take that away. Even when I was on that table, screaming and wishing I was dead, all I could think of was you. You've been with me every step of the way, and you never wavered, even when I was ready to give up. I'm sorry it's taken me this long to figure it out." He took one of my hands, holding it to his chest, his gaze never leaving mine. "So, this is me, all of me, forever. No more looking back. No more regrets. From now on, vampire girl—" he lowered his head, brushing his lips across my skin "—I'm all yours."

My throat closed up, and my eyes went blurry. Relief and emotion rushed through me, making me want to laugh, cry and hug him all at once, but all I could manage was a weak smirk and a strangled "It's about damn time."

Zeke blinked, then, very slowly, he smiled. A real smile, one I hadn't seen since that horrible night when he had died. And for a moment, everything Sarren had done to him, to us, fell away completely, and he was the same boy I'd met in that abandoned town: charming, determined, ever hopeful. Leaning in, he kissed me, long and deep, and I wrapped my arms around his neck, pulling him closer. He backed us up until I was against the wall, rough concrete pressing into my coat, feeling every part of him against me and needing more. His lips trailed a path from my mouth to my jaw and neck; I gasped and arched my head back, feeling the lightest scrape of fangs against my skin. And that hunger flared up again.

With a growl, I shoved away from the wall, pushing him toward the bed in the corner of the room. He sank easily onto the mattress, taking me down with him, wrapping his arms around my waist. I set my elbows on either side of his head and kissed him, feeling his hands slide over my back, skimming under my coat. The dark, tattered material was suddenly too constricting; I pulled back and shrugged out of it, letting it drop to the floor. Zeke gazed up at me, blue eyes serene, no traces of doubt or fear shadowing his face.

"Allie." His voice was a breath, a quiet murmur, as I dropped to kiss him again, pressing my lips to his jaw. He groaned and arched his head back, baring his throat, and I felt my fangs lengthen in response. He was so close, the scent and feel of him filling my senses, but I wanted to be closer. I wanted all of him, all he could give, and everything I could offer. No more barriers. Tonight, Zeke was mine, and nothing would take that away.

I bent to his neck, kissing his throat, barely pricking his skin with my fangs. As Zeke groaned again, my hand slipped under his shirt, tracing his skin. He gasped, and I started to push up the fabric.

"Wait," Zeke whispered, sounding breathless. I pulled back to look at him, my lips just inches from his own. "Allison," he said, though his eyes were slightly glazed and the tips of his fangs glinted as he spoke. "We don't have to do this. It doesn't have to be tonight." His hand rose, pressing against my cheek, his eyes never leaving my face. "We have forever to figure this out," he said gently, "if it's not the right time…"

I resisted the urge to bare my fangs. "The last time we chose to wait, Ezekiel, you *died*." He flinched, his eyes darkening with the memory, and I clenched a fist in his shirt. "Not that I have any intention of losing you again, but right now, we're up against a madman who has a pretty good head start on creating another apocalypse. He's *not* taking this away." I did bare my fangs then, a gesture of defiance. "If the world ends tomorrow," I whispered fiercely, "if these really are the final days, then I'll be damned if I have any regrets."

Zeke's eyes gleamed. Without warning, he reached up and pulled my head down to his, crushing our lips together. Before I could react, he abruptly shifted and flipped us over so that I landed on the mattress with a thump, blinking in surprise. I'd forgotten how strong he was now. He kissed me deeply, then trailed his lips down my neck, making me gasp and arch into him. My blood thrummed, surging through my veins. I wanted him to bite me, to sink his fangs into my throat. I ached to feel him again, like his soul had merged with mine and I knew every tiny corner of his mind and heart.

I growled, clutching him close, and Zeke responded with a growl of his own, his lips on my mouth, my neck, tracing a path down my middle. I gasped and tore at his shirt, pulling it over his head. More clothes followed, both of us almost frantic to shed them, to get as close to the other as we could.

When nothing separated us, I ran my hands over his scarred back, down his tightly muscled arms, and over his lean chest, trying to memorize him with my touch.

Zeke pulled back, his face hovering close to mine, his stare bright and his fangs fully extended.

"Say you love me, vampire girl," he whispered, his voice low and husky. "Tell me...that this is forever."

"I love you," I said immediately. "And if we have forever, there's no one else I want to spend it with."

He lowered himself onto me, and I bit my lip, digging my nails into his back. It hurt, but I'd felt far worse pain then this. As he bent to kiss me again, I closed my eyes, surrendering to sensation. We were so close; it felt like I was on fire, heat singing through my veins. But there was still something missing.

Closer, I thought through the haze. *Get closer, Zeke. It isn't enough.*

Zeke suddenly clutched me tight, a breathless growl escaping him. As I gasped, arching my head back, he bent his head and *finally* sank his fangs into my throat.

I cried out, gripping his shoulders, a hundred emotions coursing through me. I felt him everywhere, within and without. I felt his fear, the desperation that he might lose me, either to Sarren's hand or his own failings, and then he'd be left to deal with the monster he'd become, alone. I felt his anger, his rage at his sire, the demon who'd destroyed his family, who had hurt so many people and wasn't finished yet. His determination to succeed, to keep as many people safe as he could. And...his love for me, intense and powerful and almost frightening. It was an endless well, a cocoon that wrapped around us both, warm and strong and intoxicating. It brought tears to my eyes, and they spilled down my cheeks as I lay there, unable to move. Not wanting to move. Willing to stay here like this, forever.

Zeke pulled back, retracting his fangs, and gazed down at me. I met his eyes and saw they were a little red, too.

"I never...thought it would be like that," he whispered in an awed voice. Placing a hand on my cheek, he trailed his finger down the red tracks, his expression anxious. "Are you all right?" he asked. "Did I hurt you?"

I reached for him, sliding my fingers into the hair at the base of his skull. "Come here," I whispered, tugging him toward me. He complied instantly, and when he bent down, I rose off the mattress, lifted my face to his neck, and sank my fangs into the side of his throat.

Zeke gasped. His blood flowed over my tongue, hot and sweet and powerful, searing through my veins. I sensed every emotion from him once more, feeling his blood mingle with mine, merging us together. Zeke trembled, holding me close, eyes shut in complete surrender.

When I pulled back, dawn had broken the horizon outside; I could feel the light just beginning to spill over the trees and the rest of the world. Retracting my fangs, I gazed sleepily up at Zeke, who met my stare with a look of complete adoration.

We didn't need to say anything. Bending down, Zeke placed a gentle kiss on my lips and settled behind me, pulling the covers over us both. I leaned into him, feeling his blood and emotions swirl through me, drowning even the monster, and for the first time since the death of my mom when I was ten years old, I relaxed completely in someone else's arms.

I awoke lying on my side under the covers, a cool, solid weight pressed against my back, Zeke's arm curled tightly around my waist. The room was still; no sounds filtered in from the lighted crack below the door, and by my internal clock, the sun had just gone down. My sword lay abandoned and forgotten under the bed, my clothes in a crumpled heap beside it. Normally my weapon would be the first thing I checked when I woke up, but right now, it didn't seem that important.

The events of the night before came back to me, emotional and surreal, making me shiver. Last night…with Zeke's blood and emotions coursing through me, I'd never felt so close to anyone in my life. It had been intense and thrilling and completely terrifying, seeing the deepest parts of him laid bare, knowing the depth of his feelings. Realizing he saw past my wall, too.

But now, it was another night, and we had a crazy vampire to stop and a virus to destroy. Kanin and Jackal would certainly be waiting for us, ready to set out for Eden. Briefly, I wondered if either of them could feel what I had been doing last night through our blood tie. For a moment I was horrified, then decided that I didn't care. It wasn't anything I was ashamed of, and besides, if Jackal had decided to check up on me and gotten more than he bargained for, well, that was *his* fault for spying.

But I still didn't want him banging on my door.

Taking Zeke's wrist, I started to lift his arm away, intending to slip from the bed and back into my clothes, but there was a faint growl behind me, and the arm at my waist tightened, pulling me back.

"No," Zeke murmured into my hair. "Don't go yet. Just a few minutes longer."

I glanced over my shoulder at him. His eyes were closed, his face serene, except for the faint, stubborn set of his jaw. I smiled, poking the arm holding me captive. "Kanin and Jackal will be waiting for us, you know."

"I know," Zeke muttered without opening his eyes, though his brow furrowed slightly. "Two minutes," he pleaded, stubbornly holding on. "I just want to lie here like this with you.

Before we have to leave and face that whole huge mess waiting outside this room."

I turned, shifting in his arms to face him. His eyes finally opened, that clear, piercing blue, watching me intently. I stroked his jaw, wishing we *could* lie here all night, that we didn't have to worry about deadly viruses and insane vampires who wanted to destroy the world.

"We'll beat him," I whispered, a promise to Zeke, myself and everyone. "This isn't the end, Zeke. Whatever happens, I'm not giving up our forever without one hell of a fight."

Zeke smiled, his face peaceful, and placed a lingering kiss on my mouth. "All right, then, vampire girl," he whispered, his eyes shining with determination. "Let's go stop the apocalypse."

PART III

⁜

EDEN

CHAPTER 16

"There it is," muttered Kanin.

I looked up from the railing, icy wind whipping at my hair and clothes, spitting water and flurries in my face. Around us, the black, roiling expanse of Lake Erie stretched on forever, unchanging. The waves tossed our little boat, bobbing it like a cork in the water, and I kept a tight hold on the rusty metal rail surrounding the deck. Kanin stood up front, arms crossed and eyes forward, a motionless statue against the churning waves and black sky. Jackal leaned against one of the rails and alternated between gazing out over the water and shooting me knowing smirks. When Zeke and I first arrived at the dock, my blood brother had taken one look at us and barked a laugh, though, shockingly for him, the only comment he made was a rather triumphant "About bloody time." I'd been waiting for him to say something else, bristling and ready for a fight, but so far he remained mute on the subject, which was rather disconcerting.

I tried to ignore him as I gazed out over the water, squinting in the direction Kanin was facing, searching for the island. At first, I didn't see anything but waves and flurries, swirling endlessly in the void. Then I saw it, a glimmer of light, cutting through the snow and darkness, beckoning like a distant star. As we got closer, more appeared, until I could vaguely make out the island, a black lump speckled with dancing lights against an even blacker sky.

Zeke moved behind me, slipping his arms around my waist and laying his chin on my shoulder, gazing toward the distant Eden. I laid my arms over his and leaned into him, feeling his solid presence at my back. "Home," I heard him mutter, his voice pitched low. "I wonder what it looks like now. If anything can ever go back to normal."

I didn't know the answer to that, so I just squeezed his arm, watching the lights of Eden get brighter through the snow.

The boat bounced over a wave, coming down with a jolt that snapped my teeth together, and Zeke's hold on me tightened. The shadowy mass of the island loomed closer, the outline of trees and rocks taking shape through the darkness.

The boat finally came to a drifting, bobbing halt, several feet from land. A snow-covered shoreline, probably a beach, stretched away to either side, glittering coldly under the stars.

"This is as far as I go," the pilot said, his voice low with suppressed fear. "I don't want them monsters swarming my boat if I get too close." He pointed toward Eden with a gnarled finger. "Township and docks are in that direction, along the western side of the island. But we stopped unloading people there because of the rabids."

"Thank you for your assistance," Kanin replied, finally moving from his spot at the front of the boat. "We'll continue on foot from here. Allison, Ezekiel." He glanced back at us. "Let's go."

Jackal snorted, pushing himself upright as we moved to follow Kanin. "What am I, chopped liver?" he muttered, and swung his long legs over the railing. There was a muffled splash as the raider king dropped into the water and waded toward shore.

Zeke and I followed Kanin, stepping from the boat into the black waters of Lake Erie. Almost as soon as we were off the deck, the engine rumbled, and the boat turned around in a spray of icy mist, heading back toward the mainland. Apparently, no one was sticking around to take us back. We'd have to find our own way off Eden.

Curling a lip at the rapidly disappearing boat, I struck out for shore. Water sloshed against my legs and drenched the bottom half of my coat, bitingly cold even though the chill didn't affect me. Waves smacked against my arms, and the ground under my feet kept shifting as I marched doggedly toward Eden.

I was relieved when my boots finally hit solid ground. Ice and pebbles crunched under my feet as I walked up the shore with Zeke, joining Kanin and Jackal at the edge. Beyond the embankment, a dark line of trees shimmered with distant lights twinkling erratically through the branches. Aside from the churning of waves on the beach and our footsteps in the snow, everything was silent and still, as if the island itself was holding its breath.

Kanin's eyes, dark and solemn, bored into Zeke as we drew close. "Where would Sarren be?" he asked, and even his quiet voice sounded unnaturally loud in the stillness. Zeke paused, staring into the trees, his eyes narrowed in thought.

"The lab," he said after a moment. "The place where the scientists were working on a cure. That's where he'll be. I'm sure of it."

"Well, then," Jackal said, with a very slow, evil smile that glinted with fangs, "if the psychopath is expecting us, we shouldn't keep him waiting."

Sarren, I thought, as the anger, the rage I thought I'd for-

gotten, surged up with a vengeance. Everything that led to
this moment—Kanin's torture, the New Covington plague,
Zeke's death and Turning—all pointed to the madman who
waited at the end of the road. *This is it; we finally made it to
Eden.* Looking at Zeke, Kanin and Jackal, my small, strange,
indisputable family, I clenched my fists. *I won't let him win. One
way or another, it ends tonight. We won't get another shot.*

Kanin turned to Zeke again. "This is your island, Ezekiel,"
he said. "Your territory. I expect you know where to go."

Zeke nodded. "This way," he murmured, leading us up
the bank. "There's a road ahead that will take us to the city.
We'll have to go through Eden proper to get to the lab, but
there's a lot of open space between us and the city. We could
be fighting rabids the whole way there."

Let them come, I thought, following Zeke up the rise. *We're
in Eden. We finally made it. Do you hear that, Sarren? I'm here.
I'm coming for you.*

Slipping into the trees, we found a narrow strip of pavement
that snaked away into the darkness, and we headed deeper into
Eden toward the madman at the end of the road.

It was quiet, far too quiet, on the small paved road that cut
through the fields, passing distant houses that sat empty and
dark at the edge of the lots. Past the beach where we'd come
in, the trees thinned out, becoming large open pastures beneath undisturbed blankets of snow. The few homes I saw,
though they were neat and tidy, not falling to ruin under years
of neglect and decay, didn't account for the large number of
people at the checkpoint.

"I thought Eden was a city," I whispered to Zeke,

"It is," Zeke replied in an equally low voice. We hadn't
seen any pale, skeletal forms lurking in the shadows or distant buildings, but we knew they were out there, somewhere.

"We're on the outskirts of Eden proper right now. Most of the surrounding areas they use for farmland, as much as they can spare. The city itself is farther in."

I gazed out over a snowy field, empty now due to winter, I guessed, and remembered my own days as a Fringer, starving and scavenging to survive. Even the registered citizens of New Covington were barely given enough supplies to live, unless you made it into the Inner City, of course. How did Eden provide enough food for her people? From what I'd seen at the checkpoint, there had to be a few thousand survivors.

"These aren't the only farms," Zeke explained when I finally asked him. "Only a small percentage of food comes from Eden itself. There are three smaller islands—we passed them on the way here—that are solely for growing crops and raising livestock. A handful of farmers and ranchers live there year-round and ferry supplies to Eden every couple weeks." He gazed into the field, watching the wind swirl ice eddies through the pasture. "I was only here a few months," he admitted, "but from what I learned, the people here take care of each other, so no one really goes hungry for long, even in the lean times."

"Huh," I remarked, wondering what that must be like: never going hungry. Never having to worry where your next scrap of food would come from, if you could scrape enough together to stay alive another day. And even more shocking, the people here helped each other, looked out for one another, instead of hoarding their supplies or scheming ways to get more from those who had them. I'd never experienced that. Everyone in my world, before Zeke anyway, looked out only for themselves. "Sounds like they have a pretty good life here."

"They did," Zeke muttered. "Until now."

The road continued farther into Eden, and we soon left the fields and farms behind. Houses and buildings became more prominent, simple but sturdy homes that faintly resembled the rows and rows of urban dwellings in the abandoned cities. Only these were whole and unbroken, with well-tended yards, walls that weren't crumbling, and roofs that hadn't fallen in. The houses were packed together, people literally living on top of each other in two-and three-story dwellings. Still, it was a much nicer place than anywhere I'd seen before. It was crowded, sure, but it was better than the shoddy, ramshackle settlements I'd seen outside the vampire cities, buildings thrown together with whatever happened to be lying around. These homes had been carefully built and carefully maintained, like the real towns had been before the plague. Not a hastily constructed settlement that would vanish in a few years.

Though the utter silence and emptiness made it even more eerie. Like this place was *supposed* to be bustling, full of people and noise and life, and it wasn't. The world outside had been abandoned for decades, and it showed in every collapsed building, every rusted-out car, weed-choked highway, or rooftop split with trees. Everything was dark, broken, empty of life, and had been for a long, long time.

But here, there were subtle hints of a life before. A blue bicycle, leaning against a fence post, old and faded but still in working condition. A car parked on the edge of the road, doors open, dried blood spattering the front seat. A doll lay in the middle of the sidewalk, as if it had been dropped and its owner had either left it there or been hurried away. A few buildings were still lit from the inside, spilling soft orange light through the windows.

"The power plant is still running," Zeke said, glancing at a streetlamp that flickered erratically on the corner. "That's a good thing, I suppose."

I peeked through an open door creaking softly on its hinges and found a small, quaint living room, a stone fireplace in one corner and a green sofa in front of it. The sofa was the only thing in the room that wasn't overturned or destroyed. Shattered plates littered the floor, chairs were knocked over and smashed, and ominous brown streaks covered one part of the wall. I took a quick breath and smelled what I feared: that hint of decay and wrongness, lingering on the air like an oily taint. They were definitely out there, lurking in the darkness. I wondered why we hadn't run into any of them yet.

We hadn't gone far into the city when we stumbled across the first rabid corpse.

It lay in the road, the snow falling around it, its white, emaciated body curled up like a huge spider. Its skull had been crushed, either by bullets or something heavy, and the snow beneath it was stained black. I curled a lip, Kanin ignored it, and Jackal gave it a smirk as he stepped over the broken body and continued down the road.

As we went farther into Eden, and the buildings to either side grew taller and more crowded, the number of bodies increased. Rabids lay in the road or on the sidewalk, riddled with holes or blown apart. The military forces had not gone quietly and were probably the reason so many made it out of Eden alive. There were no human corpses in the road, the fallen having been torn apart or eaten by rabids in short order. But the telltale signs of the massacre were still there. Bones lay scattered amid rabid corpses, the tattered, bloody remains of clothes still clinging to them. A body, more skeleton than flesh, lay half in, half out of a broken store window. I couldn't tell if it was a man or woman because it was so savaged. The smell of blood, rabids and unrestrained gore was overpowering, and had I been human, it would have made me violently sick.

"Well, someone's been having fun," Jackal remarked as we edged around a pile of dead rabids, the street and walls riddled with gunfire. A large camouflaged vehicle lay on its side by the curb, windows smashed, blood streaked across the windshield. "This place is screwed even worse than New Covington. All we need now is a mob of bat-shit-crazy humans tearing their faces off."

Faint scratching sounds interrupted him. A rabid lay beneath one of the huge tires, its lower half crushed by the vehicle, long arms clawing weakly at the pavement. It spotted us and hissed, baring a mouthful of jagged fangs, right before Jackal drove the heel of his boot into its skull. There was a sickening pop, and the rabid stopped moving. Jackal curled a lip and scraped his foot against the curb.

"You know what? Never mind. I can do without the bat-shit crazy. This place is screwed enough."

Kanin ignored him, turning his attention to Zeke. "How much farther to the lab?"

"Not far," Zeke confirmed. "The docks and the town square are about a mile that way," he went on, nodding toward the west side of the island. "According to the mayor, that's where the barge crashed and the rabids came pouring out, so I'm trying to avoid the main strip by taking us around. The lab is on the outskirts of the city, near the power plant and the old airport."

"Then lead on."

The road continued deeper into Eden, cutting through canyons of buildings and apartments, beneath bridges and walkways from the levels above. Streetlamps glowed dimly on corners, and lights shone above us from windows and doorways, casting weird shadows over the empty streets.

"Still no rabids?" Jackal mused, gazing into dark alleys and shadowy buildings. "I thought this hellhole was so infested they couldn't throw a rock without hitting one. Where's the crazy keeping them all?"

"I'm sure we'll find out soon," Zeke muttered. "I'm surprised we haven't run into anything else. If Sarren knows we're coming, I would've thought he'd set up at least a few—"

And at that moment, of course, my leg brushed against something: a hair-thin wire stretched across the road near the ground, almost invisible in the blackness. As soon as I felt it, I froze, but it was too late.

A bloodcurdling scream rang overhead, making me jump back with a snarl, unsheathing my blade. Zeke and Jackal drew their weapons, and we pressed back-to-back, gazing around for attackers. There was no body, human or rabid, on the balconies above, no movement in the shadows. But the scream continued, frantic and terrified, echoing through the street and over the rooftops, making me cringe.

"Where is it coming from?" I snapped, wishing I could see whoever was screeching just to shut them up. In the deathly stillness, the screams pierced the night like gunfire and probably echoed for miles. But I still couldn't see anyone.

Kanin abruptly swooped down, snatched a loose brick from the sidewalk, and hurled it into the darkness. I saw the projectile flash through the air and hit something small on the corner of a roof. There was a crunch and then a garbled buzz. Pieces of wires and machinery fell into the road, fluttering like dead moths, as the scream sputtered into silence. Though the echoes still lingered, bouncing off the walls and ringing in my ears.

And now there was a new sound, rising over the rooftops, getting steadily closer. A skittering, hissing, scrabbling noise, the sound of many things closing in. Jackal bared his fangs in a silent snarl and hefted his ax.

"Well, ask a stupid question…"

"This way!" Kanin barked, turning down a side alley. "Before they're all over us!"

A white skeletal figure dropped onto the road from an overhead balcony, eyes blazing, and lunged at me with a wail. I tensed, but Zeke's machete flashed between us, and the rabid's head hit my boots as it collapsed. "Allie, go!" he snapped as the roofs, walls and streets began to swarm with pale, spindly bodies. "I'm right behind you!"

We ran, following Kanin down the narrow, winding streets, ducking into alleys and through buildings, a screaming, hissing mob at our heels. Claws snatched at me from a side street, snagging the edge of my coat. I spun and lashed out at the same time, cutting both arms from the rabid's body before sprinting on.

A rabid leaped atop a car hood, hissing. Jackal snarled and brought his weapon down with a vicious crunch, crushing metal and the rabid's spine equally. "Starting to feel like a rat in a maze, here," he said, glaring at the mob closing in around us. "If anyone has an idea beyond 'run in circles and kill everything that fucks with us,' I'd love to hear it."

Zeke dodged a rabid that leaped at him, and swung his blade into another's neck, severing it neatly. His backswing hammered into the first rabid as it lunged at him again, slamming it into a wall. "Where are we?" he growled, casting a quick look at a street sign on the corner. A rabid tried charging at him while he was distracted, but met a katana instead as I ripped my blade through its middle and cut it in half. "Centre Dyke and Sandpoint," Zeke muttered, and took a step back. "Okay, I know where we can go. Everyone, follow me!"

He took off down another side street, the rest of us close behind, cutting down rabids that got too close or blocked our path. Zeke and Jackal led the way, the machete and fire ax working in tandem, slicing through bodies or bashing them aside. Kanin hung back with me and covered our escape, his thin, bright dagger lethally accurate as it flashed through the air.

The streets opened up, and right ahead of us, a small stone building sat within a wrought-iron fence at the end of a small grassy lot. As we fought our way toward the gate, headstones became visible through the neatly cut grass, crosses and angels rising into the air, and Jackal gave a snarl of disgust.

"Oh, sure! Of course it would be a damn church. What else was I expecting?"

Zeke, slicing his way through two more rabids that came at us, didn't slow down. "If you're worried about bursting into flames if you cross the threshold, feel free to stay outside," he said without looking at Jackal, who snorted and rammed the hilt of his ax into a rabid's face, flinging it back.

"Hey, not to rain on your little parade, but I think you've forgotten something." He swung his weapon in a vicious arc, striking an attacker down with bone-crunching force before turning on Zeke. " You're a demon now, puppy, same as the rest of us. I wouldn't be so smug—you're just as likely to get the lightning bolt when you step through those doors."

"Then I'll know where I stand," Zeke muttered, and hit the cemetery gates, pushing them back with a creak. The rabids followed us across the lawn, between headstones and angel statues, scrabbling over the graves to get to us. We fought our way up the steps of the small church, toward the heavy wooden doors at the top. With the church at our back, the monsters were forced into a bottleneck as they pressed up the stairs, making it easier to deal with them. But there were still a lot of the bastards, and they were stupidly persistent. While Kanin, Jackal and I blocked the stairs, Zeke turned to open the doors. They rattled when he tried the handle, but didn't budge.

"Locked," he growled. "Someone's already sealed the way in." He bashed his shoulder into the doors, putting his con-siderable vampire strength behind the blows. The heavy doors shuddered violently, but didn't move. "Dammit! It's blocked off. Something is on the other side. I can't move it."

The rabids shrieked and pressed forward, as if sensing blood and knowing we were trapped. Kanin stabbed one through the eye and drew back a step, sheathing his blade. "Hold them off," he ordered, and whirled around, joining Zeke at the entrance. Jackal snarled a curse and slid toward me, closing the gap. The rabids hissed and clawed at us, surging forward, and we desperately fended them off.

"You know," Jackal said, kicking a rabid in the face, sending it reeling, "it seems that whenever I'm with you, I'm constantly fighting my way into places I really don't want to be. The sewers, the Prince's tower, a bloody freaking church." A rabid clawed at him from the side of the stairs, and he slammed its head into the railing. "If I ever need a favor, sister, I hope you'll remember this shit. All these life-threatening situations? Not really my thing. I should've cleared out a long time ago."

"Why didn't you, then?" I snapped back, dodging a rabid's claws to my face. "No one was stopping you. You could've left anytime, just like that time in New Covington. Or are you waiting until you find the cure to jump ship?"

He snarled, whirled around, and smashed the rabid leaping at me to the concrete. "You are so bloody frustrating!" he roared, back fisting another rabid with the axhead. "Do you really think the cure is worth *this?* You think I'd be here now if that's all I wanted?" He turned and sliced his weapon through the air, beheading one rabid and sinking it into another. "Get your damn head out of your ass, sister!" he seethed. "And give me a little fucking credit. That's not why I'm here."

A hollow boom interrupted anything I was going to say. Kanin and Zeke both hit the doors at the same time, and the added strength of a Master vampire shattered whatever was on the other side. The doors flew open with a crash, the sound of rubble scattering across the floor.

"Go," Jackal spat at me, and we swiftly backed toward the doors, where Zeke and Kanin stood just inside, ready to slam them shut. I crossed the threshold, and Jackal turned, flinging himself through the opening, his ax thudding against the floor as he rolled.

Screeching, the rabids surged forward. Zeke, Kanin and I slammed the doors, and the blows of the mob vibrated through the wood. But the wood was thick and reinforced with iron bands that could weather the relentless assault. Leaping forward, Jackal grabbed a snapped beam from the floor and shoved it between the handles, barring the doors shut. They rattled, shaking violently, but held.

Backing away, I looked around the room. Wooden pews filled the interior, some overturned or broken, but most intact. The windows were high and narrow, and had metal frames that once held stained glass, broken now, but too small for rabids to squeeze through. From the smell of death and the few rabid corpses littering the floor, it looked like people had tried to hole up here, just as we were doing, but hadn't succeeded. Either someone inside had been bitten and Turned, or the rabids had gotten in another way. Dried blood streaked the walls, benches were in pieces, and bloody bones were scattered here and there. Several pews had been piled in the corner in what looked like a makeshift barricade, but in the end, it hadn't helped.

"Well," Jackal muttered, dusting off his hands, "here we are. In a church. Vampires taking refuge in a church—that's gotta be the most ironic thing of the decade. Puppy, you'd better tell me this place has a back door."

Zeke had started across the room but suddenly paused near the front, his gaze falling to an overturned pulpit. Bending down, he picked up a book from the wreckage, a small black book with a gold ribbon dangling between pages. The corner was soaked red, and he closed his eyes.

Behind us, the door boomed, making me jump. "That won't hold them for long," I said. My gaze fell on a pew lying a few feet away, and I started toward it. "Zeke, help me move this! We have to brace the door or they'll break it down in a few minutes."

Zeke blinked, then shook himself out of his trance. "No," he said, stopping me. Gently placing the book on a pew, he turned, eyes hard. "We can't hole up. There's no time. This was just to give us an out, to slow them a bit. Follow me."

He turned and jogged across the room, weaving around pews and rabid bodies, toward the makeshift barricade in the corner. Puzzled, I followed, Kanin close behind. Jackal snatched an oil lamp that had been lying, remarkably unbroken, on a pew, before trailing after us.

A massive blow echoed through the church, and the door bowed inward. Rabid faces peered through the crack, vicious and snarling, their claws and fangs starting to rip the wood to pieces. I hurried after Zeke, hoping he knew what he was talking about, that there was another way out of here.

Behind the barricade, Zeke ducked into a short hall and opened the door at the end, revealing a set of narrow, wooden steps, twisting up into darkness. "This way," he urged, and disappeared through the door. I was right behind him, following the stairs as they spiraled upward through a stone tower and ended at a wooden ceiling with a trapdoor. Zeke pushed it back, and we scrambled into a tiny open-air room. Above us, a large brass bell sat silent and dark, and through the curved stone windows, I could see all of Eden spread out below.

"There's the power plant," Zeke said, pointing to a scattering of lights beyond the city. A set of massive smokestacks rose skyward, looming over the buildings and billowing white clouds into the air. "The lab is right next to the—"

A crash from below warned us that we were out of time. "Quickly," Kanin said, taking command, and leaped from the tower into the branches of the single huge tree sitting beside the church.

"Go, Allie," Zeke urged, and I went, getting a running start before flinging myself off the edge of the tower. For a second, I could see the church directly below my feet, and a huge horde of rabids surrounding it, swarming through the door. Then branches filled my vision, and I grabbed at the first one I saw, clinging desperately as it swayed and gave an ominous groan, but didn't snap.

Pulling myself up, I looked back for the rest of our party. Zeke was at the edge, preparing to jump, but Jackal hadn't moved from the open trapdoor. He still held the oil lamp he'd picked up earlier, and as I watched, he raised it over his head and flung it through the opening. There was a faint crash, and Zeke whirled at the noise.

"Jackal, what are you doing? Come on!"

A hiss, and a tiny flame appeared between Jackal's fingers. For just a moment, it flickered over his sharp features and the evil grin spreading across his face, right before he dropped it through the hole. There was a sputter, and a bright orange glow flared to life through the trapdoor.

The shrieks and screams coming from within suddenly took on an alarmed note. I looked down to see several rabids shoot out the building, clawing frantically at the rest of the horde to get free, before skittering off into the darkness. Smiling, Jackal kicked the trapdoor shut and sauntered up to join Zeke, who was glaring at him with unmistakable menace.

"You didn't have to do that."

"Hey, it got the rabids off our backs, didn't it?" Jackal's grin was insufferably smug as he stepped to the edge of the tower. "I would think you'd be grateful, puppy. Kill some rabids, burn down a church—I don't see a downside here, do you?" And he leaped to the branches before Zeke could respond. Zeke snarled at him, fangs bared, but he jumped off the roof as well, landing beside me on the narrow limb.

"Come," Kanin murmured when we had all converged in the tree. Below us, the rabids had all but fled, slipping back into the ravaged city, while smoke trickled out of the bell tower and the first tiny flames began to flicker through the windows. "We'll take the rooftops as far as we can," Kanin went on, nodding to the edge of an apartment building beyond the fence. From here, it would be quite the jump, but we could make it. "Hopefully we can circumvent the rabids and any other surprises Sarren has left us by avoiding the streets. Let's go."

He turned and walked gracefully down the narrow branch, as easily as he would the sidewalk. Jackal pushed himself off the trunk and started to follow, but Zeke paused, casting one final glance at the doomed church, a flicker of sorrow and guilt crossing his face. I reached out, gently brushing his arm, and he turned back with a pained smile.

"Sorry." He drew back, turning away from the church, though his face was still dark. "Just...memories. I spent a lot of time in that building after we came here, praying for guidance, asking where I should go next. It's also one of the few places where I got to see Caleb and Bethany and the others. They'd attend Sunday morning service, and sometimes their parents would invite me home, just for the afternoon. All the other days, I'd be so busy at the lab, working with the scientists, I didn't see much of them at all." He sighed, glancing back once more, watching the flames flicker through the tower windows. "Lots of memories there. It's hard to see it all burn."

"It's just a building, Zeke. It can be rebuilt."

"Yeah." Zeke nodded and turned away. "You're right. It's just a building." His voice grew stronger, more determined. "Eden can be rebuilt. We can start over. We just have to make sure there *is* a new beginning to look forward to."

We came to the end of the branch, Kanin's and Jackal's dark silhouettes waiting for us on the nearby roof. Zeke went first, leaping into the air, farther than any human could hope to accomplish, landing easily on the other side. I gathered myself and followed, my coat flapping behind me, feeling a momentary thrill as my body propelled itself through open space and hit the edge with room to spare.

Kanin took the lead again, and we moved quietly over the rooftops of Eden, heading toward the huge billowing smokestacks in the distance. I walked next to Zeke, watching him from the corner of my eye. His expression was grim and determined, but composed. Given the state of his home and all the horrors he'd seen and been through, I thought that was pretty remarkable. I hoped it wasn't just a stoic front, a serene mask like the one Kanin wore all the time, and in reality he was about to fall apart. His city, his home, was in shambles, and everything he knew had been turned on its head. I knew what that was like, all too well.

Walking closer, I gently brushed his arm. "You okay?" I murmured.

He nodded once. "Trying not to think about it," he said. "About...them. About everyone. Mostly Caleb and Bethany, and how they used to sit next to me in church and tell me everything their goats did that week. And... I just failed spectacularly, didn't I?" He gave a humorless chuckle and hung his head, running his fingers through his hair. "They're the last ones, Allie," he said, his voice pained as he raised his head. "They can't be gone."

It was hard to think anything could still be alive out here. It was foolish to hope, and to offer hope, when reality was dark and cruel and didn't care about human attachments, or emotions, or what was right. I had dared to hope before, and it had nearly killed me. It went against everything Allie the Fringer believed; nothing lasted in the world, and the only way to survive was not to care, about anything.

But Allie the Fringer was dead. And Allison the vampire had a family now. A strange, undead, sometimes infuriating family, but she was no longer alone. She had lost the human boy she loved, only to find him again, back from the dead. And, somehow, though he'd sworn that he would rather die than become a vampire, he was still here, walking right beside her.

So…maybe it was okay to hope, to trust that things could work out. Maybe…maybe that was what had kept me human all this time, that faith that I could be more than a monster. When I lost that hope—that was when the monster won.

I shook myself. Epiphanies aside, I could not let myself be distracted. And I couldn't let Zeke be distracted, either. If there *was* hope for a future, for all of us, we had to stop Sarren, before he destroyed all hope, forever.

"They're tough," I told Zeke. "Those little kids followed you all the way to Eden, through rabids and wild animals and the psycho raider king himself. If they're alive, we'll find them."

"But Sarren comes first," Zeke finished, nodding gravely. "I know." Meeting my gaze, he offered a grim smile. "Don't worry about me, Allison. I have my priorities straight. I know what we have to do." He paused, then added in a very soft voice, "But you have to be ready to do the same."

I frowned at him, confused. "What are you talking about?"

"Hey, puppy." Jackal's voice echoed over the rooftops, inter-

rupting us. He and Kanin stood at the edge of the roof, looking back at us. In the distance, wisps of smoke writhed into
the air from a much closer power plant. Jackal's eyes glowed
yellow, and he crossed his arms with a smirk in Zeke's direction. "When you're done making goo-goo eyes at my sister,
why don't you step on over here and show us where we're
supposed to go?"

Zeke gave me an apologetic look and moved forward, joining Kanin and Jackal at the edge of the rooftops. I followed,
peering down from our perch, curious as to what lay below.
Several yards from where we stood, the crowded apartments
ended, and a chain-link fence separated the buildings from a
large, flat field. Across the open lot, surrounded by another
fence, the power plant glimmered like a metal castle, wreathed
in billowing smoke. Smaller buildings surrounded it, long and
white, and Zeke pointed to one on the very corner, engulfed
in the shadow of the plant.

"There," he said, his voice grim. "That's the laboratory."

Where Sarren will be, I added to myself, feeling a chill crawl
up my spine. *Waiting for us.* I swallowed as the realization hit
hard: this was it. We were going in to face the terrifying, brilliantly insane vampire who wanted to destroy the world. No
telling what we would find when we went in, but it would
probably be awful, dangerous and as horrifying as Sarren's
twisted brain would allow. *I hope you're ready, Allie. The last
time you went down into his lair, one of you didn't come out.*

Kanin, standing motionless at the edge of the roof, observed
the lab with impassive black eyes and nodded once. "Let's be
careful," he said quietly, echoing my thoughts. "Sarren knows
we're here and that we're very close. He has had time to prepare for our arrival. When we go into the lab, it is likely that
he will attempt to whittle us down first, either with traps or
living creatures. We must be prepared to face whatever hor-

rors he is sure to throw at us. Sarren himself is at his most dangerous face-to-face, and his mood can shift in the blink of an eye. Even after decades of knowing him, learning his patterns and how his mind works, I still could not tell you exactly what he will do in a fight."

"Well, I can answer that," Jackal said breezily, and bared his fangs in a lethal grin. "He can die. Painfully. After I rip his other arm from the socket and shove it so far down his poetry-spouting piehole that he chokes on it. What I don't understand is why we're standing up here yapping away when we should be down there kicking in his door. So, come on, team." Jackal's gaze was mocking but dangerous. "Let's go kill ourselves a psychopath."

The lab was quiet as we scaled the chain-link fence and made our way toward the long white building at the end of the lot. Nothing moved; no rabids roamed around the lab, at least not on the outside. The windows were empty and dark, but the closer we got to the building, the more convinced I became that Sarren was watching us. Kanin avoided the front doors, taking us around the back, though I didn't know why we bothered with stealth. If Sarren knew we were here, we might as well kick down the doors and start killing anything in our way.

Instead, Kanin used his elbow to break a window, somehow managing to do it silently, and we slipped into the dark rooms of a madman's lair.

Once inside, Kanin turned to Zeke.

"Where to now?" he asked softly, as I scanned the room warily. It was white and sterile, with long counters lined with many small things that glinted in the darkness. I shivered, remembering another lab, another set of precise, sharp instruments, winking at me from a pool of Zeke's blood.

"I'm not sure," Zeke whispered back, unaware of my sudden, gruesome recollections. "But if I had to guess, I would say the basement level. That's where the scientists did a lot of their experiments. Where I stayed most of the time when I was here."

My stomach turned, thinking of all the things they might have done to Zeke, but Kanin only nodded. "Then lead the way," he said, nodding to the door. "And let's be careful."

We slipped into the lab, following Zeke down endless narrow hallways, through white sterile rooms filled with counters, computers and strange machinery. Nothing looked broken or out of place. There were no bodies, no blood, no hints that anything was out of the ordinary. Except for the emptiness and eerie stillness, you wouldn't guess that anything was wrong.

And yet, the lab still made my skin crawl. It was *too* clean. Everything was overly white and gleaming and polished, smelling faintly of chemicals and disinfectant. Not only sterilized, but lifeless. My world—the world outside—was broken and falling apart, full of rust and rubble and decay. But, despite that, it was still alive. This place was almost offensively pristine and undamaged, too perfect to be real. It felt like a hospital, cold and antiseptic and dispassionate, as if terrible things had happened here but were quickly scrubbed away and forgotten.

Somehow, it was even more disturbing than if we'd opened that door to find blood-drenched walls and mutilated corpses. I expected that of Sarren. Carnage, not cold, polished rooms and silence. He was changing the rules on me, and I didn't like it.

Apparently, I wasn't the only one who thought so.

"Huh," Jackal remarked, his voice echoing weirdly down the empty hall. "Well, that's kind of disappointing. We come all this way to kill Sarren, and he can't even be bothered to leave a few traps or bleeders wandering around? I'm almost offended."

"Maybe he didn't have time," I mused hopefully. "Or maybe he's not here after all."

Kanin shook his head.

"No." The Master vampire gazed around the silent lab, narrowing his eyes. "Do not be deceived by this tranquility. Whatever Sarren was planning here, he needed to ensure that he was not interrupted. That's why he set the rabids loose on Eden. With all the chaos outside, he could work in peace, unchallenged and undisturbed. He has had plenty of time to prepare for our arrival. I expect we will discover what he has in store for us anytime now."

"Let's hope so, old man," Jackal said, and casually knocked a case of vials to the floor, where they shattered on impact, scattering bits of glass across the tiles. I tensed, half expecting the room to erupt into chaos with the sudden noise, but everything remained as still as ever. Zeke shot him a look of annoyance, and Jackal grinned. "I didn't get all dressed up for nothing."

We came to the elevators and found they still worked, though both Kanin and Zeke were leery of going into a small, enclosed metal box with nowhere to escape to. It would be the perfect spot for a trap, an explosive, or another nasty surprise. It would be, Zeke pointed out, the spot where *he* would set up a trap for vampires; a mine on the underside of the box would be lethal in such a tight, cramped space. Or if they decided to climb down the shaft, one spark in a metal tube filled with hydrogen would produce a firestorm that would turn even a group of vampires to ash instantaneously.

That pretty much convinced us to take the stairs. Though we were still extremely cautious as we made our way down, remembering that the last time we'd been in a tight stairwell looking for Sarren, it had exploded. But nothing happened, no explosions, no traps, nothing. We came to a door, opened it easily, and stepped into a labyrinth of dark, empty hallways. The silence was deafening here, and Jackal turned to Zeke.

"Are you sure you have the right lab, puppy?"

Zeke nodded, leading us forward. "I'm sure."

The door shut behind us with a hiss, plunging the corridors into absolute darkness. My vampire sight shifted to compensate, and we trailed Zeke through the long, narrow halls that crisscrossed each other and angled around corners, passing swinging doors and pitch-black rooms, until I was completely lost.

"Getting tired of this, puppy," Jackal muttered as we turned down another hallway, identical to all the others. "Do the bloodbags here have some sort of complex, or do they *like* living like rats in a maze? Feels like we're walking in circles."

"I know where I'm going," Zeke replied coolly.

"Good to know. Maybe there'll be a piece of cheese waiting for you at the end."

"Did you hear that?" I whispered into the stillness.

Everyone froze. Silence descended, throbbing in my ears. But just ahead, around the next corner, I heard the faintest swish of a door closing.

My skin prickled. Weapons out, we edged up to the corner, Kanin leading this time, and peered down the hall. A simple gray door sat at the end of the corridor, swinging slowly into place. We weren't alone down here.

Kanin motioned us to stay put, glided silently to the door, and pushed it open to look through the crack. I gripped the hilt of my sword as he peered into the darkness, waiting for something to explode through the frame or yank him through the door. After a moment, Kanin glanced back and motioned us forward. Behind me, Jackal let out a sigh.

"Aw," he said, walking forward. "That's disappointing. I was so hoping something would jump out and go 'boo.' I'd sell my city to see the old man shriek like a little—"

Something slammed into Jackal with a scream.

Jackal hit the ground and instantly rolled, trying to get to his feet, as whatever had jumped him screamed again and tore savagely at his back. It was a rabid, blank-eyed and mindless, and the stench of rot, decay and blood suddenly filled the corridor. I yelled and brought my katana down, aiming for the spindly body, but the rabid dodged and leaped back with shocking speed, faster than I'd seen one move before. Raising its head, it bared jagged fangs and hissed at me, and my stomach twisted in horror.

It's eyes were gone. The white, pupil-less orbs had been clawed to ragged holes, along with the rest of its face. Deep gouges, bloody and black, ran down its cheeks, jaw, forehead, and eyeholes, and its chest had been scratched to ribbons. It screamed and leaped at me, raking bloody talons at my face and neck, and I slashed at it almost desperately. The katana met a bony forearm and sheared it off at the elbow, but the rabid didn't even flinch. Zeke lunged forward and swung his machete, sinking it deep into the monster's neck, nearly severing it. The rabid whirled like a snake and darted forward, snapping and flailing, and Zeke had to scramble back to avoid the claws. One talon struck his face, laying his cheek open, and I roared.

Leaping at its back, I raised my weapon and brought it down with my all my strength, aiming for the rabid's spine. The katana edge sliced through bone, flesh and muscle before striking the floor, and the rabid collapsed in a spatter of blood, severed from the waist down.

And still, it continued to fight, long arms dragging itself across the bloody floor, heedless that it was missing its lower half. Reaching for me, it gave one last, chilling scream, right before Jackal's fire ax hammered into its skull, crushing it like a melon, and it finally stopped moving.

I shuddered and staggered away from the body, resisting the urge to bare my fangs and kick it away as hard as I could. Was *this* what Sarren was doing? Turning rabids into...whatever that was? But why? For what purpose, other than completely freaking me out?

"Well, that was...interesting." Jackal's tone didn't quite match the look on his face, angry and terrifying. His fangs were bared, lips curled back in a silent snarl. Shouldering the fire ax, he composed himself and turned to glare at Kanin, who stood a few feet away. The Master vampire had probably come as soon as the rabid hit, but everything had happened so fast, the rabid was dead before he could join us. "Thanks for the help, old man," he sneered. "Next time, I think I'll be the one to investigate strange doorways while you stay back here with the runts." He rubbed at his neck, wincing, and I saw a smear of blood on his fingers as he lowered them.

"You're bleeding," I said, suddenly alarmed, though I didn't know why. "Did that thing bite you?"

"Aw, sister, are you worried about me?" Jackal wiped the blood on his duster. "Your concern is touching, but this isn't my first rabid bite. I'll be fine, trust me."

"But...something was wrong with it!" I remembered the bleeders of New Covington, ripping out their eyes as they attacked. I remembered the vampires infected with their blood, rotting away from the inside. If it was the same with the rabids... "What if it was sick?" I told Jackal. "What if you're—"

"What would you do, anyway?" Jackal challenged, sounding impatient. "Got a cure up your sleeve? Or are we wasting time talking about this?" I blinked at him, and he waved his hand. "It's done, sister. You wanna help me? Find Sarren and hold him down so I can rip his heart out through his teeth. Let's keep moving."

I looked at Zeke, wondering if he had any ideas, but shrieks rang out behind us, and two more rabids skittered past the end of the hall, vanishing around a corner. My stomach churned. There were more of them out there, in the hallways with us. And, vampire or no, I did not want to face those things again. Fighting rabids was one thing; fighting rabids that clawed themselves to bloody strips, moved insanely fast, and didn't die unless you literally hacked them to pieces was something else altogether.

"Zeke," I hissed. "Get us out of here now."

He nodded, and we slipped quietly into another hallway, moving fast, as the shrieks and hisses of Sarren's rabids began to echo all around us.

We managed to avoid running into any of the monsters as Zeke led us to a pair of doors at the end of the hall. Moving swiftly to the frame, he tried pushing back the doors, but they didn't budge. Zeke frowned.

"Locked," he muttered, and narrowed his eyes. "This is it. There's no other exit from this room." His face grew dark, and he stepped back. "Sarren is here. He has to be."

Moving him aside, Kanin put his shoulder to the wood, slammed into it a couple times, and the doors flew open. We started forward, but Zeke suddenly grabbed my hand, making me look back. His expression was hard, intense, as his gaze met mine.

"Remember, Allie," he whispered, squeezing my fingers. "Whatever it takes, you have to stop him. Even if that means going through me."

Apprehension flared, and defiance, but Zeke let me go and turned away before I could answer, following Kanin and Jackal through the doors. Raising my weapon, vowing it would not come to that, I stepped into the darkness.

Cautiously, we eased into the shadowy room, weapons out. The room beyond was similar to the ones we'd seen: tile floors, long counters, strange instruments. Everything looked as coldly pristine as before.

But Sarren had definitely been here. The place reeked of blood, though there were no traces of it or the insane vampire anywhere in the room. The Hunger stirred, and I shoved it back impatiently. I had to stay focused. If Sarren was close, I had to be ready for whatever he had planned.

Kanin looked to Jackal and waved at him to follow. He went deeper into the room, heading to the left. Zeke nodded to me, then tilted his head to the right side of the door. We stalked along the walls, scanning the darkness, looking for any signs of Sarren or whatever horrors he might have left in his wake.

A stainless-steel door, polished until it gave a warped reflection of reality in the dim light, dominated the end of the room. It had a simple pull-lever latch, like a meat locker or one of the vampire Princes' blood storage facilities. There was a place for a padlock on the latch, but instead of a lock, a screwdriver had been shoved into the openings and bent into a crude C shape.

I looked at Zeke, and he looked back. We didn't need to speak. Someone had wanted this door to stay closed. That someone could only have been Sarren. He slipped his pistol from its holster and raised it, taking a bead on the door. I hefted my katana in my right hand, and reached out with my left. With a silent snarl, I wrapped my fingers around the handle of the screwdriver and pulled. With a tortured squeal of metal, the shaft straightened, tearing free from the locking mechanism. My fingers closed around the latch.

I opened the door, and a body tumbled out of the refrigerator, landing at my feet with a gasp of pain.

CHAPTER 17

✦

"Dr. Richardson!" Zeke exclaimed, hurrying forward. I backed up as Zeke pulled the human away from the fridge, sitting him against the counter. He was an older human, with hair as white as his lab coat and sharp black eyes. His skin was pale, his lips blue as he gasped and coughed, sucking in deep, shuddering breaths. Zeke knelt beside him, waiting patiently until the fit had passed, and the human looked up at him in surprise.

"Mr....Crosse?" the man wheezed, staring at Zeke as if he couldn't quite believe it. Zeke gave a faint smile, and the human shook his head. "You're back. When...did you get here?"

"A couple days ago," Zeke answered and leaned forward. "I came as soon as I could. Dr. Richardson, what happened here? Where is Sarren?"

"Sarren?"

"The vampire," I supplied. "Tall, bald, scarred-up face?" *Wants to unleash a supervirus to destroy the world?*

"Sarren." The scientist's face, though pale, drained of its remaining color. "So that's the demon's name." His eyes glazed over, unseeing, as he stared at the wall. For a moment, I thought he might faint. "God help us all."

"He was here, then," Zeke prodded, and the human nodded, still in a daze. "Where is he now?" The man didn't reply, and Zeke leaned forward even more, his voice calm but firm. "Doctor, there's no time. Please, tell us what you know."

"He never told us," the scientist whispered. Abruptly, he turned and grabbed Zeke's arm, his expression pleading, almost wild. "He never told us anything," he insisted, "except what he wanted us to do. When we finally realized what was happening, what we were helping him create…" The man shuddered so violently the back of his head hit the counter, but he didn't seem to notice. Zeke gently pried the hand off his arm, his gaze intent.

"What was he creating?"

"We tried to stop him," Richardson said, still staring at nothing. "We tried to resist, to get him to see reason, but he was insane, raving mad. He…he started killing people, civilians, that he took from the city. Said he would torture and kill someone every hour, and make us watch, unless we agreed to help." Dr. Richardson covered his face with his hands. "What could we do?" he moaned. "There were children in the group."

Zeke went motionless, his eyes and expression dark. I knew what he was thinking, and hoped, desperately, that it was not the case.

"Dr. Richardson," Kanin said, his voice low and deliberate, "you have been through much, but we need to know. What, exactly, were you helping with? What was Sarren creating?"

"*Requiem.*"

The word was a whisper, barely audible. But it sent a cold lance through my insides, freezing everything around me. I remembered. I could see Sarren, looming before me with bright, mad eyes, his voice a slow croon. *The requiem has started, and when the last melody plays, the only applause will be sweet, eternal silence.* Dr. Richardson's voice echoed dully, seeming to come from far away. "He called it… Requiem."

For a moment, there was quiet. Then Kanin's voice came again, low and calm, as the Master vampire stepped forward. "And what is Requiem?"

Dr. Richardson slumped against the counter, rubbing his eyes. Dropping his hands, he took a deep breath, as if steeling himself for a confession.

"It's a virus," the scientist said, confirming what we all knew. "A mutated strain of the original Red Lung virus." He seemed to regain his composure; his expression became less wild and staring, though his voice remained grave. "I'd never seen it before, but somehow, this version has mutated so that it affects both live and dead cells. So, not only is it fatal to humans…"

"It affects vampires, as well," Kanin finished, and the scientist nodded wearily. "Was anything changed? Did Sarren mutate it further?"

Dr. Richardson wiped his brow, then continued in an overly clinical voice. "There are a lot of technical terms and scientific jargon, but I'll try to explain this as simply as I can," he said, glancing at me, as if I wouldn't understand if he used a lot of big words. I bristled, but kept silent as he continued.

"The mutated strain the vampire brought in could be transmitted via airborne pathogens," Dr. Thomas began, "much like the original Red Lung virus, or the common cold. That's how Red Lung spread so quickly sixty years ago. But the mutated virus could not be transmitted from a live host to an undead one except through internal consumption of the host's blood."

"Meaning, the vampire would have to bite the infected human to get sick," I said.

"Yes," Dr. Richardson agreed, looking impressed that I was following along. "Vampires can't catch a cold—they don't breathe or cough or share toothbrushes. And the fact that they are, technically, dead makes it impossible for diseases to incubate. A virus needs living cells to survive. But Sarren changed that. First with the mutated Red Lung virus, and then with Requiem."

"What did he do?" I asked when the human paused. Dr. Richardson swallowed hard.

"You know that the mutated virus already attacks vampires." He gazed around at all of us, his expression grave. And I realized that he knew what we were. Maybe not Zeke, but he had definitely guessed that the three dark strangers looming over him were vampires. "Well, Sarren took it a step further. I don't know what he was thinking, but the madman infected the rabids."

"Yeah, we kinda figured that out," Jackal broke in impatiently. And, though his words were mocking, his voice was tight, as if he was in pain. Alarm flickered through me as he put a hand to his neck, wincing. "On account of the damned things running around in the halls. You're not telling us anything useful, bloodbag."

The human's eyes widened. "They're out there?" he breathed, sounding horrified. He scrambled to his feet, and Zeke grabbed his arm to help him up. "Were you bitten?" the human asked, staring around at all of us. "Were any of you bitten?"

Jackal's gaze narrowed, and he went very still. "Why?"

The man stumbled away from us, one hand to his mouth, the whites of his eyes showing above his fingers. "You have to leave," he said, still backing up frantically. "Now. You must go, you can't be here—" He hit the wall, then trailed off, dropping his arm from his face. "Oh, what does it matter?" he whispered, sinking to the floor. "We're dead. Everyone is dead. There's no stopping it now."

Jackal stalked up, grabbed the man by the collar and dragged him to his feet. "I don't feel particularly patient right now, doctor bloodbag," he growled, baring his fangs as the rest of us started forward. "Wanna tell me exactly what you mean by that?"

The human stared at Jackal wearily, seemingly unconcerned with the fangs inches from his face. Brazenly, he reached out and grabbed the vampire's shirt collar, pulling it away from his neck.

My stomach twisted as Jackal's pale skin was bared to the light. The puncture wounds at his throat had darkened, the flesh around them turning a familiar, decaying black. Black veins were crawling up his neck from where the rabid had bitten him, spreading across his jaw like inky spiderwebs.

"You're infected, vampire," Richardson stated in a flat voice, and looked past him at the rest of us. "That's what Sarren changed. Requiem can be spread between undead creatures and living beings alike. If an infected rabid bites you, you get the virus. If you feed from an infected human, you get the virus. If an infected vampire feeds from a human, that *human* contracts Requiem, which can then be spread to other humans via airborne pathogens, just like the common cold." The scientist gave a short, slightly crazy laugh. "Oh, and the most interesting fact? The virus spreads between rabids and humans in the same way. So, if one rabid contracts Requiem..."

"They all do," I whispered.

I felt dazed, the ground unsteady beneath my feet. So, this was how Sarren was going to end the world. With a virus so devastating, nothing would be alive when it was done. If Requiem got off the island, if Sarren unleashed it on the outside world, it was over. For everyone, vampires, rabids, and humans alike. No one would survive that plague. Eventually, we would all be dead.

Jackal gave a vicious, almost desperate growl and shook the human in his grasp. "What about a cure?" he snarled. "There has to be a cure. You meatsacks worked on this virus right beside Sarren. You have to have made something to counter it."

"There is no cure," Dr. Richardson whispered, shaking his head. "No cure. We tried. When Sarren wasn't looking, we tried to develop something to counter it. But we didn't have enough time."

"What about him?" Jackal demanded, jerking his head at Zeke. "He survived Sarren's first plague. Whatever you gave the little bloodbag seemed to have worked."

"It's different now," the human said. "The virus is different, much stronger. If we had more time…" He closed his eyes. "But it's over. Sarren destroyed the experimental cure and all the research we had accumulated—everything we'd learned up until now is gone. We were so close," he choked out. "So close to finding a cure. The vaccines we gave Mr. Crosse were almost successful. If we only had vampire blood…that was the only thing we were missing. But it's too late."

"Are you blind, meatsack?" Jackal said, still baring his fangs. "You have four vampires standing right here."

"There's no time!" Dr. Richardson burst out. "The research is gone! Everything we learned, wiped clean. Sarren left a few minutes before you showed up, with the virus! And once Requiem hits the world, it'll be over. It's done, vampire. This is the end."

Jackal snarled and hurled the human away. He flew across the room, struck the computer desk on the far wall, and slumped to the floor, moaning.

The monitor on the desk suddenly flicked on. As Zeke hurried over to help the scientist, I stared at the computer and the image that appeared on the screen. For a second, I watched it move, puzzled at what it could mean. When I figured it out, my blood ran cold.

"Kanin," I whispered as the Master vampire turned, his gaze narrowing. The screen was dark, except for a set of tiny red numbers in the very middle, counting down.

2:46.
2:45.
2:44.

"Huh," Jackal muttered as the whole room realized what was happening all at once. "That clever sonofabitch."

Kanin spun on all of us. "Everyone, move!" he roared, and we scrambled to obey. Zeke paused to drag Dr. Richardson to his feet, looping an arm over his neck, but Kanin swept up, plucked the human from Zeke's grasp, and tossed the semi-conscious man over one shoulder as easily as a grain sack.

"Go," he ordered, and Zeke went, joining me as I waited impatiently for them both at the door. Together, we fled, following Jackal out of the room and into the maze of hallways, before Zeke took the lead. I hoped we would not run into rabids while fleeing for our lives, but apparently that was too much to ask.

A rabid appeared at the end of the hall, its face a mess of blood and gaping wounds, one eye clawed from its socket. Seeing us, it gave a shriek that echoed off the walls and sprang forward, jagged, infected teeth going for my throat.

I didn't slow down. Drawing my katana, I met the rabid head-on, slashing through its bony chest even as we collided and it sank curved talons into my shoulder. It clung to me, ripping and clawing even though its lower half was gone. Snarling, I threw it off and kept running. More rabids blocked our passage, and we cut our way through, ignoring the claws that ripped at us, dodging the teeth snapping at our necks. A rabid sank its fangs into my sleeve, barely missing my skin, and I tore it free impatiently, pausing only to slice the thing's legs out from under it. Infections and viruses be damned; if I was bitten I'd worry about that once I got out of here.

Bursting through the lower level doors, we fled up the stairs, the screams of rabids echoing behind us. We didn't look back or slow down. The entrance loomed at the end of the foyer, thick metal doors that were probably locked or sealed shut. Jackal and Zeke hit them at the same time, driving their shoulders into them, and the doors flew open with a bang. We leaped the steps and tore across the empty lot...

...and a tremendous *boom* erupted from the lab behind us, the shock wave slamming into my back, knocking me off my feet. An intense wave of heat followed, and bits of glass, rubble and flaming wood showered me as I rolled, trying to keep my head covered. Finally, I pushed myself to my knees, avoiding the glass and bits of fiery debris scattered around me, and looked back at the building.

Not surprisingly, it was demolished. The roof was gone, the windows blown out, and the remaining walls were blackened to a crisp. Flames roared through the windows, sending black smoke into the sky, as the last hope for a cure burned with the laboratory.

Wincing, I looked around for the others. A few yards away, Zeke lay on his stomach, and Jackal was struggling upright. Kanin, already on his feet, walked over to examine the body of Dr. Richardson, lying on his back on the pavement.

Wincing, I crawled over to Zeke, praying he wasn't badly

hurt, but he groaned and pushed himself to a sitting position, staring bleakly at the burning lab.

"Zeke." I put a hand on his shoulder, peering at him carefully, searching for wounds. "Are you hurt? Were you bitten?"

"No." He shook his head numbly. The firelight danced in his eyes, casting flickering shadows over his face as he gazed at the inferno. "That's it, then," he whispered. "The research is gone. There's no hope for a cure. No hope for anything now."

No. A growl rumbled in my throat, and I grabbed his arm, dragging us both to our feet. Anger and determination burned hotly in my stomach as I turned him to face me. "Sarren is not going to win," I said, making Zeke blink. "I am *not* giving our forever to that sick bastard. This isn't over yet."

A groan echoed nearby, as Dr. Richardson shifted and struggled to a sitting position, Kanin looming over him. He tried to get up, but gasped and grabbed his left arm, cradling it to his stomach. The elbow was soaked with blood, and something sharp poked out from beneath his lab coat.

"Broken," he gritted out, clenching his jaw in pain. "I don't think I'll be going anywhere with you, vampires." He looked past Kanin, to the burning lab, and grimaced. "Though I do thank you for not leaving me to that."

"Dr. Richardson," I said, sweeping up to him. "You said that Sarren left not long before we arrived. Do you know where he went? Where he is now?"

The human nodded. "He's going to spread that virus," Richardson murmured darkly, his expression taut with pain. "But he needs to get off the island first. So, there's really only one place he could go."

"The docks," Zeke said, his voice suddenly hard. "He'll be at the docks. If we catch him there, we can still stop this."

I blinked. The lab was gone, the research destroyed, and the cure was lost. A second ago, he'd seemed ready to give up. I'd thought I would have to convince him to keep going. But he didn't look defeated or horrified anymore. He looked like a pissed-off vampire. His fangs were out, and his eyes gleamed with anger and determination as he backed away, beckoning to us all. "We're not far," he said. "I know the fastest way." He paused, giving the human a solemn look, as if realizing we couldn't take him with us. "Dr. Richardson…?"

"Go," the scientist whispered, waving us on with his good hand. "Don't worry about me. Stop Sarren. Stop Requiem. Nothing else matters."

Zeke nodded once, and we went.

The streets were chillingly empty of rabids as we fled back the way we came, following Zeke down the narrow, twisty roads of Eden. I wondered where they all were, until I took a quick breath, searching for hints of rot and decay on the wind, and caught a trace of fresh blood in the air. No wonder the streets were empty. Wherever that smell was coming from, that was where we'd find the rabids.

Zeke turned a corner, and the rows of buildings suddenly ended, coming to a stop at the edge of a road. Across the street, I could see a parking lot surrounded by a chain-link fence, and beyond that, a long cement pier stretching out over Lake Erie.

It was empty.

We hurried on to the dock, leaping the fence, and ran to the end of the pier, frantically gazing around. Several boats bobbed on the surface of the water, simple rowboats, probably used for fishing and now forgotten in the chaos. But Sarren wasn't in any of them.

Then Kanin gave a weary sigh and pointed out over the lake. "There."

We followed his gaze. Far away, over the vastness of Lake Erie, I could just see the hull of a massive ship, vanishing into the darkness. Even from this distance, it was huge, one of those enormous barges like the one outside Old Chicago that held all the raiders' bikes and vehicles. I glared at the ship, frustration and helpless despair threatening to crush me. We were too late. Sarren had been right here, and we'd let him get away.

"Shit." Jackal's voice was tense. He kept one hand at his neck, his voice tight with pain. "Looks like our ship just sailed." He grimaced and leaned against a post, looking exhausted as he stared after the vanishing ship. "Though why the psychopath would use a slow-ass barge to get off the island is beyond me. Unless…"

He trailed off, as the realization hit us all at the same time. Behind us, Eden lay empty and abandoned…because Sarren had loaded a huge barge full of rabids and sailed it right into the heart of the city. And now…

"Oh, God," I whispered. "The checkpoint. That's how he plans to spread Requiem. He's taking the infected rabids *back,* to turn them loose on the refugees. Once that barge hits the checkpoint…"

It would be over. Requiem would be loosed on the world. The rabids would slaughter the refugees and then spread out, carrying the virus to every rabid and human they came across. It would be the end of everything, just like Sarren said.

"No," Zeke growled, heading back the way we'd come. "It's not too late. We can still catch up. Follow me!"

He led us down the pier to another set of docks, where several smaller boats bobbed in the water, small, sleek crafts with engines instead of paddles, built for speed. Steel drums stood at the edge of each pier; fuel for the boats, I guessed. But instead of heading toward the docks, Zeke jogged up to a tiny building at the edge of the pier, almost a shack. It had a simple wooden door on the side and a window with a counter at the front, and I had no idea what it was for.

"Zeke, what—"

Ignoring the window, Zeke walked up to the door of the small hut and kicked it open, flinging it back with a crash. "The boats on Eden are communal property," he stated as we ducked inside. Jackal and Kanin hovered in the frame, as the room was barely big enough for two people. Fishing poles, spears, nets and other supplies leaned against the walls or on shelves, and a single stool sat before the window. "Anyone can use them," Zeke continued, "as long as they bring them back. This is where they record which boats are gone and when they're returned."

A panel hung beside the counter with several keys dangling from hooks in the board. Snatching one, Zeke checked the tag that hung below it and nodded before turning around. "All right, let's go."

A shrieking sound interrupted him and made my blood freeze. From a nearby warehouse, rabids emerged, a pale swarm against the darkness. I drew in a breath, and the scent of blood hit me like a slap in the face, coming from the long metal building. Sarren had been one step ahead of us, again.

The rabids screamed and turned toward us, and my skin crawled. It was the same pack from earlier that night, except for one thing. Several of them had fresh gouges down their arms and faces, and many were ripping at their skin even as they came forward, moving like jerky puppets.

"Shit, they're infected," Jackal snarled, and shot a hard glare at Zeke. "Come on, puppy, let's move!"

We ran across the pavement, the mob of screaming, infected rabids at our heels. Swerving onto a wooden dock, we followed Zeke over the water to the very end of the pier, to where a small, faded white boat sat bobbing on the waves. Leaping onto the boat, Zeke hurried to the front, jamming the key into the ignition, while the rest of us huddled at the edge of the planks and watched the rabids swarm closer.

"Come on," Zeke muttered behind us as the boat engine gave a raspy cough and died away. "Come on, turn over." He wrenched the key again; the engine gurgled, sputtered and faded out again. "Dammit."

"Get out of the way." Jackal stepped onto the boat, shoving him aside. "I'm guessing you know as much about boats as you do bike engines." He crouched down, his face intense. "Just keep the crazies off my back for a few seconds."

A scream at the other end of the docks made me jerk up. The rabids leaped onto the pier, screeching and hissing, tearing at themselves. I drew my katana, roared a challenge, and stepped forward to meet them.

The first rabid leaped at me, swiping at my face with terrible speed. I jerked back and cut the head from its body, knowing that was the only way to make it stop. Another sprang over the first one's corpse and lunged at my throat, but Kanin was suddenly there, stabbing his thin blade through the creature's temple, kicking it off the platform.

"Jackal!" I snarled, desperately fending off a rabid reaching for my face. It hissed and scrambled over my blade, heedless of the edge cutting through its chest. "Not to rush you, but if we don't get out of here soon it won't matter if Sarren gets away or not, because we'll be dead. Hurry up!"

A shot rang out from Zeke's pistol. I heard it strike the barrels on the corner of the docks, clanging off the metal. I glanced back, and saw him standing at the back of the boat, arm raised toward the end of the docks. He fired again, puncturing the drum, and a stream of clear liquid began to stream from the center.

A searing pain erupted from my neck, making me gasp. In that split second of distraction, a rabid had gotten through my defenses and sunk its fangs into my throat. With a desperate hiss, I slid the katana between us and shoved hard, cutting off its head. The monster fell away, releasing my neck, but I stumbled in pain, seeing the rest of the horde closing in. Zeke shouted something, maybe about getting back, but the agony and screaming rabids made it hard to hear what he was saying.

Another monster sprang forward, lashing with its claws, but Kanin spun, knocking it away, and grabbed me around the middle. As he pulled me back toward the boat, I looked up at Zeke, still at the back of the boat, and saw him raise his arm. A strange, bright orange gun was clutched in his hand, and he fired a single shot at the pier.

The shot flared a brilliant orange-red in the darkness, hissing and sparking, trailing a stream of fire as it streaked through the air and struck the barrel he'd shot at earlier. There was a flash, and a massive fireball erupted into the night, sending rabids flying into the water. I felt the blast of heat from where I stood with Kanin, and turned away, shielding my eyes.

When I looked back, the end of the pier blazed with tongues of fire, licking at the posts and snapping hungrily over the wood. My vampire instincts cringed back, urging me to get as far from the flames as I could, that even this distance was too close. Beyond the roar of the inferno, I could hear the rabids screaming.

"There," Zeke growled as he stepped back, the flare gun dropping from his hands. "That should hold them off long enough to—"

And the rabids came right through the flames.

I jerked, barely getting my katana up in time as the entire swarm, not just one or two, sprang through the fire like it wasn't there and rushed the docks again. I slashed wildly at the first rabid who lunged at me, its back and arms wreathed in flames, and my vampire instincts shrieked in utter terror.

"Jackal!" I shouted as Kanin kicked a burning rabid into the water, spun, and smoothly beheaded another. From the corner of my eye, I saw Zeke leap from the back of the boat, sail over the water, and slam his machete into a rabid as he landed beside me. "You can get that boat started anytime now!"

"Not if you keep bitching at me!" came the terse reply from the boat helm. The rabids screamed and pressed forward, crowding the pier, claws and teeth raking me from all sides. I caught flashes of Kanin and Zeke beside me, fending off the rabids that surrounded us, but in a few seconds we'd be overwhelmed.

"Got it!" The boat gurgled, roared and died away just as quickly, killing my sudden surge of hope. "Well, damn. False alarm! What the hell do these bloodbags use for fuel, their own piss?"

"Jackal!"

No reply, but a second later the engine sputtered, coughed and finally roared to life in a plume of white smoke. "All right!" Jackal called as we started edging back from the relentless press of rabids. "The last ship from bat-shit crazytown is sailing, so cut the ropes and let's get the hell out of Dodge."

Kanin threw a rabid off the platform, turned and slashed through the rope tying it to the dock. The engine gurgled, and the boat began to pull away, moving down the pier and out into the water. We fought our way to the very end of the dock, Lake Erie at our backs and a murderous swarm of monsters still coming forward, while the boat pulled even farther away. We needed to jump, but the rabids would pull us down as soon as our backs were turned.

"Jackal!" I yelled, cutting a monster's head from its neck a second before its teeth would've found my skin. "If you leave us, I swear to God whatever is left of me will hunt you down and strangle you in your sleep!"

A laugh rang out behind me, and from the corner of my eye Jackal appeared at the side of the boat, which continued to drift over the lake. Something small and orange flashed in his hand as he raised his arm.

"Oh, sister. You really have no faith in me at all, do you? Duck."

The flare exploded from Jackal's hand, streaking past me as I cringed, and tore into the mob of rabids in a flash of heat and light. "Jump!" Kanin ordered over the screams, the rabids flailing back in blind confusion, and I did. Turning, I hurled myself over the water, hitting the boat railing and grabbing it with one hand, clinging desperately to my katana with the other.

Fingers clamped around my wrist, and someone dragged me over the edge and into the boat, setting me upright. Jackal smirked and dropped my arm as Kanin landed gracefully on deck and Zeke pulled himself up the side of the railing.

I looked up at Jackal and winced. This close, I could see the black circles under his eyes, the skin that was paler than normal. The ominous black veins had spread, crawling over his throat, and his golden eyes were bright with pain even through the ever-present smirk. My stomach twisted. The infection was spreading fast. At this rate, Jackal might not last the night.

"Don't look at me like that, sister." Jackal gave me a sneer and stepped back. "You forget—I always come out on top, no matter the circumstances. So, don't worry your pretty little head. I'll survive. I always find a way." His eyes narrowed, flicking to the blood staining my neck. "You, however, might need to get to Sarren quickly. Mocking the puppy just won't be the same without you around."

A rabid exploded from the water before I could answer, latching on to the rails and baring its fangs in a scream. "Oh, for the love of fuck!" Jackal snarled, whirling and smashing a coil of rope across its face, sending it crashing back. "The bastards don't give up, do they?"

More rabids clawed themselves onto the deck, dripping wet and snarling. It seemed their fear of deep water had vanished along with their aversion to fire. "Get us out of here!" I snapped, and leaped to help Zeke and Kanin kick rabids off the boat. A pale face heaved itself over the railing, hissing at me, and I split it in two before moving on.

As Kanin, Zeke and I darted from one side to the other, repelling our inhuman boarders, the boat jerked forward, picking up speed. As the docks receded, the rabids fell away, and I watched Eden grow smaller and smaller until it was swallowed by the darkness. Jackal turned the boat toward the southwest, and we sped off through the waves, the wind and spray whipping at our faces, praying we'd catch our target in time.

The race to stop the End of the World had begun.

CHAPTER 18

✦

"There's the barge!" Zeke called, peering over the front of the boat. I joined him at the railing, watching the massive rectangular ship get closer and closer, looming to an impossible height against the sky.

"It's huge," I whispered as Kanin stepped up beside me, silently assessing the enormous task before us. "How are we going to stop it?"

"We can't stop it," Kanin said, his eyes narrowing as he surveyed the vessel and its inexorable push toward the land.

My stomach lurched. Were we too late, then? Had we come this far, fought all this way, only to lose?

"We don't have to stop it," Kanin said. There was a flatness in his voice, a finality. "We need to turn it around. If we can get to the helm, we should have enough room left to bring the barge around and head it back to Eden. If we can ground it on the island, we should be able to contain things." He paused, and I saw something in his eyes that I couldn't quite define. Sadness? Resolve? "We can deal with the rabids then, but the most important thing is not to let them escape to the mainland."

I nodded, and Zeke glanced at the raider king, standing at

the helm. "Get us close," he called, and the boat surged forward, bouncing through the waves left in the barge's wake.

As we closed the distance, the shadow of the huge barge looming over us, a tall, pale figure suddenly appeared, leaning over the railings. My lips curled back from my fangs, and I felt Zeke stiffen beside me.

Sarren, the scarred, brilliant, crazy psychopath himself, walked calmly along the top deck, smiled and waved to us.

I snarled, hatred, fury and determination flaring up at the sight of the deranged vampire. There'd be no easy way around. Sarren was waiting for us, and we'd have to deal with him before trying to stop the ship from plowing its way into the checkpoint.

Then Sarren raised his hand and pointed a long, bony finger into the air, at something along the side of the ship. I flicked a glance at where he was pointing, and gripped the railing hard enough to feel it bend beneath my fingers.

A metal pole hung over the edge of the barge, away from the side of the ship. A net swung from that pole, dangling over the foaming water. Inside, two small, terrified faces peered out at me, and my stomach dropped.

"Caleb!" Zeke surged forward, looking like he might jump the railing, his horrified gaze on the net swinging precariously over open water. "Bethany! Hang on! I'll be right there!"

A faint scream came from the kid's direction, Caleb's high-pitched voice crying out for Zeke. I could see both children now, tied back-to-back with heavy chain, their faces streaked with tears. Eight-year-old Bethany, golden-haired, fragile and shy, but who had still survived the entire nightmare-filled journey to Eden. And Caleb, six years old, resilient beyond his age, and the only person in the entire group who had never been afraid of me because I was a vampire.

Horrified, I looked back at Sarren, and he gave me a wide,

evil smile, fingering a rope that had been tied to the railing.
The rope stretched back toward the barge, pulled taut up the
side of the ship and toward the metal pole. Everything inside
me went cold.

Don't, I thought desperately. For Zeke, for Caleb and Bethany, and everyone else caught in Sarren's ruthless sights. *For
the love of God, if you have some sliver of humanity left in you, any
at all, don't do it.*

Sarren raised his left arm—the arm I'd sliced off with my
katana the last time we met, severing it just above the elbow.
A viciously curved blade had replaced the forearm, attached to
his elbow with metal clamps and straps. Sarren smiled at me
over the edge of the weapon, holding my gaze, then brought
it slashing down toward the railing. The rope snapped, and the
kids screamed as the net plummeted into the foaming water
like a stone and sank from view.

"No!" Zeke gave a strangled, desperate cry and glanced
back at me. His face was tortured, eyes bright with anguish.
He knew we had to stop Sarren. He knew that if Requiem hit
land, everything would be over. But he was still Zeke. The
Zeke who protected his own, who refused to leave anyone
behind, who loved his people fiercely and would give his life
to keep them safe. If Caleb and Bethany died, even if we saved
the world, Zeke would never forgive himself.

"Go," I told him, and he spun, leaped the rails, and dove
into the frigid water without hesitation. Surfacing, he struck
out for the place where the net had sunk below the surface,
fighting waves and current and the foaming wake of the barge.
I watched him, the boat carrying us swiftly away, until a wave
broke over the lean, bright form cutting through the water,
and Zeke was lost from sight.

I swallowed the sudden terror that I'd never see him again
and turned back to the barge. Jackal pushed the boat faster,

and we closed the distance, the waves bouncing us so hard I felt the deck rattle when we came down.

"Get around it," Kanin told Jackal, who nodded grimly and spun the wheel. The boat angled off and began following the sides of the great ship. "The pilothouse is at the front. We need to steer this thing away from land."

A scream interrupted him. I looked up just in time to see a rabid fling itself from the top of the barge and land on deck. It gave a shriek and lunged toward Jackal, but Kanin intercepted it, driving his blade deep into the side of its neck and ripping it out the front. The rabid's head toppled backward, and Kanin kicked the monster over the railings, into the lake.

"Shit!" Jackal yanked the wheel, and the boat veered away from the side. Chilled, I looked up the barge to see a huge horde of rabids swarming the platform, shrieking and hissing and tearing at themselves. They weren't locked away in a hold or in cages; they were loose on the deck. And already infected.

We passed the open platform, the rabids screaming and hissing at us from the edge, and drew alongside the front of the barge. Waves tossed the boat, the foaming wake of the huge ship plowing through the water, but Jackal maneuvered us until we were just a few feet from the wall. A set of rusty metal rungs were welded to the side, leading to the top of the deck

Kanin turned to me.

"Let's go."

He leaped from the edge onto the ladder, shimmied up the side, and vanished over the rails. I followed, flinging myself over the water, grabbing the rungs as I came down.

Turning, I searched for Jackal, expecting to see him right behind me. He still stood at the helm, his lean body hunched over the wheel, almost leaning against it. I swallowed hard.

In all the time I'd known him, he had never shown signs of pain or weakness, until now.

"Jackal!" My voice carried weakly over the waves. My brother didn't move, and my fear increased. Sarren was on the other side of the barge, and there was a horde of screaming, infected rabids between us, but I knew he'd show up soon enough. "Come on! Jump! Before Sarren gets here."

Jackal raised his head, eyes gleaming, gave me a strained smile. Black veins crawled up his throat and jaw, and the skin on one cheek was beginning to darken.

"Yeah, about that." His voice made my stomach sink. It was tense, tight with agony, but resolved. Like he had just come to a conclusion, and knew we weren't going to like what came next. "Sorry, sister. But you're going to have to fight this one without me."

"You can't be serious! You're going to leave *now?*" I gaped at him, not knowing whether to be stunned, furious or terrified I would never see him again, because he'd be dead soon. "After everything we did to get here? When you know what Requiem will do once it hits land? You're still going to bail?"

He smirked, and the boat veered away. "It's what I'm best at," he called without an inkling of remorse. I stared after him, disbelieving, and he grinned. "Don't worry, sister, I'm sure you and the old man will be able to beat Sarren on your own. But I can't fight Sarren like this, and I've survived this long by knowing when the odds aren't in my favor. So I'm afraid I'm going to have to fold."

"You can't run from this, you idiot! You're infected with Requiem! Where are you going to go?"

"Don't worry, sister." Jackal's smirk was more of a grimace. "What do I keep telling you? I always come out on top. You just worry about beating Sarren. Kick him in the teeth a few times for me, would you? I'd appreciate it."

"Jackal..." Desperate, I stared at him, wishing I knew what to say to stop this. "You won't survive. If we lose, if Sarren wins, everyone will die."

Jackal gave me a wry, humorless smile. "Then I'll see you both in hell," he called, and sped off, pulling ahead of the barge and vanishing into the black. Numb, I stared after the boat until it was lost to the waves, as Jackal disappeared into the unknown once more, then I scurried up the ladder.

Kanin waited for me on top, saying nothing as I climbed over the railing to join him at the edge of the barge. We stood on the front deck, the wind whipping at our clothes as the huge vessel sliced unerringly through the water. Several yards away, the pilothouse rose into the air, and beyond that, the deck dropped away to the huge floating platform that made up the rest of the barge. Long metal containers were scattered across the platform, creating a labyrinth of aisles and corridors, and also a walkway the rabids couldn't reach from below. Of course, one wrong move or slip meant you would fall to a grisly death. A pair of containers had been stacked together and shoved against the wall closest to the pilothouse, preventing the monsters from climbing onto the front deck. Sarren was nowhere in sight.

"Jackal..." I began, not knowing what to say.

"It doesn't matter," Kanin said, moving swiftly toward the pilothouse. "He made his choice, and it is up to us now. If we can reach the controls and turn this ship around, there will be time to deal with the rabids and Sarren. But we must stop Requiem from making landfall. If the rabids escape to the mainland, it will be over."

"Oh, Kanin," purred a familiar, instantly terrifying voice,

from somewhere overhead. I looked up, and there was Sarren, standing atop the pilothouse, his bladed arm glinting in the moonlight, a steel ice ax in his remaining hand. His smile was viciously inhuman. "Did you really think it would be that easy?"

Leaping down, the tall, bony vampire swung at me with savage force, and I barely brought my katana up in time to block. The curved, pointed head of the ax struck the blade and sent me reeling back a few steps, and Sarren instantly whirled to deflect Kanin's blow with his other arm. The weapons met with a raspy screech, and I leaped back into the fray, snarling my hate for the insane vampire. As his blade sliced at me, I ducked and slashed up with my katana, aiming for his throat. He smoothly moved his head back just enough to avoid it, blocked Kanin's stab with his arm, and hammered me in the gut with the blunt end of the ax. Something inside me snapped, and pain exploded through my middle, nearly dropping me to my knees. As I staggered, Sarren swung his blade arm at my head, aiming for my neck, and for a split second, I thought I had lost. That he'd behead me and I would die the final death.

Then Kanin ducked beneath Sarren's ax, lunged and slammed into him, knocking him back. The very point of the blade slashed my throat, drawing blood, but leaving my head firmly on my neck. Sarren gave an annoyed hiss and dropped a bony elbow into Kanin's spine, then swung the ax up into his jaw as he staggered. Kanin reeled away, blood pouring from his mouth and chin, and I caught him before he could fall.

"Kanin!"

"I'm fine." The vampire spat blood, then glanced at Sarren, who waited for us calmly, a pleased smile on his scarred face. He didn't seem to be in any hurry to engage us. "That was very close, Allison," Kanin murmured, giving me a look that was both anxious and stern. "I taught you better than that. Calm your rage—don't let Sarren bait you into attacking blindly. Remember how important this is."

I nodded. I had been careless and was certainly paying for it now. My ribs throbbed, and every movement sent a jagged shard of pain through my middle, making me grit my teeth. Something was definitely broken inside, maybe multiple somethings. I was healing, albeit slowly, but we had a long fight ahead of us. And not much time to finish it.

Unlike Sarren, who had all the time in the world.

"Can you hear it?" Sarren whispered, his eyes shining with glee and madness as we approached again, cautiously this time. He raised his bladed arm to the front of the boat, a look of ecstasy crossing his face. "The song, the requiem—it calls to us all. The end draws ever closer, one final note, to sing this world to sleep." His gaze shifted to me, and he smiled. "You cannot stop it, little bird. You can only beat your wings against the bars of your cage, and you don't even realize you are trapped. You do not see the sickness, the corruption, all around you, twisting everything it touches. Requiem will set you free. It will set us all free."

"Death isn't the answer," I growled, gritting my teeth through the pain in my ribs. "Destroying everything, letting the world start over, isn't the answer. You're just giving up. But there are still things worth fighting for, things worth *living* for."

Sarren gave me a look of genuine pity. "No, little bird," he said, shaking his head. "You are still an infant demon, far too young to know the truth. Eternity is not a gift. It is a curse. The longer you live, the bleaker and darker the world becomes, until you are stumbling around, blind, in the shadows. Kanin knows, don't you, old friend?" He looked at my sire, smiling faintly. "You long for oblivion, for an end to your eternal wandering. But you're afraid of what comes after, that the evil staining your soul will send it to damnation. And so, you continue to live, to exist, in the hell you created, hoping to atone for what you have done." Sarren chuckled, and it sent a chill up my spine. "But there is no redemption for us, old friend," he whispered. "Nothing can wipe away what we have caused, the centuries of blood and death. How can we cleanse our souls, when the very world around us pulses with rot and filth and decay?" Sarren's lip curled in a snarl of disgust. "No, it is time to end it. It is time to wipe the sickness clean, once and for all. And you, little bird, will not stop it!"

He lunged, coming in fast, swinging his blade at my face. I hadn't forgotten how quick the insane vampire really was, but knowing how fast Sarren could move did me no good here. Even though I was expecting it, I barely managed to leap back, desperately swinging my katana to keep him at bay. At the same instant, Kanin stepped in with his knife, cutting at his throat. But Sarren blocked my swing, dodged Kanin's weapon, and lashed out with a kick, striking me in the chest. As I was hurled away, I saw Sarren spin toward the other vampire, whirling his ax in a vicious arc toward his neck. This time, Kanin ducked beneath his arm, stepped in, and plunged his blade into Sarren's stomach, ripping it out the other side.

Sarren roared. As I staggered to my feet, feeling the sharp throb of my ribs explode with pain, the vampire lunged at Kanin, striking him a glancing blow across the temple even as Kanin responded with a stab to his chest. I started forward, intending to jump back into the fray, but Kanin spared me a split-second glance as Sarren reeled back. "Get to the wheelhouse!" he ordered as Sarren hissed like a furious snake and came at him again. "Don't worry about me—turn the barge, Allison!"

Sarren roared again, his mad eyes snapping to me, and I took off, running full tilt for the pilothouse. I saw the crazy vamp start toward me, but Kanin lunged at him with a terrifying snarl of his own, forcing him to turn. Hitting the stairs, I leaped up to the third floor, ignoring the rabids, who screamed and hissed at me from below, trying to scramble up the metal barrier. I reached the last deck, where a line of dark windows surrounded a tiny room with a metal door, grabbed the handle, and wrenched it down.

It didn't budge. I twisted it again, putting all my vampire strength into turning it, but the door didn't move. I looked closer and saw the metal along the edge of the door had been fused together, welded shut, and the windows had thick iron beams running across them from inside.

"No, no, little bird," hissed Sarren's terrifying voice, and the vampire heaved himself onto the deck one-handed. Blood covered his face, running down his white skin, seeping into the web of scars. "That is not for you."

I snarled my fear and swung at him wildly; his free hand shot out, grabbed my wrist, and wrenched me off the deck, hurling me into space. I felt a stab of instant terror as the swarm of screaming, infected rabids rushed toward me as I plummeted, before I struck the edge of the metal container with a jolt and a fresh blaze of agony.

Wincing, I looked up to see Sarren descending toward me, his blade scything down at my head, and threw myself aside. The vampire hit the container with a thud and a ringing screech, sending sparks flying off the metal.

My katana lay a few feet from my arm. I reached for it, but Sarren stepped up and brought his foot smashing down on my elbow. Bones snapped, but my scream was cut off as the vampire kicked me in the ribs, driving me into the railings and shattering my world into shards of agony.

A roar echoed across the deck. I looked back to see Kanin, his face and arm streaked with blood, descend on Sarren like an avenging angel, driving him back. For a few brief, frantic moments, the two vampires snarled and fought each other at the very edge of the container, one step away from plummeting into the swarm below. I tried to get up, to help Kanin, but though my wounds were healing, the bones slowly knitting back together, I could barely move more than a few inches without gasping in pain.

Kanin's dagger suddenly got through, plunging into Sarren's chest; the vampire howled. Before Kanin could pull back, Sarren grabbed his wrist, sinking the blade deeper into his own body while slashing at Kanin's throat. Kanin threw himself to the side to avoid it, leaving his dagger embedded in Sarren's chest, and stumbled to edge of the platform.

I cried out as for a brief second he teetered there, looking like he would fall. I heard the rabids erupt into a frenzy of screeching, knew they were leaping and clawing for the vampire overhead. All Sarren had to do was shove him back, and Kanin would fall off the edge to his death.

But Sarren reached out, snagged Kanin by the collar, and threw him away from the ledge. Kanin hit the ground and rolled, coming to stop a few feet from me, a split-second look of astonishment crossing his face.

Sarren shook his head at us.

"Ah, ah," he crooned, waggling a bony finger. "None of that. Can't have you spreading your nasty sickness and ruining the symphony. We're just getting to the climax." Reaching for the dagger still stuck in his chest, he pulled it loose, regarded it calmly, and dropped it to the deck. "And now, I think it's time I killed you, old friend," he mused, starting forward. "Once and for all."

Kanin straightened calmly, unarmed, and watched the mad

vampire stalk toward him. Clenching my jaw, I pushed myself upright, gritting my teeth to keep the scream contained.
Every movement still stabbed like a knife, and my right arm
dangled uselessly, but my left one still worked. Enough to
hold a sword, anyway. Taking one step forward, I put myself
between Sarren and my sire and bared my fangs. "You'll have
to get past me," I snarled, raising my katana. Sarren looked at
me in amused surprise, then chuckled.

"Oh, little bird. I see now." He nodded slowly, smiling almost to himself. "I see why Kanin chose you. You don't know
when to stop. You continue to rage against the inevitable, beating your wings against the coming darkness, even as it drags
you down into its sweet, eternal embrace." His fangs gleamed
through the shadows at me. "You have such fire, such…hope.
And for someone like Kanin…it must have been irresistible.
Even though he told himself it was futile to hope." Cock-
ing his head, he regarded me intently. "So…you must repre-
sent everything he believes in. Everything he longs to atone
for."

I spared a glance at Kanin, a few feet from the railings,
watching us. His expression was blank, but I met his dark
gaze and saw a hundred different emotions staring back at me.
Something inscrutable passed between us, a fleeting understanding, almost too fast to be real. Whether it was through
our blood tie or something else, I wasn't certain, but I knew
what I had to do.

I gave a tiny nod, and turned back to Sarren.

"What would it do to him," Sarren mused, unaware of
our brief connection, "if I destroyed you right here? Right
before his eyes. Everything he hopes for, gone in an instant.
I might not even have to kill him afterward. With his little
bird gone, with her song silenced forever, there will be nothing to save him from his own despair." He finally glanced at

Kanin, a truly evil gleam in his eyes. "How does that sound to you, old friend?"

I took one step forward and bared my fangs.

"Hey, psychopath," I snarled, and Sarren's gaze flicked to me. "Why don't you stop talking already? You're worse than Jackal ever was, and unless you intend to yap me to death, let's get on with it." I raised my katana one-handed, giving him a challenging sneer. "I'm not dead yet."

Sarren laughed and faced me fully, his fangs sliding into view. "Very well, little bird," he whispered as I gripped my sword and prepared myself. "If you are that eager for death, I will oblige you. Your prince is gone, your brother has deserted you, and Kanin will not be able to save you. You are alone. Think on that, as I send you to hell."

He attacked, his sword arm a streak of metal in the darkness, coming right at me. I didn't try to block, or counter. As Sarren stabbed forward, I leaped back and half turned, tossing my blade aside.

To Kanin.

Sarren's eyes widened as he realized what was happening. He spun, the blade missing my head by inches, to face the unexpected attack from behind. But Kanin was already moving, the katana cutting a deadly arc through the air, right at Sarren's neck, and the mad vampire desperately lunged back to avoid it.

Too late. The edge sliced into his throat in a spray of crimson, opening a huge gash below his chin. Sarren's head fell back, the gaping wound streaming blood down his entire front, as his mouth made harsh gurgling sounds and his hand groped at his opened throat. He staggered away, hit the railings, and tumbled over the edge of the barge, vanishing into the foaming waters below.

★ ★ ★

Sarren was gone.

I slumped against the railing, shaking with relief, as about a thousand different hurts decided to make themselves known. My arm throbbed, and I didn't know how much was broken inside, but it felt like my entire rib cage was in pieces, stabbing me with every motion. I was healing; I could feel wounds closing, bones knitting back together, but it was agonizingly slow, and the Hunger had roared up full force with the damage. I needed blood, but there was no one around. No one human, anyway. And we couldn't relax just yet.

Setting my jaw, I pushed myself upright, gritting my teeth against the instant flare of pain, and looked around for Kanin.

He stood at the side of the barge, still holding my katana in one pale hand, his dark eyes staring at the place Sarren had fallen. His expression was unreadable, and for some reason, it sent a twist of fear through my stomach.

"Kanin?" I limped up to him, searching his face. His eyes were glazed, and he didn't seem to have heard me. My fear increased. Something was wrong. We had to stop this ship before it plowed straight into the refugee camp and set Requiem loose on the world. Kanin knew that. Why was he just standing there?

"Hey." I grabbed his arm, and he jerked, finally looking down at me, though his expression was still distant, far away. "We have to stop the ship," I told him. "Kill the engine, turn it around, something! How do we do that? Tell me what to do."

He blinked at me. "The pilothouse," he said, as if just coming out of a daze. "Get inside, turn the ship, if Sarren hasn't locked in the controls. Go," he continued, pushing the katana into my hands. "You might still have enough time."

I started off but paused, remembering the welded door, and

turned back to look at him. He had left the railings, and was gazing at the end of the platform, where the infected rabids screeched and clawed at themselves below. For a moment, he hesitated, then stepped toward the edge.

"Kanin!" I lunged back, grabbing his arm. "Are you crazy? What are you doing?" My sire gazed down at me, his expression resigned, and I tightened my grip on his sleeve. "You know something," I guessed, searching his face. "You were going to do something without me."

He didn't reply, and I met his eyes, pleading. "Kanin," I whispered. "Please. It's just us now. Tell me what's going on."

Kanin sighed, and his shoulders slumped as he bowed his head. "It's me," he finally whispered, almost too soft to hear.

I frowned in confusion. The barge lurched forward, relentless, and a few yards away, the screams of the infected rabids echoed from the bottom of the ship, but Kanin seemed to have forgotten all of them.

"What do you mean?"

"I figured it out," he went on, his voice barely above a murmur. "What Sarren meant, why he didn't let me fall." I still stared at him in bewilderment, and his gaze drifted to the edge of the deck, where the rabids waited on the other side.

"The cure," he whispered, making my stomach twist. "Dr. Richardson said they were missing vampire blood to finish the cure. That research is gone now, but they gave what they had to Ezekiel, before he left Eden to find you." His gaze returned to me, dark and intense. "And in New Covington, when I was dying from Sarren's first virus, you injected me with Ezekiel's blood, and it saved my life. It was enough to cure the sickness." He lightly touched his chest. "That research flows through me now, through my blood."

And what Kanin was saying hit me like a ton of bricks, and

I stared at him in shock. "The blood of a Master vampire," I whispered, stepping back. "That means, the cure…"

"Is me," Kanin said again. "The cure—for Requiem, for Rabidism…is in me."

I gaped at him, staggered by the implications. The cure! The cure for Rabidism at last. Sarren had fought so hard to destroy it, to kill any hope that one could be found, and it had been in Kanin all along. The blood of a vampire, combined with the research—the vaccine—that had been given to Zeke just before he'd left Eden to find me.

Would it really work? It seemed too good to be true, almost too easy. But Zeke had survived Sarren's first virus, and Kanin was one of the few vampires who could still produce offspring without creating rabids. His blood was strong, the blood of a Master vampire; it just might be enough.

"That's amazing, Kanin," I whispered, still reeling from the discovery. "We just have to stop the ship, find a way to get you to a lab. If the cure is in you, we just need your blood to end Rabidism for—"

"Allison." His voice made me freeze, the words dying in my throat. Kanin peered down at me, gentle and resolved. "There is no time," he murmured, shaking his head. "Look."

I stared over the railings, into the night. At first, there was nothing. Then, through the waves and shadows, a light winked in the darkness, and my heart plummeted.

That was the checkpoint, and landfall. We were closer than I thought.

"We're too close," Kanin said, his voice unnaturally calm. "Even if Sarren has not locked in the controls, there is no time to turn the ship around. And once it runs aground, the rabids will escape, and Requiem will still destroy the world once it begins to spread. We cannot risk the virus reaching land. We must stop it here." He paused, his next words very soft, but filled with resolve. "*I* must stop it here."

"How?" I asked, without really thinking about it.

Kanin smiled down at me, a faint, sad, gentle smile, and the world just stopped.

"No." I stepped in front of him, horror flooding my veins, turning my insides cold. My sire only continued to watch me, and I grabbed the front of his shirt in desperation. "Kanin, no! You can't. There has to be another way."

"There is no other way." His voice was calm, subdued. He put a hand on my arm, as if to push me off, and I tightened my grip. I didn't care what he thought. I wasn't going to let him do this. I'd lost so many; even Jackal, the blood brother I'd never thought I would miss, was gone, probably to his death. I could *not* lose Kanin, the last member of my family, the one who had given me a second chance and a family in the first place.

"Allison." Kanin gazed down at me, his dark eyes gentle but intense. He didn't shove me away, or pry me loose, though he could've freed himself as easily as opening a door. "Let me do this." I shook my head, unable to speak, but his voice never wavered. "It has to be me. Requiem cannot be allowed to spread. The cure is inside me, and the rabids have to receive it before this ship runs aground. That's what Sarren was talking about. He knew. He knew that if my blood got into their system, his plan would fail. With the rabids' accelerated healing, the cure will spread through them very quickly, and Requiem will be destroyed."

"We don't know that," I choked out as my eyes started to burn. "We don't know what Sarren really meant. You could be throwing your life away, Kanin."

"No." Kanin shook his head, almost in a daze. "It makes sense. The blood of a Master is the only thing strong enough to counter the virus. Sarren knew that whatever was in Ezekiel was the key to the cure. The only thing missing...was vampire blood." His eyes closed, his head tilted back toward the sky. "I've searched so long," he whispered. "So long for a way to atone, to be forgiven for what I caused. And now, everything has come full circle, as it should. This is my redemption." Opening his eyes, his hands rose, coming to rest on my shoulders, squeezing gently. "I started this, Allison. It's only fitting that I end it, as well."

"Kanin." Tears were streaming down my cheeks now, bloody and hot, making it difficult to see. Leaning forward, I collapsed against him, clutching at his shirt. "You can't," I choked out, knowing it was futile. That he'd already made up his mind. "Don't...leave me. What am I going to do... when you're gone?"

Very slowly, his arms slid around me, holding me against him. "You won't be alone," he murmured, bending his head close to mine. "You have Ezekiel. The road will be hard, and you might have to save each other from time to time. But Ezekiel has surprised me, and you are one of the strongest vampires I have ever seen. I've taught you everything I can." He pulled back, smiling down at me. "You don't need me anymore."

I couldn't speak. I could barely see him through the tears. Silently, I let my hands drop from his chest, desperation giving way to despair. Kanin held me a moment longer, then lowered his arms and stepped back, his stare appraising.

"You are my last offspring," he murmured. "My legacy to this world." His eyes went solemn, and he brushed a knuckle across my cheek. "You're a Master now, Allison," he stated simply. "Possibly the first to have been created since the Rabidism plague. I've known it since that night in Old Chicago, when you came out of hibernation—only a Master vampire would revive so quickly. And you will continue to grow stronger and stronger, until you are a match for even the Princes of the cities." I blinked in surprise, and he gave a faint smile as he stepped away. "Now, it is your turn to leave your own mark on the world."

"Kanin, wait," I whispered as he started to turn. He paused, and I swallowed the tears to clear my throat. "I never...got the chance to thank you," I said shakily, facing my sire for the very last time. "For everything. What you taught me—that I can choose what kind of monster I am... I won't forget it."

Kanin leaned forward, bent down, and very lightly touched his lips to my forehead. "I am proud of you, Allison Sekemoto," he whispered as he drew back. "Whatever you decide, whatever path you choose to take, I hope that you will remain the same girl I met that night in the rain. The one decision for which I have no regrets."

Then he turned and walked away, pausing only to grab his blade from where it lay on the deck, where Sarren had dropped it. I watched him, unable to move, unable to stop the flow of tears, as Kanin walked calmly to the edge of the platform and gazed down at the rabids below.

For just a moment, he stood there, a Master vampire, my sire, teacher, mentor and friend, silhouetted against the night sky. Then the bloody tears filling my eyes blinded me; I blinked them away, clearing my vision...

...and the ledge was empty when I looked back.

A chorus of mad screams and howls rose from the edge of the platform, vicious and bloodthirsty. I turned my face into the wall, clenching my teeth and squeezing my eyes shut, trying to block out the sounds. The screams from the rabids intensified, surging into the air, and the sudden smell of blood laced the wind, making me cry out and beat my fists against the wall, but Kanin made no noise. No cries of pain, no snarls of rage or hate, nothing. Only at the end, when the scuffles had died down, did I feel a last, brief stab of emotion from a dying Master. It wasn't fear, or anger, or regret.

It was...contentment. Kanin was finally at peace.

Then the feeling flickered and died, and I felt our blood tie fade away, as the vampire who had damned the world, who had made me immortal even as he searched for a way to cleanse his soul, finally found his redemption.

CHAPTER 19

I was alone.

I couldn't move. I couldn't think. I could only kneel there on the cold deck, feeling the wall of the pilothouse press into my cheek, and sob. Behind me, the rabids hissed and clawed at each other, their harsh voices rising into the air, but I couldn't even hate them. I couldn't feel anything through the numbing grief, the horrible, aching knowledge that I had let my sire die. The fact that he had given his life to stop Requiem wasn't lost on me, but I didn't care. He had died saving the world, he had found his atonement, but all I knew right then was that Kanin was gone.

"Allie!"

I felt a presence drop beside me, and strong arms on my shoulders, pulling me back, away from the wall. I looked up and met Zeke's blue eyes, peering down anxiously. He was soaked, his clothes drenched, and his skin was like ice, but it didn't seem to affect him.

"Are you all right?" Zeke whispered, pressing one palm to my cheek, his gaze searching for wounds. I couldn't answer, and his expression grew alarmed. "Allie, talk to me. Are you hurt? Where are Kanin and Jackal? Where's Sarren?"

"They're gone," I choked out. "They're all gone. Jackal took off again. Sarren got his stupid crazy head sliced off and fell overboard. And Kanin..." My gaze went to the edge of the deck, at the spot where Kanin last stood, calm and resolved, accepting his fate.

"Kanin...figured out the cure was inside him," I whispered, feeling a fresh flood of tears press behind my eyes, even as I tried to compose myself. "Sarren told him as much. The cure was inside him, and he knew Requiem had to be stopped, before it could reach land. So...so, he..."

Zeke let out a slow breath. Reaching out, he pulled me against him, holding me as tightly as he could. "I'm sorry, Allison," he murmured into my hair. He didn't say anything else; there was nothing to be said. For a moment, we knelt there, clinging to each other, as the rabids shrieked below us and the ship plowed on, unconcerned with the passing of one of the last Master vampires.

Finally, I pulled back, wiping my burning face. "How did you get here, Zeke?" I murmured. And then, suddenly remembering why he had gone into the lake, gasped. "Where... where are Caleb and Bethany?" Desperation flared up again, as I realized he was alone. If, on top of everything else, those two little kids had drowned...

"They're all right," Zeke assured me, easing my panic. "I got to them in time." He nodded to the second floor of the pilothouse, where two small white faces peered down at us. "They're freezing," Zeke muttered darkly, "and terrified, but they'll be all right. At least for now. Had to piggyback them all the way here, and then find the ladder up, with them clinging to my back the whole way." He shook his head ruefully. "I think it's the first time I've been grateful to be a vampire— we wouldn't have made it, otherwise."

At the sight of the two kids, my Hunger surged up and

roared to life. But Zeke's fingers dug into my arms, and his voice became urgent. "Allison," he said, as I clamped down on my bloodlust, trying to focus, "we're not done yet. We have to stop the ship." He nodded toward the edge of the deck. "There are still a lot of rabids down there. Even if they're not infected, if this thing hits the checkpoint, it'll be a massacre."

I looked over the barge to where the lights of the checkpoint gleamed straight ahead. There didn't seem to be enough time, and I was tired, hurt and starving. My sword arm still ached; I could just now flex my fingers, and there was still a shattered bone lodged somewhere in my chest. I wanted to lie motionless until whatever was broken inside me healed. I wanted to find the nearest human and plunge my fangs into their throat. And I wanted to find a quiet place to curl up and mourn my sire. Instead, I nodded and pulled away from Zeke, wiping the last of the blood from my eyes.

"Come on, then," I told him, making my way around the pilothouse, toward the stairs to the top deck. "The door to the controls is welded shut, but if we can get it open, we might be able to stop this thing."

I hurried up the steps, ignoring Caleb and Bethany's small, shivering figures as they huddled together on the second floor, desperately keeping my Hunger under control. The demon screamed at me to attack, to leap down and rip open a child's throat, knowing it would soothe the pain stabbing me from inside. It took all my willpower to keep going when Caleb called out to me, waving a pale, twiggy arm in my direction.

We reached the door to the pilothouse. I put my shoulder to the metal and slammed into it, ignoring the pain that rocketed through my body. It didn't budge, and Zeke joined me, slamming into the door, trying to break it open.

"No good," he muttered after we'd crashed into it a few times to no avail. "It's not going to open."

I glared at the door, anger and desperation rising up to dance with each other. *I'm a Master vampire,* I thought, clenching my fists. Though the notion was still hard to believe—me, a Master vampire like Kanin? Like a Prince? But I trusted my sire, and I knew he would never lie to me. *Kanin would be able to get through. And I'm not going to let those people on shore die just because of a damn door. So, open up, you stupid thing!*

I bashed into it once more, putting the last of my strength behind the blow. The impact jarred my body, sending a flare of pain through my almost-healed ribs, but the door flew open with a crash, and I stumbled inside.

The moment of triumph soon faded, though, once we were in the pilothouse. The controls, complicated and unfamiliar already, had been smashed and bent beyond repair. The wheel had been ripped off, broken, and was lying in pieces in the corner. Sarren had locked his course in, just as Kanin had guessed, and there'd be no changing direction, not from here, anyway.

"Dammit!" I snapped, gazing around helplessly. Through the window, the lights of the shoreline glimmered frighteningly close. "What now?"

"The anchor," Zeke said, pointing to a metal box on the wall, with a single button in the center. "Drop anchor—it might be enough to turn this thing so it doesn't crash into the checkpoint."

I slammed my thumb into the button. There was a click, but nothing happened. The barge continued to plow toward shore with no signs of slowing down.

"He must've cut the chain," Zeke growled, running both hands through his hair. "And there's no time to get to the engine room, even if we could get in." He closed his eyes, pressing his fists to his forehead. "What are we going to do?"

Desperate, I gazed at the barge, past the rabids milling

below on the platform, to the back of the ship. I spotted the chain Zeke was referring to, the one that was supposed to be attached to an anchor, lying in a neat coil on the deck. There was no anchor, obviously, but there were a pair of open metal containers lying close by, identical to the ones the rabids were prowling through below. And the ghost of an idea went through my mind. It was a gamble, and we'd have to get past that huge mob of rabids, but there were no options left. We were out of time.

"Come on," I told Zeke, backing away from the controls. "I just thought of something."

I whirled toward the door, but froze when I saw Caleb in the frame, pale and shivering, gazing up at me with big, dark eyes.

"Allie," he said, a shaky smile spreading over his face. "I kn-knew it. I knew you'd come back."

The demon surged up with a roar. Before I could move, Zeke sprang forward and grabbed me around the waist even as my fangs slid out and I tensed to lunge, to pounce and rip open the child's throat.

"Caleb, get back!" Zeke shouted, and Caleb's eyes went huge with fear. Zeke held me tight, his arms like steel bands around me, even as I squeezed my eyes shut and turned into him, fighting for control. "Go down to the bottom floor with Bethany and stay there," Zeke ordered, his voice firm, as I clenched my fist in his shirt and pressed my forehead to his chest. "When we leave, you and Bethany come into this room, bar the door and don't open it for anyone but me, you hear?"

My demon howled, and the Hunger ripped and tore at my insides, both driving me insane. I heard Caleb sniffle, heard his frightened voice start to protest, and Zeke's voice hardened. "Now, Caleb!"

The child broke into hiccupping sobs and fled. Zeke didn't

relent until the footsteps on the stairs disappeared, then very carefully loosened his grip, though not enough to let me go.

"Allie?"

"I'm okay," I said through gritted teeth. The Hunger burned through my veins, relentless and terrible, but I forced my fangs to retract and stilled the thoughts of pouncing on a child and sinking my teeth into his throat. "Thanks for catching me."

"Always, vampire girl." Zeke pressed his forehead to mine. "Just promise me you'll do the same. We'll catch each other." He glanced up, making sure Caleb was gone, then pulled away. "But right now, we have to stop a ship. What were you planning to do?"

Oh, yeah. The ship. "This way," I said, leading him back down the stairs. I smelled Caleb and Bethany, somewhere close by, but I couldn't let myself think of them right now. Back on deck, I gazed across the platform and the maze of shipping containers below, to the other side of the ship. A chill ran up my spine. Rabids screamed and hissed at us from below, and the shoreline was frighteningly near. We had a few minutes at most.

"What's the plan, Allison?"

I pointed across the chasm. "The chain," I said, and his gaze fell to the heavy coils by the side of the ship. "The anchor is gone, but if we attached the chain to that container and push it over the side…"

"It might be enough drag to turn the barge," Zeke finished. "Especially when it fills up with water. It won't stop the ship, but it just needs to turn it so that it misses the checkpoint." He nodded slowly, though his expression was unsure. "It just might work, but that container is huge, Allie. Can we move it?"

"We have to," I growled, and he didn't argue. Reaching back, I pulled my sword, my fingers still stiff from when Sarren had broken my arm. "We'll have to go through the rabids," I said, as Zeke drew his machete, as well. "If we stay on top of the containers, they shouldn't be a problem. But we have to reach the other side. Nothing else matters now."

Zeke nodded and raised his weapon. "Go," he said, nodding to the edge of the deck. "I'm right behind you."

I stepped to the edge of the platform and surveyed the labyrinth of containers, trying to gauge the best path to the other side. Instantly, the rabids surged forward with screams and wails, clawing at the wall, trying to leap at me. Their numbers were smaller now, I realized, and pale bodies were scattered about the deck, twisted and in pieces. The Master vampire, though severely outnumbered and intending to die, had not gone quietly into his eternal night.

I deliberately kept my gaze from straying to the suspicious dark blot in the center of the platform. The place my sire had fallen.

Taking one step back, I gathered myself and leaped off the deck, aiming for the top of the nearest shipping container. I hit the roof with a ringing clang, and the rabids immediately swarmed around it, their talons screeching off the sides. One of them clawed its way up the backs of its fellows, hissing as it scrambled up beside me. I cut the head from its shoulders with a quick slash of my blade, and it tumbled back into the masses.

Zeke landed behind me with a clang, and together we fled for the opposite side, the rabids screeching and swarming below us. Leaping from container to container, we crossed the platform with only a few pale monsters managing to claw their way onto the roofs. Screaming, they hurled themselves at us, blind with rage, but we cut them down and kept going.

Reaching the edge of one container, I skidded to a halt. This was the last roof we had to cross, and there was one final, very high jump we had to make before we reached the other side of the barge. To even have a chance I needed a running start, but two rabids blocked my way, hissing and snarling as they came forward.

Or one of them did, anyway. The other staggered, looking confused. As the first rabid lunged and met a swift end on my katana, the second shook its head, nearly falling off the edge of the roof. Its face had been clawed open until it was more skull than flesh, but small patches of skin were starting to grow over the gaping wounds.

The rabid shook itself and came at me again, hissing, but it was slower now, its movements not nearly as frantic as before. I easily cut it down and kicked it off the edge of the roof, letting it drop to the swarm below.

"You all right?" Zeke asked, coming up behind me. Dark blood streaked his arms, face and machete, but it wasn't his own. His fangs glinted as he spoke. "What happened?"

I shook my head, wanting to explain what I'd seen with the rabid, but there was no time. "Nothing," I said, facing the edge of the deck, and the long jump before it. "Ready for this?" I asked, shooting a quick glance at Zeke. "Can you make it?"

A rabid clawed its way up behind us and shrieked, and Zeke tensed. "I don't have a choice. Go!"

I ran for the edge of the container and flung myself into empty space. Maybe it was the new knowledge that I was a Master vampire, or maybe I was just desperate, but it felt like I leaped higher than I ever had before. I struck the top of the deck with room to spare and instantly whirled, lunged forward, and grabbed Zeke as he fell toward the edge of the platform, yanking him to safety.

We sprawled on the deck for only a moment, tangled in each other, our fingers interlocked, before scrambling upright. The open container sat at the edge of the barge, empty and hollow in the moonlight, and I sprinted toward it.

"Grab the chain!" I told Zeke, snatching a length of the massive, heavy links myself. The coils were huge, individual links larger than my fist. It wouldn't snap, that was for certain. I just had to make sure it wouldn't break from the container. Dragging it to the metal box, I searched for something to attach it to. Thick steel bars ran vertically up the back of the open doors; I wound the chain through them, then looked around for something to secure them in place.

"Allie!" Zeke tossed me a pipe. I grabbed it, shoved it through the metal links and, gritting my teeth, bent the pipe around the chain, twisting it several times.

There, I thought, taking a step back, surveying my handiwork. The chain was attached to the container, the doors already open. Now all we had to do was shove it overboard and hope that a huge metal box filled with water would be enough drag to turn the ship.

Something moved from the corner of my eye, and the blood froze in my veins.

No. It can't be. He should be dead.

I whirled, shouting a desperate warning, and Zeke glanced up from where he was unwinding the heavy coils of chain. Too late.

A long, curved blade erupted from Zeke's chest, punching into the air and gleaming in the moonlight, and Zeke screamed. Sarren, dripping wet, fangs bared in a terrifying snarl, lifted him off his feet, pushing the impaled vampire into the air, and I roared.

Drawing my katana, I flew at Sarren, who swung his arm and hurled Zeke's body away before turning on me. Zeke crashed to the deck several yards away, crying out in agony, and I closed on Sarren.

"Why won't you just die!" I screamed, slashing my blade at the mad vampire, intending to cut him in half. No more taking chances; this time I'd sever his head, his legs, his other arm, his spine. I'd slice him into a dozen pieces and scatter them to different ends of the earth to make certain he was dead.

Sarren blocked my swing with his sword, lunged in, and grabbed my throat. Still insanely fast. I felt my feet leave the ground as my opponent lifted me up and slammed me onto the deck with a crash that made my head ring.

Sarren knelt above me, still pinning me by the throat. His face was pulled into a vicious snarl, his eyes blank and terrifying. Fear lanced through my stomach. There'd be no words this time, no toying with his prey, no taunts or hints or creepy poetry. I faced the true demon now, and it wasn't interested in words. All it wanted was to rip me apart.

Sarren's grip tightened, bony fingers closing like a vice, crushing my windpipe and turning the world red with pain. One knee pinned my sword arm to the deck; I couldn't move my arm, and watched as Sarren raised his sword, angling it toward my neck.

With a defiant snarl, I clenched my free hand into a fist and punched the arm at my throat as hard as I could, striking the elbow. There was a snap and Sarren toppled forward, the pressure at my throat loosening as he was thrown off-balance. I shoved hard with my legs, bucking him over my head, then scrambled upright with my sword.

I barely had time to turn before he was on me again, hissing and baring his fangs. I dodged the first savage blow, deflected the second, and was hurled back as Sarren lunged in and kicked me in the chest. I hit the deck, rolled to my knees, and stabbed up as quickly as I could, almost without thinking. A jolt went up my arms as Sarren hit the point of my blade, impaling himself through the stomach. He glanced down at the weapon through his gut, bared his fangs, and stepped forward, sliding along the katana edge and slashing his sword arm at my face.

I jerked back, managing to keep ahold of my weapon, wrenching the katana free in a spray of blood. Sarren didn't even slow down as he attacked once more, driving me back across the deck. Blood drenched his front, dripping to the metal, but his eyes were crazed and glassy, beyond any pain. Past his head, I caught a split-second glimpse of land, of the lights of the checkpoint, nearly upon us.

Snarling, I knocked away Sarren's blade and slashed in with my own, desperate to end this. He dodged, the edge missing his head by centimeters, and lunged forward with an inhuman shriek. I jumped back, but hit the wall of the engine room, striking my head against the metal. In that moment of shock, Sarren stabbed forward, and the tip of his blade slammed into my shoulder, sinking deep and pinning me to the wall.

Agony flared. I howled and slashed at him, but his free hand shot out, striking my wrist as the blow came down, and my sword was knocked from my grasp, skidding across the deck. Turning back, Sarren hissed and shoved the blade in deeper, twisting it as he did, and I screamed.

Zeke suddenly rammed into Sarren, hitting him from the side as he brought his machete slashing down at his neck. The impact sent another blaze of agony up my shoulder, setting it on fire, as the blade pinning me to the wall snapped with a metallic ringing sound, and Sarren lurched away with half a sword. Roaring, the mad vampire spun on Zeke, who faced him with his machete in hand, the other pressed to his chest. His clothes were drenched with blood, and he could barely stand, his jaw clenched with pain and determination.

Zeke bared his fangs and slashed viciously at Sarren's face, but his swing was wild, hindered by pain and blood loss. Sarren blocked easily and grabbed Zeke by the throat, lifting him up with a snarl. I grabbed the blade in my shoulder and, ignoring the jagged edge slicing my fingers, pulled it free, lunged at Sarren, and sank it into his back.

He whirled with a roar, backhanding me in the jaw, sending me flying. I hit the deck and rolled into the railing, crying out as everything blazed with pain. I couldn't keep this up. I was just about done. But I had to keep fighting. For Zeke, and Kanin, and everyone in Eden, I couldn't let Sarren win.

I raised my head and caught a glint of metal, lying an arm's length away. My sword. I tried to move, to reach for it, but footsteps echoed over the deck, and a shadow fell over me.

I looked up. Sarren stood there, pale and terrible in the darkness. He held Zeke against him, one arm circling his throat, gazing down at me over his shoulder. Zeke's hands were empty of weapons, and he clawed futilely at the arm around his neck, his face tight.

"Now, little bird." Sarren's voice was a rasp, and he wrenched Zeke's head back, exposing his throat. I could only watch as Sarren raised his sword arm, the jagged, lethal edge glinting evilly as it prepared to strike. "Watch as I destroy everything you've ever loved."

A barrage of gunfire echoed from the shore ahead, ringing through the darkness and sparking off the deck and railing. Sarren jerked in surprise, hissing as he glanced toward the checkpoint. For a split second, I met Zeke's eyes, and he gave a tiny nod.

I lunged, snatching my weapon from the deck, and as Sarren turned back, stabbed up with all my might. Through Zeke's stomach and into Sarren's heart. Zeke cried out, and Sarren went rigid, his eyes bulging in shock and pain. I yanked my sword free and, as Zeke fell, crumpling at my feet, brought the blade slashing across Sarren's neck, cutting off his head.

I collapsed to the deck beside Zeke as my strength gave out, as Sarren's body collapsed like a jerky puppet and went still. His bald head bounced on the deck, rolled over several times, and came to rest a few yards away, the scarred face frozen in an expression of surprise. This time, finally, he wouldn't be getting up again.

"Zeke." I pushed myself to an elbow and put a hand on his chest, my voice a ragged whisper. He lay on his back in a pool of blood, his eyes glazed as they stared at the sky. "Can you hear me?"

He grimaced, clenching his jaw, his fangs fully extended in pain. But his hand sought mine and gripped it tightly, his voice urgent as he turned to stare at me.

"Stop the barge, Allison." A trickle of red streamed from his mouth, and he gritted his teeth. "Hurry. There's…no time left. I don't think… I can get up right now. Please." He squeezed my hand. "It has to be you."

I nodded wearily. I was so tired. Everything hurt, and I didn't know if I had the strength to stand, much less turn an entire barge. But I pushed myself to my knees, and then, clenching my jaw, shoved myself upright. Hunger roared like fire through my veins, and every step was torture, but I staggered across the deck and practically fell against the open shipping container we had chained to the deck.

Putting bloody hands against the wall, I pushed. Nothing happened, except the bright jolt of agony slicing through me like a knife, and the Hunger that shrieked in my veins. Gritting my teeth, I tried again, closing my eyes against the pain, but the box stubbornly refused to budge.

I slumped against the wall, closing my eyes. I couldn't do it. I was too weak, in too much pain, and I had no strength left. *I'm sorry, Zeke,* I thought, sliding down the metal, despair and grief clogging the back of my throat. *I wanted to spend forever with you.*

You can do this.

Blinking, I opened my eyes. The deck was empty, I was alone on the side of the ship. But I was almost certain I'd heard *his* voice, low and confident, like he was standing right beside me.

You are my last offspring, my legacy to this world. You are a Master vampire, Allison. I hope that, whatever your choice, whatever path you choose, you will remain that same girl I met that night in the rain. The one decision for which I have no regrets.

"Kanin," I whispered, my throat tightening once more. Glaring at the metal wall, I bared my fangs. "I won't let you down."

Putting my shoulder against the steel once more, I closed my eyes and pushed, ignoring the pain, the Hunger that consumed me. For seconds, the container didn't move. Then there was a rusty screech as the box shifted, just a few inches, but it was enough. I threw myself into the task, pushing with all my might, thinking of Kanin, Zeke, Caleb, even Jackal. All the people who had brought me this far. I would not fail them. I would, as a now-dead psychopath had put so eloquently, beat my wings against the coming dark until it swallowed me whole, or I drove it back entirely.

The metal container screeched horribly as it slid across the deck, stopping at the very edge of the barge. I paused, gathered the last of my strength, and shoved as hard as I could. The huge box tipped on its side, seemed to teeter at the edge of the deck, and finally went over, hitting the dark waters with a tremendous splash.

I crumpled to the deck once more, listening to the chain rattle over the side as the container sank beneath the surface, hopefully filling with water. It was done. I didn't know if I'd gotten to it in time, if it would be enough to turn the barge, but there was nothing more I could do. As I lay there,

I thought I could feel the barge turning…turning…agonizingly slow. But I couldn't be certain.

And then there was a deafening, grinding crunch that shook the deck, as the huge ship finally ran aground. The barge shuddered violently, metal screeching, wood snapping, sounding like it was tearing itself apart, before it finally stopped moving. I thought I heard shouts and cries from the shore, gunfire booming into the night, and knew I should get up, try to help. I ached, badly, but I was healing, and in no danger of hibernation. At least not yet.

But, Zeke…

Suddenly frantic, I pushed myself upright and half crawled, half staggered over to where Zeke lay, collapsing beside him. His face was slack, but at my touch, he stirred, and his eyes opened. Bright with Hunger, glazed over with pain, but alive.

"Allie?" His gaze sought mine, worried and anxious even through the Hunger. "Did it work?" he whispered. "Did you turn the ship in time?"

"I don't know," I whispered back. Raising my head, I stared past the deck, but couldn't see anything beyond the railing but trees. "I did everything I could."

"Well, you did cut it a bit close, there, runts," said a clear, familiar voice, as a shadow fell over me. "Another couple hundred feet, and it would've been a massacre. Which, don't get me wrong, I'm usually all for, but not when I'm on the losing side."

I looked up. Jackal stood over us, wearing his usual smirk, an assault rifle held casually to one shoulder. Raw, open wounds glimmered on his cheeks, and the sickly black veins had spread from his jaw to the side of his face, but he stood tall and proud there on the deck, shaking his head at me. His duster billowed out behind him, and his gold eyes shone in the darkness.

"Jackal," I whispered, as he raised a sardonic eyebrow. "You're...still here? I thought you took off...."

He snorted. "With Requiem on the loose? Where would I go, exactly? We had to stop it here, but I figured if Sarren killed us all, the damn plague would begin the second the barge hit land and the rabids got loose. I knew I wouldn't be any help in taking on the psychopath. So, I implemented a backup plan. That way, if he managed to kill you all, at least I could warn the meatsacks what was coming."

"That was your plan?" I glared at him, remembering what he'd said on the boat, right before he pulled away and vanished over the waves. "I thought you were abandoning us! Why didn't you just tell me that earlier?"

Jackal gave me a smug grin. "And miss out on those lovely rants you do so well? What fun would that be?"

"Wait a minute." Zeke struggled to sit up, his expression incredulous and skeptical. "You...you're telling me you left to warn the town. To save the humans?"

"Don't read too much into it, puppy," Jackal sneered. "I don't want Requiem to spread any more than you. It would put a rather large damper on my plans if everyone up and died. So, yes, I left to warn the bloodbags, who all agreed that we should try to stop this thing. Maybe pick off as many rabids as we could before they hit shore." He raised his assault rifle. "That's when I saw you and your girlfriend on deck with Sarren, getting your asses kicked, and thought I'd intervene. You're welcome, by the way. I'm just a little sad I didn't get to see Sarren's face when it finally left his scrawny neck." He snorted and looked at the pale, crumpled corpse lying several yards away. The head was nowhere in sight, having rolled off the deck when the ship ran aground. One corner of Jackal's lip curled in a satisfied grin, before he sobered. "Too bad the old man never got to see it."

A lump caught in my throat, even as I blinked at him. "You know."

"I have a blood tie, too, sister." Jackal smirked at me, though it lacked the bite of before. "I felt when the old bastard finally kicked it. It seemed to be what he wanted, so I'm guessing Sarren wasn't the one who did him in. How'd it happen, anyway?"

I swallowed hard. "Kanin," I began, trying to keep my voice steady, "discovered the cure…was inside him." Jackal's eyebrows arched, and an incredulous look crossed his face as I continued. "That he carried the cure for Requiem in his blood. He gave his life to make sure the virus wouldn't spread to the rest of the world, that it would end right here." My eyes went blurry, and I blinked hard to clear them, my voice coming out a little choked. "He saved us. He saved everything."

"Huh." Jackal blinked at me, his expression unreadable. Turning, he gazed back toward the platform, where the rabids had been minutes before. "Well, old man." He sighed, and his voice wasn't smug, or sarcastic, or mocking. "You've been waiting for this day since the rabids were first created. I hope you found your peace."

Suddenly, he winced, sinking down on the deck, the assault rifle clattering beside him. Alarmed, I straightened, reaching out to steady him, but Jackal slumped to his back on the deck, putting an arm over his face. I could see the ugly bite wound on his neck, glimmering and black, turning the skin around it dark.

"Well, isn't this fucking hilarious." He sighed as the wind blew over the railing, swirling around three vampires slumped together on deck. "We saved a bunch of bleating meatsacks, killed a psychopath who is older than dirt, stopped another world-destroying plague…and we still don't have the cure. God really does hate us, after all." He sighed again, letting his other arm rest on his stomach, like he was just getting ready to take a nap. "Seeing as this is probably my last hurrah, I don't suppose I could get you two bleeding hearts to massacre a village with me? For old time's sake."

"No," I said, as Zeke frowned beside me. Though I *was* starving, and I would have to feed soon, as would Zeke. Hopefully, Dr. Thomas could spare a real blood bag or two. "You're not going to slaughter the humans we worked so hard to save," I told Jackal, who snorted without looking at me. "Besides, you're not going to die."

"Oh?" He lowered his arm, eyeing me with resignation. "Got the cure up your sleeve, then, sister?"

"Actually, I think I do."

They both stared at me. I looked at Zeke, and Jackal, and felt that tiny flicker of hope grow steadily into a rising flame. Kanin had been injected with Zeke's blood in New Covington, but he wasn't the only one. Just to be certain, I felt along my neck where the infected rabid had bitten me, finding smooth, unbroken skin, and smiled.

"I'm a Master vampire," I said, to their stunned expressions. "The cure is inside me, as well."

CHAPTER 20

❖

I woke up on a table.

Opening my eyes, I winced as an overhead light blazed down on me, making me hiss and turn away, shielding my face. The surface under my back felt hard and smooth, metallic. Confused, I struggled upright, squinting against the brightness, wondering where I was.

"Ah, Miss Allison. You're awake."

A man came forward, dressed in a long white coat, the light reflecting off his glasses. His arm hung in a sling, and a bandage covered one side of his head, but I blinked in recognition. "Dr. Richardson?"

He nodded, and the rest of the room came into focus, small and white, with tile floors and shelves full of sharp instruments. The surface I lay on was a metal table, shiny and smelling faintly of chemicals and blood. My stomach gave a jolt as I realized where I was. Somehow, I was back in the lab.

I groped back for my sword and found it missing, as well. Glaring at the scientist, I growled and bared my fangs. "You should've tied me down if you thought you were going to keep me here," I said as the human's eyes widened.

"Easy." Richardson held up his uninjured hand. "Calm down, girl. It's not what you think."

"Where are Jackal and Zeke?"

"They're fine! They're both fine. Please, calm down."

"Both of them?"

"Yes." The scientist gave a firm nod. "Both of them." He sighed as I relaxed a bit, retracting my fangs. They were okay. Even Jackal was all right. "And we're not going to keep you here," Richardson went on, gesturing to the door, which lay open and unguarded. "You can leave whenever you want. Just hear me out."

"Where are we?" I asked, trying to remember the final few minutes of the night before. After the ship had run aground, most of the rabids had fled into the woods or joined the swarm still lingering around the checkpoint gates. Jackal, I discovered later, had taken a small boat out to the crippled barge rather than fight his way through the horde. We'd returned to the checkpoint the same way and found a platoon of soldiers waiting for us, thankfully with an ample supply of blood bags and no citizens around to tempt us. Jackal, apparently, had told them what to prepare for when we returned.

After downing two—just enough to heal and keep the Hunger at bay—I had returned to the hospital with Jackal and Zeke. Hendricks had been waiting for us, but with Jackal in such a bad way, I'd sent Zeke to deal with the mayor while I hunted down Dr. Thomas and forced him to help the sickening vampire. The little human hadn't said anything when I'd ordered him to draw my blood and inject it into Jackal, clearly terrified now that there were *three* vampires to contend with instead of only one.

After that, with dawn less than an hour away, the rest of the conversation had become somewhat of a blur. I remembered meeting with Mayor Hendricks and Zeke, remembered telling them about the cure, and the mayor had asked if I was willing to offer a bit of my blood for research. After making him swear that they would not be using me for a lab experiment, I'd agreed.

And then I'd woken up here.

"Is this Eden?" I asked in amazement, but Dr. Richardson shook his head.

"No, this is still the checkpoint," he answered, and offered a wry smile. "Trust me, I was just as confused when I woke up in the hospital and not on the island. After you four vampires left me at the lab, I thought I was going to die. I holed up near the power plant until I passed out from blood loss." He shook his head. "But, as it turns out, it wasn't quite my time. A squad came for me early this morning, said that one of the vampires had told them where to find me, and that Mayor Hendricks had personally ordered my retrieval."

"Why?"

"Because of you, vampire." The scientist's voice was grave. "Because of what you told them, about Requiem. About the cure. They needed someone who understood the research, who worked firsthand with the virus. I came here with a slight concussion and a broken arm, and they still had me begin work as soon as the painkillers kicked in, and I was lucid enough to stand." His eyes gleamed behind his glasses as he stared at me. "Of course, if I'd realized what they had, what they wanted me to do, I would've started as soon as I woke up, broken arm or no. To think…" He stared at me, appraising. "After all this time, the answer was right in front of us. If we'd only understood vampires a little more."

"You mean the research," I guessed. "The failed vampire experiments."

"Yes." Richardson nodded. "The key was vampire blood. That's what we always thought, but we were only half correct.

Normal vampire blood wouldn't do it. Type 2 and 3 vampires still create rabids when they try to produce offspring. We needed something stronger, something more powerful, to overcome the Rabidism virus. But you know that now, don't you? You realized the missing link."

Before I could reply, he turned and stepped to the counter behind him, picking up something with a clink. When he turned back, a vial glinted from his fingers as he held it up, full of something that shone a dark red under the lights.

"Your blood," he murmured. "The blood of a Master vampire, combined with the experimental vaccinations we gave to Zeke Crosse before he left, all those months ago. It hasn't been tested yet, not on a human, anyway. But you already injected that Jackal fellow, and he's on his way to a full recovery now. So, based on that, and the research I was able to perform..." He paused, staring at the vial, his voice going faint with awe, with hope. "This...is our cure. We finally have a cure."

Eden celebrated that night. Somehow, though the mayor and the doctor had wished to keep it quiet for now, word of the cure had leaked out of the hospital and spread like wildfire through the masses. Despite near-starvation circumstances, cases of alcohol were mysteriously unearthed from somewhere, and hunting parties had managed to return with several deer that afternoon, so the mood of the camp was jubilant. Bonfires were lit throughout the camp, and humans milled around and laughed and talked, uncaring of the few vampires who walked among them now.

I hung back from the crowds, leery of the huge fires but also not wanting to be around that many humans drunk on alcohol and giddiness. Their excited voices trickled to me as I moved through shadows, hearing snippets of conversation, about the cure, and Eden, and going home.

I couldn't join their celebration. We had a cure. The one thing both humans and vampires had searched for, sought after, desperately needed, for six decades. Dr. Richardson had told me that, if the cure worked as he expected, any human injected with the vaccine should be rendered immune to Rabidism. It wouldn't "cure" the rabids and turn them human again; the rabids were already dead, and death was the one thing you couldn't cure. But it would nullify the disease and make it so the rabid couldn't pass Rabidism on to living creatures. If you could get close enough to inject it with the cure, anyway. And a vampire who was given the vaccine would no longer be a carrier of Rabidism and would, in theory, be able to create offspring again. It wasn't perfect, but it was a start. I should've been happy.

But the cost was high. For me, anyway. The humans didn't know. They would never understand the sacrifice that had been made so that they could live—so that we all could live.

I wished he could be here now, to see it.

Wandering the perimeter of the camp, I spotted the person I was looking for near the edge of the light and made my way toward him. Zeke also hung back from the crowds, talking to a pair of humans in the shadows. As I got closer, I recognized them, or one of them, anyway. Silent Jake, tall, dark and leaning on a crutch, shook Zeke's hand before hobbling away with a dark-haired woman, her arm wrapped protectively around his waist. Zeke smiled faintly as I approached, his gaze distant as he watched them limp away.

"Hey, you," I said softly, touching his elbow.

"Allie." His voice was low, relieved, as he turned. Without hesitation, he stepped forward and kissed me, one hand pressed to the small of my back, the other against my cheek. I closed my eyes and relaxed into him, letting myself feel safe, that we had won, if only for a moment.

"Dr. Richardson told me you were awake," he said as we pulled back, his blue eyes intense as he gazed down at me. "Are you all right?"

I nodded. "What about you?" I asked, running a hand across his chest, the place he'd been run through, twice. He seemed fine now. No wounds, no scars or even bloodstains. For the first time, I was relieved that Zeke was a vampire. Had he been human, he would definitely have been killed.

Zeke smiled grimly. "I'm all right. Took four bags of blood before I felt normal again, and I gave Dr. Thomas the shock of his life when he came to examine me. Mayor Hendricks didn't mind, because we'd just saved his town but... I think it's safe to say that everyone knows I'm a vampire now."

I stroked his cheek, my voice sympathetic. "Are you okay with that?"

"It's getting better." He leaned into my touch. "The people here don't trust me anymore, but I don't blame them. They knew me as a human, but now that I'm a vampire, they don't know what to think. I guess I'll have to prove myself to them, to everyone, just like you did with us."

"You plan to stay, then."

He nodded. "Until Eden is back on its feet, at least. After that..." He shrugged. "I don't know. I don't know if they'll let me stay here, if they'll let *us* stay here. I guess we'll have to play it by ear, then."

"Zeke Crosse?"

We turned. A woman stood behind him, not old but quite weathered, looking battered by hardship and life. Her light brown hair was pulled behind her, and her left hand was wrapped in bandages. Zeke broke away from me, his eyes going wide as he faced her.

"Mrs. Brooks! I didn't know you were here. They said you had gotten off the island, but..." He paused, raking a hand through his hair, his voice thick with guilt. "I'm so sorry about your husband. And…and Matthew. I should have been there—"

She raised her hand. "Is it true what they say?" she almost whispered, though her voice was matter-of-fact. Zeke winced, shoulders hunching, as the woman continued. "That…that you're a vampire now. Is that true?"

He bowed his head. "Yes, ma'am."

She trembled, looking like she would flee if she could, but didn't back away. "You've killed people," she prodded, like she desperately hoped Zeke would disagree, prove her wrong. "To…to feed yourself."

"Yes."

Her face went pale, the last of her courage seeming to disappear. "Monster," she whispered, and I had to bite my lip to keep myself from pushing forward and snarling in her face. *You want a monster?* I thought furiously. *I'll show you a monster. You're looking at the wrong person.* But Zeke didn't say anything, only stood there with his head bowed, accepting the accusation. The woman didn't turn and flee, either, staring at Zeke as if trying to see the demon in him.

"And yet…" She hesitated a moment. "Caleb and Bethany tell me that you saved them on Eden. Saved them from that horrible vampire who wanted to kill everyone. Who killed my husband and son…" She broke off with a sob, wiping her eyes, before composing herself. Zeke peeked up, his eyes cautiously hopeful, but the woman didn't see.

"If that is true," she went on, "if you saved the other half of my family, then I can't hate you, Zeke. Even if you are a vampire. But… I do fear you. I'm afraid of what you might do to my children. They think so highly of you. They don't understand what could really happen."

"I would never hurt them," Zeke said huskily.

"I know you believe that." She nodded, looking defeated. "They want to see you," she went on, and Zeke jerked up. "Caleb…is quite insistent. They were both devastated when you left, and I don't feel right, keeping them away from the boy who brought them to Eden, who looked after them their whole life. You were their family before I was. I can't keep them from you."

She sniffled and looked behind her, to where a female soldier stood a little ways away, holding the hands of two familiar faces. Caleb beamed and waved wildly to us, and his mother gave Zeke a pleading, teary look.

"Please, don't hurt my children, Ezekiel," she whispered, and moved back as the soldier released the kids. Bethany hesitated, but Caleb pelted forward at full speed, coming right at us. Zeke stiffened, and I quickly moved behind him, placing a hand on his back.

"You're okay," I breathed so that only he could hear me. "I'm right here."

And then I had to move aside, as Caleb crashed into Zeke, wrapping both arms around his legs and rocking him back a step. "Whoa! Hey, easy there, rug rat." He steadied them both, though I could see his shoulders were tight, his face carefully controlled. "Man, you've gotten big. What've you been eating lately?"

"You left!" Caleb accused, peering up at him, his jaw set and angry, and Zeke blinked in surprise. "You left me," the boy went on, though he still didn't release his grip on Zeke's legs. "Just like Ruth. Just like Allison." He spared me the glare of an indignant six-year-old, before turning on Zeke again. "You promised we'd all live together in Eden. Why did you go?"

Zeke sighed. Gently freeing himself, he knelt so that he was face-to-face with Caleb. Bethany, coming up behind him, waved shyly, and Zeke smiled at her, holding out an arm to draw her close.

"I had to," he explained to them both. "I had to go find Allison and bring her back. You understand that, right? I wasn't going to leave forever."

They nodded, though Caleb's bottom lip still jutted out stubbornly. "You guys have a family now," Zeke continued. "You have parents, and goats, and a house, and everything. Allie didn't have any of that. That's why I wanted to bring her to Eden. She needed a home, just like you."

I smiled wistfully. Home and family. Zeke had known, even before I did, how important that was. That I'd longed for both; a family that wouldn't leave me, and a place to belong. I'd found them, with Zeke, Kanin, even Jackal. I was a vampire, and I belonged in the darkness, but that was all right. I wasn't alone anymore. And my path, as my sire always told me, was my own.

Bethany nodded silently, accepting Zeke's explanation, but Caleb looked thoughtful. "Are you a vampire now?" he asked simply, gazing up at Zeke with wide, innocent eyes. "Like Allison?"

Zeke flinched, but nodded. "Yes," he said softly. "So, that means I can't be around you guys as much anymore, okay? You might not see me for a long time, but that doesn't mean I left, or that I don't care about you anymore. It just means… that I'm a vampire. I don't want to hurt you."

Caleb chewed his lip for a moment, pondering this. Bethany looked a little frightened at the mention of vampires, but with everything she'd been through, you couldn't blame her. Even if this was Zeke.

"Do you have fangs?" Caleb asked suddenly. Zeke blinked, gave him a wary look.

"Yes."

"I wanna see."

Now he did pull back, stiffening. "Caleb..."

"I wanna see!" Caleb pressed forward, his face earnest. "The pastor says vampires are bad and evil, but I don't believe him. Allison is a vampire, and she's not bad. But everyone is scared of you now, even Mom." His lip stuck out defiantly. "Show me, Zeke. I wanna see if it makes you different."

Caleb's mother had come forward, her face tight with fear, but Zeke held up a hand. "It's all right," he said, glancing at her. "Let me show him. Maybe he'll understand better, then."

Her face turned white, but she gave a stiff nod. Zeke sighed, bowing his head, then raised it again, curling his lips back. His fangs gleamed in the darkness, bright and lethal, and Bethany skittered back with a shriek.

Caleb didn't move. He faced Zeke calmly, regarding the fangs bared in his direction with a furrowed brow, as if searching for something.

Slowly, one small hand rose, touching Zeke's jaw, and Zeke jerked back, his eyes going wide with astonishment. Caleb held his gaze, frowning, then shook his head.

"No," he said simply, as if this was something he'd known all along. "You're still the same."

Zeke's eyes closed. With a short breath, he pulled Caleb against him, bowing his head. After a moment, Bethany stepped up to join them, leaning against his shoulder, and he wrapped an arm around her, as well. I blinked red from my eyes and stepped back to give them space.

A dark, lean shadow moved across the trees, away from the crowds, heading in the direction of the lake, and I frowned. It was Jackal. I hadn't seen my blood brother since he'd been injected with my blood, and I'd been intending to check how he was doing once I caught up to Zeke. I was less worried about him than I had been; even wounded in a city of unsuspecting mortals, he'd proven he knew how to control himself, sometimes even better than me. The only question was his willingness to behave, to not give in to the monster.

Where was he going now?

Curious, I followed, pausing only once to glance back at Zeke and the children. He was on his feet again, talking to Caleb's mother, the two kids pressed close. He met my gaze over her shoulder, smiled and nodded for me to go on. He'd be all right. The monster had no hold on him, at least not right now.

I slipped down the bank, following the shoreline past the dock, to where a lone, tall figure stood at the edge of the water. The breeze tugged at his dark hair, and his duster billowed and flapped behind him as he gazed out over the waves. A strange prickle ran up my spine. For just a moment, with him standing motionless and silent at the water's edge, he reminded me, very faintly, of Kanin.

I shook myself, wondering where *that* had come from, and stepped forward.

"Hey," I greeted, making him turn. The black wounds were still there, on his cheeks and brow, but they were mere shadows of what they had been, and the dark veins covering his neck were gone completely. "Looks like you survived."

"Disappointed, sister?" Jackal smirked at me, looking like his old self. "I told you, I always come out on top, no matter what."

"Like a bad penny." I looked past him and saw a rowboat a few yards away, ready to be shoved into the water. My heart gave a lurch with the realization, surprising me with its reluctance to see him go. "You're leaving, I suppose."

"Yeah." Jackal glanced behind him, staring over the waters of the lake. "Past time, I think. We killed Sarren, found the cure, and saved the world from another superplague. I'm about to choke on all this goodwill." He turned back to me, grinning. "Figured I'd leave before I got too bored and started making my own fun. You and the puppy probably wouldn't like that."

"You could still stay," I said. "Help rebuild Eden."

He snorted a laugh. "Please. Stay and help a bunch of sweaty meatsacks with manual labor? Not my scene, sister. You should know me better by now."

"Yeah, silly me, thinking you might not be a complete bastard after all." I smiled and rolled my eyes. "So, where are you going? You've been cured of Rabidism. I suppose you're off to raise that vampire army."

"Well...." Jackal scratched the side of his neck. "I've been thinking about that. And I realized, to make it work, I'd have to get a whole new batch of minions. I'm certainly not going to use my former toadies, not when the little shits tried to kill me. I'd have to go back to Old Chicago, kill everyone there, and start over from scratch. And that seems like a hell of a lot of work." Jackal shook his head. "Ruling a city of murdering, backstabbing humans sounds a lot easier than ruling a city of murdering, backstabbing vampires. And I think I deserve a vacation. Maybe I'll revisit the idea in a century or two. Right now, I'm going to take a break from all this saving the world shit and relax. Maybe travel awhile, see what's out there. I always wanted to see Europe. Apparently, the vampires there are the real deal. Some of them can trace their bloodline all the way back to the first bloodsucker himself. It'd be interesting to see what they can do, how they run things." He grinned at me, showing fangs. "I don't suppose I could get you to come with me."

"No." I shook my head. "I'm staying in Eden with Zeke, until the city is back on its feet, anyway."

"Ah, well. Can't say I didn't try." Jackal stepped back, raising a hand in a mock salute. "See you around, sister. Have fun with your bloodbags. And tell the puppy that if he ever wants my head, I'm ready for him anytime."

"Hey," I called, as he started toward the boat. He turned back, raising an eyebrow: a tall, lean vampire silhouetted against the night, golden eyes shining in the dark. "Thanks," I said quietly. "For sticking around."

My blood brother snorted. "Don't go soft on me, little sister," he warned, and his tone was only half teasing. "You're a Master now. If we ever run into each other again, I won't go easy on you."

I smiled. "Looking forward to it."

Then I turned and walked away, and Jackal stepped up to the rowboat, shoving it into the water. I didn't stop, continuing up the bank, back to Zeke, the humans, and the light. Jackal—my blood brother, Kanin's other prodigy, and the raider king of Old Chicago—continued to glide into the darkness. I felt the pulse through our blood tie drifting farther and farther away, until I could barely sense him anymore.

It took several weeks before people could return to Eden. Even with Sarren dead and Requiem halted, Eden was still infested with rabids, and none of the humans could return until they were destroyed. Digging them up during the day would take forever, but going after them at night was extremely dangerous. We could have waited for Requiem to run its course; eventually the rabids would have died from the disease, but there were no supplies left at the checkpoint, and the mayor didn't want to risk a rabid getting off the island now that their fear of deep water was gone. Plus, it seemed to be taking an abnormally long time for the rabids to succumb to the virus, longer than it had taken the bleeders or even the infected vampires to die. Perhaps that was part of Sarren's design, his plan to spread Requiem as far as he could, but whatever the reason, the mayor wanted the rabids destroyed as soon as possible. So of course, we volunteered.

It had been Zeke's idea to set a trap; use blood to lure the horde to where we wanted them, then ambush and kill them all. The flames from the burning building stung my skin and could be seen for miles, and the stench of charred rabid flesh lingered on the wind for hours afterward, but it took out a sizable chunk of the horde. After several more forays into the city, hunting down the remaining rabids, making certain we got them all, the mayor finally announced that people could return to their homes.

Even then, it would still be a long time before Eden got back to normal. Many lives had been lost, homes and families torn apart, and devastation left in the wake of the attack. Zeke and I helped where we could, but it was obvious that the people of Eden were still leery of us, despite the mayor giving us full citizenship, and our presence was often looked upon with fear and anger. For all we'd done for Eden, we were still vampires.

Still, we stayed, through the winter and on into spring. Sometimes, I thought of Kanin, and wondered what my sire would think if he could see me now. Zeke reconnected with his family and visited Caleb and Bethany when he could, though never alone, and never for long. He was at peace with himself now, content with his new status as a vampire, but he never forgot what he truly was, and what he could do. I made a few friends on Eden, Mayor Hendricks, for one, and Dr. Richardson, who seemed fascinated with vampires and wanted to learn all he could about them. He also provided Zeke and I with blood bags as often as we needed them. And as time passed, the people of Eden began to see us less as monsters and more as curiosities; we were dangerous, yes, and could easily kill a human, but we also guarded and protected the city. Not to mention, we had saved it from a superplague and driven off all the rabids. So, we couldn't be completely evil. Eventually, Zeke and I were granted a very cautious acceptance and became just another part of the city. Eden's resident vampires.

Zeke and I were together constantly. It was strange; the more times we shared blood, shared ourselves and our emotions, the deeper the bond grew and the harder I fell for him. I'd once wondered if I could ever trust someone enough to stay with them for a lifetime; now, forever with Zeke didn't seem nearly long enough.

Still, even though I was happy with Zeke, more content than I'd been in a long time, I was restless. The laboratory had been fixed, one of the first buildings to be restored, and every human in the city was in line to receive the vaccine as often as it could be synthesized. Eden would soon be immune to Rabidism, but what about everyone else? The rest of the world knew nothing about the cure, that it even existed. Who would tell them? Who *could* tell them, with the country so infested with rabids, vampires and other monsters?

I knew the answer, of course. Though it was hard to think about; the enormity of the task was simply staggering. If the world was ever going to be normal again, someone had to go out there and take the cure to everyone. Eden shone like a beacon of hope in the darkness, a safe haven for its residents, but it couldn't reach the whole world. No, that burden would have to fall to someone else. Someone who cared about saving both humans and vampires. Someone with a lot of time on their hands.

Now, it is your turn to leave your own mark on the world.

So, I would.

★ ★ ★

I stood at the edge of a lonely dock, cool wind tugging at my hair and coat, gazing over the dark waters of Lake Erie. Beside me, a simple rowboat bobbed up and down on the waves, knocking quietly against the planks. Empty but for a tiny cooler with a couple blood bags, a handful of syringes, and a case with several vials of the precious vaccine. Dr. Richardson couldn't spare much of the synthesized version, but I wasn't worried about running out. As long as I was alive, so was the cure.

A breeze hissed across the lake, warmer now, hinting of rain. Winter was nearly over. It had been almost a year since I'd become a vampire. A year since that night in the rain, where I'd died in Kanin's arms and begun a new life. Who would've thought that cynical, jaded street rat would end up here, a vampire ready to set out into the world, following the footsteps of her sire?

Can you see me, Kanin? I thought, gazing into the darkness. Overhead, the night sky glittered with a million stars, and a full moon peered down at me, a halo of light around it. *I hope I'm doing what you wanted, what you tried to teach me. It's going to take a long time, but I won't give up, just like you didn't give up. And I pray that, wherever you are, you've finally found your peace.*

Footsteps thumped behind me, and Zeke slipped his arms around my waist, drawing me against him. I reached back and looped an arm around his neck as his lips traced my jaw, brushing it softly. My blood stirred at the contact, reacting to his presence, as if recognizing the other half of itself. A feeling of deep contentment stole over me, and I leaned against him.

"Are you sure you want to do this?" I whispered, closing my eyes against his touch. He nodded.

"We've done all we can here," he murmured back. "Eden is safe. Mayor Hendricks told me the last of its citizens will receive the vaccine tomorrow. Most the buildings have been repaired, and they have enough supplies to last the rest of the winter. Spring is coming," he added, brushing a kiss against my ear. "The planting season will start soon. They don't need vampires for that."

"Have you said goodbye to Caleb and Bethany?"

"Oh, yes." He chuckled. "You should've heard the tantrum Caleb threw. Guilt, tears, the whole song and dance. He even threatened not to like me anymore if I left. But I promised we'd come back. Someday." He sounded amused and sad at the same time. "Though he might be grown up with kids of his own when I see him and Bethany again."

Feeling a little guilty, I turned in his arms, gazing up at him. This was Zeke's home. I didn't want to do this alone, couldn't imagine being without him, but I wouldn't drag him on an endless journey if he wasn't absolutely sure he wanted to go.

"Are you really certain this is what you want?"

"Yes, Allison." Zeke put a hand on my cheek, his eyes intent. "I'm certain. We finally have a cure, but the rest of the world needs to know about it. It's up to us to spread the word, to let humans know they don't have to live in fear. Eventually, people will populate the world again, and things can be like they were Before. They'll have to figure out how to live with the vampires, how to coexist, if that's even possible. But it has to start somewhere." He took my hand and held it to his chest. "This is the beginning, right here. With us."

"It could take a long time," I said, not to discourage him, but as a warning. "A very, very long time. We might never be finished, Zeke. It could take forever."

He smiled, lowered his head, and kissed me. Long and lingering, a promise full of love, and courage, and hope.

"I love you, vampire girl," he whispered as he drew back. "And forever is exactly what we have."

★ ★ ★ ★ ★

ACKNOWLEDGMENTS

It appears I have come to the end of another series, the first since the Iron Fey, and I have a lot of people to thank for it. For without them, Allie, Zeke, Jackal, and Kanin's story wouldn't have made it onto paper.

Thanks always to my editor, Natashya Wilson, who pushes me to do better, to really think about my characters and their motivations, and who catches things I never would've given a second glance to. (Balloons in the apocalypse, who would've thought?) To all the people at Inkyard Press; I am supremely lucky to be a part of such a wonderful, supportive group. Here's to many more years with you.

Thanks to my agent, Laurie McLean, for keeping me sane during Crazy Deadline Panic Time. Maybe someday we'll be able to take that break.

Eternal gratitude to all my readers. As you probably know by now, your tears feed my muse.

And, of course, my deepest thanks goes to my husband, Nick, who continues to be my best support, inspiration, and logic-hole spotter. Still couldn't have done it without you.

DAWN

OF

EDEN

CHAPTER 1

In the summer of my twenty-third year, the Red Lung virus began its spread across the eastern United States. Flulike symptoms evolved to raging fever, necrosis of the lungs and finally asphyxiation, as victims choked and drowned in their own blood. By the time government officials knew anything was wrong, the virus had already made its way overseas and was rapidly decimating Europe and parts of Asia, with no signs of slowing down. A worldwide emergency was called; towns had been emptied, cities lay in ruins and the virus continued its deadly march toward human extinction.

We thought Red Lung was as bad as it could get.

We were wrong.

"Kylie! It's Mr. Johnson!"

I spun from Ms. Sawyer's cot, nearly beaning Maggie in the nose as I whirled around. The intern looked frantic, her eyes wide over her mask, her face pale as she pointed to a cot along the far wall. Two masked interns were struggling with the body of a middle-aged man who was spasming and coughing violently, trying to throw them off. Blood flecked his lips, spattered in vivid patterns across his sheets and hospital robes.

His mouth gaped, trying to suck in air, and his breathing tube lay on the ground in a pool of blood and saliva.

I rushed over, snatching a syringe from my lab coat and dodging the intern, who stumbled back as the man flailed. Grabbing the patient's arm, I threw my weight against him, which didn't do much as Mr. Johnson was a big guy and frantic, and I weighed about one hundred ten sopping wet.

"Hold him down!" I called to Eric, the intern who'd been flung back, and he pounced on the man again. Blood streamed from the man's nose and flew in arcing ribbons across the bed as he coughed and flailed. I uncapped the syringe and plunged it into his arm, injecting eight mms of morphine into his veins.

Gradually, his struggles ceased. His eyes rolled back, and his head lolled to the side as he passed into unconsciousness.

At this stage of the infection, he would probably never wake up.

I sighed and brushed away a strand of ash-blond hair that had come loose from my clip during my struggles with Mr. Johnson. My hand came away sticky with blood, but I was so used to that now, I barely noticed. "Keep an eye on him," I told Eric and the other intern, Jenna, who looked on with weary, hooded eyes. "Let me know if there's any change, or if he wakes up."

Jen nodded, but Eric made a disgusted sound and shook his head, his dark curls bouncing.

"He's not going to wake up," he said, voicing the fact that everyone knew but was too numb to think about. "We've seen this a thousand times, now." He turned accusing eyes on me, gesturing at the unconscious patient. Though he slept now, we could hear the gurgling in his throat and lungs, the rasp of air through a rapidly flooding windpipe. "Why did you even waste a shot of morphine on him? We're almost out, and it could've been used on someone who has a chance. Why not put the poor bastard out of his misery?"

"Keep your voice down," I said in a cool, even tone, giving him a hard glare. Around us, our patients coughed or slept fitfully, too drug-addled to really understand what we said, but they weren't deaf. And the other interns were watching. They were just as discouraged and frightened and exhausted, but I could not show weakness, especially now.

"It's not our place to say who lives or dies," I said quietly, looking at Eric but speaking to all of them. "We have a responsibility to these people, to fight for them. To not give up. That's why we set up this clinic, even though all the hospitals in the city have probably shut down by now. We can still help, and we will not abandon them."

"You're crazy." Eric finally looked up at me, his face bleak. "This is crazy, Kylie. Everyone is gone, even Doc Adams, and he set this whole place up. You might not want to accept it, but it's time to face facts." He nodded at Maggie and Jen on the other side of the bed. "This is futile. We're the only ones left, and we can't save anyone. We lost. It's time to throw in the towel."

"No." My voice came out flat, cold. "This isn't a stupid boxing match. These are people's lives. I'm not going to abandon them. Even if I can only give them a peaceful last few days, that's better than doing nothing." Eric snorted, and I stared him down. "But I'm not keeping you here." I pointed past him at the entrance to the makeshift clinic, the opening covered with plastic strips. "You can walk out anytime. If you want to leave, there's the door."

He glared at me before he reached up and tugged down his mask. I could see the grim line of his mouth and jaw, and my heart sank, but I kept my expression calm.

"You expect miracles," he said, taking a step back. Glancing around the small, cloth-walled room, the patients huddled beneath the bloodstained sheets, he shook his head. "You can stay here until the city crumbles around you, and the stink of dead bodies makes your insides rot. You might not have a family, but I haven't seen mine in weeks, and I don't even know if they're still alive." His face crumpled with worry and fear, and I felt a stab of guilt before he curled a lip and sneered at me. "So you stay here with your cadavers and the virus until one of them kills you. I'm done."

He spun on his heel and walked across the room, pushed through the door in a swoosh of plastic, and was gone.

I wanted, badly, to sink into a chair, to rub my tired eyes and even get a little sleep, but that wasn't an option. Glancing at the two remaining interns, I gave them what I hoped was an encouraging smile.

"Maggie, go check on Ms. Sawyer," I said, and she nodded, looking relieved to do something that didn't involve large, violent patients. "Jen, why don't you check the supplies, see what we have and what we're running out of. I'll keep an eye on Mr. Johnson."

They hurried off, and I hoped I'd managed to hide the worry and constant strain of keeping this clinic alive, the despair that another had gone, given up, and the secret fear that he was right. I noted the hopeless slump of their shoulders, the exhausted way they carried themselves, and knew they wouldn't last much longer, either.

Walking to our tiny operating room, I turned on the sink and ran my arms beneath the cold water, letting the dried blood swirl into the basin. I glanced up, and a thin, pale girl stared back at me from the mirror, blood speckling her face and streaked through her fine blond hair, which hadn't been washed for days. Dark circles crouched beneath green eyes, the telltale marks of exhaustion, her cheeks gaunt and wasted.

"You look hideous," I told my reflection, which nodded in agreement. "You're going to have to sleep sometime or you'll be fainting on the patients."

But there was no time for rest, no time to take a break, especially now that Eric was gone. This small clinic, hastily set up on the edge of urban D.C., was the last hope for those infected with Red Lung, the virus that had decimated the city and turned the downtown area into a war zone. Makeshift clinics had been constructed around the city to help with the overwhelming number of sick, but it was never enough. As more people died and civilization broke down, chaos and riots had spread rapidly with nothing to stop them, the worst of mankind coming to the surface. All the other hospitals had closed down, the dead left to rot in their rooms, or laid out in rows in the parking lot. As the city had emptied, even the other clinics had begun to vanish, the doctors and staff either dying or giving up in despair. As far as I knew, this was one of the last, but there were still infected people out there, and they deserved some kind of hope. Even if it was very slim.

Splashing water on my face, I rubbed my tired eyes. Now, if I could just cling to a bit of that hope myself.

"Hello?" A deep voice cut through the beeping machinery and coughing of patients. "Anyone here?"

I jerked up. Hastily I dried my hands, scrubbed the towel over my face and hurried out to the main room.

Two strangers stood just inside the entrance flaps, both young men, one leaning on the other with an arm around his shoulders. I blinked in shock; the second man had on a stained white lab coat much like mine. He had light brown hair and glasses, and even across the room, I could see he was badly hurt; his shirt was torn, especially his sleeve, and his arm looked as if he'd stuck it in a meat grinder. The other was tall and broad-shouldered, holding his friend's weight easily. His shirt and jeans were stained with blood, though I suspected it wasn't his own. His gaze met mine, dark eyes appraising beneath a mess of short, mahogany-colored hair.

"Can you help us?" he asked, his voice rough with worry. "We saw this place from the road. Is there a doctor around?"

"I'm in charge," I said, stepping forward. "But this is a quarantined zone. You can't be here—you'll both be exposed to the virus."

"Please." His brown eyes grew pleading, and he glanced down at his friend, who seemed barely conscious, hanging from his shoulders. "There's nowhere else to go—the other hospitals are empty. He'll die."

I sighed and gave a brisk nod. "In here," I ordered, and he followed me into the operating room, hefting his friend onto the table as gently as he could. The other moaned, delirious, and his arm flopped to the counter. His skin was flushed, feverish, his face tight with pain.

I cut away his shirt and coat, revealing an upper torso that was pale and slightly overweight, but he didn't seem to be wounded anywhere else. I would examine him thoroughly later, but the arm was the most pressing concern. Gently, I lifted the mangled limb from the table to study it. Several torn, bloody holes ran up the limb from wrist to elbow. The flesh around the wounds was hot and puffy, deep punctures well on their way to infection.

"These are teeth marks," I said, frowning at the strangely symmetrical patterns through the mess of blood and shredded skin. "What attacked him?"

"I don't know." The voice behind me was husky, evasive, but I wasn't really listening. I studied the arm further, trying to match the bite patterns with what I'd seen before: dogs, cats, even a horse, once. Nothing fit.

Except...

"These...almost look like human bite marks." But that wasn't right, either, not with this type of deep puncture wound. The thing that had left these marks had long canines like a predator. Human teeth were not capable of this.

The stranger's voice was stiff, uncomfortable. "Can you save him?"

"I'll try." Turning, I fixed the stranger with a firm stare. He gazed back, eyes hooded. "What is your relation to this man, Mr....?"

"Archer. Ben Archer. And we're not related." He nodded to the body on the table. "Nathan and I... I worked for him. He's a friend."

"All right, Mr. Archer. Not to be rude, but you can either help me or get out. I can't be tripping over you every time I turn around. If you think you can take direction and do exactly as I tell you, you're welcome to stay."

He nodded. I pointed to the counter behind us. "Get some gloves on, then. This is going to be messy."

He turned, and I blinked. Blood covered one side of his shirt, and the fabric was torn, sticking to the skin. Several deep gashes were raked across his shoulder blade, still raw and bloody, though he didn't seem to notice them.

"What happened to your back, Mr. Archer?"

He jerked up, wincing. "Ah," he muttered, not meeting my gaze. "Nathan was attacked and... I got it when I went to help. It's nothing, not that deep. Please, help him first."

"I intend to, but as soon as we're done here, you need to let me take care of that. And you *are* going to tell me what happened when we're done, Mr. Archer."

He nodded, and we worked in tense, determined silence,

broken only by me barking orders, directing my helper to hold this or fetch that. I didn't mince words or attempt civility; my focus was on saving this man's life. But my impromptu assistant took all direction without comment until the task was complete.

"There." I pulled the final stitch shut, tying it off with a short jerk. The man lay on the table, disinfected, bandaged and sewn up the best I could manage with such limited supplies. "That's it. We'll just have to keep an eye on him, now."

Ben Archer stood behind me. I could feel his hooded gaze on the table in front of us. "Will he make it?"

"He's lost a lot of blood," I said, turning around. "He needs a transfusion, but there's no way we can do that now. The wounds haven't gone septic, but I'm mostly worried about his fever." The man's face fell, and I offered a kind lie out of habit. "We'll have to wait and see if he survives the night, but I think he has a chance of pulling through."

"Thank you," he murmured. He seemed relieved but shifted restlessly at the edge of the counter, as if he expected something to come lunging through the operating room doors any second. "I didn't get your name, Doctor…?"

"Just call me Kylie." I really looked at him for the first time, seeing the stubble on his chin, the haunted look in his dark brown eyes. His shoulders were broad, his arms muscular under his shirt, as if he was used to hard labor.

"Miss Kylie." He shot a glance at the tiny window, at the late-afternoon sun slanting in through the glass. "I'm grateful for your help. But we have to go. Now."

"Excuse me?"

"We have to leave," he repeated to my astonishment. "We can't stay here. I'm sorry, but we have to go."

I scowled at him. "You're not going anywhere, Mr. Archer. Your friend is still badly hurt, and you don't look so good yourself. What you're *going* to do is sit down, let me take care of those lacerations on your back, and tell me what the hell happened to your friend."

He flinched, one hand going to his shoulder, but shook his head. "No," he whispered, and the guilt on his face was overwhelming. "We can't stay here," he protested in a stronger voice. "We have to leave the city." His gaze flicked to mine, intense. "You should come with us. Everyone should—everyone who can still walk needs to go. It...isn't safe out there anymore."

"When was it ever safe?" I murmured. He took a breath to argue again, but my voice grew sharp. "Move him now, and your friend will die," I stated bluntly. "With that fever and those wounds, he'll be dead by morning. You leave, you kill him. It's as simple as that."

He slumped, the fight going out of him. I gestured to the stool, and he sank down, his posture defeated. "If you would take your shirt off, Mr. Archer," I urged, trying to remain businesslike as I fished a needle and thread from my coat pockets. He blinked, pulling back a little, and I sighed. "I don't have the time or patience for modesty, Mr. Archer. And we ran out of hospital gowns the first week we were here. So, please." I gestured with the needle. "Take off your shirt."

Wearily, he complied, pulling the garment over his head without so much as a wince. I kept my expression professional, but my gaze roamed over the tanned, powerful shoulders and sculpted chest as he dropped his shirt to the floor. Things were bleak, but I wasn't blind. Ben Archer was gorgeous; you didn't need a Ph.D. to see that.

He didn't move as I walked up behind him, examining the five deep lacerations that ran from his shoulder nearly to the center of his back. They looked like...claw marks. I shivered. Something was very wrong here.

"What happened to you and your friend?" I began, dabbing the wounds gently with an alcohol wipe. He didn't flinch, though the lacerations were quite deep, and I knew the alcohol stung. "Did you hear me, Mr. Archer?"

"Ben. Just Ben."

"All right, Ben." I wiped the last of the blood away and reached for the needle and thread. "You still haven't answered my question. Those bite wounds on your friend, they aren't normal. What happened?"

I felt him hesitate. My voice grew a little harder. "Don't lie to me, Mr. Archer. If I'm going to help him, I need to know exactly what happened. Any information you withhold could end up killing him, or my other patients. Now—last time— tell me what happened."

"We…" Ben paused, as if fighting himself, struggling to get the words out. "Nathan and I…we were attacked," he finally admitted.

"Yes, that I gathered," I said, gently touching his shoulder. His skin was warm, and he finally flinched at my touch. "I'm going to start stitching now, so brace yourself."

He nodded.

"So, something attacked you," I continued, sinking the needle into the smooth, tanned skin, talking quickly to keep him distracted. "What was it?"

"I… I don't know."

"What do you mean, you don't know?" I frowned as I pulled a stitch closed, seeing him grit his teeth. "Something obviously savaged your friend and tore the hell out of your shoulder. What was it?"

"I didn't see it very clearly," Ben muttered. "It was dark, and the thing moved so fast." He shrugged, then grunted in pain as the motion pulled at the stitches. "I thought it was human, but…" He trailed off again, and I frowned over his shoulder.

"Ben, your friend was bitten by something with canines at least an inch long. Humans don't have teeth like that."

He raised his head just as I looked up at him, and for a second, our faces were inches apart. Guilt, horror and fear lay open on his face; he had the look of a soldier who had seen far too much and would be eternally haunted by it.

"You should leave," he whispered once more, his voice like a ragged, open wound. And my stomach flip-flopped at the look in his eyes. "Don't ask questions, Kylie, just trust me. Get out of here as soon as you can. Go home, leave this place, and don't look back."

I took a deep, steadying breath.

"I can't leave," I told him firmly. "I won't leave my patients, so that's out of the question. Besides, I don't have a home to go back to." He looked away, and I wished I could turn his head back, force him to meet my gaze. "You're not telling me everything," I said, and his face shut down into a blank mask. My eyes narrowed. "What are you hiding?"

"Miss Kylie?"

Maggie appeared in the door. Seeing Ben, she blushed and looked down at her feet. "Ms. Sawyer was complaining that it hurt to breathe. I gave her a shot of morphine for the pain and a sedative to help her sleep."

"Good girl," I said, feeling a lump rise to my throat. The final stages of Red Lung, before the victim began coughing uncontrollably and drowning in their own blood, was difficult, painful breathing.

I felt Ben's eyes on me, sympathetic and knowing. Suddenly self-conscious, I drew away. I didn't need his pity or his advice to leave—as if I could just walk out. And it was clear I wouldn't be getting anything further out of him, at least not now. "I have to get back to my patients," I told him, beckoning Maggie into the room. "I'm sorry. Maggie, would you mind taking care of Mr. Archer, please?"

"Sure." Maggie smiled at Ben, and he gave her a tired nod. I left them together and wandered back to the main room, checking the rows of patients along the makeshift walls. For now, everyone seemed okay; comfortable and in no pain, at least. Except for Ms. Sawyer's raspy breathing and the occasional bloody cough that I couldn't do anything about, the clinic was quiet. An event that occurred less and less, as Red Lung continued its war on the human body and continued to win.

I pondered what Ben had told me. He and his friend had been attacked, there was no mistaking that. It wasn't uncommon, sadly. With the breakdown of normal society, human beings reverted to their base instincts and started preying on each other. In the early days of the plague, not a day had gone by that I hadn't heard gunshots, screams or other sounds of distant chaos. I didn't doubt they'd been attacked, but the wounds on Nathan's arm and Ben's shoulder didn't look like anything I'd seen before.

What was Ben Archer hiding? What wasn't he telling me?

"Kylie." Jenna appeared as I made another circle through the rows of cots. The intern had been training to be a nurse and was older than me by several years, but always took my instructions without fail or complaint. Her gaze was sympathetic as she pulled me aside. "You're exhausted," she stated, blue eyes appraising, and I didn't argue with her. "How long since you slept last?"

I shrugged, and she patted my arm. "Go lie down. Maggie and I can take care of things for a few hours."

"I don't know. Ms. Sawyer—"

"You've done everything you could for her," Jenna said in a low voice. "Seriously, Kylie, get some sleep. While you still can. You're going to fall over if you don't rest soon, and no one can afford that. I promise, we'll come get you if anything happens."

I nodded. It was getting close to eighteen hours with no sleep, and I *was* tired. But before I left the room, I made a note to check on my newest patients, make sure Nathan was comfortable at least. And maybe, I could get the last of that story out of Ben Archer.

I didn't quite get that far. Instead, I went to Doc Adams's old office and collapsed on the cot against the far wall, pulling the sheet over my face. I thought I wouldn't sleep with all the dark thoughts swirling through my head, but I was out almost before I touched the pillow.

CHAPTER 2

It seemed only a few minutes had passed before someone touched my shoulder, jostling me awake. Blearily, I opened my eyes and glanced up at Maggie, who stood over me with a half-worried, half-reluctant expression.

"Yeah?" I mumbled, struggling to sit up.

"Sorry, Miss Kylie." Maggie bit her lip. "But, I wanted to let you know, Mr. Johnson just passed away."

I sighed, scrubbing a hand over my eyes, grief and anger and disappointment flaring up momentarily. "All right, I'll be right out. Thank you, Maggie."

She nodded and scurried away. Standing, I put my fingers to my temples, massaging the headache pounding behind my eyes.

Dammit. Another one lost. Another life taken by the plague, and I couldn't do anything about it. Eric had been right; this was futile. Those people out there, coughing and gagging and fighting to breathe, they wouldn't survive. Not at this stage of the virus. But I couldn't abandon them. I'd promised my patients I would fight to the end, and that was what I was going to do.

Grabbing my coat, which I'd tossed on the desk before falling into unconsciousness, I walked out of the office.

And ran smack into a large, solid chest as I emerged, yawning and rubbing my face. With a yelp, I stumbled back, looking up into Ben Archer's worried brown eyes.

"Sorry." His deep voice held traces of alarm, and I gave him a wary look. "I need to talk to you. Something is wrong with Nate, and I don't know what to do for him."

My head pounded. The stress, disappointment, and looming sense of pointlessness were starting to get to me, but I put my feelings aside to focus on what I had to do.

"Walk with me." I started down the hall, and he followed at my side. The clinic was dark now, as evening stole in through the door and cloaked everything in shadow. I could hear the generators out back, humming away, but we were running out of gas, and not much power was left for lights.

We reached the spot where Nathan was being kept, one of the smaller rooms that was separated from the main wing, away from the sick. A chair stood in the corner, probably where Ben had been sitting. Jenna hovered next to the patient, looking grim.

The man on the bed groaned, sounding delirious. He was definitely paler, and blood had soaked through the bandages on his arm. But what was most worrying was the red fluid seeping from beneath his eyelids. It oozed slowly over his cheeks, cutting two crimson paths down his skin, and it could be only one thing.

I swabbed it with a cotton ball, just to be sure. Yes, it was definitely blood. Ben came up behind me, peering over my shoulder.

"What's wrong with him?"

"I...don't know." Though I hated admitting it. Peeling back his lids, I shone a light over his pupils, checking for wounds or scratches. Nothing. "The only thing I can think of is a sub-conjunctival hemorrhage, or Ebola, as unlikely as that is. Sadly, the only way to know for sure would be to conduct blood tests, but we don't have any way to do that here. We'll just have to keep him under surveillance and see what happens."

I caught a whiff of something foul, rotten, like the stench of a decaying animal, and my heart sank. Frowning, I shooed Ben out of the way and bent over the wounded man, gently unwrapping the gauze to see the wounds on his arm.

The wounds were clean. The skin around them was still puffy and red, but the bites themselves looked fine. Or at least not infected. And yet, I could still smell the faint stench of rot and decay that suggested gangrene or wounds that had gone septic.

Then I realized it wasn't coming off his arm, but the body as a whole.

Puzzled, I cleaned and rebandaged the arm, feeling Ben's worried eyes on me the whole time. Nathan groaned and tossed restlessly, and I finally gave him a shot of morphine to calm him down. As his tortured thrashing stilled and he drifted into a drugged sleep, I heard Ben take a ragged breath.

"He's getting worse."

I turned to face him, wiping my hands. "There's no infection, as far as I can see. His fever is getting worse, yes, but we've done all we can for him now. We just have to wait and see if he pulls out of it." Ben sagged, looking lost and hopeless, unsure what to do. Sinking into the chair, he ran both hands over his face and sighed.

I hesitated. Then, not really knowing why, I walked over to him and put a hand on his shoulder. "I'm not giving up," I told him softly. "And you shouldn't, either. Why don't you get some sleep? There's an extra cot in the office if you need it. I'll let you know if there are any changes."

He looked up with a faint, grateful smile. "Thank you," he murmured. "But, if it's all the same, I'd like to stay. I should be here if…anything happens to him."

"Miss Kylie." Maggie walked into the room. The petite intern smiled shyly at Ben before turning to me. "Sorry to interrupt, but Jenna wanted to know if you'd like us to move Mr. Johnson's body to the back lot now or down to storage."

I stifled a groan. "I don't think Mr. Johnson will fit in any of the storage units we have down there," I said, aware of how morbid this must sound to Ben. It had become so common-place to us now, we didn't even think about it anymore. "If you and Jenna will get him on a gurney, I'll take him out back."

She nodded and padded away, and Ben gave me a worried look. "Out back?"

"There's an empty lot we've been using for body stor-age," I said tiredly. "When the freezers downstairs get full, we move them outside. This place was set up pretty fast, so it didn't come with a proper morgue. We've had to improvise."

"You're going outside? Now?"

"I can't leave a cadaver lying on a bed all night."

He rose swiftly, his gaze narrowing. "I'll come with you."

I frowned at his sudden change of mood. "There's no need. I'm capable of handling a dead body by myself. Besides—" I glanced back toward the bed "—I thought you wanted to stay with your friend."

"Please." He took a step forward, not intimidating, but in-tense. "Let me help. It's the least I can do."

There was more to it than that, I thought. I wasn't stupid. He was still hiding something, and I was going to find out what. Just not tonight. I was tired, my head hurt and I didn't want to fight him. "All right," I sighed. "If you think you can stomach working with a dead body, then I'll put those muscles of yours to work. Follow me."

We walked back to the main room, where Maggie and Jenna were struggling to load the body onto a gurney. In times past, I'd had a couple of the male interns perform this task. But they were gone now; it was just the three of us left.

Plus Ben. Who didn't flinch as he hefted Mr. Johnson onto the cart, handling the body like he might a sick calf. His face remained businesslike as he laid the corpse down gently, and Jenna and Maggie gaped at him.

As I covered the body with a sheet, I caught a faint hint of rot coming off the corpse. What the hell? It hadn't even been an hour since Mr. Johnson had passed; there was no way the body would start to decompose so quickly.

"What is it?" Ben asked quietly. I shook my head.

"Nothing." I flipped the sheet over the body's head, and the smell vanished. Maybe I'd imagined it, or maybe I was smelling something else: a dead animal outside. I maneuvered the gurney around him and the interns, ducked through the curtains surrounding the bed and headed out the back door. Ben followed.

Outside, the temperature was cool, chilly even. Which was a good thing, given the number of dead things lying everywhere around us, hidden away in houses and beds; the ones who had died alone and forgotten. As it was, the stench coming from the back lot was always there, drifting in the clinic when the breeze blew just right. If it had been high summer, the smell would've been unbearable.

As we made our way down the sidewalk, I was struck again by how quiet everything was. Not long ago, the sounds of sirens and cars, screaming, gunshots and breaking glass, had been constant. Just across the river, in monument D.C., the city had been a war zone. Now, an eerie silence hung over everything, and the buildings around us were dark. Of course, our small clinic was located just outside the city limits, so I didn't know what was happening closer to downtown. Occasionally, I heard screams or the roar of a distant car engine, signs that there was still human life somewhere out there. But the city seemed abandoned now, left to the desperate and the dying.

I sneaked a glance at Ben, walking beside me, one hand on the corner of the gurney. His gaze scanned the buildings and the shadows around us, every fiber of his body on high alert. The same look he'd had in the clinic when night was starting to fall, only amplified a hundred-fold.

He didn't come out here to help me, I realized with a cold feeling in my stomach. *He's afraid there's something out here now.* I pulled the gurney to a halt in the middle of the sidewalk. "Ben…"

Something big slipped from the shadows into our path, making us both jump. I flinched, but Ben lunged forward and grabbed my arm as if prepared to yank me behind him. A stray dog, big and black, drew back when it saw us. It dropped what it was carrying and darted out of sight between two cars, its tail between its legs.

Ben relaxed. Quickly, he dropped my wrist, looking embarrassed. "Sorry," he murmured, staring at the ground. "I'm not usually this jumpy, I swear. Are you all right?"

I rubbed my arm, wincing from the strength in those hands. "I'm fine," I told him, and was about to ask him why he was so twitchy. But then I noticed what the dog had been carrying and stifled a groan.

"Is that…an arm?" Ben asked, peering past the gurney.

"Yeah." I sighed, knowing where the dog had probably gotten it. As we got closer to our destination, the smell began to permeate the darkness around us. That familiar knot of dread, guilt, sorrow and anger coiled in my stomach. "Just a warning," I told Ben, "this isn't going to be pretty. Steel yourself."

"For what?"

I smiled humorlessly and turned the corner of the alley.

From the corner of my eye, I saw Ben straighten, though he didn't say anything. The drone of insects was a constant hum over the hundreds of bodies lined up in neat rows up and down the empty lot. Most were covered with sheets and tarps, but several covers were torn off or had blown away, leaving the corpses to stare empty-eyed at the sky. And, from the looks of the older, "riper" corpses, the scavengers were already gathering en masse.

Ben made a sound in the back of his throat, as if he was struggling not to gag. For a moment, I was sorry for bringing him out here, letting him see the stark reality we faced every day. But he set his jaw and walked with me to the edge of the last row, where I'd laid three people—a mother and her two sons—side by side last week. I tried not to look at them as we lifted Mr. Johnson's body up in the sheet and set it on the pavement. But it was hard not to remember. I'd stayed up countless nights with that family, trying desperately to save them, but the virus had taken the mother first and the boys hours later, and that failure still haunted me.

Ben was quiet as we left the lot and pushed the empty gurney back to the clinic. He didn't say anything, but instead of scanning the streets and shadows, he appeared deep in thought, brooding over what he had just seen. It *was* pretty sobering, when you realized how much we had lost, how insidious this thing was: an enemy that couldn't be stopped, put down, reasoned with. It made you realize…we might not make it through this.

"How do you do it?"

I blinked. I'd gotten so used to his silence; the question caught me off guard. Strange, thinking I knew a man after only a few hours with him. His brown eyes were on me now, solemn and assessing.

"Because you have to," I said, ducking through the back door with him behind me. "Because you have to give people hope. Because sometimes that's the only thing that will get them through, the only thing that keeps them alive."

His next words were a whisper. I barely caught them as we moved through the main room into the dark hall beyond. "What if there is no hope?"

I shoved the gurney against the wall and turned, pinning him with my fiercest glare. "There is *always* hope, Ben. And I will thank you to keep any doom-and-gloom observations to yourself while you're here. I don't need my patients hearing it. Or my interns, for that matter."

He ducked his head, looking contrite. "I'm sorry. It's just... it's hard to keep an open mind when you've seen...what I have." I raised an eyebrow at him, and he had the grace to wince. "And...you've seen a lot worse, I know. My apologies. I'll...stop whining, now."

I sighed. "Have you had anything to eat lately?" I asked, and he shook his head. "Come on, then. We don't have much, but I can at least make you some coffee. Instant, anyway. You look like you could use some."

"That would be nice," Ben admitted, smiling, "but you don't have to go to the trouble."

"Not at all. Besides, *I* could use some, so keep me company for a while, okay?" He nodded, and we headed upstairs to the small break room and dining area that hadn't seen much use since the clinic opened. The fridge and the microwave hadn't been used since the power had gone out and we'd switched to the generators, but the gas stove worked well enough to heat water. I boiled two cups of bottled water, spooned in liberal amounts of instant coffee and handed a mug to Ben, sitting at the table.

"It's not great, but at least it's hot," I said, sliding into the seat across from his. He smiled his thanks and held the mug in both hands, watching me through the steam. Taking a cautious sip, I scrunched my forehead and forced the bitter swallow down. "Ugh. You'd think I'd get used to this stuff by now. I think Starbucks ruined me for life."

That actually got a chuckle out of him, and he sipped his drink without complaint or grotesque faces. I studied him over my mug, pretending to frown into my coffee but sneaking glances at him every few seconds. The haunted look had left his face, and he seemed a bit calmer. Though the worry still remained in his eyes. I found myself wishing I could reach over the table, stroke his stubbly cheek and tell him everything would be fine.

Then I wondered what had brought *that* on.

"Tell me about yourself," he said, setting the mug down on the table, suddenly giving me his full attention. "No offense, but you're awfully young and pretty to be running a clinic alone. And you don't wear masks like the others. Aren't you afraid you'll get sick, too?"

Absurdly, I blushed at the compliment. "I caught Red Lung early," I told him, and his eyebrows arched into his hair. "From one of the patients at the hospital where I worked. Kept me in bed for three days straight, and everyone thought I would die, but I pulled out of it before my lungs started disintegrating."

"You're a survivor?" Ben sounded shocked. I nodded.

"One of the lucky sixteen percent." I looked down at my hands, remembering. Lying in a sterile hospital room, coughing bloody flecks onto the sheets. The worried, bleak faces of my colleagues. "Everyone was surprised when I pulled through," I said, taking another sip of the stuff that claimed it was coffee. "And afterward, I felt so grateful and lucky, I volunteered to help Doc Adams when he set this place up. Especially after…" I trailed off.

"After?" Ben prodded.

I swallowed. "After I found out that my family all passed away from the virus," I muttered. "They got sick when I was in the hospital, only they never recovered. I found out when I was released and planned to go home, only I didn't have a home to go back to."

I thought of the little home in the suburbs, the place I'd spent my childhood, with its tiny front yard and single-car garage. My mom's small but perfect flower garden, my dad's ancient leather armchair. My old room. It had just been the three of us; I didn't have any brothers or sisters, but I'd never been lonely. I'd had friends, and my parents had filled whatever void was left, encouraging me to chase my dreams. Dad had always said he knew I would become something big, either a doctor or an astronaut or a scientist, and pretty much let me do whatever I'd wanted. I'd left for college as soon as I'd graduated, eager to see what was out there, but had always come home for breaks and holidays. Both Mom and Dad had been so proud, so eager to hear of my life at school. It had never crossed my mind that one day they would just be…gone.

When I'd returned to the house after my parents had died, I'd stood in the living room, with its empty armchair and ticking clock, and realized how much I had lost. Curling up in my Dad's old chair, I'd cried for about an hour, but when it was over, I'd left the house with a new resolve. I couldn't save my parents, but maybe I could save other people. Red Lung, the silent killer, was my enemy now. And I would do whatever I could to destroy it.

Across from me, Ben was quiet. I kept my gaze on the table between us, so I was surprised when his rough, calloused hand covered my own. "I'm sorry," he murmured as I looked up at him. I smiled shakily.

"It's okay. They went quickly, or at least that's what the doctors said." My throat closed, and I sniffled, taking a breath to open it. Ben squeezed my palm; his thick fingers were gentle, his skin warm. A shiver raced up my arm. "What about you?" I asked, as Ben pulled his hand back, cupping it around his mug again. "Where's your family? If it's not too personal?"

"It's not." He sighed, his face going dark as he looked away. "My family owns a big farm out west," he said in a flat voice. "Nathan and I were on our way there, to see if anyone survived. They're pretty isolated, so we were hoping the outbreak hadn't reached them yet. I don't know, I haven't seen them for a while."

A farm. That fit him, I thought, looking at his broad shoulders and calloused, work-toughened hands. I could imagine him slinging bales of hay and wrestling cows. But there was something else about him, too, something not quite so rough. "What were you doing in the city?" I asked, and his face darkened even more. "You said you haven't seen them in a while. How long has it been?"

"Four years." He set his mug down and put his chin on his hands, brooding over them. "I moved to the city four years ago, and since then I haven't even talked to my folks. They wanted me to take over the farm, like everyone before me, but I wanted to finish school at Illinois Tech." He gave a bitter snort. "My dad and I got into a huge fight one day—I even threw a punch at him—and I walked out. Haven't seen them since."

"I'm sorry, Ben." I thought of my family, my dad who had been so proud I was going into medicine. My mom who always told me to dream big. "That has to suck."

He hung his head. "I haven't spoken to them in years. Mom

always sent me Christmas cards, telling me how the farm is doing, that they miss me, but I never answered. Not once. And now..." His voice broke a little, and he hunched his shoulders. "With the plague and the virus and everything going to hell, I don't know how they're doing. I don't... I don't even know if they're alive."

He covered his eyes with a hand. I stood, quietly walked around the table to sit beside him, and put my arm around his shoulders. They trembled, though Ben didn't move or make a sound otherwise. How many times had I done this; comforted a family member who had lost someone dear? More times then I cared to remember, especially with the rapid spread of the plague. But it felt different this time. Before, I had been there to offer support when someone needed it, not caring if it was from a virtual stranger. With Ben Archer, I truly wanted to be there for him, let him know there was someone he could lean on.

I still didn't know where this was coming from. The man was a virtual stranger himself; I'd known him only a few hours. But I stayed there, holding him and saying nothing, as he succumbed to his grief in the small, dirty break room of the clinic. I had the feeling he'd been holding this in a long time, and it had finally broken through.

Finally, he took a ragged breath and pulled away, not looking at me. I rose and went to refill our coffee mugs, giving him time to compose himself.

"Thank you," he murmured as I handed him the filled mug again, and I knew it wasn't just for the coffee. I smiled and sat down, but before I had even settled myself, footsteps pounded outside the door, and Maggie rushed into the room.

"Miss Kylie?"

I stifled a groan even as I rose quickly to my feet, Ben following my example. "Yes, Maggie, what is it?"

"It's Mr. Archer's friend," Maggie said, and Ben straightened quickly. The intern shot him a half-fearful, half-sorrowful look and turned back to me. "I'm so sorry. He slipped into a coma a few minutes ago, and we can't wake him up."

CHAPTER 3

✦

"We've done everything we can for him."

I wiped my hands on a towel, gazing wearily at the man beneath the covers, so pale he could have been made of paper. His limp hair and clothes were the only things of color left, and the skin on his face had shrunk tightly to his bones, making him look skeletal. His bandages had been changed again, IV tubes had been put in and I'd given him several shots of antibiotics to try to help with the fever. The smell—that ominous, disturbing smell of rot and death—still clung to him, though I'd checked and double-checked for any sign of gangrene. There was none that I could see, but that wasn't what worried me most.

Nathan lay on his back beneath the sheets, his shallow and raspy breathing the only indicator that he was still alive. Blood flecked his lips, making my stomach knot in dread. Jenna's sad, knowing eyes met mine over the patient. I didn't need to listen to the gurgle in his chest to know. He was infected with Red Lung. The virus had gotten him, too.

Ben stood in the corner, looking on with hooded eyes. I didn't know how to tell him. "Ben…"

"He has it." Ben's voice was flat, his eyes blank.

"I'm so sorry." He gave no indication that he'd heard. "We'll keep him under surveillance and make him as comfortable as we can, but…" I paused, hating that I had to say the next words. "But I think you should prepare yourself for the worst."

Ben gave a single, short nod. I shooed the interns out of the room and walked up to him. "Does he have any family that you are aware of?"

"No." Ben sank down in the chair, running his hands over his scalp. "Nate's family all lived here and…they were gone before we started out." I put a hand on his shoulder, and he stirred a little. "Sorry, but could I have a few minutes?"

"Sure," I whispered, and walked out, leaving him alone with his friend. As I ducked through the frame, I heard the thump of his fist against the armrest, a muffled, broken curse, and swallowed my own frustrated tears as the door clicked behind us.

Maggie and Jenna looked so disheartened when I returned to the main room that I told them both to get some sleep.

"I can handle the patients alone for a few hours," I said as Jenna protested, though Maggie looked ready to fall over. "They're not going anywhere, and I'll call you if I need assistance. Get some rest."

"Are you sure, Kylie?" Jenna asked, even as Maggie stumbled away, heading for the few extra cots upstairs. "Maggie and I can take turns, if you want one of us down here with you."

I opened my mouth to answer and caught the subtle hint of rot, drifting from the beds along the wall. My stomach turned over, and the scent vanished as quickly as it had come.

"I'll be fine," I told Jenna firmly. "Go get some shut-eye. Lie down, at least. That's an order."

She looked reluctant but left the room after Maggie. When

they were gone, I hurried over to Ms. Sawyer, slipping through the curtains to the side of her bed.

Her skin was chalky white, and the faint smell of decay clung to her, as it had to Nathan. Looking at her face, my blood ran cold. Though her chest rose and fell with shallow, labored breaths, her eyes were half open, and red fluid seeped from beneath the lids.

Just like Nathan.

As I went to wipe the blood from her other cheek, Ms. Sawyer jerked in her sleep, lunging toward my hand without opening her eyes. A short hiss came from her open mouth, and I yanked my hand back, heart pounding, as she sank down, still unconscious.

She didn't move again, and about an hour after midnight I woke Jenna, helped her move the body onto a gurney, and took it down to storage. Then, because the freezers in the basement were full, we woke Maggie and began the painstaking task of moving all the bodies to the back lot, freeing up space for future victims. We didn't know then how soon we would need it.

The epidemic began several hours later.

It started with Ms. Sawyer's bed neighbor, a middle-aged man who had been clinging stubbornly to life and who I'd hoped had a good chance of pulling through. An hour or so before dawn, he started bleeding from the eyes and rapidly went downhill. He was dead two hours later. Then, one by one, all the patients began weeping the bloody red tears and coughing violently, causing Jenna, Maggie and me to scurry from bed to bed, trying desperately to slow the flood. By the time the late-afternoon sun began setting over the tops of the empty buildings, half our patients were gone, with the other half barely holding on to life. We didn't even have time to move the corpses from their beds and resorted to covering them with sheets when they died. As evening wore on, the number of bodies under sheets outnumbered the living. With every death, my anger grew, until I was swearing under my breath and snapping at my poor interns.

At last, the flood slowed. The patients still bled from the eyes, and the smell of decay had permeated the room, but there was a lull in the storm of coughing and gasping and death. As the sun set and the light began fading rapidly, I called Jenna and Maggie into the hall. Jenna looked on edge, and Maggie had succumbed to exhausted tears as I drew them aside, fighting my own frustration and the urge to lash out at everything around me.

"Where is Mr. Archer?" I asked in a low voice. I'd never seen a roomful of patients decline so rapidly, and I had a sneaking, terrible suspicion. I hoped I was wrong, but I needed answers, and there was only one person who could give them to me.

"I think he's still in the room with his friend," Maggie sniffled. "We haven't seen him all day."

I spun on a heel and marched down the hall. Blood from the eyes, the strange bite marks, the rotten smell without the infection. Nathan's symptoms had spread to my patients, and Ben knew what it was. He knew, and I was fed up with this hiding, keeping secrets. Less than a day after Ben Archer had stepped into my sick ward with his friend, I had a roomful of corpses. He was going to tell me what he knew if I had to beat it out of him.

I swept into his room, bristling for a fight, and stopped.

Ben sat slumped in the corner chair, eyes closed, snoring softly. Exhaustion had finally caught up to him, too. Despite my anger, I hesitated, reluctant to wake him. Sleep was a precious commodity here; you snatched it where and when you could. Still, I would have woken him right then if I hadn't seen what had happened to the body in the room with us.

Nathan lay on the bed, unmoving. Unnaturally still. The faint smell of rot still lingered around him, and in the shadows, his skin was the color of chalk. I moved to his bedside, and a chill ran up my spine. His eyes were open, gazing sightlessly at the ceiling, but his pupils had turned a blank, solid white.

The chair scraped in the corner as Ben rose. I held my breath as his footsteps clicked softly over the linoleum to stand beside me. I heard his ragged intake of breath and glanced up at him.

He had gone pale, so white I thought he might pass out. The look on his face was awful; grief and rage and guilt and horror, all at once. He gripped the edge of the railing in both hands, swaying on his feet, and I put a hand out to steady him, my anger forgotten.

"Ben."

He glanced at me, a terrifyingly feverish look in his eyes, and his voice was a hoarse rasp as he grabbed my arm. "We have to destroy the body."

"*What?*"

"Right now." He looked at the corpse of his friend and shuddered. "Please, don't ask questions. We need to burn it, quickly. Does this place have an incinerator?"

"Ben, *what are you talking about?*" I wrenched my arm from his grasp and glared up at him. "All right, this has gone far enough. What are you hiding? Where did you and Nathan come from? He was sick, wasn't he?" Ben flinched, and my fury rose up again. "He was sick, and now I have a roomful of dead patients because you're hiding something! I want answers, and you're going to tell me everything, right now!"

"Oh, God." If possible, Ben paled even more. He glanced down the hall, running his fingers through his hair. "Oh,

shit. This has all gone crazy. I'm sorry, Kylie. I'll tell you everything. After we destroy the body, I'll tell you everything I
know, I swear. Just…we have to take care of this now. Please."
He grabbed my arm. "Help me, and then I'll tell you anything you want."

I clenched my fists, actually tempted to hit him, to strike
him across that ruggedly handsome face. Taking a deep breath
to calm my rage, I spoke in a low, controlled tone. "Fine. I
don't know what this is about, or why you want to deface
your friend, but I will help you this one last time. And then,
Ben Archer, you are going to tell me what the hell is going
on before you leave my clinic forever."

He might have nodded, but I was already marching back
into the hall, fighting a sudden, unexplainable terror. The unknown loomed around me, hovering over Nathan's corpse,
the sick ward full of the newly dead. The body on the table
looked…unnatural, with its pale shrunken skin and blank,
dead eyes. It didn't even look human anymore.

The sick ward was eerily silent as I walked in, searching for
the gurney I'd left at the edge of the room. In the shadows,
bodies lay under sheets in their beds, mingled with the few
still living. Jenna glanced up over a patient's cot, her cheeks
wasted, her eyes sunken. Lightning flickered through the plastic over the front door, illuminating the room for a split second, and thunder growled a distant answer.

Something touched my arm, and I jumped nearly three
feet. Bristling, I spun around to come face-to-face with Ben.

"Sorry." His gaze flickered to the darkened sick ward, then
slid to me again. "I just… How are we going to do this? Do
you need help with anything?"

I yanked a gurney from the wall. "What I *needed* is for you
to have told me why you were here the first time I asked, not
when all my patients started bleeding from the eyes and dying

around me." He didn't respond, too preoccupied with the current tragedy to take note of my anger, and I sighed. "We'll transport the body to the empty lot," I explained, pushing the cot back down the hall, Ben trailing after. "Once we're there, you can do whatever you want."

"Outside?"

"Yes, outside! Preferably before the storm hits. I'm not starting a fire indoors so my clinic can burn down around me."

He seemed about to say something, then changed his mind and followed me silently down the hall, our footsteps and the squeaking of the gurney wheels the only sounds in the darkness.

I sneaked a glance at him. His face was blank, his eyes expressionless, though I'd seen that look before. It was a mask, a stoic front, the disguise of someone whose world had been shattered and who was holding himself together by a thread. My anger melted a little more. In my line of work, death was so common, but I had to remind myself that I wasn't just treating patients; I was treating family members, friends, people who were loved.

"I'm sorry about Nathan," I offered, trying to be sympathetic. "It wasn't your fault that he was hurt, that he was sick. Were you two very close?"

Ben nodded miserably. "He was my roommate," he muttered, briefly closing his eyes. "We went to Georgetown together. I was working on my Masters in Computer Engineering, and he got me an IT job at the lab where he worked. I was never about that biology stuff. When the virus hit, the lab threw everything else out the window to work on a cure. They kept me on for computer stuff, but Nathan was with them for the really crazy shit. He couldn't tell me much—everything was very hush-hush—but some of the things I heard…" Ben shivered. "Let's just say there were some very dark things happening in that lab. Even before the—"

He stopped in the doorway of the last room, his face draining of any remaining color. Blinking, I looked into the corner where Nathan's bed sat, where the corpse had been lying minutes ago.

The mattress was empty.

CHAPTER 4

I stared at the empty bed, the logical part of my brain trying to come up with a way for a dead body to vanish from a room in a few short minutes. One of the interns must've come in and moved it. Perhaps Maggie had whisked it down to storage, by herself, without a gurney. Improbable. Impossible, really. But that was the only thing that made any sort of sense. It wasn't as if the corpse got up and walked out by itself.

Ben staggered back, shaking his head. I could see he was trembling. "No," he muttered in a low, anguished voice. "No, it isn't possible."

"I'm… I'm sure there's a rational explanation," I began, trying to ignore the chill creeping up my back. "Maggie probably took it away. Come on." I turned, suddenly eager to leave to room. The silent, empty bed, sitting motionless in the shadows, was starting to freak me out. The once-familiar walls of the clinic seemed darker now, closing in on me. "We'll check storage," I told Ben, leading him back down the corridor. It seemed longer, somehow. I could hear the groans of my patients, drifting to me from the main room. "This is nothing to worry about. She's probably down in the basement right now."

Ben didn't answer, and my words felt hollow as we reached

the stairs to the sub-basement level. The door at the bottom of the steps was partially open, creaking faintly on its hinges, and the space beyond was pitch-black.

I fished the mini-flashlight from my coat and clicked it on, shining it down the stairwell. That faint smell of rot lingered in the corridor, but it could be coming from the bodies in storage.

I pushed the door to the basement open and was hit by a wave of cold, dry air that made me shiver. As usual, the scent of death was thick down here, like stepping into a tomb, and tonight it seemed even more ominous. There was no light, no need for electricity except to keep the freezers running, and everything was cloaked in suffocating darkness.

"Maggie?" My voice was a whisper as I eased inside, Ben following at my heels. The door groaned as it swung behind us, closing with a soft click. I swept the flashlight around, scanning the rows of cluttered shelves, the thick white columns that held up the building. I'd never thought about what a maze this place was until tonight. Against the far wall, barely discernible in the weak light, the huge freezers with their grisly contents gave off a faint, low hum.

"Maggie?"

Something clinked to the floor nearby, and an empty can rolled out from between the aisles, stopping at my feet. It caused a chill to skitter up my back.

"Maggie!" I hissed again, sweeping the light around. "Are you down here? Maggie!"

"Yes?"

Ben and I both jumped, swinging around as Maggie stepped between the aisles, holding several sets of folded sheets, a mini-flashlight stuck between them. She frowned at our reaction, looking confused. "Sorry, Miss Kylie. We ran of sheets to cover the bodies, so I came down to get some more. Are you all right?"

"Geez, Maggie!" I released Ben and slumped against the wall, my hand going to my heart. "You scared me half to—"

Something lunged between shelves and slammed into the girl, dragging her down with a screech. Her flashlight spun wildly, clinking to the floor before flickering out. Stumbling back, I caught a split-second glance of a spindly, emaciated creature that faintly resembled a man before it bent its head and sank its teeth into Maggie's throat.

I screamed. Maggie's body jerked and flopped to the cement, twitching, and the coppery smell of blood filled the room. My mouth gaped again, but nothing came out. In the flashlight beam, the thing raised its head and stared at me with Nathan's face, no recognition in its dead white eyes, nothing but the flat, glazed stare of a predator. It hissed, and I couldn't tear my gaze from its gleaming, jagged fangs, smeared with the blood of my intern.

My mind had gone blank. This wasn't happening. That thing couldn't exist, it was dead! The stress had finally gotten to me, and my mind had cracked.

Frozen, I stared at it, subconsciously knowing I was about to die. But the thing turned and started savaging Maggie's corpse, tearing her open with long fingers, ripping into her with its fangs. Blood splattered everywhere, painting the walls with wet ribbons, and I threw myself backward, hitting the edge of a shelf.

Something grabbed my wrist, yanking me away. I cried out and fought to break loose, hitting the arm with the flashlight, barely conscious of what I was doing, until I realized it was Ben. He dragged me across the floor and up the staircase, his eyes hard, his mouth pressed into a thin white line.

We ducked into the stairwell, the smell of blood clogging

our nostrils and the sound of ripping flesh following us out. Ben slammed the door behind us and leaned against it, gasping. I stood there, shaking, trying to gather my thoughts. Rain pounded the ceiling overhead, and lightning flickered erratically over the wall, reflecting the pulse at my throat.

Maggie. Maggie was gone. And that *thing*, that horrible, pale thing, had been Nathan. It couldn't be real! I had seen him die. I knew he was dead, but now...

This had to be a nightmare.

"Kylie." Ben's voice was low, hoarse. I blinked, attempting to focus. "We have to get out of here, now. Do you have anything you have to take, anything you absolutely can't leave behind?"

"Leave?" I stared at him, still reeling. "I can't leave. What about Jenna?"

"We'll take her, too."

"But my patients! What about the survivors? I can't leave them—"

"Kylie!" Ben pushed himself off the door and took my upper arms, forcing me to look at him. "They're dead," he whispered, his eyes dark with sorrow and guilt. "Everyone here is dead, or they will be. There's nothing you can do for them anymore. But we have to get out of here now, if we want to survive ourselves."

A crash from the main room startled me upright. Lightning danced over the walls, the flash revealing eerie dark spatters that hadn't been there before. Fear, cold and acute, stabbed through me. Ben followed my gaze, his muscles coiled tight beneath his shirt.

"Come on," he whispered, leading me down the hall. "My truck is out front. Let's find Jenna and get out of..."

He stopped. I looked down the hall, and everything inside me went cold.

Ms. Sawyer's gaunt, wasted body stood silhouetted in the doorway to the sick ward, still in the hospital gown she had died in. Blood stained her face and hands, smeared around her mouth and the fangs that protruded from her upper jaw. She carried something in her hands, something round and dripping, the size of a basketball.

Lightning flashed again, and I saw that it was Jenna's head.

I might have gasped, or gagged, for the thing that had been Ms. Sawyer looked up, and her dead, blank eyes flashed to mine. Her mouth opened, fangs gleaming, like jagged bits of glass. She screamed, a wail unlike anything remotely human, and charged toward us.

Ben yanked me across the hall, ducked into Doc Adams's office and slammed the door. A booming thud rattled the frame just as he threw the latch and looked frantically around for something to brace it with.

Another bang on the door, followed by the screech of the thing on the other side. I fell back in terror. Ben pulled me aside, dragged the old wooden desk from the corner and shoved it across the tile, pushing it up against the door.

"Kylie, come on!" His voice snapped me out of my daze. Crossing the room, he yanked back the curtain on the window, revealing the full fury of the storm outside. "Hurry, before it claws its way in."

The door jumped inward a few inches, scraping the desk back, and nails clawed at the opening. More voices joined the one beyond the frame, terrifying shrieks and howls, as if a whole pack of the things were clustered outside. The door shook and began to open as pale arms and shoulders shoved their way inside.

Ben threw up the window with a blast of rain-scented wind. "Come on!" he yelled at me, and I threw myself forward. His hands grabbed my waist as I scrambled for the opening, pushing me through. I fell on wet pavement, gasping as my elbow struck the hard ground, and then Ben collapsed beside me, rolling to his feet.

He dragged me upright, and through the window, I saw the door burst inward and a host of pale, shrieking bodies spill into the room. Former patients, people who had died that very afternoon, reanimated and somehow transformed into bloodthirsty monsters. Their empty white eyes scanned the room, catching sight of us outside the window, and they lunged forward with vicious wails.

We ran.

My shoes splashed over the wet concrete, cold rainwater soaking my hair and clothes. The storm raged around us, forks of lightning slashing the sky over the buildings. Behind me, I heard the monsters' savage cries as they leaped through the window and skittered after us.

I followed Ben around a corner, dodging a rubble pile, and nearly ran into a small white pickup parked between two buildings. I waited, heart hammering, as Ben fiddled with the keys, hands shaking as he tried to unlock the door. A monster leaped to the top of the rubble pile, hissed when it saw us and sprang forward.

Ben yanked open the door, reached in and pulled a shotgun out of the front seat. The monster leaped onto the hood, snarling, as Ben aimed the muzzle at it and pulled the trigger point-blank.

A flash and a deafening boom rocked the alley, nearly making my heart stop. The creature was hurled away, crumpling into the wall and slumping down, a bloody mess. But then it staggered to its feet, hissing, though there was a massive gaping hole that went right through its chest, showing jagged ribs. It shrieked again, sounding more pissed than hurt, and lurched forward as several others came around the corner.

Ben pushed me into the truck and lunged in after me, slamming the door just as Ms. Sawyer crashed into the glass. She shrieked at us, clawing the door with bony talons, as Ben jammed the keys into the ignition and the truck roared to life. The monster with the bloodied chest scrambled onto the hood again and lunged at me. Its head bounced off the windshield, and a spiderweb of cracks spread out from the impact. More creatures crowded the truck as Ben threw it into Drive. The vehicle lurched forward, striking several monsters as it roared out of the alley. The creature on the hood slipped and rolled off the side as Ben slammed his foot onto the gas and sped into the road.

I turned to look through the back window, watching the clinic and the pale, spindly creatures swarming from it like ants, until Ben turned a corner and the building was lost from view.

CHAPTER 5

We drove for nearly an hour in frozen silence. Ben kept his gaze on the road, swerving around rubble and debris, easing through oceans of dead cars that had clogged the street. The city loomed above us, dark and menacing in the rain. Except for a few flickering streetlamps and several dying traffic lights, the streets were black, the buildings empty and dark. I remembered, when I first came here, how bright and busy the city had felt, even at night. Now, it was like driving through a war zone. Most everyone had fled or succumbed to the virus. There were a few stubborn hangers-on, those who had nowhere to go, or worse, those who stayed behind to prey on what was left. But for the most part, the city was empty of life, and just a few short months after the catastrophe hit, it was already beginning to crumble.

But *things* moved in the shadows, pale and terrifying, skirting the edges of the light. They skittered through alleys and between aisles of dead cars, sometimes alone, sometimes in small packs. Every time I saw one, my stomach convulsed in dread, and I couldn't move. How long had they been here, roaming the city, with me oblivious to the monsters right outside my door? Or was this something new, some awful, mutated side effect of the virus?

We drove on, through the city limits, though progress was slow. The road out of the city was clogged with cars, crashed into railings and each other, some upside-down or on their sides. Hundreds lay in ditches, and a few sat burned and blackened in the middle of the road. After weaving around this endless obstacle course of steel and glass, Ben finally pulled his truck off the pavement and drove through the dirt and trees.

It seemed to take forever, but the sea of cars finally thinned, then stopped altogether. After a few miles of nothing, Ben took the next off-ramp and parked the truck at an abandoned gas station.

"Stay here." His voice was hoarse. Turning off the engine, he grabbed the door handle, not looking at me. "We're almost out of gas. I'll be right back."

"Ben, wait!" My words came out harsh and sharp, startling us both. Ben flinched, then slowly took his hand from the door, turning to face me. His eyes, his face, his entire body, were slumped and resigned, as if he'd been waiting for this moment, dreading it.

"You promised me answers," I whispered. The numbness inside was fading, the horror and fear slipping away into something that felt close to rage. I could barely force the words out, but I did. "You promised you would tell me what's going on. I'm not going another step with you until you start talking."

"All right." Ben took a deep breath, let it out slowly. "All right, Kylie, I'll tell you everything I know. I don't have all the details, because I wasn't close to it, not like Nathan. But what I did find out…well, you'll see why I couldn't tell anyone."

"You know what those monsters are," I guessed, and it was an accusation. Ben hesitated, then nodded slowly.

"I've seen them before," he began, gazing out the window.

"It was one of those things that attacked Nathan, in the lab." He looked at me, suddenly pleading. "I swear, I didn't know it was transferable. Not like that. Nathan was bitten, but I didn't know the disease could spread to others, Kylie. If I'd known that, I would have never brought him in."

"Disease?" My mind was spinning. "Ben, what *are* those things? I just watched my dead patients come back to life and attack me! Are they...some sort of zombies?" The words sounded ridiculous out loud, but what else could I think? I'd only seen this happen in horror movies.

"No." Ben rubbed the stubble on his chin, clearly uncomfortable. "Not...zombies. From what I understand, they're more of a hybrid. Of human, and..." He trailed off, bring his lip.

"And?" I prompted.

"Vampire."

Ben grimaced, even as he said the word. I blinked. The implication hung between us, impossible. Ridiculous. Vampires didn't exist. They were movie monsters, Halloween costumes. Never mind that a second ago I'd seriously considered the zombie apocalypse. My logical doctor's brain scoffed at the idea of fanged, undead creatures that came out at night and drank the blood of the living to survive.

And yet... I'd been attacked by people who had died. I'd seen the corpses, lying in their beds that very afternoon, before they'd sprung to life. Corpses that moved at lethal, frightening speeds. That had ripped apart two humans as easily as paper, that had smelled of death and rot and decay. Corpses that had fangs.

"Vampires," I said slowly, still trying to decide what I thought about this, whether to accept, question or scoff at the claim. "You mean...like Dracula? The drinking-blood, turn-into-bats kind?"

Ben sighed. "I know how it sounds," he muttered. "And that's why I couldn't tell you before. You would've thought I was insane. But...yes, vampires are real. They don't turn into bats or wolves or mist, as far as I know, but everything else—the drinking blood, the coming out at night—it's all true." My face must've betrayed my disbelief, because he shook his head. "I know. When Nathan told me, I thought the chemicals in the lab were affecting his brain. I told him he needed help. But then he showed me, once, what they were keeping behind closed doors." He visibly shivered. "And that was enough to convince me."

"Why..." I couldn't believe I was asking this. "Why were they keeping vampires down there, anyway? I thought you said Nathan was part of a team searching for a cure."

"He was. And they were." Ben looked disturbed now, his brows drawn together in a frown. "I didn't get this out of Nathan until later, but...they were experimenting on the vampires. They were using vampire blood to try to develop the cure."

"Why?"

"Because vampires were immune to the Red Lung virus," Ben replied solemnly. "Nathan told me they didn't know if it was because the vampires were, technically, dead, but none of the specimens they acquired could be infected with the virus. They were hoping to duplicate the vampire's natural immunity to disease into something that could combat Red Lung." His gaze darkened, and he gripped the steering wheel tightly. "But something went wrong," he said in a near whisper. "The virus mutated. The 'cure' they gave infected patients—*human* patients—killed them. And turned them into those...things." He shuddered, running a hand through his hair. "I was there the night they escaped. No one knows how it happened, but Nathan was attacked, bitten. Everything was chaos. We got out, came here. But I had no idea the mutated virus was air-borne, that it would spread just like Red Lung."

"Then…" My stomach felt cold as the implication of what he was really saying hit me like a load of bricks. The virus was airborne, seeping across the country like a spill of blood. "Then, you're saying that everyone who is already infected with the Red Lung virus…"

Ben didn't meet my gaze. His hands gripped the steering wheel so hard his knuckles turned white. His face was ashen, and for a moment, I thought he might actually pass out.

"Oh, God," he whispered, closing his eyes. "What have I done? What have *we* done, Nate?"

My hands were shaking. I clenched them in my lap and took a deep, calming breath. I'd seen what Red Lung could do to a person, I knew how fast it spread, I'd heard how entire com-munities and towns had vanished off the map in the space of a week. I imagined those towns now, only instead of bodies lying in their homes, I could see pale, screaming abomina-tions filling the roads, destroying anything they came across.

And it had started right here. With the person in the seat next to mine.

No, that wasn't entirely fair. Ben Archer hadn't performed those experiments on—I stumbled over the word—*vampires.* Ben hadn't created the retrovirus that was spreading across the country, turning the sick into bloodthirsty undead. He wasn't responsible for the creation of those monsters, he wasn't even a scientist. I knew that. My doctor's brain accepted that.

But the part of me that felt responsible for Maggie and Jenna, that had worked like a dog to save those patients, that viewed Red Lung as an enemy that had to be destroyed—that part of me hated him. He'd brought a hidden virus into my clinic, and because of him, my patients were all dead. Worse than dead, they were monsters, rabid beasts. If Ben Archer had never darkened my doorstep, they would still be alive.

My heart pounded. Anger and rage coursed through my veins, turning them hot. Ben's shotgun lay on the seat between us; without thinking, I grabbed it and flung open the door of the truck, leaping to the pavement.

"Kylie!"

Ben scrambled after me. I heard his footsteps round the hood of the truck, and though my hands were shaking, I planted my feet, spun around and raised the muzzle of the gun, leveling it at his chest.

He stopped, raising his hands, as I took a step backward, glaring at him down the barrel.

Lightning flickered, distant now, the storm having moved on. The lingering rain felt like cold spider webs falling across my skin.

Ben took a slow, careful step forward, still keeping his hands raised. I bared my teeth and shoved the muzzle at him, and he stopped.

"Stay back!" I hissed, knowing how I must look: wild and desperate, the whites of my eyes gleaming in the darkness. I felt crazy, out of control. "You stay right there, Ben Archer. Don't move, or I swear I'll kill you!"

"Kylie." His voice was low, calming, though he didn't move from where he stood. "Don't do this. Please. You can't survive out there alone."

"You," I snarled, curling my lip back, "have no right to tell me anything! You brought this down on our heads. My patients are dead because of you! Maggie and Jenna are dead because of you! The whole city, the whole world, maybe, is going to hell. Because of you!" With every accusation, he flinched, as if my words were stones smashing into him. My throat closed up, and I took a breath to open it. "All my life,"

I whispered, "I wanted to help people, save people. That's why I became a doctor, so I could make a difference. I wanted to beat this thing, so badly. And all it took was you waltzing into my clinic with your demon friend to destroy everything I worked for!"

"Then shoot me." He dropped his arms as he said it, regarding me with dead, hooded eyes. I blinked at him in shock, but he didn't move. "You're right," he said in a quiet voice. "What we did, what happened at that lab, there's no excuse. We unleashed something that could destroy everything. And if I..." He paused, closing his eyes. "If I deserve to die for that, if killing me will make things right for you, then...do it." Opening his eyes, he met my gaze, sorrowful but unafraid. "If this will bring you peace," he rasped, "for Maggie and Jenna and everyone, then do what you have to. No one will fault you for pulling that trigger."

My arms shook, and the gun was cold in my hands, the curved edge of the metal trigger pressing into my skin. It would be so easy, I realized—a quick pull, barely a motion in itself. I gazed down the barrel at the body in the rain, my throat and chest tight, my mind spinning. No one would hear the gunshot this far from the city. And even if they did, no one would care.

Ben stood there, unmoving, the rain falling lightly around his shoulders, waiting to see if I would kill him.

God, Kylie, what are you doing? You're really going to murder this man in cold blood? Horror, swift and abrupt, lanced through me. I was a doctor, sworn to save lives, regardless of circumstances or personal feelings. Ben had saved *my* life. If he hadn't been there when those things attacked, I would be a pile of blood and bones on the clinic floor. Just like Maggie and Jenna.

And then, all the fear, frustration, sorrow and guilt of the past three days rose up like a black wave and came crashing down. Tears blinded me, my throat closed up and the world went blurry. The gun dropped from my limp grasp, falling into the mud, as, to my horror, I started to cry.

Strong arms wrapped around me a moment later, pulling me to a broad chest. For a heartbeat, anger flashed, but it was immediately drowned by everything else. I had failed. I had lost everything, not only the patients whom I had sworn to save, but my family, my friends and, very nearly, my humanity. And now, the world was filled with monsters and things I didn't understand, I had nearly been *eaten* by my dead patients and I had nowhere to go, nowhere left that was familiar. I leaned into Ben and sobbed, ugly, gasping breaths that blotched my face and left the front of his shirt stained with tears.

Ben didn't say anything, just held me as I cried myself out, the rain falling around us. My back and shoulders were cold and damp, but my arms, folded to his body, and the side of my face where his cheek pressed against mine, were very warm. Eventually, the tears stopped and my breathing became normal again, but he didn't let me go. One arm was wound across the small of my back, the other rested near my shoulders, holding me to him. His head was bowed, and I could feel rough stubble against my cheek.

My arms, trapped against his chest and stomach, began to wind around his waist, to pull him to me as well, but I stopped myself. *No*, I thought, as my senses finally returned. *Just because he saved you, do not excuse this man for what he has done. Jenna and Maggie are dead. If he'd never come to your clinic, they would still be alive.*

I stiffened, and Ben apparently sensed the change, for he let me go. I stepped back to compose myself, wiping my face, pulling my hair back, deliberately not looking at the man beside me. Because if I glanced up and met those haunted, soulful brown eyes, I wouldn't be able to stop myself from reaching for him again.

The shotgun still lay in the mud between us, and Ben casually reached down for it, as if it had simply fallen and hadn't been aimed at his chest a few minutes earlier. I looked at the weapon and shuddered, appalled at myself, what I had almost done.

"What now?" I whispered, rubbing my arms as the rain started to come down hard again. Ben hefted the shotgun to one shoulder, staring out into the darkness.

"I'm going home," he said without looking back. "Back to the farm. It's been…too long since I've seen everyone. If they're still there." He paused, then added, very softly, "You're welcome to come with me. If you want."

I nodded, feeling dazed. "Thanks. I… I think I will. Come with you, I mean." He finally glanced back, eyebrows raised in surprise. I shrugged, though I was a little surprised at myself, as well. "Might as well. I don't have anywhere else to go."

He didn't say anything to that, and we walked back to the truck in silence. Ben pulled open the passenger door, and I slid inside, blinking as he handed me the shotgun as if nothing had happened. Shivering, I placed it on the dashboard and watched Ben use a rubber tube to siphon fuel from one of the abandoned cars into a gas can. It was a slow, tedious process, but it couldn't be helped. Many of the everyday conveniences—like ATMs, smart phones and gas pumps—were no longer working since the plague and the collapse of society. There was no one left to keep the grids going, no one to man the towers and the internet servers. It was a wake-up call for everyone, to realize how much we relied on things like electricity, running water and easy communication, and how crippling it was to go without.

When he was done, Ben slid into the driver's seat, closed the door, and sat there a moment, staring out the glass.

"Are you sure you're okay with this?" he asked in a near whisper, glancing at the weapon on the dashboard. "I won't force you to come with me. I can drop you off anywhere between here and home."

"No." I gave my head a shake. "Like I said, I have nowhere to go. And I don't want to be by myself right now, not with what's happening out there. Not if those things could be spreading across the country like the plague." Ben looked away, hunching his shoulders, and I wasn't sorry. "I'll figure out what to do next when we get there. If your family doesn't mind me hanging around…"

"They won't. Mom, especially. She'll be thrilled I finally brought home a girl."

That tiny bit of humor, forced as it was, finally coaxed a smile from me. I settled back against the leather seat and pulled down the seat belt, clicking it into place. "Then let's not keep them waiting."

Ben nodded. Turning the key in the ignition, he eased the truck down the ramp and onto the empty road, and we roared off toward our destination.

CHAPTER 6

We drove through the night, down a road that was desolate and empty, snaking through the darkness. No cars passed us, no headlights pierced the blackness but our own. Ben and I didn't speak much, just watched the quiet, primitive world scroll by through the glass. Out here, far from cities and towns and dimly lit suburbs, it truly felt as if we were the only humans left alive. The last two people on earth.

I dozed against the window, and when I opened my eyes again, Ben was pulling into the parking lot of a small motel and shutting off the ignition. The streetlamps surrounding the lot were dead and dark but, oddly enough, a Vacancy sign flickered erratically in the window of the office.

"We're stopping?"

"Just for a bit." Ben opened the door, and a gust of rain-scented air dispersed my drowsiness a little. "It's almost dawn. I need a couple hours of sleep, at least, or I'm going to drive us off the road. This looks safe enough."

It might've looked safe enough, but he snatched the gun off the dashboard and handed me a flashlight before walking up to the office door. I followed closely, peering over my shoulder, shining the beam into windows and dark corners.

We stepped up to the porch, and my heart pounded, imagining gaunt, pale faces peering through the windows. But they remained dark and empty.

After several moments of pounding on the office door and calling *"Hello?"* into the darkened interior, Ben raised the shotgun and drove the butt into the glass above the door, shattering it. Ducking inside, he emerged seconds later with a key on a wooden peg, jingling it with weary triumph. I trailed him down the walkway to a battered green door with a brass 14B on the front and watched as he unlocked the door and pushed it back. It creaked open slowly, revealing a small room with an old TV, a hideous pink-and-green armchair and a single bed.

"Damn," I heard him mutter, and he glanced over his shoulder at me. "Sorry, I was hoping to get one with double beds. I'll see if they have the keys to another room—"

"There's no need." Bringing up the flashlight, I brushed past him through the doorway. The room was stale and dusty, and the carpet probably hadn't been cleaned in years, but at least there was no stench of death and blood and decay. "We're both adults," I said, attempting to be pragmatic and reasonable. "We can share a bed if we have to. And I... I'd feel better not sleeping alone tonight, anyway."

"Are you sure?"

"Ben, I'm a doctor. You don't have anything I haven't seen before, trust me."

My voice sounded too normal, too flippant, for what was happening outside. I felt like a deflated balloon, empty and hollow. Numb. I'd seen patients with post-traumatic stress disorder, having lost a loved one or even their whole family, and wondered if maybe I was heading down that same road. If perhaps this eerie calm and sense of detachment were the beginning.

The door clicked shut behind me, plunging the room into

darkness. I whirled with the flashlight, shining the beam into Ben's face. He flinched, turning his head, and I quickly dropped the light.

"Sorry."

"It's all right." He looked up, and I saw that his stoic mask had slipped back into place. I shivered a little. If anyone was suffering from PTSD, it was probably Ben.

I turned from that haunting gaze, shining the light toward the bathroom in the corner. "I'm…going to see if the water still works."

He didn't say anything to that, and I retreated to the bathroom, leaving him in the dark.

Miraculously, the water still ran, though the temperature barely got above lukewarm. I told Ben I was going to take a bath, then filled the tub halfway, sinking down into it with a sigh in the darkness. The flashlight sat upright on the sink, shining a circle of light at the ceiling, turning the room ghostly and surreal. A tiny bar of complimentary soap sat on the edge of the tub, and I scrubbed myself down furiously, as if I could wash away the horror, grief and fear along with the blood. I heard Ben stumble outside the door and felt guilty for hoarding our only light source, but after a minute or two I heard the door open and close, the lock clicking as it shut behind him.

Uncomfortable that he was going somewhere alone, I counted the seconds, the silence pressing against my eardrums. After a few minutes, though, the door creaked open again. I heard his footsteps shuffle around the room before the bed squeaked as he settled atop it, and finally stopped moving.

I finished my bath, slipped back into my dirty, disgusting clothes, and left the room, keeping the flashlight low in case Ben had gone to sleep.

He hadn't. He was perched on the edge of the mattress with his back to me, head bowed, slumping forward. His tattered shirt lay in a heap at the foot of the bed, and the flashlight beam slid over his broad shoulders and back. As I paused on the other side of the mattress, I saw his shoulders tremble, and heard the quiet, hopeless sound of someone trying to muffle a sob.

"Ben."

Anger forgotten, I set the flashlight down and slipped around to his side, touching a bare shoulder as I came up. A nest of bloody gauze sat on an end table, next to a bottle of peroxide. His stitches had torn open, and the claw marks were dark, thin stripes down his back.

Sympathy bloomed through me, dissolving the last of the anger as my logical doctor's brain finally caught up with my emotions. Ben was hurting, not from his wounds, but from the guilt that was tearing him apart inside. I wasn't quite ready to forgive what had happened to Maggie, Jenna and my patients, but I knew, really knew, that the horrible night in the clinic was not his fault. And if he hadn't been there, I probably would have died.

"Would you...help me?" Ben didn't even bother trying to hide the wet tracks down his cheeks, though he didn't glance up. He gestured to the peroxide and an open first aid kit on the nightstand. "I found those in the office, but I can't reach it on my own."

Silently, I picked up the first aid kit and scooted behind him on the bed. His skin was cold, but the area around the slashes was puffy and hot, though it didn't look infected. I gently wiped away the dirt and blood, watching the peroxide sizzle into the open wounds, bubbling white. Ben didn't even flinch.

"I don't blame you, you know." My voice surprised me, even more that I found it true. Ben didn't answer, and I pressed a gauze pad to the wounds, keeping my voice low and calm. "What happened back in the clinic, in the lab with Nathan, that wasn't your fault. I just… I freaked out. I reacted badly and I'm sorry for that, Ben."

"You have no reason to apologize," Ben murmured. "I should have been straight with you from the beginning, but… I didn't know what you would think. How do you explain zombies and vampires to someone without sounding like a raving lunatic?" He scrubbed a hand over his face, and now I felt a tiny prick of guilt. If he had told me that in the clinic, I probably *would* have scoffed at the idea, or assumed he was on drugs. Whose fault was this, really? "But I should have told you," Ben went on. "Nate…he was the smart one, the one who could explain anything and have it all make sense. In fact, I was hoping he would wake up so he could tell you what was going on. If that's not a selfish reason…" A soft, bitter laugh, ending in a muffled sob. "It should've been me," he said in a near whisper. "I should've been the one who died."

"No." I slid off the bed and walked around to face him. Crouching down, I peered at his face, putting a hand on his knee for balance. "Ben, look at me. This isn't your fault," I whispered again, as those tortured eyes met mine. "It isn't Nathan's fault. Ben, the virus is killing us. The human race is facing *extinction,* though no one is willing to admit it. Something had to be done."

"Something was," he muttered. "And now things are even worse. I don't know if we can survive this. And just thinking that I was there when it happened, that maybe if I'd done something a little different, I could've stopped them from getting out—"

"You couldn't have known what would happen." I kept my voice calm, reasonable, my doctor's voice. "And those scientists, they were only doing what anyone would do to save our race. We had to try something. It isn't our nature to roll over and die without a fight." I smiled faintly. "Humans are stubborn like that."

He held my gaze, the light reflected in his eyes. Very slowly, as if afraid it would scare me away, he reached out and took a strand of my hair between his fingers. I held my breath, my heartbeat kicking into high gear, pulsing very loudly in my ears.

"I don't know how you can stand to be around me," Ben murmured, staring at his hand, at the pale strings between his fingers. "But...don't go. Don't leave. You're the only thing keeping me sane right now."

Maggie and Jenna's faces crowded my mind, angry and accusing. My patients rose up from the darkness to stare at me, their gazes vengeful, but I shoved those thoughts away. They were gone. They were dead, and I couldn't honor their memory with anger and blame and hate. The world was screwed, monsters roamed the streets and I had to cling to my lifelines where I could. I was sure everything would hit me, hard, when I had the chance to breathe. But right now, I had to make sure I—we—kept breathing.

Gently, I placed a palm on his cheek, feeling rough stubble under my fingers. "We'll get through this," I promised him, feeling, absurdly, that I was *his* lifeline right now, and if I left he might take that shotgun and put the muzzle under his chin. "I'm not going anywhere."

For just a moment, Ben's gaze grew smoldering, a dark, molten look that swallowed even the anguish on his face, before he straightened and pulled back, looking embarrassed.

Turning away, he gingerly bent to scoop up his shirt. "I'll take the chair," he offered in a husky voice, rising to his feet. I stood as well, frowning.

"Ben, you don't have to—"

"Trust me." He slipped into his shirt, grimacing. "I think I do."

I didn't think I would sleep, but I did drift off, listening to Ben's quiet snores from the chair in the corner. I awoke the next morning to sunlight streaming in through the dingy curtains and Ben emptying a bag of junk food onto the table.

"Morning," he greeted, and though his voice was solemn, it lacked the despair of the night before. "I thought you might be hungry, so I raided the snack machines by the office. I, uh, hope you don't mind Doritos and Twinkies for breakfast."

I smiled and struggled to my feet, brushing my hair back. "Any Ho Hos in the bunch?" I asked, walking up to the table.

"Mmm…no, sorry." Ben held up a package. "But I do have Zingers."

We smiled and ate our hideously unhealthy breakfast without complaint, knowing food was an unknown equation. The days of easy access were over. Places like McDonald's or Wendy's, where you could just walk in and order a hot breakfast, were a thing of the past. And many of the big superstores had been raided, gutted and picked clean when the chaos began. I wondered how long it would be before things went back to normal. I wondered if things would ever go back to normal.

"How far is it to your parents' farm?" I asked, once the chip bags were empty and plastic wrappers covered the table. Ben handed me a Diet Coke, and I washed down the cloying sweetness in my throat.

Ben shrugged. "About a fourteen-hour drive, if the roads are clear. We should get there by this evening if we don't run into anything."

Like rabid zombie vampires. I shivered and shook that thought away. "You'll be home soon, then. That's good."

"Yeah." Ben didn't sound entirely convinced. I glanced up and saw him watching me intently, his chin on the back of his laced hands. A flutter went through my stomach. Abruptly, he stood and started cleaning up the piles of wrappers scattered about the table, before he stopped, shaking his head. "Sorry. Old habits. Mom would always have us clear the dinner table for her. Come on." He grabbed the shotgun and opened the door for me. "Let's get out of here. The sooner we're on the road, the sooner we'll arrive."

We piled into the truck, after stashing the shotgun safely in the backseat, and Ben stuck the key in the ignition. "Home," he muttered in a voice barely above a whisper, and turned the key.

Nothing happened.

CHAPTER 7

My heart stood still. Ben swore quietly and turned the key again. Same result. Nothing. The engine lay still and cold and dead, and no amount of jiggling the key or pumping the gas pedal seemed to revive it.

"Dammit." Ben jumped out of the driver's seat and stalked to the front, opening the hood with a rusty squeak. I watched him through the window, obeying when he told me to slide into the driver's seat and try the ignition again. We worked for nearly twenty minutes, but the old truck remained stubbornly silent.

Ben dropped the hood with a bang, his face sweaty and grim. I peeked out the driver's side window, trying to stay calm. "No luck?"

He shook his head. "Fuses are blown, I think. That, or battery is dead. Either way, I'm not going to be able to get it started without jumper cables and another running engine. Dammit." He rubbed his jaw. "Looks like we're hoofing it."

"To Illinois?" The thought was staggering. "A fourteen-hour drive will probably take us a week or more of walking, and that's if we don't run into anything."

"I don't see any other way, do you?" Ben looked around

helplessly, hands on his hips. "We'll look for another vehicle down the road, but we can't stay here. I know, it scares me, too. But we have to get moving."

Daunting was the word that came to mind—hiking across a lawless, empty, plague-ridden country, where society had broken down and humans were just as likely to turn on you as help—it was a frightening thought. Especially now, with those…things out there. But Ben was right; we couldn't stay here. We had to continue.

Ben dug an old green backpack out from under the seats, and we raided the broken vending machines again, stocking up on sweets, chips and soda, as much as the pack could carry. Hefting it to his back, slinging the gun over one shoulder, he beckoned to me, and we started down the empty road, feeling like the only two people left on Earth.

The highway continued, weaving through hills and forest, past side roads and off-ramps that led to unknown places. Occasionally, we passed cars on the road, pulled over on the shoulder, abandoned in ditches, or sometimes just stopped in the middle of the lane. Once, I thought I saw a person in one of the cars in a ditch, a woman slumped against the dashboard, and hurried over to help. But she was long dead, and so was her little boy in the backseat. Sickened, I turned away, hoping their deaths had been swift, and the images continued to haunt me the rest of the afternoon.

Ben inspected every car we came across, searching around the dashboard and glove compartments, hoping for a lucky break. But except for the dead woman's car, none of them had keys, and hers was too damaged to use. Another, a van, seemed to be in good condition, but the tires were flat. I asked him once if we could hot-wire a vehicle into running, but neither of us had a clue how to do that. So we kept walking as the sun slid across the sky and the shadows around us lengthened.

"Here," Ben said, handing me an open can of Sprite when we stopped for a break. I took a long swig and handed it back as he sat beside me on the guardrail. We'd been hiking uphill for what had seemed like miles, and I could feel the heat of his body against mine, our shoulders and arms lightly touching. My stomach did a weird little twirl, especially when his large hand came to rest over mine on the railing.

"I think we're coming up on a town," he said, after finishing off the can and tossing it into the ditch. "If we are, it might be a good idea to stop and look around for a car. And food. Real food, anyway." He glanced at the backpack, lying open at our feet. Twinkies, Snowballs, chips and candy wrappers stood out brightly against the dull gray of the pavement. "I might slip into a sugar-induced coma if I eat one more Twinkie."

I smiled, liking this lighter, easygoing version of Ben. Out in the sunlight, away from all the blood, death, horror and despair, things didn't look as bleak.

I grinned at him, bumping his shoulder, just as he looked back at me. And, very suddenly, we were staring at each other on a lonely, empty road, miles from anywhere.

The late-afternoon sun slanted through the branches of the pine trees, turning his hair golden-brown, his eyes hazel. I could see rings of amber and green around the coffee-colored irises. They were beautiful, and they held my gaze, soft and tender, and a little bit afraid. As if Ben was unsure where we stood, if this was all one-sided.

My heart pounded. Ben waited, not moving, though his eyes never left mine. The ball was in my court. I licked my lips and suddenly found myself leaning toward him.

The growl of a car engine echoed, unnaturally loud in the silence, making us both jerk up. Gazing down the road, I saw a flash of metal in the sun, speeding toward us, and my heart leaped. Ben stood, grabbing the shotgun from where it lay against the railing, as a rusty brown pickup roared around the bend and skidded to a halt in a spray of gravel.

My senses prickled a warning, and I moved closer to Ben as the doors opened and three big, rough-looking guys stepped out into the road. They looked related, brothers maybe, blond and tanned, with the same watery blue eyes. I caught the stench of alcohol wafting from the cab as they sauntered to the edge of the pavement and grinned at us.

They all had guns, one rifle and a couple pistols, though no one had raised a weapon yet. My stomach clenched with dread.

"Hey there." The closest guy, a little bigger than the other two, leered at me. His voice was lazy and drawling, and a little slurred. I saw his gaze rake over me before he turned a mean look on Ben. "You two lost? Kind of a bad spot to be stranded—never know what kind of crazies you'll run into out here."

The other two snickered, as if that was actually funny. Ben nodded politely, though his arms and shoulders were tense, his finger resting on the trigger of the shotgun. "We're not lost," he said in a cool, firm voice. "We're just going home. Thank you for your concern."

They hooted with laughter. "Ooh, listen to him, all dandy and proper," one of the others mocked. "A real gentleman, he is."

"Now, now, be nice, Bobby," the leader said, turning to grin at the one who'd spoken. "They said they're trying to get home, so let's help 'em out." He turned and smiled at me, blue eyes gleaming, as inviting as a snarling wolf. "We'll take you home, darlin'. So why don't you just hop in the truck, right now?"

Ben's weapon came up instantly, as did the other three. I

gasped as a trio of deadly gun barrels were suddenly trained on Ben, who had his own pointed at the leader's chest.

Time seemed to stop, the air around us crystallizing into a silence that hovered on the edge of chaos and death. I froze, unable to move, shocked at how quickly the situation had descended into another horror film. Only the guns pointed right at us were real.

"Ben," I whispered, placing a hand on his arm. My legs shook, and a cold, terrified sweat dripped down my spine. "Stop this. You'll be killed."

"Listen to your girlfriend, boy," the leader said, smiling as he leveled the pistol at Ben's face. "There's three of us and only one of you. Odds ain't in your favor." His eyes flicked to me, and he jerked his head toward the open truck door. "Just come along quietly, missy, and make it easy on you both. Unless you want your dandy boyfriend pumped full o' holes in about two seconds."

"I'll go," I told both of them, though my eyes still pleaded with Ben. I felt sick, knowing what they wanted, what would happen to me the second I went into that truck. But I couldn't let them shoot Ben. "Ben, don't. Please. They'll kill you."

"Stay where you are." His voice, low and steely, froze me in my tracks. He hadn't moved through the whole encounter, and his stare never wavered from the man in front of him. "There's three of you," he agreed, still locking eyes with the leader. "But I can still kill one of you before the others get their shots off. And the odds aren't in *your* favor, are they?" The leader stiffened, and the barrel moved with him, just enough to keep him in its sight. "Do you know what happens to a body shot point-blank with a shotgun?" Ben asked, his voice cold as ice. "You'll have to be buried with your truck, because they'll never get all the pieces out of it."

"Fuck you." The leader pulled the hammer on his pistol

back, aiming it at Ben's face. Ben stared him down over the shotgun, not moving, never wavering, while my heart hammered so hard against my ribs I thought I might pass out.

Finally, the leader slowly raised his other hand, placating. "All right," he said in a soothing voice, and lowered his weapon. "Everyone just take it easy, now. Relax." He shot the other two a hard look, and they reluctantly lowered their guns. "This is what we're gonna do. Give us that pack full of stuff, and we'll be on our way. That sound like an okay trade, boy?"

"Fine," Ben said instantly, not lowering his weapon. "Take it and go."

The leader, still keeping one hand in the air, jerked his head at one of the other two, who edged around the truck and snatched the bag from the ground. Ben kept his gaze and his weapon trained unwaveringly on the leader, who smirked at us and slipped back into the truck, slamming the door as the others did the same.

"Well, thank ya kindly, dandy boy." He grinned as his friends hooted and pawed through the bag, snatching at Twinkies and cupcakes. "You two have fun, now. Run on home to mommy. It'll be dark soon."

The truck peeled away in a squeal of gravel, the echoes of their laughter ringing out behind them.

Ben let out a shaky breath and finally lowered the weapon. I could see his hands shaking as he leaned back against the rail, breathing hard. "Why did you do that?" I whispered, my heart slamming against my ribs. "You could've been killed."

"I wasn't going to let them take you."

My legs were trembling. I took a shaky step toward him, and he reached out with one arm, pulling me close. I felt his heart, beating frantically through his shirt, and wrapped my arms around his waist, clinging to him as fear and adrenaline slowly ebbed away, and my heartbeat slowed to normal. Ben leaned the shotgun against the railing and held me in a fierce, almost desperate embrace, as if daring something to try to rip me away. I relaxed into him, felt his arms around me and, if only for a moment, let myself feel safe.

"Come on," he whispered, finally drawing back. "Let's try to make town before nightfall."

It wasn't quite dusk when we stumbled off the main highway, following an exit ramp into the ruins of a small town. The late-afternoon sun cast long shadows over the empty streets and rows of dark, decaying houses, their yards overgrown with weeds. We passed homes and streets that must have been a nice little suburban community. Yards had been well-tended once, and the driveways were full of station wagons and minivans. I kept looking for signs of life, hints that people still lived, but except for a small orange cat, darting away into the bushes, there was nothing.

"What are we looking for?" I asked Ben, my voice sounding unnaturally loud in the stillness. The sun hovered low on the horizon, a sullen blood-red, like a swollen eye. Ben gave it a nervous look, then gestured to a building as we reached a crossroad. "Something like that."

A gas station sat desolately on a corner, windows smashed, gas hoses lying on the ground. We approached cautiously, peering through the shattered glass, but it was empty of life and most everything else. Inside, the shelves were stripped clean, glass littered the floor, and most of the displays were tipped over. Others had been here before us. Fleeing town, perhaps, when the plague hit. Though I didn't know where they thought they could run. Red Lung was everywhere, now.

"Been pretty picked over," Ben muttered, stepping around downed shelves and broken glass. He nudged an empty display that had once held energy drinks and shook his head. "Let's not waste too much time looking; I want to get out of here soon. This place is making me jumpy."

Me, too. Though I couldn't put my finger on why. The town seemed lifeless. We rummaged around and found a few meat tins, jerky rolls and a bag of Doritos that had been missed. We tossed our findings into a plastic bag, the rustle of paper and plastic the only sounds in the quiet. Outside, the sun dipped below the horizon, stealing the last of the evening light, and a chill crept through the air.

"All right," Ben said, rising to his feet, "I think we have enough, for a little while, at least. Now, I wonder how hard it will be to find a car...?"

A woman shuffled past the broken window.

I jerked, grabbing Ben's arm, as the figure moved by without stopping. My stomach lurched. "Hey!" I called, hopping over shelves and broken glass to the door, peering out. The woman was walking down the sidewalk, stumbling every few steps, and didn't seem to have heard me.

Abruptly, she put a hand against the wall and bent over as violent coughing shook her thin frame. Blood spattered the ground beneath her in crimson drops, and I stumbled to a halt.

Ben came up behind me and took my arm, moving me back. The woman finally stopped coughing and slowly turned to face us. I saw the thin streams of blood, running from her eyes like crimson tears, and my insides turned to ice.

"Oh, my God." I looked at Ben, saw the same horror reflected on his face, the realization of what was happening. Not Red Lung. The other thing. It was already here. "How could it spread this fast?"

He grabbed my wrist as the woman gagged on her own blood and collapsed to the gutter, twitching. "The whole town could be infected. We have to get out of here, now!"

We turned and fled, our footsteps pounding the sidewalk,

echoing dully in the stillness. Only…the town wasn't as empty and still as I'd first thought. As the light vanished from the skies and streetlamps flickered to life, things began moving in the darkness and shadows. Moans and wails crept from dark houses, doors slammed open and pale, shambling figures stumbled out of the black. Terror gripped me. We were out in the open, exposed. The second that one spotted us, we would be run down and torn apart. The only saving grace was that the creatures seemed groggy and confused right now, not completely alert. If we could get to the edge of town without being seen—

Ben jerked to a halt in front of a line of cars as one of the creatures, long and thin and terrible, leaped onto the roof with the ease of a cat. It peered at us with blank white eyes and hissed, baring a mouthful of jagged fangs. My heart and stomach turned to ice. Gasping, we turned to run the other way.

Three more of the monsters leaped over a fence, hissing and snarling as they crept forward, blocking our path. One of them had been a woman, once; she wore a tattered dress that dragged through the mud, and her hair was long and matted.

Oh, God. This is it, we're going to die.

One of the creatures screamed, sounding eerily human, and rushed Ben. It moved shockingly fast, like a monstrous spider skittering forward. Ben barely had time to raise the shotgun, but he did bring the muzzle up just in time, and a deafening boom rocked the air around us. The creature was flung backward, landing in the bushes with a shriek, and wild screeching erupted from the shadows around us. Pale things scuttled forward, closing in from all directions, teeth, claws and dead eyes shining in the darkness.

"This way!"

The deep voice rang out like a shot, startling us both.

Whirling around, I saw a tall, dark figure emerge from the shadows between two houses, beckoning us forward.

"Hurry!" he snapped, and we darted toward him, following his dark shadow as it turned and vanished between houses, seeming to melt into the night. The shrieks of the monsters rang all around us, but we trailed the figure through a maze of overgrown yards and fences until he fled up a crumbling set of stairs into the ruins of a brick house.

The door slammed behind us as we ducked over the threshold. Gasping, we watched the figure throw the lock, then stalk to the front windows and yank the curtains shut before turning around.

Muffled silence descended, broken only by the shrieks and wails outside. I blinked, my eyes slowly adjusting to the darkness. The man before us was enormous; not overly tall or heavy, just physically imposing. He wasn't that much taller than Ben, but he possessed a definite quiet strength, the bearing of someone who knew how to handle himself. His skin was the pale color of a man who spent all his time indoors, someone who didn't see a lot of sun, though his broad chest and corded muscle hinted at the power underneath. His hair was dark, and his eyes, when they turned on us, were blacker than the shadows that surrounded him.

"Stay back from the windows," he said in that deep, powerful voice. "We should be safe here, but the rabids will tear down the walls if they see us. Move back."

"Rabids?" I whispered. The man shrugged.

"What some have taken to calling them." His piercing gaze lingered on me, assessing. "Have either of you been bitten?"

"No," Ben said, holding his shotgun in both hands, I noted. Not pointing it at the stranger but not relaxing it, either. I held my breath, but the stranger didn't press the question. He simply nodded and moved away from the door, heading toward the dilapidated kitchen.

"If either of you wish to be helpful, you might want to start covering any windows that you find." His voice drifted back from the hall. "Just don't let the rabids see you, or we'll have to find a new place to hole up. I'm afraid you're rather stuck here until morning."

Ben and I shared a glance, then did what we were told. For several minutes, we concentrated on fortifying the house, making sure there were no windows, gaps or open spaces through which the monsters—the rabids—could climb in or see us. When we had made the house as secure as we could, closing curtains, shoving furniture in front of doors, we returned to the kitchen, which was small and had no windows to speak of. The dark stranger was there, leaning against a counter, watching us with fathomless black eyes.

"You might want to turn the flashlight off for now," he said, nodding at the light in my hands, the feeble ray barely piercing the shadows. "There are candles in the drawers if you need light, but be cautious where you set them out. Make sure they are in a spot where the rabids cannot see them."

I watched him carefully, shining the light for Ben as he rummaged through the drawer across from the stranger, pulling out three short candles and a book of matches. He stood there, motionless as a statue, his stark gaze not even on us anymore. He seemed distracted, as if we were only shadows, moving around him, not part of his world at all.

There was the sharp hiss and sizzle of a match flaring to life, and I clicked off the flashlight as Ben set the lit candles on the counter. The stranger's attention finally shifted back to us, and he looked almost surprised that we were still there. Ben stared back, his expression cautious, all the muscles in his body rigid.

"You can relax," the stranger told us with the faintest hint of a smile. "It was pure coincidence that I stumbled upon you this evening. I did not lure you here to kill you in your sleep." His smile faded, and he turned away. "I mean you no harm tonight, I give you my word."

Tonight? I thought, not knowing why that sounded odd to me. *What about tomorrow night, then?* "We don't mean to be ungrateful," I said, as Ben slowly relaxed his grip on the shotgun. "It's just been a rough couple of days."

"Yes, it has." The man scrubbed a hand across his face, then pushed himself off the counter. "There's food in the cupboards," he announced, sounding tired. "And I believe the stove is gas. It might still work. I'd advise you *not* to open the refrigerator—the electricity has been out for a couple weeks, by the looks of it."

"Thank you," Ben murmured, setting the gun on the counter as the stranger moved toward the door. "I'm Ben, by the way, and that's Kylie."

The stranger nodded. "I'll check the closets for blankets," he continued, as if Ben hadn't spoken at all. "Make yourselves as comfortable as you can."

With a nod to me, he turned and left the room, making absolutely no noise on his way out.

He didn't, I noticed, offer his name.

I found several boxes of macaroni and cheese in the cupboard, along with a few cans of vegetables, and cooked them in the darkness with Ben hovering beside the stove. I found myself wondering who had lived here before, what had happened to them. Had they fled town, leaving their house and all their possessions behind? Or were they now a part of the horror...outside?

"Your carrots are boiling over," Ben commented, and I

jerked up with a whispered curse. Water was bubbling over the rim of the pot and flowing down to the stovetop. "Sorry," I muttered, moving it to a different burner. "Cooking is not my strong suit. Most of my dinners come in microwave boxes." The macaroni suddenly followed the carrot's example, hissing as it overflowed its container. "Dammit!"

"Here." Ben gently moved me out of the way, turning down the heat and maneuvering the pots around with the ease of familiarity. I watched him stir in the cheese, spoon the noodles and carrots onto tin plates, and wondered at the surreal normalcy of it all. Here we were, cooking macaroni and having dinner, while outside the world was falling to the vampire-zombie apocalypse.

No sleep for me tonight, that's for certain. Think about something else, Kylie.

"Wow," I said, as Ben put the bowls on the table, "a man who can shoot a gun *and* cook? Why are you still single, Ben Archer?"

I couldn't be positive in the flickering candlelight, but he might've blushed. "Mac-n-cheese is *not* cooking," he said with a small grin. "And, I don't know. I've never found the right girl, I suppose. What about you?"

"Me?" I sat down at the table, picking up the spoon left on the cloth, hoping it was clean. "I never had the time for…anything like that," I admitted, as Ben sat down across from me. "It was either work and study or have a life, you know? I never thought about settling down or having a family. I wanted to concentrate on finishing school, getting a good job. Everything else sort of took a backseat."

"What about now?" Ben asked softly.

I fidgeted. He was giving me that intense, smoldering look again, the one that made my insides do strange twirly back-flips. "What do you mean?"

He gave me a you-know-what-I-mean look. "What do you want to do, now that the world is screwed over?" He jerked his head at a window. "Everything is different, and it won't be normal for a long time, I think. Do you…" He paused, playing with his fork. "Do you ever think you'd want to…settle down? Find a safe place to wait this out and start a family?"

"You mean pull an Adam and Eve and populate the world again?" He didn't smile at the joke, and I sighed. "I don't know, Ben. Maybe. But I also want to see if I can help. I know everything is screwed up right now, but I'd like to help out where I can." I shrugged and prodded my food. "I haven't really given it much thought, though. Right now, all I want to do is stay alive."

"An admirable plan," came a voice from the doorway.

We both jumped. The dark stranger stood in the frame, the light flickering over his strong yet elegant features. I hadn't even heard him approach; the space had been empty a moment before, and now he was just *there*.

"Next time, though, perhaps you should avoid going into any towns or settlements at night," he said. "The rabids are everywhere now, and spreading. Just like the virus. Soon, nowhere will be safe, for anyone."

His voice was dull, hopeless, and though his face remained calm, I could see the agony flickering in his dark eyes. As if his mask was slipping, cracking, showing glints of guilt, horror and sorrow underneath. I recognized it, because Ben had worn the same mask when he'd stepped into my clinic that day, a stoic front over a mind about to fall apart. This stranger looked the same.

Ben gestured to the chair at the end of the table. "There's plenty of food, if you want it," he offered.

"I've already eaten."

"Well, join us, at least," I added, and that black, depthless gaze flicked to me. "You sort of saved our lives. The least we can do is thank you for it."

He paused, as though weighing the consequences of such a simple action, before he very slowly pulled out a chair and sat down, lacing his fingers together. Every motion, everything he did, was powerful and controlled; nothing was wasted. His eyes, however, remained dark and far away.

A moment of awkward silence passed, the only sounds being the clink of utensils against the bowls and the occasional shriek of the rabids outside. The man didn't move; he remained sitting with his chin on his hands, staring at the table. He was so still, so quiet, if you weren't looking directly at him, you wouldn't know he was there at all.

"Where are you headed?" the stranger murmured without looking up, an obvious attempt at civility. Ben swallowed a mouthful of water and put the cup down.

"West," he replied. "Toward Illinois. I have family there, I hope." His face tightened, but he shook it off. "What about you? If we're headed the same direction, you're welcome to come along. Where are you going?"

For a few seconds, there was no answer. I wasn't sure the stranger was even paying attention, when he gave a short, bitter laugh. My gut clenched with horror and fear. In that moment, his mask slipped away, and I saw the raw agony beneath the smooth facade, the glassy sheen in his eyes that hovered close to madness.

"It doesn't matter," he rasped. "Nothing matters anymore. No matter where I go, I'll be hunted. I could flee to the other side of the world, and they would find me. I thought…" He covered his eyes with a hand. "I thought I could change things. But I've only made it far, far worse."

"What do you mean?" I asked.

The stranger drew in a deep breath, appearing to compose

himself. "I've...done something," he admitted, lowering his hand. He stared down at the table, the candlelight reflected in his dark eyes. "Something I will never be forgiven for. Something that will likely cause my death. A very painful, drawn-out death, if I know my kin." Another of his short, bitter laughs. "And it will be completely justified."

Outside, something shrieked and slammed into the side of the wall. We froze, holding our breath, listening, as the body scrabbled around the base of the house, watching its jerky movements through a slit in the curtain. Finally, it shuffled off, vanishing into the night, and we started breathing again.

I glanced at the stranger. "Whatever it was," I began, knowing he probably wouldn't tell me the details, "it can't be *that* bad, right?"

No answer. Just a tight, bitter smile.

I took a breath. "Look," I began, wondering why I wanted to help him, to ease the darkness in his eyes, on his face. Maybe I was trying to return the favor, or maybe I felt that I was seeing only a hint of the agony beneath that cool, flinty shell. The reasons didn't matter; I reached out and put a hand on his wrist. "Whatever you've done, or think you've done, it's over now. You can't go back and change it. What you do about it, right now, from here on out, that's the important thing."

I felt Ben's eyes on me and realized I could be talking to both of them. And myself. I *couldn't* go back and change anything. Maggie and Jenna were gone. The world was full of monsters, or it would be soon. I could not dwell on the past, what I had lost, who I had failed. From here on, I could only move forward.

The stranger blinked, staring at my fingers on his wrist as though surprised to find them there. His skin was pale, smooth and oddly cool.

"Perhaps...you are right." He straightened, giving me an

unfathomable look. "I cannot escape what I have done, but perhaps I can make up for it. I still have time. It shames me that a...stranger...must tell me what should be obvious, but these are unusual times." He stared at me, and that faint, bemused smile flickered across his face. "Incredible, that after all these years I can still be surprised."

He rose, startling me with the smooth, quick motion. "There are stairs to a finished basement down the hall," he said, back to being matter-of-fact, his mask sliding into place once more. "It will be the safest place for you to spend the night, I believe. If you want to get some sleep, I would do so there."

"What about you?" Ben asked. The stranger gave one final faint smile.

"I will be up all night," he said simply, and left the room.

Ben put the dishes in the sink, despite the futility of it all, and in the flickering candlelight, we found the stairs leading to a bedroom on the lowest floor. I caught sight of the stranger as we left, sitting in a living-room chair facing the door, his fingers steepled in thought. Strangely, the notion that he was on guard duty made me feel that much safer.

The walls downstairs were made of concrete, with no windows and a single queen-size bed in the corner. It was dry and cool, the cement floor covered with several thick shag rugs, muffling our footsteps. It felt more secure than any place we'd been so far. I set my candle on a nightstand by the bed and clicked on the flashlight to see better, shining it around the room. Ben shut the door, locked it and then pushed the dresser up against it, the scraping sound making me grit my teeth.

"There," he muttered, once the heavy piece of furniture was butted firmly against the wood. "Only one way in, and if anything tries to get through that, at least we'll hear them coming."

He turned just as I did, shining the beam right into his face, and he flinched away. "Sorry!" I whispered, lowering the beam. "I'm not doing that on purpose, I swear—"

I stopped at the look on his face. He crossed the room in two long strides, took the flashlight from my hands and pulled me to him, pressing his lips to mine.

His lips were warm, soft and hard at the same time, and something inside me, some dam or wall or barrier, shattered. I thought I'd be shocked, at least surprised, but my arms wrapped around his neck, and I rose on tiptoes to kiss him back. Ben groaned, sounding almost like a growl, and crushed me to him, nearly lifting me off my feet. I met him with equal passion, fisting my hands in his thick hair, pressing my body to his. My brain jangled a warning, but it was rapidly shutting down; I had to say something before it powered off completely and my body took over.

"Ben," I breathed, as his mouth dropped to my neck, searing the flesh along my jaw. "Wait, we shouldn't…there's still that guy upstairs. And the rabids. If they hear us…"

"I can be quiet," Ben whispered against my skin. His hands were roaming down my ribs to my thighs, and mine had somehow slipped beneath his shirt to skim his muscular back. "But it's your call," he panted. "Tell me to stop, and I will."

Yes, stop! my logical doctor's brain was screaming. *This is crazy! You don't know this man, the house is surrounded by zombies and there is a scary, I-might-be-a-serial-killer stranger in the front room. This is not the time for…this!*

I ignored the voice. God, I *did* want this. I wanted *him.* If only to feel something again, to convince myself that I was alive. The past few days—hell, the past few *months*—had been a nightmare, and I'd felt like a zombie myself, shambling from place to place, numb. Barely alive. Ben had reawakened something inside me, and I didn't want to let it go. Dammit,

I'd nearly been killed tonight. One night of letting go wasn't too much to ask.

"No," I rasped, clutching at him. "Don't stop. We just… have to be quiet."

Kissing me fiercely, Ben drew back just enough to push my coat off my shoulders and tug my blouse over my head. I did the same, freeing his shirt from the waistband of his jeans and pulling it from his broad shoulders. He bent over to help, shrugging free, and his tanned, muscular chest and stomach were suddenly bared in the glowing candlelight.

Oh, my. I scarcely had time for a complete thought before he was on me again, kissing, nipping, devouring. His strong arms wrapped around my waist and lifted me off my feet, moving me back to the bed. I braced myself to be dropped, but he laid me on the quilt very gently and straddled my head with his elbows.

I looked up at him, at his face inches from mine, at the hazel eyes gone dark with passion and want. But he was hesitant now; a little of that worry had trickled back, filtering through the desire. He licked his lip and drew back, his expression shifting to guilty concern.

"Are you—" his voice was a little ragged "—okay with this? I don't want you to—"

Frowning, I slid my hands into his hair and pulled his lips down to mine. He sucked in a breath, and a low groan escaped him. "You're not being very quiet," I whispered against his mouth, and he moaned again. "Less talking, more kissing, Ben. Now."

"Yes…ma'am."

With deft fingers, Ben undid my bra and shifted it off, tossing it over the bed. His mouth left mine and trailed hot kisses down my neck, my collarbone, between my breasts. I arched my head back, biting my lip to keep from gasping, knowing especially now, we had to be silent. His lips closed over a nipple, teasing it with his tongue, and I clutched at the quilt beneath me, whispering his name. I felt alive, my body glowing, afire with every stroke of Ben's artful fingers, every brush of his lips across my skin. I trailed my hands up his arms, feeling his hard triceps, and lightly raked his back with my nails.

He jerked up, wincing, as my fingers scraped across the claw marks on his shoulder. I instantly yanked them back.

"Shit! Sorry!"

"It's all right." His voice was a ragged whisper in the darkness. "You didn't hurt me." His gaze roved over my face and bare chest, heavy with passion, as he lowered himself down. "God, you're beautiful," he breathed into my ear, making me shiver. "If I were allowed to talk, I'd tell you how gorgeous you are. But since I'm not…" His lips closed on my earlobe, and I squeaked, feeling his smile. He seemed different now, more playful and less guarded, perhaps lost to desire, same as I was.

Once more, he raised his head, mouth and hands skimming my stomach, moving slowly downward. I closed my eyes as he reached my navel, right above the hem of my jeans, and raised my hips as he undid the button and eased the fabric down. My panties and shoes hit the floor with my jeans, and I was laid out before him, naked and aching for his touch.

Abruptly, he scooted forward again, taking my lips with his own, thrusting with his tongue. I whimpered and arched into him as Ben caressed my breasts, my stomach, then very slowly moved his fingers down, slipping them between my legs, into my wet folds. I gasped into his mouth as he stroked lightly, circling gently with one finger, and I nearly came apart in his hands.

Oh, yes. I moaned softly and writhed beneath his stroking fingers. *Yes, more. I want to feel more. Shatter me. Make me feel alive.*

Somewhere outside, a rabid screamed, chilling and terrifying, but I was too far gone to even care. Ben was circling my bud; this was sweet, exquisite torture, and I could feel myself tightening, tightening...

"Come for me, Kylie," Ben crooned in a velvet whisper, and I erupted, throwing my head back and biting my lip as my insides fluttered and convulsed and I melted onto the quilt, shuddering with release.

As I lay there, reeling, Ben rolled off the bed and stood, slipping out of his jeans. The mattress shifted as he clambered back on, a smooth, muscular jungle cat. I felt his length graze my stomach as he moved between my legs, positioning himself over me, and trembled in anticipation. *Protection,* my logical doctor's brain objected, a faint, weak plea, but I shoved it aside. The world outside was ending. I was not going to worry about the future. All I wanted to feel was the *now.*

With one quick, masterful stroke, Ben slid inside me. I stifled a cry and rose to meet him, arching off the bed as his arm snaked under my back, pinning me to his chest. We began a slow, rolling rhythm that quickened and intensified with every gasp, every panting breath and muffled groan. I buried my face in his neck, biting his hot skin to keep from crying out, as every thrust brought me closer to the edge again.

The white-hot pressure building inside released, and I couldn't contain the shriek that tore free as waves of pleasure radiated out from my core. Ben gasped and followed me over, crushing me to his chest with one arm, the other braced against the mattress as he poured himself into me.

We slumped to the quilt, panting. Ben carefully eased out and settled behind me, wrapping his arms around my waist, pulling me to his chest. My body was still tingling from the aftershocks, and I could feel his warm skin where it pressed against mine. The crazy whirlwind of emotion and passion faded, and I shivered as, just outside the walls, I heard the ra-bids, shuffling around. Still out there.

Ben kissed my bare shoulder, blew out the candle, then pulled the quilt over us both. "Don't think about them," he whispered as the warmth and darkness closed around us like a cocoon. "They can't get in, they don't know we're here. Try to get some sleep."

I shouldn't be feeling this safe, but I believed him. Of course, that could be because I was completely spent, warm and satisfied, and the quilt combined with Ben's body heat was making me drowsy. I felt protected here. Ben held me tighter and, wrapped in the nest of his arms, I faded into a dreamless sleep.

CHAPTER 8

The next morning, the dark stranger was gone. He left nothing behind, nothing to indicate he had been there at all, except a short note on the kitchen table.

> *Apologies for the sudden departure, but I could not stay. There is a vehicle in the garage with enough fuel to get you where you need to go. The rabids cannot be out in the sun and will sleep when it is light out. Travel only by day and seek shelter before night falls.*
> *I will remember your words about the past and making things right. You will likely never see me again, but you've helped me more than you know. For that, you have my gratitude.*
> *-K*

We took the van, which had the keys in the ignition, probably left by our mysterious friend, and got out of town as quickly as we could. The streets and roads were eerily deserted, though subtle signs of the monsters' presence lingered: broken windows, doors with claw marks slashed across their surface. The bones and shredded carcass of an animal lying in a dark stain on the side of the road.

Rabids, the stranger had called them. It fit. I wondered where he was now, where he was going. I hoped, wherever it was, he would find his peace.

We drove all afternoon and through the evening, following the deserted highway as it wound its way through a desolate, empty world. I sneaked glances at Ben, at his rugged profile, and every time my skin flushed and my stomach squirmed. Last night... I didn't know what to make of it yet, what had come over us. I didn't know if our lovemaking had been brought on by our hopeless circumstances, a desperate need to connect to another human being when we thought we could die, or if it had been...something more.

Did I want something more...with Ben?

I didn't really have much to compare it to. I'd been in relationships before, of course, even thought I was in love, once, at the ripe old age of fifteen. But when I'd left for college, boyfriends and relationships had taken a backseat to my future career. I didn't have time for a serious commitment; my life revolved around my work and school. The couple guys I did go out with soon realized they played second fiddle in my life, and ended things after a few months. I barely gave them a second thought.

But Ben...was different.

We stopped a couple times for gas and other necessities, siphoning fuel from abandoned cars and raiding gas stations and minimarts for food. As the afternoon wore on, Ben grew increasingly nervous and quiet, brooding over the steering wheel with his gaze far away. I asked him, once, if he was afraid we wouldn't make it before nightfall, but he shook his head and said we would get there before the sun went down. When I pressed him further, asking if anything was wrong, I received a mostly empty smile and the assurance that he was fine, that it wasn't anything I should worry about.

Of course, that just made me worry more.

We stopped one last time at a gas station atop an off-ramp, and Ben siphoned gas from an old tanker while I answered a call of nature inside, despite the fact that the toilet was beyond disgusting. We hadn't spoken for nearly an hour, and I'd given up trying to draw him out.

When I returned, Ben was screwing the cap back onto the tank, so I moved past him to the door, ready to get on the road. He called my name as I went by, but I ignored him, opening the door to slide in.

He caught me by the wrist and drew me to him, wrapping his arms around my waist. I stiffened but didn't have it in me to push him off.

"Hey." His voice was quiet, apologetic. "I'm sorry. I know I've been distracted. I didn't mean to ignore you." His hand came up, brushing my hair back. "It's not you, I promise."

I slumped a bit in relief. "What's going on, Ben?"

"It's just…" He sighed. "My family. I haven't seen them in so long, I don't know what they're going to say when I come back. If they're alive at all." His face darkened, and he gazed out over the trees. "God, I hope it hasn't spread that far. I would rather they be…dead…than turned into those things." Shivering, he held me tighter. "I don't think I could handle seeing them like that."

My heart ached for him, and I reached up to stroke his cheek, bringing his attention back to me. His eyes softened, and he leaned down, kissing me gently. It was not like last night, hard and desperate and needing to feel something, anything, to remind ourselves that we were still alive. This was tender and thoughtful, a promise without words and a hint of something more, something that could be forever.

"We'll figure it out when we get there," I whispered when I could breathe again.

The road wound on, and the sun continued to sink toward the horizon, making me check its position every few minutes. It felt strange, watching the once-cheerful sun slip away like sands through an hourglass, feeling tiny flutters of panic the lower it dropped and the longer the shadows became. I was contemplating telling Ben to stop for the night, to not risk pushing further into the evening, when he suddenly turned off the main highway and onto a smaller road. We drove through a small town, chillingly empty, and continued down several winding, one-lane roads. At last, as the sun became a brilliant orange ball on the horizon, he turned off the pavement onto a bumpy dirt path that snaked between a field and a line of trees, and the van lurched to a halt.

Ben stared down the road, his face lit by the setting sun. I glanced past him out the side window and saw a battered mailbox nailed to a fence post, soggy letters hanging out the front and rotting to mush in the grass below. The side of the mailbox read *Archer* in faded white paint.

Ben drew in a deep breath, and I reached over to lay a hand on his leg. He looked at me, managed a sickly smile, and started the van again.

We bounced down that tiny path for quite some time, until we rounded a bend, and a monstrous old farmhouse rose from the sea of grass. Perched atop a hill, it looked ancient and foreboding and desolate, a faded gray-white structure against a backdrop of clouds, glaring down at the tractor supplies and rusty cars scattered around its base. A collection of whimsical statues in the front yard did nothing for its somber appearance.

"Looks deserted," Ben whispered in a voice that was half terrified, half relieved. We inched up the driveway, gravel crunching under the tires, until we reached the first of the rusty shells of cars left to disintegrate in the grass. Ben parked the van and opened the door, gazing up at the farmhouse. I followed his example.

"Hello?" Ben called, slamming the door. The sounds echoed thinly over the silent fields. "Anyone here? Hello?"

A metallic click made my hair stand on end.

A man slid out from behind a car, and another followed on the other side of the driveway, blocking our path. Both held rifles pointed in our direction. Our weapon still lay on the backseat of the van.

Ben raised his hands as the men glared at him, their faces hard. One was lanky and rawboned, the other grizzled and huge, but they both looked dangerous and unfriendly. "Don't know who you are," the big one growled through a thick brown beard, shoving the gun barrel at Ben, "but you can get in your car and drive back the way you came. We got nothin' here for the likes of you."

My heart was pounding, but Ben stared at the man with a faint, puzzled frown on his face, as if trying to remember something. The man scowled back.

"Hey, you hear what I said, boy? If you and the little lady know what's good for you, you'll hightail it outta here, before I put a lead slug in your stupid—"

"Uncle Jack," Ben breathed. The man stopped, squinting at him down the gun barrel, then his thick eyebrows arched into his hair.

"Damn. Benjamin Archer, is that you?" He snorted and lowered the rifle, and I nearly collapsed in relief. "Last I saw of you, boy, you were this sulky teenager always trying to get out of heavy work." He shook his head and gave Ben a piercing look. "We heard you ran off to the city an' broke your mama's heart, swearin' you'd never come back."

Ben shifted uncomfortably, not meeting my gaze. "Yeah, well, things change. Are Mom and Dad around?"

Before he could answer, the screen door banged open, and a man stepped onto the porch. I swallowed, glancing between the two of them. He looked like a grizzled version of Ben, with gray streaked through his brown hair and a neatly trimmed beard. Dark eyes raked over us both, hard and cold, lingering on Ben. He didn't smile.

Ben stepped forward, approaching the front door. "Dad…"

"Get out."

The command was unyielding. My stomach plummeted. Ben came to a halt a few feet from the steps, gazing up at the older man, his voice pleading but calm. "We have nowhere else to go."

"You should've thought of that before you went traipsing off to the city and left the rest of us to pick up your slack." His cold eyes flicked to me, and one corner of his lip curled. "Now you come dragging yourself back, with a pregnant girlfriend most likely, and expect us to welcome you home like nothing happened? After what you said to me, and your mother?"

I bristled, stepping forward, as well, but Ben gave me a pleading look, warning me not to get involved. "You want me to say it?" he asked, turning back to his father. His hands rose away from his sides in a hopeless gesture. "I'm sorry. You were right, and I was an ass. I should have never left."

"Four years too late, Benjamin." Mr. Archer's expression didn't change. Neither did his uncompromising tone. "You made it very clear that you are no longer a part of this family. As far as I'm concerned, you can go back to whatever city hole you crawled out of. You have no place here anymore."

I couldn't see Ben's expression, but the way his posture slumped hinted at the devastation on his face, and my blood boiled. Stepping around the van, I marched up the driveway, coming to stand next to Ben. "What the hell is wrong with you?" I demanded, and all four men stared at me in shock. I ignored them and faced Ben's father, seething, as he turned that cold glare on me. "Don't you know what's happening out there? People are dying! Cities are empty, and you're going to stand there and tell your son that he can't come home? Because of some stupid argument you had four years ago?"

"Who the hell is this?" Mr. Archer asked, not speaking to me, but to Ben. "Some tramp you picked up off a street corner?"

I took a step forward, raising my chin. "If by 'tramp' you mean 'doctor,' then yes, I am," I answered before Ben could speak. "Ben came to my clinic when his friend got sick, so let me tell you what I've seen before he showed up. I've seen people puking blood in the streets, right before they drown in it, and their bodies lying there because no one is alive to take them away. I've seen infected mothers smother their own infants with a pillow so they won't have to suffer a long, painful death. I've seen piles of bodies rotting in open pits, because there are too many to bury and everyone is too busy dying to dig more graves. *That* is what is happening out there now, and *that* is the world you're going to send Ben into. So if you want to be a heartless, stubborn bastard over something that happened *four years* ago, that's your decision. But I will tell you this right now—you're handing out a death sentence. To your son. Send him away, and you kill him."

I didn't mention the rabids, not wanting to look like a raving lunatic in front of these people we needed to convince. I suddenly understood Ben's reluctance to talk about them at the clinic; it did sound like something from a horror movie. Ben's father still wore a stone-faced expression, no crack in his flinty mask, but the other men looked rather pale and concerned, yet still unwilling to step in for us. I felt Ben's gaze on me but didn't dare turn to face him.

The tension mounted. Then the screen door banged, startling us all, and a woman rushed onto the porch. Tanned, bony, her steel-blond hair coming loose of its bun, she took one look at Ben and flung herself down the steps with a cry.

"Ben!" I stepped back as she embraced him fiercely, almost wildly, and he hugged her back. "Benjamin! Oh, you're home! Thank God, I knew you'd come home! I prayed for you every night. Samson, look!" She turned to beam tearfully at the man on the porch. "Ben's home! He's come home."

Tentative hope blossomed through me. Ben's father pursed his lips as if he'd swallowed something foul, turned and vanished inside, slamming the door behind him. Ben winced, but the woman, his mother I presumed, didn't seem to care. I felt a tiny twinge of longing, watching them, and swallowed the sudden lump in my throat. I would never see my parents again.

"Mom." Ben freed himself from her embrace and turned to me, holding out a hand. "This is Kylie. She helped me get here." His eyes met mine, solemn and grave. "I wouldn't have made it this far if it wasn't for her."

"Bless you, dear." I was suddenly enveloped in the thin, steely arms of Ben's mother. She pulled back, holding me at arm's length, sharp blue eyes appraising. "Thank you for bringing him home."

I shot Ben a desperate look, and he cleared his throat. "Mom," he began as she turned back, releasing me from her wiry grip. "What's happening? Is everyone all right?" He paled, looking back toward the house. "Rachel. Is she…?"

"Your sister is fine," Mrs. Archer said firmly, and Ben slumped in relief. I gave a little start, not having known he had a sister. "And if you're talking about that horrid sickness, we heard what's been on the news, before all the stations went down. That's why your uncle Jack is here." She nodded to the two men, who were walking back to their posts. "He lost everyone," she whispered, her voice sympathetic. "Your aunt Susan, his three boys, all the farmhands. Except Shane, there. It was so horrible." She shook her head, and tears filled her eyes. "I just thank God that it hasn't spread out here, yet. I guess because we're so isolated."

Ben relaxed, as if a huge weight had been lifted from his shoulders. "Where is Rachel?" he asked, a smile creeping onto his face. "Did she move into my old room, like she always wanted?" He looked toward the house again, excitement and longing peeking through the worry. He looked very big-brother-ish then, and I smiled.

"She went to feed the goats a few minutes ago," Mrs. Archer said, beaming. "Your sister has turned into quite the little goatherd, Ben. There's an orphaned kid who follows her around like a puppy. It's adorable, though we could do without her letting the thing sleep with her at night. But Samson can't tell her no." She sighed and pointed a finger over the distant hills, where a sliver of red hung on the horizon. "She's probably out in the far pasture right now."

A chill went through me, and by the blood draining from Ben's face, he was thinking the same thing. At that very moment, it seemed, the sun slipped behind the tree line and shadows crept over the fields like grasping claws.

"Rachel," Ben whispered, and took off, running toward the pasture and the darkness looming beyond the fence line.

CHAPTER 9

❖

"Ben! Where are you going?"

Mrs. Archer's cry rang out behind us, but Ben didn't slow down, his long legs hurrying across the field. I scrambled to keep up as he strode through the tall grass to the pasture surrounding the building and leaped the fence without breaking stride.

Squeezing between the boards, I followed. Sheep and goats scattered before us with startled bleats and watched us curiously from several yards away. A massive shaggy dog, pure white with a huge thick head, eyed us warily as we rushed across the field, but it didn't appear threatening as long as we didn't bother its herd.

In the farthest pasture, a small group of long-eared goats milled around a figure with a pair of buckets, bleating and trying to stick their heads into the containers. Just beyond them, beyond the fence line, the forest crowded forward with long, dark fingers.

"Rachel!" Ben called, and the figure looked up, a skinny girl of about twelve, light brown hair braided down her back. She gasped, dropping her buckets, which the goats swarmed over immediately, and sprinted into Ben's arms.

"Benji!"

Ben hugged her tightly, then pulled back a little, shaking his head as I came up. "Hey, Scarecrow. I told you I hate that name— Ow!" he yelped as the girl hauled off and slugged him in the arm with a small fist. "What was that for?"

"Jerkoff!" Rachel snapped, scowling at him, though her eyes were bright and glassy. "You never showed up for my birthday, or Christmas, or anytime you said you would. Stupid jerk, making Mom cry." She hit him again, and this time he accepted it, his expression going solemn. She glared at him, fists clenched, ready to continue the abuse. "Are you back for good? Or are you going to be stupid and leave again?"

"I'm back for good," Ben told her. "I'm not going anywhere this time, I promise."

That seemed to placate her, for her curious gaze suddenly shifted to me. At that moment, I noticed a small white creature sniffing around my legs: a baby goat with black legs and dark splotches down his back. It nipped the hem of my jeans, and I squealed.

"Davy, no." Rachel freed herself from Ben and gathered the goat in her arms. "He's not trying to be mean," she explained. "He's just curious."

"Benjamin? Rachel?" Mrs. Archer's voice cut across the field, and the older woman came striding up, shielding her eyes. "Are you three all right?" she asked, giving us all a worried look. "What's going on?"

Ben cast a nervous glance at the forest and took a deep breath. "Let's go inside," he suggested, leading us all away from the trees and the shadows beyond the fence. "We… Kylie and I…have to tell you something. And everyone needs to hear it."

"That's the biggest load of bull I've ever heard."

I bit the inside of my cheek to keep back a frustrated, snapping reply and faced Ben's father calmly. "That is the truth, Mr. Archer. Believe it or not, but it's true. We've both seen it with our own eyes."

We were in the Archer family's kitchen, huddled around the table. All of us, which was pretty impressive. The Archer clan, it seemed, was quite the large, extended family, with aunts, uncles, brothers and sisters, cousins, in-laws, nieces, nephews, even some farmhands, all packed into one room. When the plague had hit and people had begun dying, the Archers had sent out the call for everyone to come home, bringing the family under one roof.

Ben had not received this call.

"You're talking about zombies," Samson Archer said in disgust. "Walking dead people. Movie monsters." He sneered. "You must think we're mighty stupid."

"They killed my friend," Ben said softly, though I could hear the quiet anger below the surface. "They killed him, and he came back to life and attacked me. I have the scars to prove it." He looked around the table at the grim, skeptical faces, and his voice grew even harder. "This is real. These things are real, and they're out there, and they're coming. If we're not ready for them, they'll tear this place to pieces and everyone here will die. That's the truth of it."

Silence fell as the reality of everything sank in. I could understand their skepticism, their disbelief. One person they might've shrugged off as crazy, but two accounts made them hesitate. Even if I was a stranger, I was still a doctor, and I was from the city. And then, Ben pulled up his shirt, revealing the still-healing claw marks down his back, eliciting a horrified cry from Mrs. Archer, and that was enough to convince them that *something* was truly out there.

An older woman, one of Ben's many aunts, spoke up, her

voice shaking. "Shouldn't we leave, then? We're all alone here—"

"No." Samson Archer's voice cut through the suggestion like a knife. "I'm not going anywhere," he said flatly. "This has been our home for eight generations, and I'll be damned if some zombie apocalypse will drive me off my own land." His steely gaze went around the table, and most everyone looked away. "Anyone who wants to leave, leave. Right now. Because the only way I'll leave this place is in a long wooden box."

Or in a rabid's stomach, I thought ungraciously, but didn't voice it out loud.

Ben stood up. "We're not ready for them, not yet," he said. "We have to get this house fortified if we're going to stand a chance when they show up. We should start right away—I don't think we have a lot of time."

"Since when did you become the head of this family, boy?" Mr. Archer asked in a low, dangerous voice. "Last time I checked, *I* owned this land and this house, and you were the one who didn't want anything to do with us."

Ben paused. He took a slow breath, then met his father's gaze. "Fine. What would you have us do?"

"We'll start with the house." Samson Archer raised his voice for the rest of the group, taking charge. "Fortify the doors, board up the windows. See if we can't attach some of that old rebar to the frames from outside. After that, we'll work on the barn—the livestock will need to be protected, as well. We'll set up watches at night, and we'll have a safe room the women can retreat to if something gets inside. Everyone got that?"

Everyone did. I was surprised and, reluctantly, a little impressed. Samson Archer might be a mean, sexist sonofabitch, but he knew how to protect himself and his land. However, as everyone at the table rose, preparing to carry out his instructions, Samson gave both of us the coldest, most withering glare yet, and I knew that, even if we survived the rabids sweeping across the land, our biggest challenge was going to be the man standing in front of us.

That first night, nothing happened. We fortified the old farmhouse, nailing boards across windows and installing a bar across the front door. The next day we continued to secure the house, creating a room in the basement that we could fall back to and lock from the inside if needed. When night fell, we set up watches on the porch and the roof, as the hilltop farm offered a fantastic view of the fields all the way to the woods. If anything came shuffling out of the trees, at least we would see it coming.

Nothing happened on the second night, either.

When the house was secure, we moved on to the barn where the goats and other livestock would be kept at night, closing all windows and reinforcing the heavy sliding doors. The barn became a virtual fortress; the livestock had to be just as well-protected as the humans, as they were the key to our survival now that the outside world was in turmoil. No more running to Walmart for steaks, eggs and milk. At least, not for a long time.

After the third night, people began to mutter. What if we were wrong? What if the house was too isolated to be in any real danger? What if all this work was for nothing? As the nights wore on, tension flagged, nervousness disappeared and people began to revert to their old habits and routines.

Ben and I kept pushing, however. Just because the rabids hadn't found us yet didn't mean they weren't out there. During the day, Ben helped the men fortify the property, while I stayed in the farmhouse and helped the women as they gathered food supplies, water, medicine, candles, soap and other necessities. At night, when Ben wasn't on watch, I would curl up with him beneath the quilt in the guest bedroom and we would make love, pressed tightly against each other in the darkness. And I would fall asleep wrapped in Ben's arms, listening to his slow, deep breathing and basking in the warmth of his body.

One morning, about a week after we'd come to the homestead, I walked out onto the porch to find Ben and his father standing in the driveway. By Ben's frustrated, angry gestures and Samson's cold glare, it was obvious they were in the middle of an argument.

"And I'm saying we shouldn't leave the farm," Ben said, stabbing his finger down the driveway. "Dammit, you haven't seen these things. You don't know what they can do, how many of them are out there. Sending people into town is going to get them killed."

"We're low on ammunition," Samson said in his flinty voice. "And the women are complaining that we're running out of certain things. We need more firepower if we're going to defend this house from your monsters. The town isn't far— if we leave now, we can get the supplies we need and make it back by sundown."

"You're going to get everyone killed."

"I don't need your opinions, boy." Samson narrowed his eyes. "This is happening, whether you like it or not. I've seen no evidence of your walking zombies, and the people in this house have to eat. We're going into town, so get out of the way."

"Fine." Ben raised a hand. "Then I'll come with you."

"No, you will not." Samson's mouth curled into a sneer, and Ben took a breath to argue. "I won't have you whining at us the whole trip," he said, overriding Ben's unvoiced protest. "We don't need you. I'm taking Jack and Shane, and you can stay here with the women. I'm sure they can find something for you to do."

Without waiting for an answer, Samson spun on a heel and continued down the driveway, where Jack and Shane waited in the back of an ancient-looking pickup. Ben watched them, fists clenched at his sides, until the truck bounced away down the gravel drive and disappeared around a bend.

"Dammit!" Ben turned and kicked the ground in a rare show of temper, sending gravel flying. "Stupid, stubborn old man!" He spotted me then, watching from the porch, and winced. "Hey. Did you hear all that?"

I nodded and stepped off the porch, slipping into his arms. "I'm sure they'll be okay," I told him, peering up at his face. "Your father is a bastard—sorry—but he knows how to take care of himself. And he knows not to stay out past sunset."

Ben frowned. "I know he's looking out for everyone, but he shouldn't compromise people's safety just to put me in my place." He sighed and gazed down the driveway. "I wonder if he'll ever forgive me for walking out on them."

I didn't have anything to say to that, so I just held him as we stood in the middle of the driveway and watched the road, as if we could will the truck and its occupants into appearing, safe and unharmed.

"I guess I should get back to the barn," Ben muttered at last. Glancing down at me, his eyes softened. "You have apple peels in your hair." He picked a sliver of red skin from my ponytail. "What have *you* been doing all morning?"

I grimaced. "Busy discovering that I became a doctor for a reason, since the mechanics of turning fruit into preserves is completely lost on me. I think your aunt Sarah was just about to ban me from the kitchen permanently."

Ben laughed. Pulling me close, he kissed me deeply in the middle of the driveway. My stomach did a backflip. I slid my hands up his back and held him tight, feeling the hard muscles shift through his shirt. I wanted to take away his pain, the guilt still lingering in his eyes. Because, even though he was home, he wasn't part of the family; as long as Samson kept him at arm's length, he would always be an outcast. Just like me, a city girl and an outsider. Someone who didn't know the first thing about goats, or chickens, or making preserves.

That was fine with me. I could learn. And Samson would eventually forgive Ben, or at least start treating him like a human instead of the mud on his boots. And if he didn't, that was fine, too. We would be outsiders together, and maybe together we could save this stubborn family.

Ben suddenly pulled back, his gaze intense. One hand rose to stroke my cheek, sending little flutters through my stomach. "Kylie, I—"

"Kylie, dear?" Aunt Sarah appeared in the doorway. In one hand she held a long wooden spoon, covered in bits of fruit mush. "Oh, there you are. Are you ready to give this another go?"

We both sighed.

"You go on," Ben said, reluctantly pulling back. "I have some work to finish." He caught my hand as I drew away. "Will you tell me when Dad and the others get back? I'll be checking in every five minutes, otherwise."

"Sure."

He looked as if he wanted to kiss me again, but Sarah was still watching us, so he gave me a quick peck on the cheek and left, striding away toward the barn. I stifled a groan and returned to the kitchen and the torture of canning.

The afternoon wore on, and Samson did not return.

A tense silence hung over the farmhouse that evening. Everyone knew the three men had gone into town, and by now, even if they didn't quite believe the rabids were out there, we had at least made everyone nervous about the sun setting.

Said sun now hovered over the distant hills, dangerously low and sinking lower with every minute. As Mrs. Archer and some of the women bustled about the kitchen making dinner, I busied myself with setting the table, finally free from my disastrous canning attempts. But every thirty seconds or so, someone would glance out the window and down the road, searching for headlights or listening for the rumble of a distant engine. Dinner was solemn, and afterwards, as the kids and women cleared the dishes, some of the younger men began arguing about sending a search party. Surprisingly, Ben was the one to talk them down, saying that we had to give them until sunset, that if we left now, we wouldn't make it back before dark.

Restless, needing to get out of the tension-filled farmhouse, I wandered onto the front porch, breathing in the cool evening air. A breeze whispered through the grass, moaning through the trees surrounding the field, and I shivered. Rubbing my arms, I glanced toward the sun and found only a half-circle of red, sliding behind a cloud. As I watched, unable to look away, it shrank to a crescent, then a sliver, then finally vanished altogether.

"Kylie?"

I jumped, spinning around at the deep voice. A shimmering blob of color hovered in front of my vision, and I had to blink several times before I could see who it was.

"Geez, Ben. Sneak much?"

"Sorry." He joined me at the railing. "What are you doing out here?"

"Just needed some air." I rubbed my arms and nodded to the darkening sky, trying not to shiver. "Sun's gone down, Ben."

"I know."

"Your father isn't back yet."

"I know." He ran his fingers through his hair, looking uncomfortable, as if there was something he didn't want to tell me. I was afraid I already knew what it was.

"You're going after them, aren't you?"

Ben nodded. "I figured we'd give them until sunset to make it back," he said, glancing at the fading orange glow on the horizon where the sun had been. "But we can't leave them out there now, even though it'll be full dark when we make it to town. We have to go look for them."

"You know I'm coming with you."

"Kylie—"

"Don't you dare give me any crap about this, Ben Archer." I glared at him. "I am a doctor, and it's my duty to help people. What if someone is injured, or bleeding? I am not going to sit here and wash dishes while you go off to face these things alone. So save your 'I am a manly man' speech, because you're not getting rid of me that easily."

He looked torn between amusement and exasperation. "I know that," he snapped, matching my glare with his own. "I wasn't going to tell you to stay here. I already told Donald and Chris that you'll be coming with us. That's not what I was going to say."

"Oh," I said, faintly embarrassed. "Well…what were you going to say, then?"

For some reason, this seemed to fluster him more, and he scrubbed a hand over his face, wincing. "Christ, this is going badly. Kylie… I know we've just met, and everything has gone crazy, and I probably shouldn't even be thinking of this right now, but…" He looked down, swallowed, then met my eyes. "I want to know what your plans are…with me."

"You?"

"I'm staying, Kylie." Turning away, he gazed over the fields, resting both hands on the railing. "I want to build a life here, if I can," he murmured. "No more running, or fighting with my past. I'm done. Dad can rake me over the coals all he wants, but I'm staying here. This is where I belong."

I was glad to hear it. Family seemed important to Ben, even if certain members made life difficult for everyone. But despite the tension and occasional argument, this was a strong community, and I was glad that he had found his place, that he was finally home.

"Except," Ben continued, facing me again, "I don't know what your plans are. You once said you didn't know if you could settle down. And I wouldn't force you to do anything, but…you could have a place here, if you wanted it. With me."

"What do you mean?"

My heart pounded. This sounded very much like a proposal without the words. I didn't know what to say or think. Ben wanted to build a life together…but was it only because he recognized the need to keep the family strong? We'd only known each other a short time, barely more than a week. What did Ben really want from me? And what did I really want, from him?

Ben moved closer, sliding his hands up my arms. "Kylie, I…"

A shot rang out in the darkness.

We jerked, all senses rigidly alert, listening as the echo of the gunshot faded away. Ben's hands were clenched on my arms, squeezing painfully, but I barely noticed.

More shots, several this time, rapid, frantic. Ben released me, ran into the house and emerged seconds later with the shotgun. My heart clenched as he leaped off the porch, sprinting down the driveway. After a second's deliberation, I followed.

"Kylie, go back to the house!" he growled, sparing a glance over his shoulder. I ignored him, and he spun, grabbing my arm again, his face tense.

"Don't!" I snapped before he could say anything. "I'm coming with you, so don't waste time telling me I'm not."

His eyes darkened, but then the shots came again, closer this time, followed by a scream of anguish. Ben gave me one last angry look and sprinted down the driveway again, me trailing doggedly behind.

We neared the road, and I gasped. Samson and Ben's uncle Jack were staggering up the driveway, weapons drawn, gasping for breath. Samson was covered in blood, though he didn't look injured, and Jack's face was so pale it almost glowed in the twilight. As Ben jogged toward them, I looked around, hoping to see their final member limping frantically up the driveway, but he was nowhere in sight.

"What happened?" Ben demanded, taking Jack's weight as the big man stumbled and nearly fell. "You were supposed to be back hours ago. Where's Shane?"

Samson's eyes were huge, scary orbs in his bloody face. His beard and hair were streaked with crimson as he pointed down the road.

"Truck broke down a few miles from town," he panted, shaking with gasps as Ben grabbed his arm. "We had to abandon the supplies...try to make it back on foot. They were everywhere, came right out of the fucking ground. Shane... didn't make it." His face crumpled with anger and grief, before he shook himself free. "Hurry, I think they're right behind us."

"Samson, you're hurt," I said, remembering, for one horrible moment, Nathan's snarling face as he'd lunged at me, eyes empty of thought or reason. I remembered the wound on his arm, the seeping bite mark that had been the start of everything. "Did one of them bite you?"

"Dammit, girl! There's no time!" Samson gave me a wild glare and started limping up the driveway. "Get everyone inside!" he ordered as we hurried to catch up. "Lock the doors!"

he bellowed as several people crowded onto the porch, wide-eyed. Mrs. Archer and Rachel were among them, with Davy, the goat, peering at us from behind her legs. She scooped him up and fled inside. "Secure the barn," Samson continued as we staggered up the steps. "Close the windows, and get all the women and kids into the basement!" He turned to me and Ben, his dark eyes intense. "Everyone grab a weapon, because I think there's a lot of them."

An eerie wailing rose from the trees around us, making my hair stand on end. We lurched through the door and slammed it behind us as the chilling cries drew closer, and we prepared for what might be our last night alive.

CHAPTER 10

They slid out of the darkness like wraiths, a pale, monstrous swarm, cresting the rise at the top of the driveway. Even huddled behind a window, peering through the slats in the boards, I could see their faces, their dead white eyes and slack jaws bristling with fangs. Most of them still wore the clothes they had died in, torn and filthy now, some with darker, more ominous stains spattered across the fabric.

"Mother of God," one of the men swore beside me. Shuddering, I drew away from the window and turned to where Samson was giving orders a few feet away, one hand planted against the table to keep himself upright.

"Douse all the lights," he hissed at a nephew, who scrambled to obey him. "Make sure everyone has a weapon, but, for the love of God, don't fire unless they're coming in through the walls! Let's keep our heads, people!"

"Samson," I said, stepping between him and Ben. "You need to let me examine you. If you've been bitten—"

"I'm fine." Samson smacked my hand away. "Get downstairs with the rest of the womenfolk, girl. You'll just be in our way up here."

I bristled, but Ben put a hand to the small of my back. "She can help," he said quietly. "She knows how to shoot, and if anyone gets hurt she can patch them up quicker than anyone here. She stays."

Samson glared at us both, then snorted. "I don't have time for this. Fine, give the woman a gun if she wants, and tell her to stay back from the windows. Everyone else, *shut up!*" His voice hissed through the room, quieting the mutters, the terrified whispers that we were all going to die. Silence fell, and Samson glowered at the small group of frightened humans. "We all knew this was coming. You all had the choice to leave, but you stayed. We are not going to lose our heads and make stupid mistakes. The survival of this family depends on us, and we will make our stand here."

A soft, drawn-out creak echoed from outside, as the first of the rabids eased onto the porch.

Everyone froze or silently ducked behind cover, as the pale, hissing swarm crowded the front door. Ben and I peeked around the kitchen doorway, seeing them through the slats over the windows, watching as they poked their claws between the wood, testing it. No one moved, not even when one of the rabids pressed its face to the wall and peered in with a bulging white eye, scanning the room. With a hiss, it pulled back and shuffled off, and the mob on the front porch slowly cleared out. We could still hear them, though, stalking the perimeter of the house, searching for a way in. But, for now at least, they hadn't seen us. I hoped they couldn't smell us, though it was obvious they knew something was inside. Maybe they had no sense of smell if they were already dead? I didn't know, and right now, I couldn't worry about it. Samson was hurt, and stubborn ass or no, he needed help.

"Ben," I whispered when everything was still again. "I have to check your father. He needs medical attention, whether he likes it or not. You saw what happened…with Nathan."

He nodded stiffly. "I know." For a moment, that ugly pain was there again, darkening his eyes. Then he shook it off, and an iron determination took its place. "What do you need me to do?"

"See if you can get him into the bathroom. There are no windows there, and I'll need a light to see what I'm doing." I peeked into the front room again, checking for rabid silhouettes in the windows. "I'll need to go to our room and get my medical supplies. See if you can convince the stubborn fool to let me take care of him before—"

A thud echoed through the darkness, and everyone jumped, raising their weapons. Ben and I rushed into the room to find Samson collapsed under the table, moaning softly. The rest of the men gaped at his body and at each other, looking lost.

Ben stepped forward, smacking one of the men on the shoulder as he passed. "Dale, help me get him up. The rest of you, go back to your posts. The rabids are still out there. Kylie..." He glanced back at me, and I nodded.

"I'll get my bag."

Minutes later, the three of us huddled on the bathroom floor, with Samson slumped against the tub and Ben shining a flashlight over my shoulder. The older man had regained consciousness, but seemed oddly complacent as I cut off his shirt, only commenting once that a knife would work better. Ignoring him, I gingerly peeled back the fabric, revealing a dark mass of blood and mangled flesh below his ribs. Ben drew in a sharp breath.

"Dad, what the hell? Why didn't you say anything?"

Samson Archer sighed. "Because I didn't need the lot of you worrying over me when we had fucking zombies coming up the driveway."

"What happened?" I asked, liberally soaking a towel in

disinfectant before pressing it to the wound. Samson hissed through his teeth, clenching his jaw.

"One of the bastards grabbed Shane. He started screaming, and I went back to help him. Then another one of 'em came right out of the ground, right under my feet. It latched on, and by the time I got it off, they'd torn Shane to pieces."

"Dammit," Ben growled behind me. "Kylie, can you tell what kind of wound it is? Is he…" He trailed off, and Samson narrowed his eyes.

"Am I what?"

"I don't know," I said, moving Ben's arm to hold the light at a better angle. The ragged flesh and blood made it difficult to determine what kind of damage it was. "Samson, do you remember if the rabid bit you?" I wasn't entirely certain how the virus spread, if it was passed on through the saliva or blood or something else. But Nathan had been bitten, and everything at the clinic started with that, so I wasn't taking any chances. "Did it bite you?" I asked again, firmer this time. "Or did it just grab you with its claws?"

"Shit, woman, I don't know. I was just trying to get the bastard off of me. I didn't ask what it was doing."

I pulled my last syringe of painkiller from my bag. I'd found it in my coat pocket a few days ago when I was gathering our clothes to wash. "This is morphine," I told Samson, holding it up. "It will help with the pain. It will also put you to sleep, so don't be alarmed if you get drowsy or light-headed."

"Don't want to sleep," Samson growled, waving me off. "Can't sleep now. Who will look after everyone with those things out there?"

"I will," Ben said quietly.

Samson's lip curled. He glanced at Ben and took a breath to scoff, but stopped when Ben didn't look away. Father and son gazed at each other for a silent moment, and I didn't know what passed between them, but I took advantage of the moment to slip the needle into Samson's arm, injecting him with the painkiller. He jerked, glaring at me, then sighed.

"Stubborn, intractable woman," he muttered, though I thought I caught the faintest hint of reluctant respect below the surface. He snorted. "Know what's best for everyone, do you? Just like this insufferable idiot. You two are definitely made for each other."

I didn't answer, not wanting to snap at an injured patient, though I could feel Ben's anger behind me. Tossing the needle away, I was reaching for the gauze when Samson's bony fingers fastened on my arm.

Startled, I looked back to find him leaning in, staring at me intently. "Take care of him," he rasped in a voice almost too soft to be heard. "If I don't make it, watch out for him. Don't let him do anything stupid. You're the only one he listens to now."

He slumped against the tub, all the fight going out of him. I sat there a moment, shocked, pondering his words. Anger flickered. Samson had no right to demand I look out for his son, not when he'd done such a dismal job of it himself. And I didn't need his orders. I didn't need anyone telling me to take care of Ben. Maybe Samson had to be reminded that you took care of the ones you cared for, even if they'd hurt you in the past, but I already knew that. I was here because I cared for Ben. I was here because...

The reason hit me like a load of bricks, and I nearly dropped the bandages. Because... I loved him. Even after such a short time. I loved his strength, his loyalty, his fierce protectiveness when the need arose. The way he looked at me as if I was the most precious thing in the world, the way his hands slid gently across my skin. Even his faults, the guilt and inner torment, the darkness that he retreated into sometimes. I loved all of that. I couldn't live without him.

I was in love with Ben Archer.

I finished bandaging the wound, my body and hands acting on autopilot, but my mind far away. Then, still feeling as if I'd been blindsided, I helped Ben move Samson into our room and laid him out on the bed.

Samson's eyes were closed, and he seemed dead to the world, which was a small kindness considering the pain he must've been in. However, when we drew back, he stirred and raised his head, muttering something insensible. Ben glanced at me, then knelt beside his father and bent close, as Samson whispered something only they could hear. Ben gave a solemn nod, and Samson's head fell back onto the pillow. He finally drifted into unconsciousness.

"I'll stay with him," I whispered as Ben stood, looking grave. "You go out there and let everyone know what's going on."

He nodded gratefully and paused as if to say something, then seemed to think better of it. Spinning around, he grabbed a long wooden box from the top shelf, set it down, and carefully opened the top.

A revolver lay there, glimmering dully in the shadows. For a second, Ben stared at the gun, a tortured expression briefly crossing his face. But then he yanked the weapon from the case and turned to me.

"Here," he said, flipping it over and holding it out to me, handle first. "Just in case."

"Ben…"

"Take it, Kylie." Ben's eyes pleaded with me. "In case I'm not here and he… Just take it. Please."

Gingerly, I reached out and took the gun.

"Ben?" I called as he went through the door. He turned,

raising his eyebrows, and I bit my lip. *Just tell him, Kylie. You might not get another chance. Tell him you want to stay here. That you want to be part of this family.*

That you've fallen in love with him.

But that question still lingered, plaguing me with indecision and doubt. Was Ben's offer based on love, or the need to continue his family line? Did he genuinely want me, or was this a joining of convenience? Ben had admitted that he needed me, and that he didn't want me to leave. He hadn't said anything about love.

I forced a smile. "Tell one of the boys to boil some water for me? I might need to do some stitching later."

He gave me a puzzled look but nodded and vanished silently into the hall.

It was a long night.

The monsters never gave up. All through the night and into the early-morning hours we heard them, circling the house, clawing at the windows and scratching at the walls. Sometime after midnight, we heard a wild screeching outside and realized that the rabids had discovered the livestock in the barn. The swarm had surrounded the building, tearing at the walls, and we heard the frantic bleats of the goats within. But there was nothing we could do except hope that our fortifications and the reinforced doors would be strong enough to keep the rabids from slaughtering everything.

Samson continued to worsen. His skin grew hot, and the wound turned puffy and red, fluid beginning to seep through the bandages. I kept close watch on his eyes and mouth, mentally preparing myself to see bloody flecks on his lips or worse, red tears streaming from his eyelids. Apart from the shuffle of the rabids outside and the occasional cough or shift from men in the living room, the house was eerily silent. Ben was a ghost, gliding from room to room, checking on everyone and calming nerves. "We're almost through this," I heard him murmur to a relative once. "They'll go away when the sun comes up. We just have to survive till then."

And then what? I thought. *What happens tomorrow night, and the night after that?*

Ben came silently into the room, startling me. I looked up from my chair as he handed me a mug that steamed and smelled heavenly of coffee.

"Thought you could use this."

"Lifesaver, Ben." I took the offered mug and sipped deeply, welcoming the hot jolt of caffeine. Ben set his ever-present shotgun aside and perched on the ottoman, regarding me with tired eyes.

"How's Dad?"

"Hasn't changed." The same answer I'd given him the past three times he'd come by. I gazed at his haggard, tousled face and had the very strong urge to kiss it. I restrained myself and sipped my coffee. "How's everyone else?"

"Tired." Ben rubbed his forehead. "At least, everyone up here is exhausted. Rachel and some of the others downstairs actually managed to get some sleep. Kylie, you never answered my question last night."

I choked on coffee, sputtering and spilling it down my chin. Setting the cup down, I wiped my mouth with the back of my hand and stared at Ben's serious expression. "Is...is this the best time to discuss that?" I whispered.

He closed his eyes briefly, as if pained. "When will I get another chance?" he murmured, scooting closer. "We're surrounded by death, afraid to even move, and they're not going to go away. This..." He let out a heavy sigh. "This will be my life, every night. Fighting these things, trying to keep my family alive. And I realize it's not fair to you. You shouldn't feel like you have to stay because of me. If the world hadn't gone crazy, I wouldn't ask anyone to go through this, especially you."

A scream echoed from outside, and on the bed, Samson groaned. Ben shot him a worried, hopeful glance, but he fell silent and didn't stir again.

"Kylie, I need you here," Ben continued in a low, intense voice. "You're the most important thing in my life now. As much as any member of my family, maybe more. But... I won't ask you to stay if you aren't certain you want to. It's your choice."

"Why do you want me to stay?" I whispered.

Ben blinked. "I...thought it was obvious."

I shook my head. "You told me you wanted to settle down, maybe even start a family. That sounds an awful lot like a proposal, Ben. But, you haven't said...how you feel about me. And I need to know, before I decide anything. I need to know if this is some partnership of convenience, or if you want me to stay because..."

Because you love me as much as I love you.

"Kylie." Ben sighed, running his hands through his hair. He looked embarrassed, uncomfortable, and my heart sank. "We've only known each other a couple weeks," he stammered, as my heart plummeted to my toes. "And after the whole Nathan situation, I was certain you hated me. I thought if I said anything, it would be too soon. That I would come across as some creepy, desperate guy and it would scare you off. And I couldn't bear the thought of you leaving, so I stayed quiet."

My heart roused a little, a tiny flare of hope lifting it up. "What are you trying to say?"

Ben swallowed. "I wanted to wait a little while. I thought that if we came here, and I convinced you to stay, I would have all the time in the world to tell you how I felt." He glanced toward the curtained window, and his face darkened. "But we don't have much time anymore, and it's selfish of me to ask you to stay here, just because I—"

He stopped. My stomach was in knots, my heart racing, hanging on for those next few words. I wanted to hear them. I *needed* to hear them. "Because you...?"

Ben slumped, letting out a long breath. Leaning forward, he eased off the ottoman but didn't stand, dropping to his knees in front of me. His calloused hands took mine and trapped them in gentle fingers, while his gorgeous, soulful dark eyes rose to meet my gaze.

"Because I love you," he whispered, and my flattened heart swelled nearly to bursting. "I am completely and irreversibly in love with you, ever since that first night in your clinic when you told me you had survived. You are the most amazing woman I've ever known, and I can say with complete sincerity that I wouldn't be here if I hadn't met you. You pulled me out of the darkness, and I will be forever grateful for that. I honestly don't know what I'll do if you leave." He squeezed my hands, his gaze never wavering from mine. "I love you, Kylie," he murmured. "Stay with me. Till the end of the world."

My eyes watered. Sliding forward, I wrapped my arms around his head and kissed him fiercely, feeling his arms yank me close. I buried my fingers in his hair and pressed myself against him, and for a moment everything—the rabids, Samson, the circle of death surrounding us on all sides—all melted away, and the only thing that mattered was the man in my arms. Let the world fall; I had my sanctuary right here. My own pocket of Eden.

"Ben?"

A soft, hesitant voice broke us apart, and we turned to see

Rachel standing in the doorway, a flickering candle in hand, staring at us. But she wasn't smirking or frowning; her eyes were wide and teary, and her free hand wrung the front of her shirt in quick, nervous gestures.

"Rachel, honey." Ben let me go and crossed the room, kneeling down to face her. "You're supposed to be downstairs with Mom and Aunt Sarah and the rest of them," he said, putting himself, I noticed, between her and Samson's body on the bed. "You need to go back to the basement, now."

"I can't." The child sniffled, biting her lip. "I can't find Davy."

"Davy? Your goat?"

A nod. "I think he slipped out when I came upstairs to use the bathroom."

Ben frowned. "Go back to Mom," he told her, and the girl's lip trembled. He smoothed her hair and gently tugged on an end. "I'll find him and bring him back, okay?"

She sniffed and nodded. Turning, she padded down the hall, and we listened until the creak of the basement door echoed to us in the silence. Ben stood with a grimace.

"Care to go goat hunting with me?"

A soft clink came from the kitchen before I could answer. Ben and I shared a glance and hurried quietly into the living room.

Sunrise wasn't far off. Instead of complete darkness, the slats over the windows let in a faint gray light, and the air held the stillness of the coming dawn. We could still hear the rabids, though, constantly shuffling around outside, sometimes passing in front of the windows, making the porch squeak. Ben had rotated the guard duty throughout the night, and the last watch huddled in the shadows and behind doorways, guns in their laps or beside them on the ground. It was lighter outside, the blackness losing ground to a muffled gray. We were almost in the clear, but we still had to be very, very careful.

I suddenly saw the kid, a glimmer of white in the shadows, trot out of the kitchen and into the front room. My heart stood still. Ben hurried forward, but before he could do anything, the frightened kid walked past one of the men, who instinctively reached out and grabbed it. The goat let out a startled bleat—and a rabid's face slammed into the window, mad white eyes peering in. It screamed, sinking its claws into the wooden slats, shaking violently, and more bodies flung themselves onto the porch. Blows rattled the doors and windows, filling the house with noise.

"Everyone, stay calm!" Ben ordered as the men jumped to their feet, grabbing their weapons. "Get down to the lower levels and block the doors. Use the staircase and the hall as a choke point if they get through." A slat ripped free of the frame, and a rabid's face became fully visible through the space, blank and terrifying. It screeched, and Ben's shotgun barked loudly, the flare from the muzzle searingly bright in the dark room. The rabid's head exploded in a cloud of blood, and it fell back, only to have several others take its place. More slats began to tear loose, and Ben turned on the men. "Move! Now!"

As they scrambled away, fleeing downstairs, Ben shot a sick, terrified glance at me. "You, too, Kylie. Go to the safe room and bar the door behind you. Don't open it for anything, understand?"

"What about you?" I gasped as he turned away. "Where are you going?"

"I have to get Dad!"

Ben fled down the hall, and I followed. Darting into the guest room, I slammed the door and leaned against it, panting, as Ben strode to the bed. Samson lay where he had all night, face up, eyes closed. But now, seeing him, I felt a chill go through my stomach. He was so very, very still. Too still.

"Ben," I warned, but it was too late. He had already grabbed Samson's arm to haul him over his shoulder. I watched, helpless, as Ben froze, staring down at his father, then slowly lowered the arm back to the mattress. His voice was a choked whisper in the shadows.

"He's gone."

Tears filled my eyes, more from the pain in Ben's voice than for the man on the bed. He would never reconcile with his father now. And Samson had been harsh, abrasive, stubborn and infuriating, but he'd loved his family and, in his own way, done everything he could to protect them. He might not have been a good man, but Ben had loved him, and had struggled hard to be forgiven and accepted.

Which made what I was going to suggest even more horrible.

"Ben," I said softly, hating that I had to bring it up. "We can't leave him like this." He gave me an anguished look, and I swallowed hard. "You have to…make sure he doesn't come back," I whispered. "You can't let him turn into one of *them,* like Nathan."

Understanding dawned on his face, followed by horror. I walked to the corner table and retrieved the revolver that Ben had given me that night. The metal was cool in my hands as I came back and stood in front of Ben, holding it out.

Ben's eyes were glassy. He looked down at the gun and drew in a shuddering, ragged breath. "I can't do this."

"Yes, you can." My own throat was tight, but I swallowed the tears and continued to hold out the gun. "He would've wanted this, Ben. It has to be done, and it has to be you. Go on." I lifted the revolver toward him. "Take it. Set him free."

A sob tore its way past his lips, but Ben slowly reached

out and took the weapon from my hands. Turning stiffly, he raised the gun and pointed it at the corpse on the bed, aiming it right between the eyes. He was shaking, trembling like a leaf, but his arm was steady. "I'm sorry," he whispered, using his thumb to click back the hammer.

Samson's eyes flashed open, blazing white. Turning his head, he screamed, baring fangs, and the boom of the revolver shook the bed and the walls. Samson fell back amid a pool of blood, the top of his head blown apart with the violent explosion, and Ben fell to his knees.

An answering screech rang out beyond the door, making me sick with fear. They were in the house! I lunged across the room and locked the door, just as a bang from the other side made me shriek in terror. I stumbled back into Ben, on his feet once more, as the door shook and rattled, and the maddened wails from the monsters grew more numerous as they crowded forward on the other side.

We pressed back into the corner by the curtained window, watching as the only thing between us and death began peeling away, shuddering under the relentless assault. Surprisingly, I felt calm. So, this was it. This was how I was going to die. At least… I wouldn't be alone.

Ben's arms wrapped around me from behind, pulling me back to his chest. I felt his forehead against the back of my neck, his warm breath on my skin. "I'm so sorry, Kylie," he whispered, his voice shaking. I turned to face him, gazing up into those haunted brown eyes, placing a palm on his rough cheek.

"I love you, Ben," I murmured, and watched his eyes widen. "I don't regret any of this." There was a splintering crack behind me, as a rabid tore a large chunk out of the door, but I didn't turn. "You gave me a home, and a family, and if I had to do it all over, even knowing how it would end, I would still follow you anywhere."

Ben leaned down, pressing his lips to mine, crushing them. I pressed forward, trying to feel him with my whole body, to merge my soul to his. We kissed one last time in that dark bedroom, the rabids shrieking at the door, Samson's bloody corpse lying on the bed a few yards away.

Ben released my mouth, but he didn't pull back, his forehead resting against mine. "They won't take you," he whispered fiercely, a bright, determined gleam in his eyes. "I won't let them. You're not going to die like that."

The door shook again, rattling in its frame. They were almost through. Ben pulled back slightly, and there were tears in his eyes now, as I felt the cold barrel of the revolver under my jaw. It sent a shiver down my spine, but I wasn't afraid. Yes, this was better. No pain, no teeth or claws tearing me open, ripping me apart. No chance to rise as one of them.

"It won't hurt," Ben promised, holding my gaze. "You won't feel a thing, I swear. And I... I'll be right behind you."

He was shaking. I wrapped my fingers around his hand, holding it and the gun steady. He was watching me, waiting for my signal, to let him know I was ready. Behind me, the rabids screamed, almost as if they knew I was slipping away, to a place they couldn't ever reach me. I almost smiled at the thought.

"Ready?" Ben whispered, and I took a deep breath. Behind him, through curtains and the slats in the window, I could see the sky, a soft dusky pink.

The window. "Wait!" I whispered, tightening my grip on his. "Ben, wait."

I pushed at the gun, and it dropped instantly as Ben yanked it down with a shudder of relief. Taking one step around him, I reached for the thick, black curtains covering the boarded window and threw them back.

Orange light streamed between the cracks in the wood, bright and promising, throwing ribbon-thin slivers of light over the floor. "Ben!" I gasped, spinning toward him, but he was already moving. Snatching the shotgun off the floor, he slammed the butt into the window, and the sound of breaking glass joined the wild screeching of the rabids.

I joined him, using a book from the shelf to batter at the wood. Frantically, we pounded at the boards over the window frame, as the rabids wailed and screamed behind us. The nails held, and the boards loosened, though they stubbornly refused to give.

With a final crack, the door burst inward. Howling, the rabids swarmed the room, flinging themselves across the floor. I cringed, bracing myself, just as Ben gave the board one last blow, and it came loose, flying out and away from the window frame.

A bar of orange sunlight spilled over the floor between us and the lunging rabids, and amazingly, the monsters skidded to a halt. Ben pressed back into the corner, holding me tightly to him as the swarm hissed and snarled at the edge of the light. I clung to Ben, forcing myself to keep my eyes open, to face the monsters not five feet away. I could feel Ben's heartbeat, his breath coming in short gasps, the strength of his arms crushing me to his chest. The rabids hissed, frustrated, and one of them inched forward, out of the shadows and into the light.

There was a different sort of hissing as smoke erupted from its white skin. The rabid shrieked, flinging itself backwards. Clawing at itself and wailing, it turned and fled the room, the stench of burned, rotten meat rising into the air. The other rabids hissed and growled and gnashed their fangs at us, but slowly followed its example, filing out of the room. I peeked out the window and saw the pale forms scramble off the porch into the shadows outside, darting into bushes and trees, keeping out of the sun.

In seconds, they had disappeared.

A hazy mist hung over the distant woods and fields, pooling in low spots and coiling through the branches. Somewhere in the trees, a bird called out, and another answered it. The rabids were gone. They would be back tonight, that was certain, but for now, they were gone and we were still alive.

Or, most of us were.

I looked up at Ben and found him staring out the window, a bit dazed. He was still breathing hard, and his heart was still pounding, but he closed his eyes and, without warning, crushed me to him in a desperate hug.

I returned it. We didn't say anything. We didn't state the obvious: they would be back tonight when the sun went down. We just held each other, content to listen to our breaths and heartbeats mingle as the sun crept farther into the sky and touched every living thing with light.

We buried Samson that morning, beneath a single pine tree that stood tall and straight in the middle of the field. The sky was clear, and the sun blazed overhead, slanting through the branches of the pine, speckling the bare patch of earth at the trunk. Ben wore a borrowed tie and jacket, and standing beside the grave, his hands clasped in front of him, he looked solemn and serious…and very much like his father.

"I haven't been back long," he said to the semicircle of kin on the other side of the mound. "I remember, just a few years ago, I was so eager to leave this place. So desperate to get away. And I did, for a while. The city was exciting and noisy and crowded, so different than the boring little stretch of farmland I left behind. I thought I would be happy there, on my own. I was wrong.

"Now," he continued, meeting everyone's gaze, "I realize what Dad was talking about. This is our home. And we're going to defend it. We will stay strong, and rebuild, and start over. We will make a life here. Whatever it takes." His gaze dropped to the mound of earth at his feet. "Dad would've wanted it that way."

He bowed his head and stepped back. Rachel and some of the other women came forward to lay flowers over the grave. I held out my hand as he rejoined me, and he squeezed my palm.

Ben sighed and closed his eyes, tilting his head to the sunlight. I watched him a moment, then bumped his shoulder with mine.

"What are you thinking about?"

He looked at me, his eyes clear and direct, as if the light had finally burned away the last of the guilt and anguish, and I was looking straight down into his soul. "Just...that everything is beautiful in the sun," he said quietly, holding my gaze. "And that I'm home, finally, and I am going to take care of this family. That's what he wanted, anyway. The last thing he said."

I remembered Samson's last words, whispered into Ben's ear, and smiled. "Yeah?"

"Well, there was one more thing." Ben stepped forward, gathering me into his arms. "He also insisted we get married in the fall, like him and Mom."

I smiled through my tears. "Bossy, stubborn man. I guess we can't say no." Ben kissed me gently, a kiss full of promise, and love, and hope. Especially hope. Taking my hand, he laced his fingers through mine, and together we returned to the open arms of our family.

A full moon glimmered over the waves as they lapped against the dock, throwing fractured sliver light over the hull of the ship tethered there. Two figures stood at the end of the pier, speaking in low, intense voices. One was a sunburned, lanky man who smelled faintly of brine and was most at home on the open water. The other was a tall man with pale skin and eyes blacker than midnight. The pier bobbed up and down on the waves, and the lanky man shifted his weight subtly to compensate, but the tall stranger was as motionless as a statue.

"The pay was acceptable?" the tall man asked in a low, almost dangerous tone. His companion rubbed his beard and sighed.

"Yeah, it was fine. Last-minute, but fine. You're lucky— I turned down the last poor sap who couldn't pay up. Idiot thought I'd let him and his kid tag along for free. I don't run a fucking charity here." He eyed the stranger's empty hands and shook his head. "Long way across the ocean, friend. Sure you don't want to take anything? This ain't a pleasure cruise, you know."

"You don't have to worry about me, Captain." A ghost of a smile tugged at the stranger's lips. "I have everything I need right here."

"Eh. Whatever. Let's get moving, then. Time and tide wait for no man."

The captain walked off, leaving the pier and striding up the ramp without a backward glance. But the tall stranger stood on the dock a moment more, letting the breeze play across his face. He turned, looking back the way he'd come, from a rabid-infested town and a small house and two humans he'd rescued on a whim. The boy was unimportant; it was *her* words he would remember, her words he would take with him on his long, impossible journey. His kin were already looking for him, vengeance and retribution foremost on their minds. He was not afraid of their wrath, but he could not allow himself to be destroyed just yet.

"I will make things right," he whispered, a promise to her,

to everyone. "The rabids are my creation, but I will atone for that mistake. And I will not stop until everything I have destroyed is returned to the way it was."

"Oy, mister!" The captain stood at the top of the ramp, glaring down at him. "You coming or not? I'm getting too old for this kind of stress."

The stranger smiled. *Don't worry, Captain,* he thought, gliding down the pier. *You won't have that concern much longer, because this will be the last trip you and your crew will ever make. I did not lie when I said I have everything I need, right here.*

Walking up the ramp, he nodded politely to the captain and continued inside. Ropes were tossed, anchors were pulled and the great ship slid easily into open water and vanished over the horizon.

★ ★ ★ ★ ★

THE HUMAN WORLD

A long, long time ago

It was almost time.

I peeked out of the bushes and grinned. The stage was nearly set. In the tiny, sun-dappled clearing beyond the trees, the crystal-clear pool glimmered, attracting all manner of life to its sparkling waters. A herd of spotted deer bent graceful necks to the surface under the watchful eye of a great stag, standing tall at the edge of the pond. A few rabbits hopped through the bracken scattered through the clearing, and a family of squirrels scolded each other in the branches of a large gnarled oak. Birds sang, wildlife meandered, and the wind gently rustled the leaves overhead. It was a blissful, picturesque woodland scene, a perfectly peaceful day in the human realm.

Boring, boring, boring.

I smiled, reached into my shirt, and pulled the pan flute into the light. It was my own design; I'd spent several days gathering hollow reeds, cutting them, binding them together, and making sure the tone was perfect. Now I was going to see what it could do.

Drawing glamour from the forest around me, I raised the flute to my lips and blew out a single note.

The clear, high sound cut through the stillness of the woods, arcing over the grove, and all the animals clustered around the pond jerked up, eyes wide and nostrils flaring. The rabbits sat up, ears twitching back and forth. The deer raised their heads, dark eyes huge as they gazed around, ready to flee. The squirrels' tails flicked as they clung to the branches, their chittering voices silenced.

In the sudden stillness, I took a deep breath, gathering my magic, and began playing.

The melody rose into the air, cheerful and fast-paced. It swirled around the pond, into the ears of every living creature. For a moment, none of them moved.

Then, one of the rabbits began tapping its foot. The others followed, thumping their hind legs in tune to the rhythm, and the deer began tossing their heads to the music. In the branches, the squirrels bobbed, tails twitching back and forth, keeping time, and the birds added their voices to the song. I bit down a smile and played louder, faster, drawing in more glamour and releasing it into the notes trilling through the forest.

With a bugle, the ancient stag reared up, tossing his huge antlers, and bounded gracefully to the center of the clearing. His sharp hooves pawed the grass, gouging the earth, as he stepped and leaped with the music. As one, his herd joined him, cavorting to his side, and the rabbits began flinging themselves in wild arcs around the stomping deer. My glee soared; this was working better than I had hoped. It was all I could do to keep playing and not let the song drop because of the enormous grin wanting to stretch my face.

Rising from the bushes, I walked toward the grove, the pan flute moving rapidly under my lips, the song rising and the magic soaring in response. My feet itched, and I started to move them, dancing to the center of the clearing. Filling my lungs, I played as loudly as I could, my body moving almost on its own, leaping and twirling and spinning through the air. And all around me, the forest creatures danced as well, hooves and horns and furry bodies barely missing me as they bounced and cavorted in a frantic circle, hurling themselves around the grove with wild abandon. I lost myself in the music, in the excitement and ecstasy, as I danced with the forest.

I didn't know how long the melody went on; half the time my eyes were closed and I was moving on pure instinct. But at last, as the song reached a crescendo, I sensed it was time to bring it to a close. With one final, soaring note, the melody died away, the wild emotions faded, and the whirlwind of magic swirling through the grove fluttered out, returning to the earth.

Panting, I lowered my arms. Around me, my fellow dancers also came to shuddering stops, breathing hard. The great stag stood a few feet away, antlered head bowed, legs and flanks trembling. As I watched, he quivered and collapsed, white foam bubbling from his mouth and nostrils as his head struck the ground. One by one, the rest of the herd crumpled as well, some gasping wide-eyed for breath, some lying motionless in the dirt. Scattered around them, furry lumps of rabbits lay in the churned mud. I looked at the trees and saw the squirrels and birds lying at the bases of the trunks, having fallen from their perches once the music ceased.

I blinked. Well, that was unexpected. How long had I been playing, anyway? I looked at the sky through the branches and saw clouds streaked with orange, the sun hovering low on the horizon. I'd come to this grove and played the very first note early this morning. It seemed our wild revel had lasted the entire day.

Huh. I scratched the back of my head. *Well, that's disappointing. I guess I can't push these mortal beasts too aggressively, or they just collapse. Hmm.* Tapping the fingers of one hand against my arm, I gazed at the pan flute in the other. *I wonder if humans would do any better?*

"Boy."

The deep, lyrical voice came from behind me, and a ripple of magic shivered through the air. I felt a stab of annoyance that someone had been watching my revel; that was why I'd chosen to do this in the human world, after all—so I could worry less about curious eavesdroppers.

I turned and saw a procession of horses at the edge of the clearing, watching me from the trees. The mounts were fey creatures, lighter and much more graceful than their mortal counterparts, their hooves barely touching the ground. The riders atop them were sidhe knights, clad in armor of leaves, vines, and branches woven together. Part of the Summer Court, I realized. I'd seen them before, as well as the knights of the Winter Court. I'd even played with a few of them in the wyldwood, though they never realized the cause of all their small, annoying mishaps was a forest boy too insignificant to notice.

But the rider at the front of the procession had definitely noticed me, and he was impossible to miss, too. His mount was bright gold, brighter than any mortal steed, but the noble atop it outshone even his mount. He was dressed in armor of green and gold, with a cloak made of blooming vines that left flowers where he passed. Long silver hair flowed from under the huge antlered crown that rested on his brow, and the piercing green eyes beneath it were fixed solely on me.

Why was *he* here? Had he heard my music and been drawn to the sound? That was unfortunate. I tried to avoid catching the eye of the Summer Court, particularly *this* faery. I hadn't been doing anything wrong; the fey cared little as to what happened in the mortal world. The deaths of a few forest creatures meant nothing to them.

But attracting the attention of one of the most powerful faeries in the Nevernever was a dangerous game. Depending on his mood, he might demand that I "gift" him the thing I'd worked so hard on, play the pipes for him and his knights for as long as he was amused, or entertain them all by becoming the next hunt. The fey lords were notoriously unpredictable, and I treated them as I would a sleeping dragon: it was okay to tip-toe around and steal their gold, as long as they didn't see you.

But now, the dragon had spotted me.

The sidhe gentry nudged his mount, and the horse stepped into the clearing, striding across the grass until beast and rider loomed before me. I stood my ground and gazed up defiantly at the noble, who was watching me with appraising eyes.

"So young," he mused. "And such an impressive use of glamour. What is your name, boy?"

"Robin."

"And where are your parents, Robin?"

I shrugged. "I live by myself. In the wyldwood." I couldn't remember my parents, if I'd even had them. My earliest memory was the tangle of the wyldwood, foraging for food and shelter, learning the skills I needed to survive. But even though I was alone, I'd never felt like I didn't belong. The forest, the wyldwood, was my home. That was how it always had been.

"Hmm." The tall noble didn't press the question. He observed me in silence for another moment, his face giving nothing away. "Do you know who I am, boy?" he asked instead.

This time, I nodded. "You're King Oberon." It was obvious; everyone knew who the Summer King was, though I'd never seen him in person. It didn't matter. I had never seen Queen Mab, ruler of the Winter Court, either, but I was certain I would know her if I did.

"Yes," the Seelie King agreed. "I am indeed. And I could use someone of your talents in Seelie territory." He raised a hand, indicating me with long, elegant fingers. "You have power—raw, unfettered Summer magic rivaling some of my strongest allies in the court. Such a gift should not go to waste in the wyldwood. You should not be living in the forest like a beast, singing to birds and squirrels. You should be part of the greatest court in the Nevernever. What say you, Robin?" The king regarded me with eyes like pale green frost. "Would you like to become part of the Seelie Court?"

Part of the Seelie Court?

Curiosity battled defiance. I was intrigued, of course. Living by myself in the wyldwood meant I could come and go as I pleased, but it was getting a bit lonely. I wanted to talk to people, others of my kind, not just forest creatures and the occasional scatterbrained piskie. And of the two courts, Summer territory sounded much more pleasant than the frozen, hostile land of Winter.

Still, it was never a good idea to take the first offer. Even I, with my limited knowledge of bargains and deals, knew that much.

"I like it in the forest." I crossed my arms and smiled at the king. "Why should I go live at the Summer Court?"

The Seelie King smiled, as if he'd expected that answer. "Because, Robin, I am king." He spoke the phrase like it was the most important fact in the world. "And as King of the Seelie, I can give you whatever your heart desires. I can grant you power, wealth, the love of as many hearts as you wish." He paused when I wrinkled my nose. "But I can see you are not interested in these things. Perhaps, then, this would be of note. I have many enemies, Robin. Both within the court and without. From time to time, these enemies need to realize that they cannot underestimate the sovereignty of Summer. If you join me... Well, let us say you will have plenty of opportunities to practice your magic on things other than common forest beasts."

Now *that* sounded interesting. I glanced back at the pond, at the motionless bodies surrounding it. Poor dumb animals. I hadn't meant to harm them, but it seemed normal creatures were very fragile. I would love to try some of my ideas on sturdier creatures, maybe even a few fey, and Oberon was dangling that big, bright carrot in front of me. He seemed to know exactly what I wanted. The only question was, did I care?

"So, Robin of the Wyldwood," King Oberon went on, peering down at me from his horse. "What is your decision? Will you join my court? I will name you court jester, and you can play your tricks and practice your magic without boundaries. All I ask is that you do me a small service from time to time. Do we have a deal?"

Something nagged at me, a feeling that this agreement wasn't quite what I thought it was. I'd made deals before, but they were with piskies and sprites and a couple local dryads. Never with someone as important as the ruler of the Seelie Court. Was I missing something? This did seem a little too good to be true.

I hesitated a moment more, then shrugged. Then again, why not join the Summer Court? What was the worst that could happen? I was aching for something new, and if I was under the protection of King Oberon himself, think of all the pranks and tricks I could play without fear of retribution.

This was going to be fun.

"All right," I agreed, grinning up at Oberon, who raised a thin silver brow in return. "You have a deal, King. I'll join the Summer Court, as long as I get to practice my magic and play as many tricks as I want."

"Excellent." Oberon nodded and raised both hands. "Then I name you Robin Goodfellow, jester of the Summer Court," he announced in sudden, booming tones, and the branches of the trees shook, as if acknowledging his declaration. Lowering his arms, the Summer King gazed down at me with a sudden, almost proud smile. "Welcome to the Seelie Court, Robin Goodfellow. Wear your name proudly. Perhaps someday the world will come to know it as well."